D0837480

burned
hearts

also by calista fox

burned deep

flash burned

burned hearts

CALISTA FOX

st. martin's griffin ≋ new york

This is a work of fiction. All of the characters, organizations, and events portrayed in this novel are either products of the author's imagination or are used fictitiously.

BURNED HEARTS. Copyright © 2016 by Calista Fox. All rights reserved. Printed in the United States of America. For information, address St. Martin's Press, 175 Fifth Avenue, New York, N.Y. 10010.

www.stmartins.com

Designed by Anna Gorovoy

Library of Congress Cataloging-in-Publication Data

Names: Fox, Calista, author.
Title: Burned hearts / Calista Fox.
Description: First Edition. | New York : St. Martin's Griffin, 2016.
Identifiers: LCCN 2016016273| ISBN 9781250072535 (paperback) |
    ISBN 9781466884212 (e-book)
Subjects: | BISAC: FICTION / Romance / Contemporary. | GSAFD:
    Erotic fiction.
Classification: LCC PS3606.O895 B88 2015 | DDC 813/.6—dc23
LC record available at https://lccn.loc.gov/2016016273

Our books may be purchased in bulk for promotional, educational, or business use. Please contact your local bookseller or the Macmillan Corporate and Premium Sales Department at 1-800-221-7945, extension 5442, or by e-mail at MacmillanSpecialMarkets@macmillan.com.

First Edition: October 2016

10 9 8 7 6 5 4 3 2 1

For my real-life hero. There are no words.

acknowledgments

I'm still so grateful my stars were perfectly aligned and brought me together with my agent, Sarah E. Younger, from the Nancy Yost Literary Agency, and my St. Martin's Press editor, Monique Patterson. I'm also thankful for Monique's assistant, Alexandra Sehulster, who always has her finger on the pulse of everything that's happening with each book.

While I will admit that writing a trilogy wasn't as easy as I thought it would be, I got wrapped up in Dane and Ari's whirlwind romance and life. I was quite sad to end the series, but then Monique embraced a fourth story, Kyle's book—which is titled *Burning Obsession*, and will release in the fall of 2016—and that made me so thrilled that I could give him the happily ever after I felt he deserved.

My readers have sent amazing e-mails, reviewers have given great praise, and I honestly just feel blessed that I was able to share this story with the world. This third book is a little more complicated, with all the intricacies of tying up loose ends and really delving into the nuances of what Dane and Ari have committed to as they've joined forces to fight the evil that still plagues them. I sincerely hope you enjoy the conclusion. It was the most appropriate ending I could think of as I finished the trilogy—and if you've read the first two books, you know I like weaving in a healthy dose of eroticism and danger! Thanks for sharing the journey with me!

burned
hearts

chapter 1

"I'm not staying here a second longer."

I tossed clothes into my suitcases, not caring in the least how haphazardly they were strewn about.

"Ari, just take some deep breaths," said Kyle Jenns, my best friend and up-and-coming Mr. Muscle Bodyguard Extraordinaire. He crossed his bulging biceps over his wide chest and pinned me with a serious look. "You're freaking out prematurely."

"Oh, yeah?" I glared at him, my pulse racing, my heart thundering. "Two diamondbacks on the Kool Deck mere feet from where I turned off the waterfalls in the pool is no cause to freak out? Come on, Kyle. Everywhere I turn, it's snakes, scorpions, and stalkers. And I am *always* the mark. I've had enough, thank you very much."

"Should have thought of that before you married Dane."

"Leave him out of this."

Kyle heeded the warning, but demanded, "Where will you go?" Concern etched his strong features. "There's nowhere else like this fortress—walls that can't be scaled, topped with high-voltage electrical wiring. We even have a watchtower, for God's sake."

"Fat lot of good that's all done. Vale Hilliard got to me anyway, didn't he?"

The man who'd once kidnapped me and unleashed unspeakable nightmares was supposed to be dead. But he was the only one who knew how to terrify me, and he'd done it again this evening. So chances were very good he had not been in the car struck by a freight train, despite earlier news reports suggesting otherwise.

Kyle gripped my shoulders and looked deep into my eyes, which were a couple of shades darker than his sky-blue ones. "Ari, chill out for a minute." He spoke with a slow, measured tone, meant to reassure me, no doubt. "I know you're scared. But whatever happened tonight, we'll get to the bottom of it. There's no better place for you to be than here."

"Yes, there is. Home."

He released me. "The Oak Creek house?" He hated that I considered it my permanent residence. He'd taken great offense when I'd moved in with Dane last fall, after only a few months of seeing each other—although it hadn't taken even that brief amount of time for us to realize we were fated, couldn't exist without each other.

"I feel safer there, Kyle." I'd never once encountered a problem inside the gated property. Yes, Kyle and I had been set up a while back and we'd nearly fallen into the trap, but the trouble had occurred on the other side of the massive security fences, not within.

He shoved a hand through his crazily mussed sandy-brown hair. Agitation turned his all-American, athletic looks stony. A former college quarterback, Kyle had taken to bodybuilding, martial arts, and target practice with the GLOCK he'd recently purchased. Over the past year, he'd turned into the quick-thinking, determined-to-save-the-day sort of man who made a walking target such as myself thankful for his loyalty. And monumentally guilty that loyalty put him in danger right along with me.

"I know Amano is grilling his security people right this very minute," I said, trying to sound reasonable and stable, though my voice faltered. "And he'll figure out how two rattlesnakes ended up on our back patio. I'm grateful for that. I'm also grateful that you're still here, when you really ought to wash your hands of the whole damn—"

"Not gonna happen, Ari." He gave me that stern yet somewhat cocky expression he'd adopted, which radiated confidence and heroic charm. The two-day stubble currently lining his squared jawline added to his rugged good looks and resolute disposition. "If you're going to the creek house, I'm going with you."

So, too, would Amano. My shadow. Kyle's mentor. A man you wouldn't want to run into in a dark alley if you'd just mugged a little old lady of her collection plate money. You'd pay dearly out of sheer principle.

"Get packing then," I told Kyle. "Because I can't stay here tonight. I can't sleep here. I can't *breathe* here."

Facing coiled and hissing rattlers was horrific enough—I wouldn't wait around for the second-string army of venomous scorpions on the attack. Tonight I'd lost my steady frame of mind when it came to this precarious situation we'd all inadvertently found ourselves in after several of the original investors in the opulent hotel 10,000 Lux had been cut from the roster for global financial and criminal corruption.

My husband, owner of the now-decimated megaresort, wasn't one to take blows without hitting back. Although he'd frightened me a bit at first with the wrath he'd let loose on Vale Hilliard when he'd found me bound and bleeding, Dane had sworn to work with the FBI to bring down the ousted investors *legally*— not with his lethal bare hands. And he was so very close to finishing what he'd started.

But while he put the heat on so, too, did the opposition.

With shaky fingers, I zipped my luggage and said, "If it was just Amano and me waiting for this to all come to a conclusion, I could stick with the plan. Sit tight in this fortress. But the circle has expanded, Kyle. To include you—and believe me, I would *never* forgive myself if anything happened to you. Neither would Dane, despite the fact that he, well . . . doesn't like you."

It was a territorial thing. Dane was the determined sort who protected what was his at all costs—so he didn't easily accept that his wife's best friend was male. A macho one at that, who was always by my side.

"I've told you a million times, Ari. I know what I'm involved with. Do I like it? Hell, no. Would I love to punch Dane in the face for all of this? Hell, yes. But I get what it is that he has to do." This came reluctantly. "He's given up everything to crack this syndicate wide open and help the Feds reel in these assholes. I can't imagine the torture of all that—knowing you're here with me, out of his reach, and the fact that your baby is in jeopardy, too."

That was the other contributing factor to my panic attack. I was five months pregnant. I'd kept the news from Dane as long as possible, so that he could concentrate on his work, not worry about me and our child. Amano—devoted to me, but loyal as a Labrador to Dane—had ratted me out. I didn't blame him. Still, it complicated matters, just as Kyle had stated.

"I don't feel safe here," I reiterated. "No offense to you or Amano, but that was a very foreboding sign on the patio tonight and I read Vale's threat loud and clear."

"Fine. If you want to leave Sedona to return to Gotham, I'll go with you. Amano will, too, but you already know that."

I smirked at Kyle's reference to the creek house. Yes, I'd gone a little Mistress of the Dark when I'd thought Dane had been killed in the explosion, but the fact was, his house comforted me.

The Mediterranean-style estate on which we currently resided was beautiful and spacious, with all manner of amenities. But I missed the lovely serenity of our home, nestled in the woods with the water flowing over smooth rocks just beyond our terrace.

"If you're sure you want to go, I admit I could use the company," I told Kyle.

"I'd pretty much follow you anywhere." He shook his head. He knew as well as I did that wasn't a sane conviction, but we were sort of attached to each other. Kyle wanted more between us and, had I never laid eyes on Dane Bax, he just might have gotten his wish. But one look at the tall, gorgeous, green-eyed brooder . . . and I'd been hooked.

There would never be anyone else for me. Ever. No matter what.

"You know that I appreciate everything you do for me—for all of us," I said. Then added, "Shit, I should pay you. Why didn't I think of that sooner? You haven't been able to work recently, because you've been dodging danger with me." The attacks had started last fall. It was now May. The trouble had only escalated.

He said, "Dane already offered."

"What?" This shocked me. "He never said anything."

"Probably because it's moot. I turned him down."

"Are you *insane*?" My husband was worth billions. That meant I was worth billions, too, but that was still a near-impossible reality to grasp, even though we'd been secretly married for six months.

"What's the big deal?" Kyle asked with the shrug of a ridiculously broad shoulder. "I made plenty at the Lux and then the physical rehab retreat when you were there to put into savings. I let go of my apartment when I moved in here. My Rubicon was bought used and is now paid for, and let's face it, I practically eat you out of house and home. Plus, I canceled my gym membership because of the fitness room we have here. I figure we're even."

"You figure *way* wrong, my friend. You deserve hazard pay. And you know Dane's going to end up compensating you, regardless of your stance on the subject. He's indebted to you. We all are."

"See?" Kyle gave his enthusiastic, engaging grin—the one I'd witnessed turn many feminine cheeks flush since we'd met. "The King of Everything is indebted to *me*. Really, that just makes my day. And I get to hang out with you."

"I am a lucky girl for that." I gave him a quick hug.

"Feeling any better?" he asked.

"A little calmer, thank you."

"Great. Why don't you take a bath, have some hot tea, and relax? We'll move in the morning."

I didn't love the plan. But the upheaval could wait until tomorrow, I surmised. Amano was doing Amano things, anyway. No need to disrupt his business, especially since he was helping Dane and the rest of us. I didn't want to hinder their progress. The quicker my bodyguard got to the bottom of the snake visit, in addition to the indictments being wrapped up, the sooner Dane could come home. For good.

I took Kyle's advice and felt a little less tense as, later on, I curled on the couch and flipped through magazines. I retired early and crawled under the covers—after I had Kyle double-check all the locks on the windows and patio doors in my room. Take a peek beneath the bed and inside the closet for critters of the reptilian variety.

My nerves were still jangled, but I was exhausted, so it wasn't too difficult to drift off.

I woke some time later, a warm body spooning me from behind, muscles surrounding me. Or maybe I was dreaming of the intimate cocoon, because Dane couldn't possibly have returned so soon. He'd just been here with the FBI when they were in hot pursuit of Vale.

"Am I imagining this hard, hunky body pressed against me?" I whispered.

"Nope." His soft lips grazed my neck. I'd pulled my long, dark-brown hair up in a messy ponytail before falling asleep.

"Who called you?"

"Kyle."

"You're kidding?"

"He was worried about you. Said you had a meltdown earlier." Dane's voice was a low rumble against my skin. Sensuous, though also tinged with concern. "That's not like you, baby. At all. And it's not like Kyle to think he can't handle on his own anything that spins you up."

My eyes squeezed shut for a moment. "I suppose he mentioned the rattlesnakes?"

"That's why I'm here."

"Dane." I sighed. Wiggling in his loose embrace, I rolled onto my other side to face him. A devilishly handsome man with strong, sculpted features and a commanding, reassuring presence.

I whisked my fingertips over his cheek, then tried to smooth away the furrow between his brows. Not much luck there.

I told him, "You can't keep running back every time something happens to me. That's why Kyle and Amano stick around. To talk me off the ledges and protect me."

"That should be my job, right?" I heard the anguish in his voice and it broke my heart.

"You have another job to do. A very important one. And they know it—they understand how risky this is for you, too. How painful, really." I thought of Kyle's words when I'd had my panic attack. He wasn't hip on admitting Dane was living the proverbial rock and a hard place existence for a valiant cause but clearly couldn't dismiss it.

"Nothing's more important than you," Dane said, his emerald eyes glowing with an intense longing that mirrored my own, deep in my soul. The slivers of moonlight filtering in through the shutters made his dark-green irises shimmer, captivating me.

"And our baby," he added as he rubbed my stomach in the slow, circular motion that always made me want to purr. No matter how wound up I was. He had a very soothing effect on me.

"I'm not arguing the fact that you're here, or complaining about it," I told him. His priorities had shifted from 10,000 Lux to me when we married. Now to include our child. Dane wasn't the type to shy away from his responsibilities, but his focus really needed to be on his work with the FBI. "I don't want to distract you."

"Too late," he murmured against my lips, sending a shiver of delight down my spine. "It's impossible to stay away from you. Impossible to get you out of my mind."

His hand slid under the oatmeal-colored Henley I wore—his shirt. Unfortunately, it smelled of fabric softener, not Dane. Though it would after tonight, and tomorrow I'd be thrilled about that when I put it on again.

He palmed my breast and gently massaged.

"You don't have to be so careful with me," I reminded him. Ever since he'd found out I was pregnant, he'd considered me fragile. I wasn't.

He caressed a little rougher and excitement shot through me.

"Better," I said on a heavy sigh.

His thumb swept over the puckered bud. Then he pinched and rolled lightly. I instantly ached for him.

"I love your body," he said as he nibbled the corner of my mouth. "I love you."

"So make me come."

A throaty sound escaped him. "You know I will. Repeatedly."

He shifted away from me just long enough to drag the Henley up and over my head, tossing it aside. My panties followed. Dane was already naked and I feasted on all those chiseled-to-perfection muscles. I traced my nails over the hard ledge of his pecs, tenderly scraping a small nipple. Making him jolt from the wicked touch.

It never ceased to amaze me that I could incite such strong physical reactions from this man. He was powerful and mysterious. A bit intimidating. Incredibly brilliant.

Perhaps what really astonished me was that he was all mine.

My fingers skimmed lower, along the ridges of his abs. Lower still, until they wrapped around his thick shaft. I held him at the root and pumped slowly.

His head dipped and his tongue fluttered over my nipple, teasing it tighter. Then he suckled. A soft cry of pleasure fell from my lips.

He eased my hand away from his cock as he whispered, "You're too good at making *me* come." His head lifted and he kissed me. Slowly and seductively at first. Then it became a hot, sizzling lip-lock. I gripped his strong biceps with a hand and plowed the other through his lush, onyx hair.

I'd married a man who innately knew how to draw me in, how to mesmerize me so that all I could focus on, all I could think of, all I could feel, was *him*. His muscles and heat surrounding me, his lips and tongue engaging me further, his hands caressing my body. One of which skated downward, over my slightly rounded stomach, to the apex of my legs. The tips of his fingers glided along my slick folds.

Breaking the kiss, I stared into his eyes and said, "I'm already wet for you."

"And you make me so damn hard. So fast." His erection pressed to my hip. Tempting me once more.

While his fingertip flittered over my clit, his mouth wreaked beautiful havoc on my neck, his teeth nipping in all the sensitive spots that lit me up. Desire rushed through my veins.

"I'm feeling less and less guilty about you returning this evening," I told him.

"Baby, I want to come back to you every night." He slipped

two fingers inside me and leisurely stroked. "Mm, this is nice, but I want you wetter."

My inner walls contracted around his fingers as my hips undulated. The slow burn was sinfully delicious. A private decadence I loved sharing with him.

"You taste so fucking good," he said, his teeth tenderly biting just below my ear. "Once you have our baby—"

"I know exactly what you're going to do to me." And that thought hitched my pulse.

"Night after night."

He liked to make me come with his mouth, his lips and tongue teasing my clit, driving me half out of my mind. My OB-GYN didn't currently recommend it, so Dane refrained. But I craved the intimate act as much as he wanted to pleasure me that way.

"I can hardly wait for you to get me off like that again," I told him. "It's always so, so good." As was his current technique. I writhed beneath him, his chest pressed to my breasts. The heel of his hand rubbed the swollen knot of nerves between my legs as his fingers continued to stroke steadily, the tempo gradually increasing.

My breathing escalated with the quickening of the sensual rhythm. His pumping became more assertive, determined.

"Yes," I whispered. "Oh, God. Dane." My lids drifted closed. Erotic sensations sparked within me, searing and scintillating. Taunting me to give in to them. But I wasn't willing to just yet.

"Kiss me," I softly demanded.

His lips skimmed over my jaw and then his tongue toyed with mine before he claimed my mouth with his. He kissed me passionately, no holding back—leaving me with absolutely no doubt that this was where he wanted to be every night. With me, pushing me higher until the pleasure erupted deep in my pussy.

I tore my mouth from his and cried out, "Dane!" The orgasm blazed through me. Radiantly. Fantastically.

I clenched his fingers, prolonging my climax as long as possible.

"Now that *really* gets me going, baby." His warm breath on my temple made my skin tingle as much as the intense release. "There's nothing quite like you falling apart for me."

I reached for his hand and pulled it away, feeling every ripple along my sensitive flesh as he withdrew. I said, "I want you inside me."

He shifted ever so slightly. His tip nudged my opening. Anticipation mounted.

"Don't play," I insisted. "You know what I want."

He gave me a sweet kiss, our lips tangling. Ironic, because I knew what he intended to do to me would be anything but sweet. Because I liked it downright dirty with this man.

He massaged my breast again, causing me to squirm beneath him. My hips rose and the head of his cock pressed farther in.

"Yes," I breathed encouragingly. "Give me all of you."

He slung my leg over his waist and palmed my ass cheek, angling my pelvis. Then thrust in.

"Oh, fuck!" I screamed as he filled and stretched me.

"Ah, Christ, Ari." His voice was heavy with arousal. "You're so tight. So perfect."

My fingers curled more fiercely around his biceps as he buried himself within me, thrusting fervently.

"Yes," I told him. "Just like that." His hips bucked and he drove heartily, setting me on fire.

"Feel me deep inside you."

"Yes," I repeated, the adrenaline raging. "Fuck me," I begged, the frenzy already ignited, my need for him already clawing at me. "Dane, you feel so incredible."

He made love to me with the kind of fervor that pushed the air from my lungs and caused my inner muscles to clutch him so firmly, sharp, primal sounds blew between his teeth. Turning me on even more. Because I knew how excited *I* made *him*.

My other hand unraveled from his hair and I gripped his ass, not quite fully cupping a cheek but holding on to the enticing flesh and muscle as his butt flexed and released with his solid pumps into my body.

We moved together with a feverish pace. I had the insane craving to feel him deeper, like I couldn't get enough of him. But he was plunging and pulsating and sending me reeling toward another powerful release.

Yet the gnawing sensation grew, as though I just wanted to crawl inside him and be a permanent part of him. I couldn't get close enough to him, even though we were melded together, our bodies moving in perfect sync with each other. I wanted to be wrapped around his heart, live within his soul, consume his mind.

That was the selfish part of an obsessive, unrelenting love. I wanted to be his every waking thought, every breath he took.

I also knew he would do anything for me, and I would do anything for him. Including making all the sacrifices that tore us apart even when all we truly desired was to constantly be drowning in private, intimate moments, as we currently were.

I sensed precisely when everything shifted within him, pulled taut, threatened to erupt. It happened inside me as well.

"Dane," I said on a breathy sigh. "Come with me."

"Yes," he ground out. "Oh, fuck, yes. Ari!"

He thrust quicker. Raspy pants of air leapt from my throat.

"So amazing," I whispered. And then I lost it completely, coming on a loud scream, followed by the only word that registered in my mind: "Dane!"

My climax was amplified by his release, the hot moisture suddenly filling me, the convulsing of his body, the throbbing of his cock.

"Oh, goddamn, Ari," he said on a harsh breath. "You can make me forget everything but you."

His face burrowed in the crook of my neck. I slipped my arms around him. Held him to me. Smiled triumphantly. I'd gotten exactly what I'd wished for.

"I could stay buried inside you forever," he whispered, tugging on my heartstrings. "There's no place I'd rather be."

Emotion welled within me, mixing with the sexy feelings he evoked. "I like your pillow talk."

"That's not all you like," he said in a devilish tone.

"So true." I kissed the top of his head, his silky hair tickling my lips and skin. "I need you, Dane. Always."

"This is all I want," he told me. "You. Our baby. Our family."

"I know." But we were currently victims of circumstance. I tried not to think of that. Instead, simply basked in the way I'd connected with this man from that first electrifying moment when our gazes had met and I'd been instantly caught up in his raw intensity, the dark beauty of him.

He'd turned out to be so much more than I'd expected. A fiercely protective husband who would give us an heir to everything that Dane stood for—everything *we* now stood for.

Feeling somewhat swept away, I said, "It'd be okay if we never left the bedroom."

He chuckled. "Careful there, sweetheart. After all this is over, I might not *let* you leave."

My smile widened. It was an alluring sentiment. Still . . . "I suppose we'd have to eat from time to time."

"Maybe Rosa will agree to room service."

"Not a chance in hell," I scoffed. The efficient woman who'd basically run our home while Dane and I had been 24-7 Lux pre-launch preparations was not about waiting on anyone hand and foot. Fine by all of us, particularly since Kyle and I liked to do the cooking. But that pretty much meant no holing up in our suite for Dane and me.

Darn.

He eventually withdrew from me and slipped out of bed to tidy up in the bathroom. I, of course, admired the view. As he walked away and when he returned, strutting toward me. I sighed dreamily. My heart fluttered. My stomach felt as though butterflies had taken flight.

He gave me a sexy grin. "You can devour me with a look."

"And my mouth."

"Yes," he added with a mischievous glint in his eyes as he climbed in next to me. "That talented tongue of yours knows a few tricks of its own."

"My body parts are quite partial to yours. What can I say?" I snuggled close to my husband, his arms around me, my head on his. I absently trailed a fingertip over one of his scars, the constant reminder of the devastation at the Lux and how it'd significantly altered our lives.

I let out a long breath, hoping to expel the anxiety that instantly besieged me when I thought of all we'd been through and all that still needed to be done.

"Someday, we'll get our honeymoon, right?" I asked.

"I promise."

I was quiet for a few moments, a little lost in thought. Mostly lost in how wonderful it was to be in his loving, reassuring embrace and to be able to touch him. Even just hearing his steady breathing warmed and comforted me.

Eventually, I said, "I don't even know where you go or what you do when you're with the FBI."

"It's not just the FBI. This is a global problem the society sparked by using my intellectual property for their personal gain. The Feds are labeling it conspiracy, terrorism, and attempted murder if they can prove these assholes were behind the destruction of my hotel. There were forty people inside when the timer on that bomb started ticking."

I knew most of this, yet my head popped up and I stared at him, not missing the fury and the agony in his voice. The bunching of his muscles all around me.

Dane gently eased me back into his arms, though his hand

stroked my hair. "Ari, sweetheart. The only reason I'm away from you and our son is because I already know the impact these people can have on the worldwide economy. I don't want anyone to suffer again. Not like in '08. Jesus. All those lost jobs, all that despair. There were suicides because of financial strains and destitution. Retirements imploded. Foreclosures forced bankruptcy and homelessness. Families—*children*—went hungry. And there are so many still trying to recover from that."

I understood this wasn't just about Dane and the loss of the Lux. His dream. The poli-econ society he'd secretly been a part of had possessed the ability to effect positive change—that had been the goal for generations. Unfortunately, with the sort of intel they'd collected and dissected it was also possible to incite financial ruin, because some members' greed overrode their good sense and intentions.

He said, "The society put extensive effort into keeping disaster from striking again. But all that information—all the tracking, trending, analysis, forecasting . . ." He let out a strangled sound that was full of agitation . . . and torment. "In the wrong hands, it starts the vicious cycle of economic downturn and the struggle for recovery all over. To the benefit of those who are pulling the strings."

I'd always found the concept of "Billionaires' Clubs" difficult to wrap my mind around. A conglomeration of the elite could throw hundreds of millions of dollars at someone in the position of political power and influence in order to advance personal agendas. Not those designed for the greater good but for individual gain.

Dane had once said money was like a drug for some. It was an addiction only sated by building bigger empires, amassing more and more wealth—and, again, gaining power and using it to one's advantage.

His purpose within the society had never been self-serving.

What Dane and the legit members of the Illuminati bloc had attempted to do was maintain a sound economic environment. There would always be an ebb and flow, but a dramatic downward swing could spiral out of control. As we'd all experienced not too long ago.

Frankly, I never wanted to see people in such dire straits again. Nor did Dane. Hence the reason the generational society had dissolved. Now it was just Dane, Ethan Evans, Sultan Qadir Hakim, and Nikolai Vasil who attempted to right the wrongs.

Something I admired greatly. Even if it did mean my husband was mostly sequestered and rarely lying next to me.

I said, "You know I support what you're doing. And though I'm thrilled you're here with me, remember that you have faith in Kyle and Amano looking after me. I don't want to cause any problems with these indictment cases you're helping to build."

"I'm grateful for that." He kissed my forehead. "But when you're so scared that *Kyle* calls me . . . That's when I know where I have to be—what my most important priorities are."

"Then I have to keep from freaking out. Because you have serious work to do. And I want it wrapped up soon. So that you can come home to me."

His fingers stroked my cheek as a few tears tumbled along them.

"Soon, baby," he murmured against my hair. "I promise."

I slept soundly in Dane's protective embrace and woke feeling much more composed. Safer. Saner.

He made love to me once more; then we showered. We headed into the kitchen and I poured orange juice while Dane went straight for the coffeemaker and popped in the bold French roast pod he favored. The aroma wafted through the air and must have drawn Kyle, because he came in seconds later.

He wore a tank top and gym shorts. His hands clenched the

ends of the towel wrapped around his neck, and perspiration beaded his hairline. I assumed he'd just finished another P90X workout. He'd had muscles to strain the hems and fabric of his short-sleeved shirts from the time I'd met him, but now, he gave Marky Mark in his immortalized Calvin Klein boxer ads a run for his money.

My husband scowled. Clearly, he didn't like Kyle flaunting his biceps in front of me. I bit back a smile. Although Kyle proved swoon worthy to most women, *everything* about Dane riveted me. At six-three and with his broad shoulders and prominent features, he knocked the wind out of me every time he was near.

Lucky me, all Dane wore this morning was a pair of black drawstring pants. His hair—as dark and luxurious as polished obsidian—was a sexily tousled mess. His emerald eyes always glowed seductively when he looked at me. Even when he crooked a brow, as he did now, as though to ask, *Does Kyle always walk around all buffed out when I'm not here?*

I ignored the burning question in Dane's gaze and kissed him on the cheek. "Behave," I murmured. To Kyle, I asked, "Are you cooking or am I?"

"I'll do it. You two"—he waved a hand at us—"spend time together. Or . . . whatever."

"Thanks for calling him," I said. "I needed a little extra assurance to keep me from imagining rattling tails all night long."

Dane took a sip of coffee, then set the mug on the Italian marble counter. "Won't be long before this is all over. There'll be another indictment any day now—Keaton Wellington the Third. That only leaves one other society member out there. And trust me, he's shaking in his Gucci loafers."

I could see Dane gleaned a bit of satisfaction that his former investors were tormented by the full-court press put on them recently. Rightfully so on my husband's part.

"So when do the trials begin?" Kyle asked as he yanked open

the door on the Sub-Zero fridge and reached for the carton of eggs. He did the most amazing things with breakfast, and I hoped he had his thick, decadent, melt-in-your-mouth French toast on the menu this morning. I could practically smell the rich Mexican vanilla and he hadn't even made his way to the spice rack yet.

"The FBI and IRS criminal investigations are still under way. Corruption and tax evasion are substantial charges on their own. The heartier chunk of the puzzle is tying them into the bombing of the Lux. That'll nail their coffins shut."

Dane's strong jawline set and his eyes flashed with the need for revenge. It set me on-edge when he looked so formidable, so intimidating. But the razor-sharp vibe was warranted when it came to his luxury resort having been blown to bits. Not to mention the treacherous situation we were all in.

Kyle cracked eggs into a bowl as he asked, "Then what? More of our version of witness protection until all the convictions are made—if they're made? Not sure if Ari got around to mentioning it, but she wants to go back to the creek house."

I shot him a sardonic look for broaching the subject ahead of me. "Thanks so much."

"I'm not opposed to that," Dane said as he slid onto a high-backed upholstered stool at the island where Kyle worked. I joined Dane, draping my arm along the top of the stool next to his and propping my hip against the seat. "That location is securely monitored. It's also a bit smaller than this estate. Easier for surveillance." His tone held a contemplative tinge, so I deduced he wasn't wholly convinced moving was a good idea at the moment, but at least he considered the possibility. I appreciated that.

Being under Amano's and Kyle's watch made me infinitely happier than if I'd been secreted away somewhere by the FBI because I was Dane's wife. It was difficult enough giving up some personal freedoms for the sake of protection.

Kyle carried the empty carton of eggshells to the trash can, tossed it, then popped into the pantry. I studied Dane.

"I feel safer at the creek house," I told him. "Calmer. I can't explain why. I just do. And I never would have left if I wasn't having so much trouble with the morning sickness and dehydration my first couple of months with the baby and needed Macy's medical retreat."

Turned out to be a wise decision to seek professional, holistic help, and I was glad Kyle had suggested I consult Dr. Macy Stevens, his aunt. Her physical rehab facility also offered inpatient care for four people. I'd been one of the four, and the entire experience had been wholly beneficial, possibly even lifesaving, given that I'd lost weight rapidly at the beginning of my pregnancy, not gained. And dehydration was never something to fool around with. Nor was the extreme grief I'd suffered when I'd believed Dane had been killed in the Lux destruction.

Now here I was entering my third trimester. That likely lent to my desire to return home.

Dane said, "I know you like it there." He brushed away a plump curl from my temple. "And you know that I'd grant you any wish. As long as I don't think it puts you in jeopardy."

"Yes." I leaned toward him and kissed him softly. Against his lips, I said, "I also know that, sometimes, I have to coax you into granting my every wish."

The corner of his mouth lifted. "This ought to be interesting."

"Well." I splayed my palms over his sculpted pecs. He was too fantastically built not to touch every chance I got. "We do have baby planning in the midst of all of this mayhem. I want the world's most amazing nursery, Dane. I want our son to open his eyes every time he wakes and see the extreme his parents would go to in order to make him happy."

Tears suddenly prickled the backs of my own eyes. Maybe I was hormonal. Or perhaps it was that I suffered from long absences from my seriously sexy husband and the fact that nothing about my pregnancy had been commonplace. I wanted everything following the delivery to be perfect. And I wanted our son to have stability in one home—not be moved from location to location because of extortion, explosions, high-speed car chases, and the like.

Dane's handsome face became a mask of hard angles. I'd seen the expression before. He went to a very dark place in his mind when dealing with this terrifying nightmare we all endured.

"Baby—"

"I'm not complaining about this house," I was quick to say. "The estate is incredible. It's just . . . not home. Not *our* home, even if you did have it built for us. We both know where we belong, Dane. And I want He-Who-Will-Hopefully-Be-Named-Soon to have roots. Not a transient life."

"I agree. If you want to go back to the creek house, we'll make it happen." He kissed me tenderly, making my toes curl. "Whatever you want."

"You and this kid will suffice," I said with a smile as my fingers swept through his hair.

Dane did his usual schooling of expressions to erase the tense one. "FYI, though. Kyle's not going to live with us. Not after I'm done with the FBI."

"I don't know," I mused. "He's really gotten into this bodyguard stuff. I think he might self-appoint for a gig looking after our so—"

"Not a chance," Dane grumbled.

I laughed softly as I reached for my glass of orange juice and sipped while Dane seethed over his mug of coffee.

I turned back to him and said, "We do have the space, that's for cer—"

"Hey," Kyle interjected as he returned from the walk-in pantry, his voice sharp, tinged with just enough *holy shit* to send a dark shiver through me. "What the hell is that red dot on Ari's forehead?"

chapter 2

Dane's gaze snapped up from his cup and he apparently saw the dot, too, because his ceramic mug went sailing across the room and he leapt to his feet, whirling around. I stood paralyzed where I was, staring at Tom Talbot, head of the watchtower security detail. He held a high-tech rifle in his hands with a scope on top. The barrel was pointed right at me.

My heart launched into my throat. Dane took one step to the side, his body shielding mine.

"Oh, hell, no!" he roared in a harsh tone. "You are *not* threatening my wife and child."

"Move out of the way, Dane," Tom said. "You're not the target."

"The fuck I'm not. She has nothing to do with this." His voice was grave and dangerous—I had no delusions his chiseled features were as well.

I could barely breathe, could barely process this new peril we suddenly faced.

Kyle twitched. Dane told him, "Don't move. Not unless he tells you to. Do whatever he says, Kyle. Don't take any risks."

Dane had read Kyle's expression, I had no doubt. My best friend would have instantly been plotting in his head what course of action to take in order to rescue me.

"He's right, Kyle," I said from behind Dane, surprised I even got the words out, I was so terrified.

"This is a huge mistake," Dane told Tom. "You'll regret even considering this. I'll make sure of it."

"She's your biggest weakness," Tom explained. "Since Vale couldn't complete his mission, I have no choice but to—"

"Vale's still alive," I said, peering around Dane's thick biceps.

"Ari," Dane all but growled.

I shifted so that I was concealed behind him again. "I'm just pointing that out."

"You're wrong," Tom said. "He *is* dead."

"But the snakes . . . ," I muttered.

I was sure my rapidly beating pulse wasn't good for my current condition, yet I couldn't slow it or pull in a full breath. Fear slithered through my veins. This was not a scenario I'd ever anticipated any of us finding ourselves in.

"Kyle, move over there with them," Tom instructed.

"No!" I cried out. "Leave him out of this! Let him go—please!"

"Shut up, Ari," Kyle grumbled. "As if I'd walk away." He joined us and swiftly pushed me backward, behind him, so I had a double layer of protection.

Tears stung my eyes—not just because of the massive scare factor of knowing that ominous red dot was now on my husband's forehead and that Kyle was in equal danger, but also because I was monumentally pissed off at how Tom had turned on all of us.

"If Vale is dead," I managed to say, "then who put the snakes on the patio?"

"I don't know," Tom told us. "Someone from the society network. I left the gate open while you were all out last night and turned a blind eye."

"You son of a bitch," Dane said.

"I had to do as instructed."

"But there's no Lux!" I shouted, the anger getting the best of me. "It's over. It's all *over!*"

"No," Dane reasoned. "Because Tom here has compromised the *entire* society network by telling them I'm still alive. Right?"

"I haven't told anyone anything. Only took the directive and said I'd eliminate Ari."

"This doesn't make any sense," I contended, trying to see around the two brick walls protecting me. "If there's no hotel, what is the point in continuing this attack on us?"

"It's the principle of the matter," Dane explained. "They destroyed the Lux as a last resort. The ultimate statement. But they didn't get the checkmate they sought, because I'm the one who produced all the evidence for the indictments. That'll be confirmed for them today, thanks to Tom. And if he doesn't take my queen in this living, breathing game of chess, he's a dead man. Aren't you, Tom?"

"I'm glad you understand. This isn't what I want," the security guard said. "But I have to do what's required of me."

"Problem is," Dane countered, "I'm the knight protecting the key component of your strategy—and you're not getting to her."

"I don't want to shoot you, Dane. But have no doubt—I will. In the leg or the shoulder. Whatever it takes to get you out of the way. Kyle, too. Ari's the mark."

I swallowed hard, understanding the motivation here was to cripple Dane for his involvement. Not physically, but emotionally. By taking his family out. Right before his very eyes.

I'd had enough exposure to the shady side of the secret society to accept that those who'd crossed the line did so with the full intention of going all the way to get what they wanted. Empires and legacies were at stake. And even those who were simply the soldiers within the network had so much to lose or gain, so much to shelter, that they'd allow themselves to be manipulated—as Tom had—just to get their piece of the pie.

It was sickening. Chillingly frightening. But not exactly a new world order. It was a different kind of gangster warfare—the billionaires' mafia.

"This isn't in your nature," Dane told Tom. "If it were, you would have taken the shot when you had it. But you hesitated, giving me the chance to intervene. So put your weapon down and we'll work this out. Otherwise . . . You realize you won't take another breath if anything happens to Ari and my child."

His menacing tone made my heart thunder and my insides seize up. I knew how deadly this could get when it came to any threat against me. With our baby involved—and even Kyle—that would make Dane even more determined to win this game. By any means necessary.

"Dane," I nervously whispered. "This is out of hand again."

"Actually, it's all coming together."

"What?" I couldn't see around Kyle's sturdy frame and that frustrated me.

Dane said, "You only get one shot, Tom."

"You're not going to be able to stop me, Dane."

"Be glad."

I heard Amano's voice across the room, in the direction from where Tom stood. He was supposed to be with Jackson Conaway, our lawyer, working out some logistics for when the trials started and Dane was fully sequestered.

In a menacing tone, Amano added, "If it were up to Dane, he'd save the bullets and kill you with his bare hands. I'll be sparing you the drawn-out agony by simply shooting you in the head."

I gasped.

Amano must have deduced from his grilling last night that Tom was the culprit, our breach in security. Now apparently

Amano had crept up behind Tom, but Christ, I couldn't see a thing! All I knew was that a standoff ensued . . . and I didn't expect Tom to amiably surrender and back away. These people didn't operate that way. It was all or nothing when it came to this precarious endeavor.

My stomach knotted. I reached out for Kyle, my fingers curling around the material of his tight tank top at his spine. I leaned toward him, needing the support. My knees nearly knocked together and I swayed a little as horror rolled through me.

Kyle muttered, "Step back, Ari."

"Behind the counter," Dane added. "Crouch low."

I was afraid to move. Too petrified to move, what with a gun pointed at my husband, and Kyle in the line of fire as well.

"Do it," Kyle insisted. "He's got no clear shot of you. Trust us."

I did—explicitly. That didn't keep me from shaking from head to toe.

"Ari," Kyle practically snarled. "Fucking do it!"

I released his shirt, hunched down, and crept to the end of the island, hunkering further, not daring to steal a peek around the corner for fear there was some small gap between Dane and Kyle that Tom could aim through to get to me.

Then I remembered there were tall glass patio doors behind me, so I spared a glance over my shoulder and watched in the reflection of the panes as the impasse unraveled.

"Stand down," Dane said to the gunman.

"You know I can't do that."

"Is whatever they're paying you really worth this?"

Tom shook his head. "It's not the money. They have *my* wife and kid."

Oh, my God!

"Dane." That one word wrenched from my mouth and filled the quiet room.

"Fuck!" he yelled, enraged. I could practically feel the angst radiating from him. "Who the hell contacted you? Was it Bryn Hilliard?"

"I don't know. He didn't say. Obviously he's high enough up the chain of command to capture Candace and Ruby, and instruct me on what to do in order to get them back safely. He put them on the line briefly and they sounded terrified, so he wasn't bullshitting me about kidnapping them."

"Goddamn it." Dane's fury reverberated within me.

"You really think I would have chosen this?" Tom insisted in a low tone. "You really believe I would do this if I had any choice whatsoever?"

"Jesus Christ!" Kyle's violent outburst scared me all the more, because he was a bit of a loose cannon while he still learned the bodyguard ropes. There was no telling what he might do to save me. The very reason I'd asked him on more than one occasion to reconsider this new quest of his to protect me when Dane couldn't be here with us and when Amano had FBI business to attend to.

"They forced my hand," Tom continued. "That's the only reason I let someone on-property to plant the snakes. The only reason I'm standing here, pointing a gun at you."

"You won't hit your mark," Dane said. "I won't let you. It was a good attempt, but you're not getting to Ari. Whatever happens to your family because you failed is on you."

"I know that."

Despite Dane's cold words, I suspected his mind worked feverishly with how to get Candace and Ruby out of the clutches of Hilliard's henchmen. Dane wouldn't let them suffer if there was anything he could do about it.

I watched as Tom's arms dipped in defeat, in surrender. My eyes squeezed shut from relief—and to fight back tears.

He wouldn't shoot Dane.

Yet a heartbeat later the sound of a gunshot ripped through the house. I screamed. The noise and the sinister, horrific implication jolted me. My eyes flew open. Dane reeled backward, plowing into Kyle.

"Dane!" I cried out.

Just as Amano slammed the butt of his gun to Tom's temple. Tom Talbot dropped to the floor.

I stood and whirled around to face everyone. Tom's rifle hit the tiles and Amano kicked the weapon away. I scrambled around the counter as Kyle helped Dane to a chair, which he slumped into.

"Oh, shit!" I stared in shock at the blood gushing from the gaping hole in his shoulder. Kyle bled, too. The bullet must have exited Dane's shoulder and grazed Kyle's biceps.

A rush of adrenaline propelled me forward. I snatched two clean linen napkins from the kitchen table where Dane sat and pressed them against Kyle's arm. "Hold these firmly."

Then I raced back to the island, jerked open a drawer, and extracted several dish towels. I hurriedly returned to Dane and held the thick material to his wound, applying as much pressure as I could with shaky hands and panic vibrating through me.

Kyle had to help me with his free hand while keeping the napkins to his arm. Dane fished his iPhone from his pocket and hit a speed dial number. Amano was on the phone, too. From the sound of the conversation, I'd venture to say he spoke with Jackson. A man who knew how to handle dire situations such as this.

I certainly didn't know what the hell to do.

Luckily, Dane had a private physician, and that was whom he called.

Amano also told Jackson about Tom's wife and daughter being in jeopardy. All the while, Amano kept his gun trained on Tom. Who didn't so much as flinch. He was out cold.

To be honest, I was surprised Amano hadn't shot him. It must have tested the very limits of his restraint not to have inflicted mortal injury when it came to someone he'd trusted with all of our lives—who'd betrayed us all. Someone who'd just threatened my life and used Dane for target practice.

"This is getting a little too real." Kyle's voice was tense, rough around the edges. "Like, seriously? Now we've reached the point of dueling over breakfast—to hell with high noon?"

"Pressure's on the society," Dane said. His gaze slid to me. "It'll get worse before it gets better. So you get your wish. Creek house. And you don't leave Amano's or Kyle's sight. Do you hear me?"

I nodded, not even capable of cracking my usual joke about whether they'd follow me into the ladies' room. Tears crested the rims of my eyes and streamed down my flushed cheeks. My heart still pounded; my pulse still raged. I was a mess. Though I tried really hard not to show Dane how freaked out I was.

"He could have killed you." I bit my trembling lower lip, desperately hoping I wouldn't fall apart.

"Don't think about that," he said.

"How can I not?" I quietly demanded. *"He actually pulled the fucking trigger."*

"He did what he had to do, without taking it to the next level. He didn't want to shoot either one of us. Hilliard will make him pay for the screwup. Either before Tom heads off to prison or while he's inside."

Dane contacted FBI Agents Daugherty and Strauss, whom he'd worked with as he handed off evidence against the society.

When Dane wrapped up the conference call and shoved the cell into his pocket, I asked, "Could it have been Wayne Horton who was sent in with the snakes? He does seem to get off on terrorizing me."

"Doubtful. He worked directly for Vale. No paycheck attached to being a lone wolf," Dane said, clearly fighting a wince of pain. And trying to keep the look of sheer agony from me as he continued to bleed—too much for my comfort. The dish towels were already coated in crimson.

He added, "I can't imagine Horton would go to all this trouble without a funding source. And Bryn wouldn't be able to count on him, since Wayne and Vale failed their mission the first time around."

"Not necessarily," I said. "Wayne could very well have been the one to bomb the Lux."

Kyle snorted. "Probably hoping Ari was inside. She's right—seems he's taken a personal interest in making her suffer."

"You think he'd come after her for the sport of it at this point?" Dane lobbed the question out there, but he didn't sound convinced Wayne would pursue this avenue without Vale to provide the directives.

Kyle said, "You didn't see Horton chasing us up the switchbacks with hairpin turns and no shoulder on her side of the car—just a forty-five-hundred-foot drop into Oak Creek Canyon."

Dane's scowl deepened. "Don't think for a second that I'm letting him off the hook. Not after all the damage he's done. That asshole's on my list, believe me."

"Dane." I didn't like that lethal blade to his voice that sliced through me.

He was slipping back into that dark and dangerous place in his mind.

I knew he wanted vengeance. And he certainly deserved it. Yet it was what he was willing to do in the name of retribution that alarmed me.

"Kyle, you're on-watch," Amano said as he gestured to Tom, then shoved his gun in his holster. "Don't touch the rifle. We don't want to smudge the prints on it."

"You got this?" Kyle asked me of Dane's wound.

"Yes." I bucked up. Forced my hands to steady.

Kyle crossed to the other side of the kitchen and said, "My GLOCK's in my room."

"You'll survive."

"Seriously, you're leaving me unarmed with him?"

"The man is unconscious, Kyle," Amano stated in a flat voice.

"Or dead," Kyle mumbled.

"He's still breathing. Just keep an eye on him. If he comes to, you know what moves to use on him."

Kyle's chest puffed out a bit. "You got that right."

Amano left us briefly, evidently to retrieve Dr. Forrester from the other side of the massive walls surrounding the estate, which sat in a secluded portion of a box canyon in Sedona. Though we were surrounded by breathtaking red-rock formations, I currently found no beauty in our grim world. Not with my insides twisted and Dane and Kyle bleeding. The scent and sight of it made me nauseous, but I tamped down the bile burning my throat.

I eyed Dane closely, seeing the rage burning within him. I had no doubt it took all the willpower *he* possessed—and then some—to keep from either shooting Tom himself or kicking the shit out of him. Good thing the man was already down for the count.

Forrester and his team arrived.

"Do something, quick!" I urged the doctor. "He's lost a lot of blood."

"Ari, baby." Dane planted his hand on my hip as I stood between his veed legs while still applying pressure to his shoulder. "I'm all right."

This made the tears fall faster. "There was a gun pointed at your head."

"There was one pointed at yours, too." His gaze locked with mine, holding it unwaveringly, conveying a wealth of emotion that tore at me.

I nodded slightly. He understood exactly how I felt—he felt the same. Had been just as horrified when I'd been the target. He just controlled his emotions better, kept a cooler head.

"Okay," I said, though my voice cracked. "I'll be calm."

It was a lie, of course. And he knew it. But what good would hysterics do us at this moment? I also had the baby to think about. I hated bad vibes coming his way. So I took several full breaths.

Dr. Forrester had brought two assistants, who joined us. One saw to Tom. The other started in with stitches to Kyle's arm. Forrester himself took care of Dane, declaring it was indeed an exit wound.

Of course, Kyle could attest to that—and did with a smirk. Knowing my courageous and somewhat crazy best friend, he likely felt heroic for taking part of the bullet. That worried me substantially, but Kyle had superman qualities springing to life around every treacherous corner. There was nothing I could do about that.

I helped Dr. Forrester move Dane to a bedroom. The physician patched him up and hooked him to an IV to replace the blood he'd lost. Apparently, Dane donated regularly to his own cause and Forrester kept the supply on-hand for him, and traveled with all the necessary equipment. A haunting thought, yet a comforting reality.

Still quaking from head to toe, I washed up at the kitchen sink, and Kyle did the same while Dane rested. The assistants donned gloves, suits, and boots to clean the mess on the floors and the island. Then they disinfected, as though hazmat duties were just part and parcel of their jobs. I didn't want to know how true that might be, given their connection to Dane's network.

"That was a little too close for comfort," Kyle said after they'd left and we were alone.

"You don't have to tell *me* that."

"I hate to admit it, but if Dane hadn't been here . . ." Kyle grimaced. "Tom wouldn't have let me near you, and you would have been a bull's-eye in a wide-open space."

A chill raced down my spine. "Nothing like one of your own turning on you." What a fucking nightmare this had became. "I know Tom didn't want to harm any of us. But what other option did he have? He can't even be sure that the people *he* cares about are okay. This is just so bad and wrong, on more levels than I can even process."

"I'm with you on all counts—including thinking that Horton might still be involved. Something has to be done about that douche."

We stared at each other as we stood at the sink, fresh towels still in hand as we dried off.

I knew precisely what Kyle meant, what he silently implied. We'd had this discussion before—right here in this very spot, in fact.

We had a plan. It'd been formulated after Kyle had learned Amano had been tracking Wayne's activity to ascertain the extent of his involvement with Vale's kidnapping plot last year. Amano had kept tabs on Wayne's comings and goings. Kyle and I both knew the results, knew Wayne's patterns.

"It's not exactly far-fetched to 'bump' into him here in town," Kyle reminded me, "since Horton has been sticking pretty close so that he could move in on us whenever Vale snapped his fingers. We know his favorite places to hang. Cliff Castle Casino being one of them."

"Dane would go through the roof that we're even talking about this," I warned. Not that I changed the subject. "Trying to get a confession out of Wayne would put me in more danger. Dane'll throttle you if anything goes wrong. Amano, too, if there's anything left of you." I rolled my eyes. "Dane would strangle you just for strategizing with me."

"Goddamn it, Ari," Kyle said under his breath. Although no one else was in the room, neither of us would be shocked if Amano lingered close enough to pick up on any scheme we might concoct to help with the investigations and do whatever we could to put an end to the reign of terror.

How could we not want to do whatever possible to help neutralize this situation?

Kyle continued. "As stealthy as Dark Knight is, Dane can't be in five places at once. There's still so much he has to do—he can't even get to the hard drive he needs that's sitting in a safe-deposit box in Switzerland, because he's supposed to be dead."

"That cover's pretty much shot to shit now." I cringed at my crappy choice of words as much as at how I feared the society might now know he was alive. With a shake of my head, I said, "We have to stick to whatever plan Dane and Amano devise, or we could throw everything out of whack."

I believed that was the only reason Amano hadn't followed through on his threat to shoot Tom in the head. The reason Dane hadn't taken matters into his own hands when he'd had the chance—and the justification—to leave Tom Talbot a bloody mess on our kitchen floor.

Kyle kept at our confession-reaping scheme. "Even Dane conceded our idea was reasonable when he'd heard of it."

Amano had not only put a stop to our plotting but also shared our tactic with Dane for good measure—knowing he would lay down the law that left no room for interpretation. We weren't to make any aggressive moves. Just follow his and Amano's lead.

He'd be pissed to high hell that we revisited this subject. Yet I was pissed, too. Had every right to be. And I wanted to do something about it.

Still, I hedged as I thought of Dane with a hole in his shoulder. It brought back too many excruciating and insidious memories of when I'd believed him dead—and when I'd seen him for the first time after months of suffering under that belief. He'd been severely injured and had the scars to prove it. I couldn't go through that again.

Bringing home the salient point that if anything went wrong on mine and Kyle's end it'd devastate Dane.

So I said, "I'm not stressing him out further, Kyle. My God. He took a bullet for me today. So did you." I gave him a contrite look. "I would try to send you away one more time, but now I'm thinking it's better you stay close. You might be a sitting duck all on your own." I tossed the towel aside and let out a sharp, humorless laugh. "You're a sitting duck by staying with us." This nearly shredded me. "Christ, Kyle. You could have been killed today."

"Wouldn't be the first time I was on the ragged edge."

"Don't act like this is some cool Vin Diesel movie," I snapped, my nerves—and my concern for Kyle's well-being—getting the best of me. "That day on the switchbacks was seriously hazardous to our health. *This* was even worse."

"Ari." He gave me an unfaltering look. "You're wigging, and I understand why. I get it, okay? This was yet another full-on game of chicken that, fortunately, we once again won." He gripped my shoulders and said, "Splash some cold water on your face and try to calm down. Then go see Dane. Just . . . not like this. Shit, you're all ghostly and traumatized."

"Everything was going so well, working out the way it should. All this time and effort Dane has put into helping the FBI yielded results. And then, *bam!* Wayne Horton strikes back? Or Bryn Hilliard? That menace to the human race should be sweating bullets over his criminal indictment, not devising ways to send one through my skull."

Kyle actually blanched. Not exactly a familiar expression for my steadfast friend. The flash of white against his tanned skin was a bit unnerving. "You can't imagine what it was like to see that infrared dot on your forehead." He had to glance away and drag a hand down his face. It took several seconds for his gaze to return. "Ari, it scared the shit out of me."

"I was scared, too. For all of us."

"Damn it!" His torment ate at me. "I know there's no fucking point to venting, no sanity wrapped around it, but, Christ. Everything that's happened so far has been complete bullshit and I'm mad as hell. What we just went through—"

He whirled around. Stalked away. Then he pulled up short at the kitchen table where the trail of blood from the island had led to the chairs and pooled at the legs. All cleaned up now, but the memory didn't fade. My stomach roiled and more fat drops welled in my eyes.

Kyle spun back to face me. "I can't leave, even though I know I should. What purpose is there to staying? Sure, maybe I can protect you, too. Then again, maybe not. I'm not two steps ahead of everything the way Dane and Amano are. I'm reacting as the shit hits the fan, not before it's even been flung."

"Don't gross me out," I complained. "All that blood made me queasy as it is."

He closed the gap between us. Kyle stared into my eyes, the way he had the night before, when I was all worked up over the diamondbacks. Only this time there was more than his perpetually tortured soul reflected in his blue irises.

"Dane's right," Kyle told me. "This *is* getting worse. And you're stuck in the middle of it all. I just want to take you away from it, Ari. I want to put you in a car—if I could just get my fucking Rubicon back from the creek house—and drive you far, far away."

My heart wrenched. "Kyle."

"I love you, Ari." The torment deepened. "But what the hell good does that do? What does it mean?" He stepped away once more, though I still felt his fury. "Not a goddamn thing."

He turned and stormed off. The breath rushed from my lungs. My heart constricted. And more tears fell.

I loathed being the source of his agony. But it seemed inescapable.

How had one chance encounter between Dane, Kyle, myself, and a snake-tatted blond at a wedding nearly a year ago turned so twisted and mangled? So hazardous and painful?

If we survived this cyclone of evil, it certainly wouldn't be unscathed. Physically or emotionally.

Not for any of us.

chapter 3

I did as Kyle had suggested and composed myself before visiting Dane, upon Dr. Forrester's approval.

I entered the bedroom but halted just beyond the threshold when I got a good look at Dane, propped up against a mound of pillows, his left biceps and shoulder wrapped in white gauze and tape, his arm in a sling. He was much paler than usual. About as ticked off as I was used to seeing him. Still, I fought the gape.

"You look like hell," I said, trying to keep my tone even.

"Well, I did just get shot," he deadpanned. "And I've still got a mind to make Tom suffer more than a concussion."

"I suspect that worrying about imminent imprisonment and the safety of his wife and daughter will be excruciating enough. Any word on them from the FBI?"

"No. And that's not my concern."

"Dane." I knew he was just being ornery. Of course he wouldn't want any harm to come to two innocent people. "Tom did what he had to—and his wife and daughter are going to pay the price?"

"Ari." Dane sighed in frustration, because I pulled all the right strings. I knew him too well. With his good hand, he gestured for me to join him. "Are you expecting me to save the world?"

"No. I already told you that, because you've been the one to take on all the burden of an epic ordeal you didn't even start." Sitting gingerly on the bed, I asked, "There is something you can do, though, right? For Candace and Ruby?"

He gave me a look that clearly said he knew leaving that potentially fatal situation up to Tom wasn't possible—if he wanted to please or pacify me.

"The FBI is searching for them. It's out of my hands now, but I did give them some leads I thought might be useful. Amano had some ideas as well." His head rolled back and forth against the pillow as he added, "Problem is, my network has been compromised, as we learned today. So I can't pinpoint a specific direction in which to go with this. I don't know who to trust at the moment."

I inhaled deeply. Tried not to panic any more than I had been all morning. He didn't need me crazed on top of everything else he dealt with—including his latest society-inflicted wound.

"How do you feel?" I asked. "Aside from wanting to rip the heads off of a hell of a lot of people?"

He snickered. "It's a little hard to see past that at present."

"I can believe that. But, Dane, you have to concentrate on healing."

"That's the doc's job—why I pay him so damn much. All I can think of is how I'm going to get my revenge on Bryn Hilliard."

I swept away some wayward strands from Dane's forehead. He usually kept his dark hair shorter but still wore the mussed style perfectly, even though it was a bit longer than normal. Sexily rakish. "I don't like you adding another layer to all of this."

He crooked a brow at me.

"I know. I hear you without you even saying a word. At the same time, you agreed to legal retribution. Not bodily harm."

His emerald gaze was a steely one. "You can't even begin to imagine how furious I am. How much what just happened—what could have happened to you and our child—terrified the hell out of me."

"Yes, I can." I swallowed a lump of emotion. "Because you were in the line of fire, too. So was Kyle." I fought the churning of my stomach. "There is nothing worse in my mind than losing you. Except—"

I spared a glance at my belly. A peculiar thought gelled in my head. One I wasn't sure he'd understand.

I said, "I don't really know how to say this, because it won't come out right. But I would sacrifice myself for you; the way you did for me. It's just that, in doing so, I'd put our son's life in danger. I wouldn't want to hurt him. Or leave you without him."

The waterworks started. All this tension couldn't be good for the baby, which aggravated me further. Made me a little irrational, so that I wasn't quite thinking straight.

I told Dane, "You'd be upset if anything happened to me, I know. But this kid . . ." I stared up at Dane and saw the raw pain in his eyes. "That would be pure hell for you."

"*All* of this is pure hell for me."

"But it's *necessary*, Dane." I emphasized the importance of what he was doing, even though it bordered on disastrous. Yet there was so much good that would inevitably come of us sticking to the plan. "I chose to travel this path with you. I'm perfectly aware of the risks. I had plenty of opportunities to step away from the flame. But I love you and I can't be without you. And what you're doing—"

I sighed, not able to latch on to the words to accurately express my admiration for his determination and resiliency. "So many people will benefit from the collapse of the society. You're the one making it happen. I'm so proud of you."

I leaned toward him and he draped his good arm around my shoulder, holding me tight. My cheek pressed to his bare pecs, his warm, smooth skin reassuring. I flattened my palm against the corrugated grooves of his abdomen and stayed nestled against him for Lord only knew how long, inhaling his delicious scent and finding the steady rise and fall of his chest soothing.

He drifted in and out of sleep, likely from the pain meds. I gleaned a huge amount of relief from his light, fluid snoring. It helped to bring my anxiety down several notches.

Amano came for us mid-afternoon, when Dane was rested.

"You're packed," Amano told me in his low voice. "Whenever you're both ready, we'll move."

"No time like the present," I said, desperately wanting to go home. I gazed at Dane, whose eyelids had fluttered open when he'd heard Amano speak. "If you're up to it, that is."

"Of course." He didn't have any trouble throwing his long, powerful legs over the side of the bed and getting to his feet. My brow dipped. Maybe he'd refused the pain meds, not wanting anything to impair his judgment or slow him down. "Let's do this," he simply said.

Dread clawed at me. He had to be hurting. Inside and out.

Amano told him, "Strauss came for Tom and the rifle. Questioned Kyle and myself. He'll be in contact with you again once he's interrogated Talbot."

"That prick had better know to stay away from my family." Dane's tone was deadly.

My stomach coiled. I figured we were due for a serious talk about all this turmoil, not just what had happened today. But now was hardly the time, so it was shoved to the back burner.

Which created a bit more internal strife. I couldn't help feeling as though our relationship, our marriage, our love grew more tenuous with every threat against us. And it was evident in Dane's eyes that this weighed heavy on his mind as well.

Yet we were too caught up in the current situation to address the overarching issue of how all of these vicious attacks impacted our life together.

We took Amano's SUV to the house in Oak Creek Canyon. He and Kyle selected rooms and assigned one to Rosa, our house manager. Amano had spoken with her and she'd agreed to a live-in arrangement. He and Dane felt more comfortable with her on-property as opposed to coming and going, possibly being followed and inadvertently putting herself in harm's way. Since she'd been with Dane for some time and didn't have kids or a husband at home, she didn't mind the employment deal. Plus, we paid her incredibly well.

The bedroom in the main wing that sat on the other side of our master suite bathroom was designated for the nursery, and I was relieved to have the impending chore of setting it up to keep my mind off everything else.

After dinner, which Kyle whipped up for everyone, since he put as much effort into being Iron Chef as he did bodyguard—a curious combination—Dane and I retired to our suite. I took a quick, hot shower just to help me relax further. Being in our home did amazing things for my psyche, and my stomach settled. I rubbed it while using my free hand to blow-dry my hair.

I couldn't imagine what this kid inside of me must be thinking. All of my agitation, jumping nerves, crying jags. Chances were good he'd want to stay huddled in his protective cocoon rather than face the big, bad world in which we lived.

But he still had four more months before making his grand entrance. Plenty of time for the mayhem to be resolved and the bad guys to be locked up. As Dane had mentioned, the trials would begin soon, and I highly doubted they'd be dragged out, given all of the evidence he'd provided.

As I thought of the decimated Lux, I felt a flutter in my belly. The first sensation of the baby stirring. I set aside the dryer and went into the bedroom, where Dane was sprawled on the California king, resting against the mound of pillows, reading a book. As I entered, he set the hardback novel aside and gave me a suspicious look.

"You're smiling."

Yeah, not exactly something I'd done of late.

I carefully sat on the mattress so as to not jar him and placed his good hand on my stomach.

"Can you feel anything?"

I knew it wasn't really a kick. My doctor had told me I'd feel a light "popcorn popping" or the fluttering I'd experienced around this time of my pregnancy, but actual kicks were still a bit off. Didn't matter. Just feeling the baby move inside me was a wonderful, reassuring sensation.

Dane concentrated hard but then gave a slight shake of his head. "Nothing yet."

"It's very subtle. But I feel it."

He raised his hand and cupped the side of my face. "That's incredible. You're incredible." Love blazed in his eyes and it warmed my heart.

"I hope I'll be a good mom."

"You'll be the best."

I inched forward and kissed him softly. "At least I know how *not* to be an evil witch from hell."

That would be my own mother. A woman who had not only destroyed my father and abandoned me years ago, until she'd discovered I had something she finally deemed of worth—money and prestige—but who also recently threatened my father's stellar reputation as a former PGA favorite in an attempt to extort cash from me. She'd even tried to collect on the tragedy at 10,000 Lux.

I didn't feel guilty that she and I were estranged, that I held no love for her. I'd had to sever that tie long ago, for my own sanity. I wasn't sure anyone could honestly say they wanted absolutely nothing to do with a parent, but sometimes it was born of sheer necessity.

I had yet to tell Dane my mother had returned to Sedona after the explosion. Kyle had helped me deal with the situation at that point. I'd needed her off my back, away from me so that she didn't create more drama and tension.

Granted, I still harbored a hint of apprehension over how she'd respond if she learned Dane was alive and that we were married. Would she darken my doorstep again? Concoct some other method to get her hands on my money?

I wouldn't spend the rest of my life paying her off; I'd already discerned that. Nor would Dane. But what if she used our secret marriage against us? Worse, what if she used my pregnancy against us?

Kathryn DeMille had proven she wasn't above dirtying her own hands to better her situation. She'd been willing to fess up to adultery for the sake of a lucrative book deal if her blackmailing me didn't pan out. Luckily, Dane had put a stop to that insidious plot.

She was definitely a piece of work.

I shuddered.

Dane frowned. His thumb whisked over my cheekbone. "Hey. What are you thinking about?"

I didn't like keeping anything from him, so I admitted, "Something I failed to tell you after I was released from the hospital and figured out you were among the land of the living, though working undercover with the FBI."

The crease between his eyes spoke volumes. If something disturbed me or posed a problem, he wanted to be the first to know. So he could deal with it.

But my independent nature forced me to try to solve my own crises. Which irked him in that possessive *it's my job to protect you, Ari* sort of way.

However, I said, "Just mentioning my mother makes me fear she's going to materialize in a plume of smoke, broom in hand."

"Thought we took care of that."

"No," I corrected with a bit of scolding in my tone that made his brow crook. "*You* took care of it, when I'd specifically asked you not to, remember?"

"Ari. The woman planned to bleed you dry. You would have been stuck signing over every paycheck to her, working your fingers to the bone for nothing."

"True," I reluctantly agreed. "Though I was formulating a strategy to—" The other brow jerked up. The double-doubt look. I laughed softly. "All right, all right. When it comes to her, I am not nearly as strong willed as I'd like to be." Not to mention, I'd do anything under the sun to keep my dad from being publicly humiliated. He'd never deserved her venomous attacks, mostly stemming from the fact that injuries had kept him from reaching the top tier of professional golf legends—thereby, in my mother's selfish opinion, precluding her from the elite status she'd sought by being his wife.

"Baby," Dane said as he slid his hand through my thick hair. "If she comes back, then—"

"She did come back," I said. And cringed.

His hand left my hair. His eyes squeezed shut briefly as he pinched the inner corners in obvious consternation. And irritation.

I sighed. I was about to get an earful.

"I didn't want to trouble you with her visits," I explained. "You had enough on your plate after the explosion—you still do."

His eyes snapped open. "Ari."

"Don't get all surly."

He speared me with a challenging look.

"Oh-kay. Too late for that." Despite the unpleasant subject matter, a smile tugged at the corner of my mouth. "I thought we already ascertained that you can't save the world."

"The world, no. My wife, yes."

I couldn't keep the grin at bay. "And I love you for your endless devotion. But my mother is the least of our problems."

He slowly shook his head. "She makes you cry, Ari. She makes you enraged and heartbroken all at once. I've *seen* how she devastates you. And she's on my list of people I'd like to—"

"Dane," I said, warning in my tone. I didn't like when he went all scary-furious.

He groaned. "Whatever. Have you heard from her recently?"

"When I was in the hospital. Then I went off the grid at Macy's retreat. Technically, she has no idea how to reach me, where to find me—where to even start looking—though when she's properly motivated anything seems possible on her end. And hey, that reminds me. I need to let my dad know we're back home."

"Jackson already took care of it."

"He thinks of everything, doesn't he?" Our attorney was as loyal as Amano and as well connected and in tune to every little component of our lives. Thankfully, no one knew his association with us outside of our small circle. That kept him and *his* wife safe.

Dane said, "If you do somehow hear from Maleficent"—one of my nicknames for my mother—"be sure to tell me. Immediately." He did a little scolding of his own.

"I swear." I kissed him again. "Forgive me?"

"It depends."

I laughed. "Liar. You wouldn't hold anything against me."

"That's probably true. But if you gave her money this last time, you're in serious trouble."

"I didn't. Kyle helped me out of the sticky situ—" My mouth clamped shut.

Oops.

Dane glowered. "That's just fucking great, Ari. Is there any job of mine he's not trying to take over?"

I thought of our confrontation in the kitchen earlier, at the estate. Kyle had told me he loved me. That had been a doozie of a revelation. Though perhaps all along I'd sort of suspected his feelings ran that deep. Likely the reason I'd been so adamant about us being *just friends* and doing everything in my power not to lead him on.

Yet it could be that all of the life-threatening and intense scenarios we'd found ourselves in for the past year had bonded us in a way that had taken his infatuation with me to a higher level.

I didn't dare mention that to Dane, though. I knew better. No need to jeopardize Kyle's health further.

"He was persuasive with her," I said. "Pretty creative, actually. I guess that's why he was so good in your Marketing department. Sadly, I can't convince him to find another position in that field, maybe in Phoenix. Away from all of this."

Dane grimaced at my cover-up. He was always on to me. But he let his angst over how close Kyle and I were slide—for the moment.

"I ought to convince him to extract himself from our dilemma," Danc said, "but he has proven . . . invaluable."

My head jerked back. "Wow. Did you really just say that?"

"Don't be a smart-ass." He pressed his lips to mine and kissed me in that territorial way that made me burn. His tongue swept inside, over mine, twisting and tangling. Exciting me.

I wanted nothing more at that moment than to strip down and show him exactly how much he thrilled me. But the man had been shot less than twelve hours ago. He needed his rest.

So I reticently pulled away. "You should sleep."

He leaned toward me and nipped at my bottom lip. "I'll recover just fine."

"With some rest," I insisted. "You either behave, or I'll sleep in another room." Lord knew we had plenty of them.

"You wouldn't."

Okay, he called my bluff. He understood how difficult it was for me to sleep without him by my side. If he had work in the middle of the night, I always woke when I subconsciously sensed his absence. I'd snuggle on the sofa with him, in front of the fire, and sleep while he was on the phone with Nikolai in Russia or Sultan Hakim in the Persian Gulf.

Thus, my threat was basically useless. Still, I held my ground. "Do as I say."

He chuckled. "Only because it's so sexy when you're demanding."

"Don't mess with me."

"Right." He grinned.

I swatted playfully at his uninjured arm. "And don't patronize me."

"Why don't you crawl in here," he said as he scooted to the other side of the bed so I could slip under the covers. I curled against his side, resting my head on his good shoulder.

"Are you in pain?"

"I'm too angry for that to even register right now."

"Maybe you should take something to knock you out." Knowing him, his mind would whirl all night long with thoughts of retaliation and how he was going to help the FBI ensure there were five convictions at the end of the day—the Honorable Bryn Hilliard (what a crock that title was), Dr. Lennox Avril, Anthony Casterelli, former prime minister Keaton Wellington III, and Admiral Robert Bent.

Six, if there was some way to prove Wayne Horton was Vale's minion and carried out his near-fatal work.

"I'll be fine," Dane told me. "I just need you here with me."

I kissed his neck, my lips gliding along his throat, down to that pulse point at the base, just above his collarbone, that I adored pressing my lips to. "I couldn't love you more," I whispered against his skin. "You know that, right?"

"Ari." He let out a long breath. His arm tightened around my shoulders. "You are *everything* to me. There are no words for how much I love you—how destroyed I'd be without you. If things had gone differently this morning—"

"But they didn't. You're to thank for that. And Kyle, too. Dane, he wouldn't let anything happen to me if he could help it. You have to accept that and maybe not be so grumpy with him."

He let out a half snort.

"Fine. Maybe just let him know that you trust him with my safety."

"I've thanked him," Dane countered.

"And offered him money. Which I appreciate, by the way."

"He's operating out of a sense of duty toward you. Probably wished like hell Tom would have taken the shot he had with me this morning so I'd be out of his way."

"That's not true. He knows I'd be a lost cause without you. He's already experienced that. He understands you're it for me." That, of course, made it more agonizing to think of Kyle's earlier declaration. But when we were past all the danger and justice was served, he'd get over me.

When I had Dane's baby and he saw our son and how this intimate connection strengthened our bond, he'd get over me.

When Dane and I were finally, totally together . . . he'd get over me.

He would *get over me.*

The crazy thing about me trying to convince myself of this was that I'd reached the point where Kyle had become such a vital part of my life—of my life with Dane, even—that I couldn't imagine what our world would be like after the bad guys were in prison, we were all safe, and he no longer had to play secondary hero/bodyguard.

Where would he go from here? The Secret Service?

I winced inwardly. I didn't like the idea of him purposely putting himself in hazardous situations. Nor did I relish the idea of him leaving our little brood.

It was a complicated predicament all the way around. One I couldn't help but grind over as Dane and I lay in the dark, each tangled in our own thoughts, yet so highly aware of each other.

His fingertips tenderly grazed my bare arm, making my skin

tingle. My fingers skated slowly, seductively, over his cut abs. Were I to slide them lower, I knew I'd find him hard and wanting me. The sexual pull between us was a powerful one, even if the emotional turmoil brewed steadily.

As much as I also wanted him, though, it was critical that he slept. Not that I expected him to, but I wouldn't hinder his healing. So I closed my eyes and tried to clear my mind. Tried to concentrate on his breathing, listening carefully, making sure it remained strong and stable.

It took quite some time, but eventually I gave in to the exhaustion created by the harrowing day. I managed to sleep soundly.

Because of Dane.

Because of Amano.

Because of Kyle.

chapter 4

Dr. Forrester arrived first thing in the morning to check on Dane. Amano escorted him into the bedroom and I settled on the sofa during the exam, breathing several sighs of relief at the nods of approval and "looking goods" from the physician. Dane, however, wore an impatient expression.

He thought he was invincible. After everything he'd been through, I sort of suspected the same. That did not keep me from worrying about him.

When the doctor was done, I left Dane with his laptop, because there was no stopping his insatiable need to continue his work. I joined Kyle in the kitchen as he prepped breakfast. My eyes nearly rolled into the back of my head with his perfectly executed eggs Benedict. He'd make some woman deliriously happy one of these days. I just hoped he accepted soon that it wouldn't be me.

Although, again, the thought of him leaving us was a tricky one to reconcile. Not that I had to resolve it this very moment.

We were all still caught in the crosshairs and he'd proven he wasn't going anywhere until all of this was said and done.

We had another visitor after lunch. Ethan Evans. He was the brilliant Harvard economics professor who'd recruited Dane into the Illuminati faction. Ethan was now retired from the university. He and Dane were close friends, and Dane had considered him a crucial mentor as he'd shaped his business goals.

Ethan was a good-natured sort with salt-and-pepper hair. Attractive, well dressed, refined. I always enjoyed his combination of impeccable manners and off-the-cuff jokes.

"You look wonderful, Ari," he told me with a kiss on the cheek.

"It's so nice to see you, Ethan. It's been much too long."

"Your husband has been busy. Just keep in mind that if there's ever anything you need, Jackson and I are both here for you."

"For which I am eternally grateful." I gave him a quick hug.

Ethan and our lawyer had been in on the secret wedding ceremony, along with Amano, Kyle, and my dad. My dear friend Tamera Fenmore had officiated, and Rosa had served during the reception and dinner. That'd been it. Seven people to bear witness to the most important and perfect day of my life.

Too bad that perfection had been shattered less than a month later. And we still hadn't put all the pieces back together.

Truthfully, I wasn't sure how we ever would. . . .

I shook that dismal thought from my head as Dane and Ethan took their intense discussion of what had transpired the day before at the estate into Dane's office. An hour or so later, I delivered a decanter of brandy and snifters. They were in the middle of a conversation about the hard drive Dane couldn't get to in Switzerland.

"It's still not public knowledge that I'm alive," he said. "I need to keep it that way for as long as possible. So my passport isn't worth shit. And given everything that's happened in the last twenty-four hours, I can't rely on help from the network to get me out of the States and into Europe. Not to mention, the bank would likely consider me an imposter if I showed up with my key."

I set the crystal on Dane's mammoth desk, made of gleaming mahogany, and poured. I handed a glass to Ethan, who thanked me and said pregnancy suited me. It was impossible not to glow—I was carrying Dane's baby, after all.

To my husband, I asked, "Have you taken any drugs today?"

He gave me a sardonic look. "No."

"Just asking." I smiled. Then poured a snifter for him.

Ethan inquired, "So what about the FBI?"

"I don't want them touching the laptop when I'm not there with them. It needs to stay intact—no one trolling through files and possibly compromising information. The truth is, I'm not even sure what all is on it. I started backing up documentation when I got suspicious of the others years ago. I need to wade through it all, figure out what's admissible in court, what will help each case, and then bring it forward."

"Risky game to play. The Feds might consider that an obstruction of justice—withholding evidence from them."

"So fucking sue me," Dane retorted. "I can always claim I had no idea what information I held in my hands."

"I don't think the federal government subscribes to the *ignorance is bliss* theory."

"With all the help I've given them, I'm sure we can come to an agreement."

"Hmm." Ethan swirled the amber liquid in the bowl of the small, intricately cut Baccarat glass. "Maybe send Amano for the laptop?"

"He's not leaving Ari's side. Especially after yesterday. And I don't trust anyone to courier the key to Nik in Russia to make the pickup."

"Then I'll retrieve it," Ethan offered. "I'll take your Lear to New York, then my Gulfstream across the pond and into Switzerland. Might throw off anyone trying to keep tabs on us."

"Better yet," Dane said, "take Qadir's plane. We'll have him meet you in New York. No. Charlotte. No one will expect you to fly from there."

As they dove into tactical details that went well over my head, I slipped out. I found Kyle in the kitchen once more, at the massive island, three iPads spread before him, all propped up on stands.

"Is this the new Rubick's Cube you kids today are trying to solve?"

"Funny." He didn't glance up. "And I'm only four years younger than you. Soon to be three, because my birthday's next month."

"Then four again, because mine is the month after that. So there."

He chuckled. A low, soothing rumble that filled the room. Yeah, I'd for sure miss him when he was gone.

I slid onto an upholstered high-backed stool, trying not to think of that. "So what's happening here?" I gestured to the tablets.

"Amano hooked me up to all of the surveillance cameras so I can monitor every inch of the property, then the entire perimeter of the bordering forest. I'm just trying to figure out how to juggle all the angles for efficiency. That's my first test."

My head tilted to the side. "Test?"

"Sure. You don't really think Mr. Intensity is going to let me go off half-cocked, do you? I have to learn touch points and weights and balances—since we have wildlife out here—and all kinds of shit I'm sure you don't want to hear about that might set off the alarms. Apparently, he's got them on an ultra-sensitive setting, so my guess is Bambi or Thumper could trip a sensor."

"And you're going to be able to discern exactly where that trip is?"

"And the source. Within a nanosecond." He beamed.

"You're a little too zealous about this." That worried me, naturally.

Without doubt, Kyle had the steely constitution for this sort of work. He was focused—likely a result of being the sort of quarterback who could step into the pocket with ball in-hand and quickly assess the field, taking his time to locate an open receiver. Or determine if it was necessary to run the ball himself.

We'd watched footage of him on wintry nights at the retreat. He'd had a very promising career, with the potential to go pro. Unfortunately, a few grueling sacks had left him with an injured knee. He'd made it through his last season, but the prognosis had not been good, and he'd decided football wasn't in his future. His ego and his sense of direction in life had taken a substantial hit. He'd spent the summer after graduation touring Europe, then decided upon returning to Arizona and going into marketing. There'd been several openings at 10,000 Lux.

He'd once confessed, though, that he regretted throwing in the towel on a pro career when he could have taken a chance and gone for the draft. I still didn't know exactly what had held him back and found it incredibly difficult to believe anything had given him pause—because Kyle didn't have a pause button. He went full throttle. Something that had saved my ass on more than one occasion. And which Dane had to respect, even if he didn't always admit it.

"So, the key here," Kyle explained with regard to the iPads, "is for me to get tuned into the cameras surrounding the property, while still keeping an eye on what's happening inside, and then expand my view to new surveillance being planted by Amano farther outside the perimeter fencing."

"Farther outside?"

"We're going to have a three-hundred-and-sixty-degree view of, like, ten acres. Fucking unreal, right?"

I stared at him a few moments, then asked, "When do you plan to sleep?"

He made a *pshaw* sound. "This is exciting, Ari. It takes my full concentration."

My eyes narrowed. "Does this have anything to do with football?"

His head whipped up. "Huh?"

"Well." I thought back to our discussions on his last year playing ball. "You were really good. But you were concerned about whether you'd be able to walk when you were thirty. You said it made you freak out a little. Like, you were supposed to not give a rip about that sort of thing when you were only twenty-one. But you couldn't get your mind off it."

He shrugged. Went back to studying the screens.

"Kyle."

With a grunt, he said, "It sucks to blow out a knee; I've told you that before. I had a boatload of cortisone injections, rehab in the off-seasons, knee braces year-round, just to cover it all up. I pretended it didn't hurt like hell. I—" He shook his head and turned away.

"Hey, what about Amano's test?" I challenged.

Kyle whirled back to face me. "I popped pills, Ari. That was the reason I spent so much time at my aunt's retreat in between semesters and during winter and spring breaks. I needed physical rehab, yeah. But I also had an addiction to kick. Exactly why I'm not taking anything stronger than ibuprofen right now when my biceps hurt like hell."

Because his shirt pulled tight against his muscles, I could see the outline of the bulky bandage covering his stitches, high up by his armpit.

"I took a ton of painkillers," he confessed. "All the time. The only thing that got me through my last two years on the field was natural talent—I can assess exactly where the ball needs to go and it's there. I just need the receiver on the other end to do his job. As for my studies . . ." He rapped his knuckles on the marble counter agitatedly.

"What about your studies?" I implored, happy he was finally opening up about all of this. "You had a fantastic GPA." I'd seen his résumé. I'd been the one to submit it to HR at the Lux, behind Dane's back, because I'd believed in Kyle and wanted him to have the chance to get his foot in the door, without being stone-walled from the onset, since he was my friend and Dane was of the superalpha variety.

"Ari," Kyle said. "I'm not really cool with talking about this."

"Did you cheat?" I asked. "Is that how you maintained a three-point-seven average?"

"I didn't cheat," he said, his tone adamant. "I did my home-work, I read the books I was supposed to read, did what I was supposed to do. It was just that . . . I couldn't quite form thoughts on paper because I was doped up. I could verbalize them. Surpris-ingly, I had a shitload to say about everything. I could pontificate until the cows came home."

I laughed. "Classy."

He flashed his megawatt grin. But it faded much too fast. "When I stared at a blank piece of paper or computer screen, though, nothing crystallized in my head. I was always looking at—visualizing—the playbook, feedback from the coach, strat-egy, you get the picture, instead of what I needed to be concen-trating on. I was obsessed with whether I'd make it through the next game. So written communication was pretty much my down-fall."

"How'd you get through your courses, then?"

He went to the double, glass-door fridge and pulled out two bottles of FIJI water. He set them on the counter, twisted the cap off one, and handed it to me. Then he uncapped the other and took a few long swigs.

Finally, he said, "I had some friends who helped with the home-work. I spewed, they typed, and then they cleaned everything up for me. Technically, it was all my cognitive thinking. I just needed someone to edit my rants."

"Girlfriends?" I asked with a lifted brow.

He snickered. "Does it matter?"

"Well, I can see how you might have your own groupies."

"Who, thankfully, appreciated the fact that I wasn't just some dumb jock."

"So they knew about the pills?"

"Yes."

"And didn't say anything—report your problem?"

"Ari." He gave me a *come on* look. "They wanted their football team to win as much as I did."

"Ah. Your groupies were cheerleaders who needed a reason to jump up and down on the sidelines in their short skirts."

"Did you even go to high school?" he quipped. Though he knew the answer to that—I'd also graduated from college with a business degree, while building my wedding consulting company, long before managing events at the Lux.

Yet I sucked down some water and said, "Sort of."

"What does that mean?"

"Nothing, really." I got to my feet.

"Oh, hell, no," he suddenly said. "You don't get to play all supersecretive. Not with me." His blue eyes were piercing, boring into me.

"Kyle."

"Tell me about it, Ari. For fuck's sake, I've *met* your mother, remember? Nut job to the extreme. And your dad's, like, so normal. Very laid-back. What the hell was he doing with *her*?"

"That's pretty much the million-dollar question." I raised my hands in the air, indicating I had absolutely no clue what my dad had been thinking when he'd hooked up with her. And even less of an idea as to why he'd married the ice queen. "My best guess is that when you're a PGA golfer and have your own high caliber of groupies it's not so difficult to lose sight of what's real and what's not. She definitely is *not*. Never was and never will be."

"That's just crazy, considering how down-to-earth your dad is."

"I know. That's what has always made this beyond annoying

for me. He'd do anything for her—he'd help anyone, whether he knew them or not. He's genuine. Totally amazing."

I loved my dad fiercely. I suddenly realized that was likely why I loathed my mother with equal passion.

"He never deserved to be treated the way she treated him," I said. "She cheated on him; she spent every penny he had when they were married, then made off with an even bigger haul when they divorced. Thanks to her and the team of lawyers my father had to pay for, he and I lived in absolute shit—I'm talking hellholes. After the divorce, she traded in the house awarded to her in the settlement and bought a gorgeous Scottsdale condo. Had it professionally decorated. I was rarely welcomed there." I shook my head. Waved a hand in the air. "Whatever, right?"

"Don't dismiss this, Ari. That's bullshit." He kept his gaze on me. "You pulled this nonchalant crap when she came at you in the hospital. Wanting to file lawsuits against the investors of 10,000 Lux—and reap the financial benefit personally, despite the fact that you were the one in the ER, bleeding, and thoroughly fucked up."

I shuddered at the reminder of that entire nightmare. "She didn't care about any of that—and, of course, she has no idea I'm married to Dane or that Amano is my bodyguard. As for the rest of it, she looked right past the stitches and bruises. Didn't see them at all. Can you imagine how rabid she'd be if she knew about the wedding? That all of Dane's money is also mine?"

Perhaps that was my poetic justice. That my mother had done her best to weasel cash from me, thinking I was only worth a small amount, having no idea what my investment portfolio really looked like.

I'd been upset at first that Dane and I were subjected to a private wedding. Being an event planner, naturally I'd wanted a magnificent ceremony and reception. Now it was a huge relief that very few people knew I was Mrs. Dane Bax—and that my mother currently thought I was unemployed because the Lux had been destroyed.

I tried to shove aside the dismay all this brought on. "Really," I said to Kyle, "the most incredible part about our seclusion is that, right now, I can phase her out. I don't have a cell phone, since I never replaced the one that went up in flames with the Lux and because our last residence had zero reception in that box canyon. And well, she has no fucking idea where I live."

I convinced myself all of that was enough to keep the wicked witch from materializing.

In fact, I patted my stomach and grinned. A little peace from Kathryn DeMille drama was a good thing.

Kyle said, "She'll never know about the kid, will she?"

"Not if I can help it. And let's face it, Dane is his own wraith. He makes 'donations' to ensure only approved photos of him and select information about his investments post to the Internet." It'd blown my mind he had that sort of influence—and financial stature—to make that happen. But I'd come to realize the importance of safeguarding one's personal details, especially when involved in such a precarious situation with an Illuminati faction. "There won't be pictures of our son on the Web, and chances are, it might never even be divulged that Dane and I are married."

"And you're okay with that? I mean, the last part?"

I'd already considered this. Sure, what woman wouldn't want to show off her tall, dark, and sinfully delicious man?

Conversely, after all Dane and I had experienced since getting together I wasn't opposed to the hush-hush relationship.

So I said, "For now it's all right. I feel better keeping all of this amongst us. It's unbelievable how the vultures circle at the tiniest whiff of blood."

"No shit."

"Dane's parents died in a plane crash when he was just a month old. To have grown up with all those vultures had to be difficult," I lamented. "Dane didn't even know at such a young age why everyone wanted to be near him, be a part of him, be included in every aspect of his life. Thank God he had Amano looking over his shoulder for him. But even so, Dane eventually had to accept and acclimate to the fact that he was a hot commodity. That couldn't have been a good feeling, knowing so much of it was based on his bank account."

I gave this further thought and conceded, "Then, later on, because he's so damn good-looking."

Kyle scowled. "That whole skyscraper height and dark, broody looks thing again." He rolled his eyes. "Whatever."

I laughed softly. Kyle was six-one, so Dane didn't exactly dwarf him. "Anyway, we're all kind of messed up in our own ways, huh?"

"Yeah. I'll give you that one."

I didn't mention Dane's childhood friend Mikaela Madsen, whom Kyle had also met. She'd had a pretty tumultuous upbringing as well. Mikaela didn't know I was pregnant or that I'd married Dane. Which meant I also had yet to share with her the miraculous news about Dane surviving the explosion. A peculiar cross to bear in that, of all people, she should be a part of those in the know.

She'd even orchestrated his memorial service at my prompting—since it would have made no sense for me to do it when no one knew Dane and I were more than just boss and employee at the Lux. I knew how torn up Mikaela was about his death. It disturbed me greatly not to be able to ease her pain. Yet there was nothing I could do about it at the moment.

"So," I ventured, wrapping up my discussion with Kyle. "Do your awesome reconnaissance and I'll get out of your hair. I have a nursery to decorate."

"You ever gonna name the kid?"

I shrugged. "Nothing's sticking. I figure it'll hit me when it's the right one."

"Sure. We'll see how that works out for you. Otherwise, we'll just go with 'Kid Bax' for the first few years."

I laughed again. "Get back to your *Mission Impossible* work."

Leaving the kitchen, I went into the room designated for Kid and eyed it speculatively, taking in every square foot. A nice, spacious area. Windows with striking scenery beyond the glass panes. Wood floors. Walls trimmed with smooth, waist-high river rock. All in all, elegantly rustic.

It occurred to me that the best way to tackle this enormous undertaking was to go at it from the stance of wedding planner. I could take a million ideas from a bride and pull together one specific theme to make it all gel once I saw the photos and concepts staring me in the face.

I grabbed my laptop, went into the great room, flipped the switch that brought to life a roaring fire in the tall hearth, and settled on one of the sofas scattered about.

A color scheme was the first order of business. That entailed envisioning what our child might look like, who he might become. I pictured Dane, of course. Our son would be strapping, powerful, gorgeous—just like his father. Girls would fall at his feet.

I frowned. That'd be quite the challenge for me. I'd always teased Dane about his possessiveness. Suddenly I realized I'd feel the same about the baby. Because he was ours.

All I could fathom was providing him with the best of everything, all the opportunities in the world. And showering him with love.

I groaned. I might *smother* rather than *shower*. I'd have to work on that. Strike a balance.

It was a strange conundrum. For me, I'd only had the love of one parent. Had, admittedly—and not at all via fault on my father's side—suffered from that. I'd grown up closed off, standoffish, a loner.

Dane had grown up with no parents. But he'd had a devoted aunt and the never-faltering Amano. Not to mention the Heidi Klum look-alike Mikaela Madsen.

Kyle had experienced as close to a perfect family unit as I could comprehend, though he'd confessed his dad preferred being a road-warrior salesman to a traditional home-at-six-o'clock-for-dinner husband/father.

I longed for a happy medium based on all the realities of life—and the fact that I still wanted a career. And once the criminal convictions came in, Dane would be on to his next big project. Whatever that might be.

Now was the time for me to seriously contemplate how to shape our future with a child being a prominent part of it—developing his own skill set, interests, passions. Feeling free to be his own person, not having to follow directly in his father's footsteps. Or, again, be smothered by a mother who adored him to pieces.

I already felt so attached, so addicted, to the baby growing inside me. How could I not be a crazed lunatic when I gave birth to him?

You'll have to chill. Let him breathe, Ari. Let him breathe.

I did just that currently. Big inhale, slow exhale.

Dane joined me on the sofa. I hadn't even realized Ethan had left us, being so engrossed in my mental debate.

"Everything okay?" Dane asked as he rested his hand on my thigh.

I cozied up to him. "Just fine. I was reminding myself not to suffocate our son with motherly love."

Dane grinned. "I doubt he'll mind."

"I don't want to be fearful of all the things he might want to do, either. It'd be cool if he rowed and boxed like you. Golfed like my dad. Played football like Kyle. Or is that too much? I want him to be well-rounded. Completely amazing. Oh! And Amano could teach him martial arts."

I stared at my husband, who raised a brow.

"I'm too weird, aren't I?" I asked. "Totally mommy-psycho."

Dane wrapped his arm around me and held on fiercely.

"Baby, I get it. Nothing weird about you. I want our son to have it all, too. Be all he wants to be, you know?" Dane paused a moment, then added, "We are going to name him eventually?"

"Have you been talking to Kyle?"

"Yeah. Sure."

Okay, the two of them discussing the baby would be the absolute *last* topic on the table.

I said, "We just might have to wait to see our son's first identifying quality before we can make a sound decision. I have no intuition when it comes to this. No name seems extraordinary enough. I mean, he'll never be a Jack or a Bill. I like Samuel, but still, not right. I want unique, but not bizarre-unique. Nothing related to fish or fruit or colors. No colors."

"Hmm . . . Pewter Bax." Dane gave me an amused nod.

"*Not.*" Shifting on the sofa so that I could cuddle deeper against him, I rested my cheek in the crook of Dane's neck. My happy spot. I said, "You haven't exactly been throwing out any bones to chew on."

"Let's see . . . Vaughn? Cagney? Something international?"

"Cagney." I let it roll off my tongue. "Interesting. Definitely unique. Manly. Strong."

"Cagney Bax," Dane said.

"Just shot to the top of my list."

"You don't have a list," he quipped.

"True. But I should have a list. *We* should have a list. Keep at it."

He kissed my forehead. "Whatever you want, baby. Whatever you want."

"That's a no-brainer." I flashed him a lascivious grin.

My palm skated over his abs. He hadn't bothered with a shirt, not even upon Ethan's arrival. Not that that would be out of the ordinary. Ethan had apparently been a regular ringside fan when Dane had boxed in college. And I certainly wasn't complaining that he strutted around with nothing more on than loose dark-gray or black pants.

As my fingertips teased his skin, Dane's emerald eyes glowed suggestively. "Why don't we take this into the bedroom?"

I kissed him, then said, "There's nothing I'd rather do than get naked with you. Except that you're seriously injured."

"And seriously wanting you."

His words and heated gaze sent a tickle along my clit, making me squirm. "Mm. Tempting."

"Then get a little closer." His arm shifted to my waist and he hauled me onto his lap, so my legs straddled him.

"Dane," I reluctantly protested. *Weakly* protested—because I wanted him just as much. "According to Dr. Forrester, you're supposed to be relaxing while hooked up to that sophisticated water-chilling contraption he brought for you to keep the swelling down."

The pad was to be placed over Dane's shoulder. Tubes connected to the pad and the box churned out frigid water to keep the pad icy cold.

He gave me a devilish look. "I promise to spend the rest of the night in bed."

"With your cold pack."

"With my wife."

He kissed me. His arm around my waist held me firmly and he stood in one graceful motion. He shifted me to his hip on his good side and I encircled his neck with one arm and clasped my hands together so I was nowhere near his injured shoulder. I gripped him with my legs.

"Hey," I said. "Let's not get all Tarzan-like. You don't have anything to prove to me."

"Ari, you're doing most of the work."

True, I clung to him, holding myself up. But still. "I'm a bit heavier than I used to be."

"Actually," he said, "it seems like you should weigh much more. You're five months pregnant, after all."

I hadn't "popped" yet. I could still pass for needing to lay off the Doritos and take a few extra laps in the pool.

"Regardless," I told him, "you shouldn't be straining yourself like this."

"Let it go."

I had no choice. I couldn't press the issue without insulting his manliness. I also suspected he liked demonstrating his virility because I spent way too much time with Kyle.

Dane and I made it stealthily down the long, winding corridor, me not the least bit worried I'd end up dropped on the stone flooring along the way. My major concern was Dane exerting himself.

He set me on the bed and I gazed up at him, asking, "Can I get you the shoulder pad now?"

"You can take your clothes off now."

Heat flashed through me. Still, I hedged. "Dane."

"Or I'll do it."

The fire in his eyes kept my insides sizzling. I reached for the hem of my shirt and peeled away the material. Then I stood and rid myself of every other article.

His gaze slid over me. "You're sensational."

Emotion welled in my throat. "You say the sweetest things."

"Just stating the obvious."

I reached for the drawstring at his waist and slid his pants and briefs down his thighs. He was barefoot, so stripping him bare was an easy task. He sank onto the edge of the bed and pulled me to him. I straddled his lap again, slowing lowering onto him, taking his thick cock deep inside me, inch by hot, solid inch.

Our eyes locked. He said, "I love that you're always ready for me."

I kissed him, then murmured against his lips, "I love that you always want me."

"More than you know." His tone was low, intimate. Sexy as hell. His hypnotic irises burned with love and lust, sending heat along my skin and searing my insides. "Every minute of the day. I could never get enough of you, Ari. Never."

His arm caged me again. I dropped my hips so he could sink into me. My inner walls clutched him firmly, holding him in place while I went up in flames. He was hard and huge, filling me completely. Feeling so damn good, I could come with just a few quick squeezes, a gentle milking of his erection.

My fingers threaded through his hair. He kissed me hungrily, as though in desperate need of me. I returned the kiss with equal fervor—desperately needing *him*. I couldn't help it. With Dane, I was insatiable.

I couldn't press my chest to his the way I craved doing, because his arm remained immobilized across his midsection. We were sealed together in all the right places, though, and I greedily took what I wanted from him. He willingly gave it.

Rocking my hips slowly at first, I felt the initial wave of euphoria flow through my veins. The erotic sensation built, drawing me in, tempting and taunting me. We fit beautifully together, and Dane continued to kiss me as though trying to convey his intense yearning for me. He succeeded wonderfully.

When I picked up the pace and we moved faster, with more insistency, he tore his mouth from mine and let out a sensual growl that reverberated in my core.

"Ari," he said on a sharp breath. "You feel incredible."

He eased back against the bed, bringing me with him. I flattened my palms alongside his broad shoulders on the mattress, again holding myself up so I didn't brush his arm or his wound. His hand at my waist shifted to my ass. He cupped a cheek and gave it a rough squeeze that excited me. His hips bucked and he pumped into me as I ground against him, my breath coming in heavy pulls.

The insane desire to claw at him welled within me. It was next to impossible to fight the craving. To refrain from pressing my fingertips into his rigid muscles and feeling them flex beneath my touch. Instead, I fisted the comforter. Not a satisfying alternative, but at least Dane was here with me, inside me, making love to me.

Still, that desperation he incited held me in a vise grip. My mouth crashed over his and I kissed him possessively, the way he always did me. His hand moved to palm my breast and he massaged with just the right amount of pressure to add to my escalating passion. Then he swept the pad of his thumb over my tight nipple before rolling it, pinching the tingly bud.

My orgasm blossomed quickly, fiercely.

I broke our kiss. "Dane." My heart hammered; my pulse raced. "I'm going to come."

He raised his head and kissed the side of my neck. Nipped at the skin. All the while, he pumped steadily, until I couldn't hold on a second longer. A rush of heat seared me as I cried out his name.

The release was thrilling, exhilarating. Scorching. I clutched his cock, taking pleasure in every second of him thrusting into me. My body trembled and little pants of air escaped my parted lips.

"I love watching you come," Dane told me in a primal tone. "I love making you come."

"You're so good at it," I managed to say as I still soared from the climax.

"And I'm not done. But damn it." He hissed out a breath. "I want to touch you with both hands. I want you pressed against me, not holding yourself away."

"Note I'm still having a moment here." My body continued to vibrate. My pussy clenched him. "I don't think you've missed a single beat."

"It's not the same."

"It's fantastic."

His hips jerked and he slid easily against my coated walls. Caressing solidly again, with purpose.

I smiled in my delirium. "Got a point to prove?"

"I don't like feeling weak."

"You're not weak. I am for letting you do this when you should be resting."

"You're what I need, not Forrester's therapy."

"I'd argue, except that what you're doing is too amazing to tell you to quit and ice that shoulder."

"Fuck my shoulder."

"Better yet, fuck me."

He pistoned into my wet depths, igniting the inferno again. My head dropped and my lips grazed his hot skin, over his collarbone and uninjured shoulder. His chest. Then upward to his throat and that pulsing vein that screamed of his vitality and always, always beckoned my attention. I swept my tongue along it, enjoying the taste of him and reveling in the fact that Dane was alive and healthy—current wound notwithstanding.

"I love you," I whispered against his lips.

"And you are more than I could have ever asked for, baby. Everything I want and need."

Emotion crept around the edges of ecstasy. Anticipation mounted. "I'm going to come again."

"Yes," he murmured. "Come for me. Come with me."

His hand moved to my ass once more and his fingers glided along the cleft, gathering moisture as he heightened my arousal.

"Oh, God, Dane." My head nestled close to his throat and I inhaled his enticing scent. Heat, expensive cologne, and pure masculinity exuded from his every pore. An intoxicating fragrance that hitched my pulse a few notches.

As he pumped with heartier strokes, one of his slick fingertips rimmed the sensitive spot between my cheeks and then carefully pressed in.

Excitement roared through me. "Dane."

"You like everything I do to you, don't you, baby?"

"I *love* everything you do to me."

The snug fit in both places was enough to push me to that sizzling precipice. But Dane maneuvered himself slightly and suckled my hard nipple, adding even more pleasure to the firestorm already raging within.

"That's so wicked," I said on a throaty moan.

He thrust deeper, his finger delved farther, and I called out his name again as I came.

"Ah, Christ. Ari."

I felt his cock throb in wild beats and then explode inside me. His body convulsed with mine, the furious tremors a testament to the fiery passion we shared.

I let my body burn. Savored every delicious, core-singeing sensation.

"Ari," Dane murmured in a raspy voice. "You can't begin to imagine how much I miss you every night I'm away from you."

"Yes, I can." I'd been just as tormented by his absence. "But once this is over, nothing will keep us apart ever again."

"Not if I can fucking help it."

chapter 5

Over breakfast the next morning, alone on the patio off from our master suite, I broached another touchy subject with Dane.

"I understand the need to keep your Phoenix-rising-from-the-ashes miracle within our tiny group, but I couldn't help but think of Mikaela yesterday."

He eyed me speculatively. "The woman who caused you to succumb to jealous tendencies—for absolutely no good reason?"

"Please. She's drop-dead gorgeous and you'd be lying if you claimed otherwise."

"She's attractive. Not my type, though." His gaze slid over me and he grinned. "And being pregnant with my son makes you even more spectacular."

"Thank you." I picked at my omelet a moment while my heart fluttered from the appreciative look Dane gave me. Then I said, "Anyway, about Mikaela. I went to see her after her Italian market opened in Old Town and I put the bug in her ear about a memorial service, which she graciously orchestrated. We've talked several times since. She's really pretty broken up about your 'death,' and I was wondering if, at some point, you intend to let her know you made it out of the Lux and that you're fully intact. Well, relatively speaking."

I spared a glance at his bandaged shoulder and fought a wince. I hated seeing him injured.

While Dane mulled over my inference of letting Mikaela in on the secret, I nibbled on my breakfast. His other shoulder bunched and I could tell it was a difficult decision for him to make.

Finally, he said, "I really don't like keeping this from her. I'd never intentionally hurt her." There was a sudden hint of regret and remorse in his eyes.

"She'll understand the reasoning behind the confidentiality issue, but still. I imagine she's pretty tortured over losing you. Sometimes, she'll bring you up and then—" I shrugged. "It's like she goes to this place somewhere distant and happier in her head and then pretends to override her misery with some outrageous anecdote. Yet I can hear in her voice it's all feigned."

He shoved back his chair. Stood and paced.

"I'm not trying to pull heartstrings," I gently said. "I just think it's something to consider. I know you too well, Dane. You'll want to be the one to deliver the delicate news first, before the media latches on to the story. You'll want to do it in person, so that she can see you're okay, that it's real."

He raked his hand through his hair, making it even more disheveled. I was momentarily sidetracked, thinking of nothing other than falling back into bed with him.

But then he said, "I trust her completely. She wouldn't do anything to compromise my safety or my work. Unless—" He shook his head, a bit agitatedly.

"Unless she told Fabrizio." Her boyfriend and business partner. It was his village in Italy where they imported a good deal of their gourmet meats, cheeses, olive oils, and sauces.

The wine they sold all came from top vineyards around Tuscany and Florence. From what I'd gleaned through Mikaela, they were on a mission to get Scottsdale society hooked on bold and expensive Super Tuscans, reigniting the market for those types of wines.

What Mikaela and Brizio knew about Sangioveses, Merlots, Proseccos, et cetera, boggled the mind. I merely collected their recommendations and gifts, having no idea myself about categorizing and rating wines—and not currently being able to sample them. Kyle and Rosa, however, enjoyed every bottle.

Really, it was one more reason to feel inferior in comparison to the uber-sophisticated and worldly Mikaela Madsen, but I conveniently reminded myself that it was me Dane had married. I was the one carrying his child. That took the sting out of Mikaela being so perfect and being so bound to Dane that she'd always turned to him for help.

He stopped his pacing and said, "Whether she could keep this from Brizio is a major concern. One small slip . . . That could be detrimental to us all. We're at a very crucial point right now, especially not knowing all that Hilliard—or the rest of the network or society—knows about my existence and my work with the FBI."

I nodded. "I haven't brought this up previously for that reason. But thought it should at least be on the table."

"I'll give it some thought." He kissed me on the forehead, then sat. "Eat the rest of your breakfast."

Later, Dane reluctantly consented to let me play nursemaid. I hooked him up to the ice machine while he sat on the sofa in our great room, his bare feet propped up on the sturdy coffee table. His computer was in his lap and I caught his frustrated groans because his one hand on the keyboard couldn't keep up with his lightning-quick thoughts.

He'd told me there were just a few dots left to connect to the indictment puzzle. He was definitely going for the jugular with the society, overturning every possible stone to make sure the maximum amount of evidence against them was brought forth. Any tiny suspicion he had he investigated. No matter what rabbit hole it led him down.

I curled up next to him and quietly searched the Web as well, looking at furniture for the nursery on my iPad. Occasionally shutting off the chilling unit. Letting a little time pass, then switching it back on. Not disturbing Dane.

Only an hour or so passed before the agitation got the best of him.

He threw off the pad on his shoulder and set his laptop on the table before him. Got to his feet. He crossed to the floor-to-ceiling doors and windows looking out on the terrace and the forest beyond. A couple of the doors were open and the rustle of leaves and the running of the rapids filtered in. Soothing sounds, though Dane's aggravation overrode the tranquility.

I flipped the cover on my tablet, left it on the sofa, and joined him.

Wrapping my arms around his waist from behind, I pressed my cheek to his warm skin, feeling his good shoulder blade flex.

"What is it?" I asked in a soft voice. "Can't find what you're looking for?"

"I'm used to the needles and haystacks by now," he told me, his voice low and tense.

"So what's got you so annoyed?"

"Not annoyed. More like . . ." He blew out a sharp breath. Shook his head. Then said, "You mentioning Mikaela earlier has me thinking about a lot of things."

"Seeing her? Letting her in on the secret while it's still a secret?"

"No, that's not it at all. I'm actually not thinking about her right now. I'm thinking about you. About us."

My stomach took a peculiar dive south. Because of his grave tone? Because I'd been thinking a lot about us lately, too? How all of this affected our marriage. Or relationship.

"I've made a million promises to you," he said. "How many have I kept?"

I closed my eyes. Tried to maintain steady breathing and calm nerves. In all honesty, I told him, "You've kept the most important one. That your heart will never belong to anyone else."

That'd been his wedding vow to me. Not the only one, which he clearly thought of now.

"I also told you that I wouldn't let you down."

"And you haven't," I contended.

"I haven't given you the life you deserve."

My heart wrenched at his silent fury. "You gave me exactly what I wanted, Dane. You."

"But I can't always be here with you. I have to allow Amano and Kyle to protect you." He let out a low growl. "Fuck. There shouldn't be anything for them to protect you from. You should be planning events at the Lux. Spending time with Meg and Sean. Grace. Tamera. Your friends. You should be out shopping and wondering if I'm going to hit the roof when I see the bill."

I couldn't help but laugh at that one. "I fear you'd only be disappointed I didn't make a dent in the bank account. Not much of a shopper. Well, except for this kid."

"You know what I'm saying."

"Yes."

"This isn't ideal, Ari."

I was quiet for a few moments. My arms tightened around him. I could feel his pain. His disconcertment. His need to give me the moon and the stars. Not nightmares.

But it wasn't Dane's fault.

I said, "You once tried to convince me you weren't the bad guy. When you'd beat the hell out of Vale for what he'd done to me. It scared me, Dane. Everything about that night and the way you responded scared me. But you rescued me. And the only reason you went off on Vale with such rage was because he'd hurt me."

Turning my head into Dane's rigid muscles, I kissed his smooth flesh. Then whispered, "You're not the bad guy. And I know it."

"I'm a bad husband, then."

That just plain broke my heart. Tears sprang to my eyes.

"No," I was quick to say. "You absolutely are not. I respect your convictions. You are solid as oak, Dane. And I love you even more for that."

"I want your life to be perfect, Ari."

"*Nobody's* life is perfect, Dane. You have all this money, these gorgeous houses, limited-edition books and cars. But you never knew your parents. You never once got to speak with them, tell them your hopes and dreams and let them admire your successes. Your strength. Your brilliance."

"That was something I had no control over. This—"

"Is something you don't have full control over, either. I chose to be with you. I knew from the beginning it was going to be dangerous. Less than ideal. But I committed to this. To you. With no blinders on, no delusions. You laid it all out for me, Dane. I am here because this is where I want to be. I'm here because you're my husband and I love you more and more with every breath I take—and I'm not going anywhere."

The tears spilled a bit faster. His hand covered mine, clasped around his midsection. He gave them a gentle squeeze.

I added, "When you're here with me, I have everything I want."

It tore me up that he was so conflicted. That such a confident, steadfast man could think for even one second that he didn't give me everything I needed, everything I desired.

But I could also understand how someone who was accustomed to being in charge of his destiny and environment would falter when it came to having the rug ripped from under-neath him. And how he'd feel he wasn't doing his marital duties justice.

I simply said, "Finish this, Dane. Come home to us. *That's* my idea of a perfect life."

The FBI showed up mid-afternoon. Agents Daugherty and Strauss had found Candace and Ruby Talbot, handcuffed to ex-posed pipes in an abandoned warehouse. I didn't need to imagine their fright—I'd suffered it once myself.

Wayne Horton, who Strauss informed us was merely a person of interest at this point, had reportedly disappeared again. According to Daugherty, our menacing ghost kept no permanent address and had numerous aliases. And likely some the FBI hadn't even discov-ered yet. That didn't bode well for tracking him down anytime soon. Yet I caught the glint in Amano's dark-brown eyes during the discussion. He lived for shit like this—the hunt was his forte. Kyle seemed to catch the fever, because he appeared equally will-ing to take a stab at sniffing out Wayne.

I fretted over the whole situation—not wanting to invite more trouble into our lives.

Dane did more pacing, this time in front of the fireplace in the great room. He said, "We need to dig up more on this guy, find out if he was the one to plot Ari's kidnapping and plant the bomb at the Lux. The snakes on the patio. All of it."

"I highly suggest we don't underestimate him," Daugherty said. He was of medium height, solidly built, with a shock of red hair against a pale complexion. "But he's not our main concern at the moment. We've got to wrap up our investigation on Admiral Bent. We want all five members going down—no one slips through the cracks. In fact—" His cell buzzed, interrupting him. He spared a quick glance at the screen. "I need to take this. I've been waiting on some information related to Bent's whereabouts. This might be it."

Daugherty stepped away from us. Strauss continued the conversation, though both Dane and I paid more attention to Daugherty and the way his casual strolling about the cavernous room turned agitated, along with his tone. He nodded sharply and then he swore under his breath.

Dane and I exchanged a look. My blood turned to ice in my veins.

Finally, Daugherty jammed his phone into his pocket and returned to our small group.

To me, he asked, "Would you mind turning on CNN, Mrs. Bax?"

I usually got a thrill out of Dane calling me that—any reference to my being his wife, actually. But right now nothing registered beyond the apprehension gripping me.

"Certainly." I reached for the remote on one of the end tables and flipped on the flat screen mounted above the fireplace. I found the proper channel and quickly read the Breaking News ticker at the bottom. "Holy fuck."

"Right," Daugherty said. "Our search for Bent's whereabouts is over. A couple of D.C. agents found him about an hour ago, hanging from the rafters of a vacant building in Georgetown."

"Suicide or homicide?" Dane asked, angst seeping into his tone. I surmised he wasn't pleased Admiral Bent might have taken the "easy" way out of all of this.

"Evidence currently points toward suicide, but of course there will be an investigation and an autopsy."

"It's not really his style," Dane offered. "He was an admiral, after all. Tough as nails."

"When the heat's on . . . ," Strauss merely said. "Desperate times and all that—people do what they have to. He wouldn't have fared well in prison. Clearly knew it."

"What does this mean?" Kyle asked. "Related to the indictments?"

Daugherty said, "My guess is the trials are going to be

moved up—they'll be starting soon. Which means you need to come with us, Dane. We'll have two more agents stake out this property."

Amano scowled. I knew what he was thinking—*not on my turf.* But he said nothing.

"I don't like this," I suddenly said to Dane, panic seizing me. "I know we've talked about it and the FBI wants you sequestered so no one can get to you, but what if they do? This has all turned so sinister that—"

"Ari," he said as he clasped my hand and stared into my eyes. "It'll be okay. You stay here with Amano, Kyle, and Rosa. Let the two other agents do their thing. Keep calm; decorate the nursery; come up with baby names. Do whatever you have to to get through the day. Do you hear me?"

I gazed up at him. "This is all happening so fast."

"That's the way of it when the dam breaks. All of the indictments have been made, since Bent is dead. It's time to move forward. And if we're really lucky, this will all be wrapped up quickly. It'll be all right."

I tried to breathe.

Daugherty said, "I assure you, Mrs. Bax, your husband will be well protected. We need him alive—nothing's going to keep us from finishing this case."

I could understand that in my head. My heart, however, did not reconcile the fact that Dane would be tucked away somewhere, likely going crazy over me as much as I did over him. That made it worse. I didn't want him stressing about what might be happening here. More than that, I wanted him safe.

I said, "I have Kyle. Take Amano."

"No, Ari. I'm not taking any chances. They both stay with you. And you do *exactly* as they say. Even Kyle."

My eyes bulged. Hadn't seen that one coming.

"He'll take care of you," Dane said with confidence, "look after you. He won't let anything happen to you."

"This is serious, Ari," Kyle chimed in. "The Feds need Dane. Even though they'll have him covered, you know he's too *Die Hard* to end up in anyone's crosshairs, now that he knows he can't trust his network. He can take care of himself."

I couldn't dispute that. It didn't settle me, though. More tears flooded my eyes. "You don't have to go right this very second."

"Actually, we do," Strauss said. He'd briefly been on his phone, issuing instructions to someone on the other end. Now he returned his attention to us and added, "Expect Agents Price and Johnson shortly. They'll coordinate with Amano. No one else comes through your gates."

"My dad!" I hastily blurted. "I haven't seen him—"

"FaceTime or Skype," Dane said. "We don't want him or Jackson anywhere near here. They've been of no interest to anyone— particularly Horton. Let's keep it that way."

"So we're sequestered, too," I lamented.

"Witness protection comes with perks," Kyle told me, trying to lighten the mood. "We haven't streamed the current season of *The Walking Dead* on Netflix."

I tried to grin. Failed miserably. "I'll stay put," I vowed to Dane.

He released my hand. Cupped the side of my face. "I need you to be safe. I need you to keep our baby safe. That's what I'm asking of you."

I choked down the emotion swelling in my throat. "Swear you'll come back. Because I know you're determined to keep your promises from now on." More tears pooled. Pain lanced through me.

"You know I will," he said with conviction in his tone, in his beautiful emerald eyes.

No, I didn't know that. But I couldn't torment him with my fears. Every tiny facet of our lives was but a thin strand of webbing that could easily be ripped away. I had to live with that reality. Because as I'd told him, *I* chose this.

"Ari, I love you."

I fought the body-wracking sobs threatening me, making me shake. I couldn't even hug him without hurting him.

"This is so fucked up," I said.

"Yes. But not for long. It's almost over. Just stay strong for me." He kissed me fiercely, to hell with our audience. Then he pulled away and added, "Stay strong for the baby. Figure out a name for him."

"We should go," Daugherty said in a quiet, respectful—even remorseful—tone.

My eyelids squeezed shut for a moment. I tried to compose myself, to no avail.

Kyle moved in, nudging me with his elbow. "He'll be back before Kid's even born and wondering what the hell you did all day when there's no nursery set up. Let's get cracking. Unless you're planning on propping up your feet and popping bonbons all day long."

I glared at him through the mist I couldn't contain. "Don't you have some squats to do? Barbells to lift?"

He laughed, albeit tightly. As though my being shredded to the core over another of Dane's absences shredded him as well.

Amano said to Dane, "I'm stuck with their bickering. I'm not sure you're paying me enough."

Dane kissed me on the cheek. "Play nice so Amano doesn't quit on us."

As if that would ever happen. The man was the epitome of devotion. But I said, "I'll try."

Once again, I watched my husband leave me. Painfully praying for his safe return.

I spent the first week restlessly prowling the house. I left CNN on every TV, in every room, 24-7. There was huge coverage of Bent's suicide and the indictments. Wild speculation. Tons of theories and a lot of political strategists, lawyers, economics experts, and talk-show personalities debating the Billionaire Effect—as it'd been dubbed—on our society and globally. They brought average Joes into the studio to relay their hardships during the '08 recession and how livid they were to possibly face another hit because those in power could influence change to their advantage, leaving the middle and lower class hanging out to dry.

This had to grate on Dane's nerves as he watched, too. Wherever the hell he was.

This was *exactly* what he fought to keep from happening.

I soaked up every tidbit I could, latched on to every estimation of when trials would begin. The climate in D.C. was intriguing to factor in, since the society's network was riddled with politicos and world leaders—whose names were slowly leaked. For better or for worse.

I wasn't sure how all of this impacted our country or others, but tensions were definitely high. There was a lot of finger-pointing going on and endless *he said, she said.*

I browsed for items for the nursery while I kept the programs on in the background. I had a stack of catalogs to peruse, and I relied on my old trick of tearing out pages and pinning them to the wall over my desk in Dane's office. I liked having the options staring me in the face. I'd eventually choose a theme, after I'd collected enough samples.

Unfortunately, baby planning didn't fully occupy my mind. I spoke with my dad only once on the iPad. Dane called on the endless stream of disposable phones Amano provided. He destroyed each of them after just one use. And I wasn't allowed to stay on for long.

Though Wayne Horton knew about the creek house, I was 99.9 percent certain there was no way he'd ever get through our gates or over our fences. That, however, didn't mean he couldn't hack phones or computers—he'd proven quite good at it. Oddly, everything in our lives had become disposable because of him.

Since I refused to sit around and twiddle my thumbs, I put time and effort into another project.

10,000 Lux.

Kyle came into the office on a rainy Sunday afternoon, propped his broad shoulder against the doorframe, and asked, "Wallpaper not in the billion-dollar budget?"

I glanced at him over my shoulder. "Ha, ha." Then I turned back to the span of wall that separated my work space from Dane's. The room was large, with distressed leather sofas and chairs scattered about, along with coffee and end tables. A gorgeous fireplace trimmed with river rock filled one corner. I kept it on a low flame for ambience.

I'd hung photos of the lobby and main building of the Lux that I'd taken last fall, when I'd had to assess all of the Christmas decorations I'd need to order prior to the grand opening of the resort. That had never actually come to fruition. Well, the decorating had taken place. But our soft launch had been thwarted by the bomb.

"So you're turning Dane's office into a Lux museum?" Kyle asked.

"Not exactly." I crossed to an oversized chair and sank into it. Kyle joined me, taking the sofa on the other side of a sturdy wooden coffee table.

"What gives, then? And does this have anything to do with that field trip we took to the hotel the night we got the snake visit?"

"Yes." I pulled in a deep breath, let it out slowly. "I want to rebuild the resort."

"Oh, Christ." He sprang to his feet. Shoved a hand through his sandy hair. "Come on, Ari. That's like *huge*. Monumental. Astronomical. Totally insane. Take your pick."

My eyes narrowed on him. "Are you saying I can't do it?"

"Where the hell would you even start?"

"Well." I'd put significant thought into this. Yet it was still daunting. I licked my lips and tried to infuse a healthy dose of confidence into my voice. "First of all, the main building is still taped off but no longer considered an off-limits crime scene, since investigators have collected their evidence and taken their photographs."

Too bad they hadn't been able to pinpoint a culprit as of now. I was further disconcerted that no one had come forward with the recovery of my wedding bracelet, despite the hefty reward offered. Luckily, I had a new engraved bracelet, which matched Dane's. Still, thirty carats of chevron diamonds were difficult to part with—not to mention the symbolism of the stunning piece of jewelry he'd originally given me. My wedding band.

Continuing, I said, "I'm not sure when we can clear the grounds, but I've already had Jackson send out a request for proposal to several companies to get a quote and time estimation on removing the debris. That's all he knows about my plans. I personally contacted the original engineers and architects. They'll have to determine if the remaining portion of the main building is structurally sound."

"Ari, a bomb went off in the lobby. Your fourth-floor office was wiped out. I'm thinking the whole damn thing has to come down."

"Not necessarily." I stood and returned to the photos, grabbing a red marker from my desk along the way. Gesturing to the largest picture of the heart of the Lux, I said, "The night the hotel was on fire, I saw this incredibly eerie similarity to another burning building." Turning to the photo, I drew a circle around the lobby. "There's a huge, gaping hole right here. It reminds me of the Pentagon after the plane crashed into it on 9/11."

"Yeah, that was all jacked up."

"But they didn't have to bring down the entire Pentagon, post-collapse. They had to rebuild the damaged portion, but not the entire structure. So, yes, the lobby of the Lux, the administrative offices in the west wing, and the hotel suites in the east wing that were destroyed will have to be restored, but maybe not the entire housing."

"And that makes it less of an overwhelming project? And when did you become an expert in the resurrection of a horrifically damaged resort?"

"I'm not. I'm the funding source. I have a list of the professionals Dane worked with and I can hire them to reinforce everything, restructure everything, whatever. I have all the original schematics from Dane's files, and while I won't be able to replace every fixture he'd had specifically crafted for the lobby, I can come up with close replicas and other items that complement his vision."

Kyle studied me a few moments, not exactly hating the idea, I could see, but not loving it, either. Finally, he asked, "Does Dane even want the Lux rebuilt?"

"I don't know. He doesn't talk about the hotel. It is literally the one and only thing he won't discuss with me."

"Maybe there's a reason for that."

"Maybe," I agreed. "But remember when Amano drove you and me out there and he said that Dane would probably just have all the other buildings and the rest of the resort mowed down and he'd sell off the land? If there wasn't a 10,000 Lux the way Dane had envisioned it, then there wouldn't be one at all?"

"Yeah, so?" Kyle asked skeptically.

"Don't you think that's a complete waste? Have you ever seen anything more extraordinary than that hotel?"

"It was pretty astonishing," he concurred.

"It still is. With the exception of our mammoth hole." I indicated the red circle again.

Kyle shook his head. "You're forgetting about all the scorched grounds from the fire. And shit, Ari. The fountains are all ruined from the debris that struck them and there's more metal and marble in the treetops than there are branches. Where the trees weren't ripped out of the ground from the flying pieces of the Lux, that is."

"I'm not saying it'll be easy clearing it all out and fixing all the landscaping—though that's something you could certainly help with, since you did such a great job at Macy's retreat while we were there."

He neither confirmed nor denied he wanted to participate in my grand plan. His blank expression gave nothing away.

So I continued. "It'll be a mammoth effort to coordinate. So will reconstructing the lobby. But it's not like we lack for time, right?" I challenged.

He regarded me again, then said, "This goes back to that discussion we had about how once you've worked at a place like the Lux nothing else compares."

"It's more than that. Yes, I want a career. No, event planning anywhere other than 10,000 Lux would never be the same. We poured our hearts and souls into prepping for a spectacular launch we never got to experience. But above all that, what I saw the night we visited with Amano was a legacy shredded. My son's legacy. *Dane's* son's legacy. 10,000 Lux was his dream from way, way back. He made it come true—then someone demolished it."

I returned to my desk and set the marker on the leather blotter, emotion creeping in on me. I took a few deep breaths, because Kyle was right about what a tremendous undertaking this would be, if I committed to it. But something ate at me, compelling me to move forward with this strategy.

I speared Kyle with an intent look and said, "What if I could give this all back to Dane?"

"Ari."

"He deserves it, don't you think? After all he's been through? Considering *all* he's doing? The sacrifices he's making, having to be away from me, especially when I'm pregnant? I can see how torturous this is for him. I see it in his eyes, even as he tries to hide it from me. And he feels as though—"

My stomach clenched, my heart constricted. I couldn't betray Dane by sharing with Kyle his insecurity that he wasn't giving me what he thought *I* deserved. A perfect life.

So I shook my head and just said, "He should get something in return for all of his suffering."

"I'm not discounting his efforts," Kyle said. "I'm just commenting on the obvious. You're talking about a multi-*billion*-dollar project. And, again, what the hell do you know about building a portion of a hotel, let alone bringing it back on-line?"

"Not much," I conceded. "But don't forget a key resource. Amano has worked side by side with Dane on *three* hotels." I smiled triumphantly.

Kyle snickered. "I'm with you, chief, but here's the thing. Asking for Amano's help leads to what?"

My smile instantly vanished. "He'd tell Dane what I was up to."

"In a heartbeat."

"Urg!" I paced the hardwood floor. How could I convince Amano to let me do this for Dane and keep it on the QT?

I'd be working with the people who constructed the Lux initially. Not exactly the blind leading the blind, right? And if the main building was structurally sound and just the lobby and its close quarters had to be restored it wasn't as though we'd be working from the ground up on an entire megaresort. Just this one area of it. Everything else was intact, with the exception of the courtyards, gardens, and fountains. Sure, they'd all have to be tended to, because they'd incurred the brunt of the debris, but that wasn't the end of the world.

The outbuildings were all in excellent condition. The conference center and ballrooms, the aquatic center with its indoor and outdoor pools and restaurants, the spa and bistros, the casitas along the five top-pro-designed golf courses—all in phenomenal shape. Never-used amenities, because the Lux had never even opened.

Hell, even the stunning perimeter fencing and columns were all standing, not the tiniest bit damaged. Of most significance, it was the once breath-stealing lobby that had suffered.

Honestly, it'd been so beautiful that I could cry over the devastation. To ruin something so soul stirring, so stunning. It was inhumane. Sacrilege.

But to resurrect it . . .

I turned to Kyle, now more determined than ever. "I remember the first time I walked through the doors of the Lux and thought nothing could be more extravagant, more glamorous, more amazing, than that lobby—and the chandeliers. Especially that ginormous one in the center, which you could see all the way out to the stone drive because it literally filled those tall asymmetrical windows." Emotion welled within me. "I have to get it all back. For Dane. For us. For Kid. Christ, throw out some names already, will you?"

"Dawson, Pacey, Joey, Mitch, Andie—"

"All from *Dawson's Creek*. You ass!" I lifted a foam stress ball from my desk and tossed it at him.

Kyle laughed. "What the hell do I know about naming a kid?"

"Clearly as much as the rest of us, so suggestions are welcomed."

"Maybe ask Amano. I bet he's got a family full of mysterious people with mysterious names."

"Oh, my God. You are *so* right. I don't even know his last name."

"Do you think he has one?" Kyle teased.

"Chances are good he doesn't. He just showed up on a riverbank somewhere as a baby, GLOCK in hand."

"Robin Hood reincarnated."

"Totally."

"Or maybe—"

"Ah-hem." I cleared my throat as the dark-haired, six-foot-six-inch bodyguard filled the doorway behind Kyle.

"He was raised by a pack of coyotes in the Sandia Mountains of Albuquerque, where he hunted wild boar with his bare hands and—"

"Ah-*hem*," I added with emphasis.

Kyle's eyes narrowed. "He's standing right behind me, isn't he?"

"Yep."

Kyle glanced over his shoulder.

Amano, not looking the least bit amused—though that was nothing new, since he rarely let an expression cross his face—said, "There are no wild boar in the Sandia Mountains."

"Right." Kyle slowly nodded his head. "Mule deer, then?"

I bit back a laugh. I swear, it was like poking a hibernating bear—that wasn't actually hibernating.

Amano tolerated Kyle, though. A hint of amusement actually flashed in Amano's eyes. So very briefly, but still. A good sign.

"Shouldn't you be monitoring the south side of the property?" he asked.

Kyle raised his iPad. "On it." To me, he said, "Back to the daily grind." He left the office.

Amano turned his steely gaze on me. "What's with the photos?"

"Just needed something on the walls," I lied. Unsuccessfully. He harrumphed, then sauntered off. I wondered if he'd tell Dane but then considered that there wasn't really anything to tell at this point.

So I went back to my plotting.

chapter 6

A month passed, and I couldn't have been antsier.

Or more paranoid.

Not just over the trials that had begun and the fact that Dane hadn't been back to visit us since he'd left, but because I didn't want Amano catching me during my secret discussions with the people who were going to help me reconstruct the lobby of 10,000 Lux.

With my new accomplice, hotel security guard John—who'd been instrumental in my rescue from Vale's kidnapping ploy— and several destroyed cell phones later, I had a plan in place.

The good news was, it sounded as though the entire structure would not have to be demoed and rebuilt.

The bad news was, we really couldn't "break ground" so to speak without Amano finding out.

I had proof I was the beneficiary of the Lux, and had the capital to do with it what I pleased, so we pretty much had the green light. I just needed to be strategic in how it all unfolded.

In the midst of sneaking around behind Amano's back so he didn't report my resurrection plans to Dane, I'd picked out the vast majority of furniture for the nursery and had it shipped to Jackson's house for Kyle to retrieve, given that Amano wouldn't allow deliveries within our gates. I also had a color scheme going on that I currently liked. I couldn't commit to it, though, because it was the fourth theme I'd fallen in love with in as many weeks. No need to get excited.

Names were grabbing me just as fast and leaving me just as furiously.

Who on earth would have thought this would be such a difficult part of having a baby? For God's sake, it was only a name.

Then again, I was a firm believer in the fact that a name helped to shape the person. Case in point, were I having a girl, I'd likely stick to the *J*s. There seemed to be a lot of strength associated around *J* names. Jackie Kennedy Onassis. Jackie Joyner-Kersee. J. Lo. JHud. J. Law. Jennifer Aniston.

I winced.

Scratch that one. She made me think of glamorous Mikaela.

Still, I felt I was on to something with the *J*s. For girls.

For boys, however, I was at a complete loss. And all over the board.

Dane called randomly—against Agents Daugherty and Strauss's advisement, but he refused to lose all connection with me—and one evening I asked, "How do you feel about 'Kennedy'?" Since the Jackie KO thing was in my head.

"As a president?"

I laughed. "As Kid's name."

"Hmm." He fell silent a moment, then said, "Gotta tell you, I'm not a fan. Everyone would call him Ken."

"Good point. Too preppy. Not at all the mysterious, edgy sound we're going for."

"That's what we're going for?"

"Sure. You really think he's going to be a normal child?"

"Well, I'd sort of hoped."

With a smile he couldn't see, I said, "I don't mean he's going to be weird, or anything. But he is *your* son. So you have to consider—"

"Baby, I have a better idea for this phone conversation."

My grin widened. "Oh?"

"Yeah." I heard the rustling of crisp sheets on his end.

"How's your shoulder?"

"Just fine." He paused a moment. When he spoke again, wickedness dripped from his sensual tone. "Where are you?"

"In bed."

"Me, too."

"Sucks that they're two different beds."

"I agree."

"And I don't even know where your bed is located," I said.

"That's why they call it witness protection."

"I wish you were here."

He was quiet again.

I sighed. "Dane."

"I've told you before. You have no idea how much I miss you."

"Tell me again. Better yet . . ." I stretched out, under the covers. "Tell me what you'd do to me if you were here right now."

"One thing I've missed doing. Not that I'm complaining. I can curb my tendencies. I definitely love you pregnant."

"Sure, what's not to love with this belly?"

He chuckled. "You're damn sexy. What Dr. Preston advised against for precautionary reasons is right at the top of my list of things I want to do to you."

"Ah, that. I adore that." I felt the wetness pool.

"I love dragging your panties down your legs, spreading your thighs, nipping at those spots on the inside that make you squirm and let out little gasps."

One escaped my lips now. "When you're between my legs—"

"When my *head* is between your legs," he corrected.

"Yeah." I sighed. "*Unbelievably* amazing."

"You have the most enticing little pink parts," he mused in his intimate bedroom voice. "I like to glide my fingertips over your soft, slick lips. Back and forth, lightly. Then sweep my tongue over the tight, moist folds. Tug gently with my mouth."

My little gasp turned into a throaty moan.

"You like it when I do that to you, don't you, baby?"

"Yes," I murmured as excitement rippled through me. "You are so good. At *everything*."

"I get turned on just thinking about you. Whether you're naked or not." His voice lowered. It made my nipples tingle. "But when my tongue is sliding along your pussy lips and then the tip is flicking slowly over your clit—"

"Lightly," I whispered. "Like butterfly wings."

"You enjoy the soft flutters at first. Then the firmer licks, the deeper suckling."

The knot of nerves between my legs throbbed.

My eyelids drifted closed. "I can practically feel you. Warm breath, soft lips, talented tongue." I writhed under the bedcovers as a thrill ribboned through me.

"I'd lift one leg over my shoulder, spreading you wide. While I continued to suck your clit, I'd slip two fingers into your pussy, pumping slowly. So slowly."

I sighed.

"Tell me you're touching yourself," Dane urged. "I can visualize it. I need to know. I need to hear."

I slid my fingertips along the folds he'd spoken of, the part of my body I knew he currently envisioned.

"It's not the same," I told him. "Nothing compares to you touching me." I wanted it, craved it.

"Imagine it's me."

"I am." I slid two fingers into my tight canal, stroking long and leisurely, matching the tone of his voice.

"I love how you taste," he told me. "And you get so wet for me."

"You're not even here and I'm wet for you."

"I want you to come, Ari. Think of me licking your pussy, my fingers plunging inside, pushing deep."

I called on erotic memories and felt the orgasm build.

"Dane." I put him on speakerphone and picked up the pace with my hand between my legs while the other one slipped beyond to the veed neck of the bodice of my nightgown. I squeezed my breast, pinched my nipple.

"You taste so damn good," he murmured. "I miss that. And the way you smell, especially when you're wearing the frankincense I gave you."

"Which you like to lick off every inch of me."

"I would if I were there."

I pictured his mouth on my body, his lips and tongue gliding over my flushed skin.

"God, I want you," I told him.

"Just think of me there, baby, sinking into you, thrusting deep."

Nothing felt as incredible as having Dane buried inside me, setting a quick, forceful rhythm that had my hips lifting and rolling to meet his exciting moves. I imagined him kissing me passionately, then staring into my eyes as he pushed us both to that ultimate pinnacle.

"Come for me, baby," he said.

I could from his voice and words alone, had certainly done so in the past. But with my fingers pumping steadily, I was instantly there for him.

"Dane." Exhilaration laced my tone. My breath hitched.

"You make the sexiest sounds when you're losing it for me."

"I want you to come, too."

"I'm thinking about those luscious lips of yours wrapped around my cock, teasing me at first with your tongue, then taking me deep, sucking me hard."

"I like making you come that way."

"You're so good at it. I love fucking your mouth."

"Oh, God." I squirmed on the bed as adrenaline rushed through me while I rubbed my clit, then plunged two fingers into my pussy again. All of the sensations converged. "Dane!" The climax took hold of me.

"That's it, sweetheart," he said in a tight voice. "I'm thinking about you taking me deeper, sucking harder." A few moments later, he let out a carnal growl. "Oh, goddamn, Ari." His breathing was jagged, matching mine.

We both panted harshly for a while, lost in our release, even if we weren't in the same bed. While I longed for his heat and powerful body, just listening to his labored breaths made me smile.

Eventually, he said, "Damn, baby. You made a mess."

I laughed. "That's the problem when you're not here with me."

"That's going to change soon."

I'd long since stopped hanging my hat on that hope. No one could really predict how long the trials would last or when the verdicts would come in.

As I thought of this, I heard the faucet running in the background, then Dane said, "Again, this is less than ideal."

"Don't grumble. You just had an orgasm."

"It's not the same without you."

"I know. But nothing to scoff at. I feel wonderful."

"Glad to be of service."

"Too bad that hunky body of yours isn't curled around me."

"I'll make it up to you for the next several decades."

I smiled. "I'm definitely holding you to that."

"You didn't just cringe and think, 'Oh, fuck, I'm stuck with this guy for the rest of my life'?"

"No, I just got another thrill over being stuck with this guy for the rest of my life."

He grunted. "I wouldn't go that far, all things considered."

I knew he thought of our current predicament and our last conversation. I chose to think beyond it all. "I would."

"You and your silver linings."

"They've worked out well for me thus far. You'll come back safely to us, Dane. That's all I want. All I need."

"I love you, baby."

"I love you more."

"Not a chance."

I settled deeper in the covers and said, "I don't want to hang up, but we shouldn't stay on the line any longer."

"I'll call you when I can."

"Be careful."

"You, too."

chapter 7

My dad visited the following week, despite initial instruction otherwise. He'd said it was urgent that he see me.

I'd been alarmed from the moment he'd called the landline, so the first words out of my mouth when he came through the front door were, "Are you okay? What's happened?"

He did a double take at me in my yoga suit and blurted, "Wow, you're about to have that kid!"

"Not yet." Though I'd finally popped. "Another six weeks."

He whistled. "I'm thinking linebacker."

"Me or the kid?"

With a kiss on the cheek, my father said, "You look fantastic, as always. I guess I just wasn't expecting you to be so, so—"

"Big?" I offered.

"Well." Holding his hands out, he seemed to sort of gauge the size of my belly. "You went from not-so-much there a little over a month ago to *oh, wow—you really are pregnant!*"

"You don't know the half of it. Feet and ankles swollen, nothing fits. I'm *this close* to resorting to wearing Dane's drawstring pants and T-shirts." Not that I didn't already wear his Henleys with my stretchy yoga pants to bed.

As we left the foyer and entered the great room, my dad chuckled. "You've even got the waddle down pat."

"Would it be rude of me to say *shut up*?"

He laughed heartier. "I'd find your sarcasm biting were it not for the fact that you are beaming. Seriously, sweets, you glowed the last time I saw you. Now you have this incredible brightness that really suits you."

"He kicks now. Like, a lot. I love it. Every time my mind wanders to Dane being gone or some other dreary thing, he gives me a jolt and I get giddy over the fact that I have this tiny person inside me, demanding my attention." I patted my stomach. "He's a bit hyperactive, but so awesome."

My dad kissed my forehead. "You're going to be a wonderful mom."

"Time will tell. Now, what's going on? You said it was urgent."

His good mood instantly dissipated. "Speaking of moms."

My spirits plummeted as well. "Oh, no."

"Oh, yeah."

We took the sofa in front of the fire and Rosa served me iced tea and my dad a beer. He sucked down half of it before continuing. That was alarming unto itself.

"You're making me nervous," I told him.

He set aside his pilsner. "So she has this crazy idea about writing a book."

"That again?"

His gaze snapped to me. "You know about this?"

Uh-oh. "Um. Sort of?"

"Ari." He reached for the beer and drained it. That pretty much summed up his state of mind. My father wasn't a big drinker.

Unless it was Dane's fifty-year-old scotch. "Do you *really* know what she's up to?"

"Sadly, yes. Except, I don't think there's actually a book, Dad. It's a threat."

He whipped out his cell and handed it over. "Scroll through."

The pages were already pulled up in his e-mail, and I skimmed the first chapter of drivel. Trashy drivel. Name-dropping, party-hopping, designer-wearing Mother in all her "*fabulous*" glory. She'd glammed herself to the hilt and dove right into the famous men she'd slept with while my dad was on his PGA tours.

Anxiety roiled through me. Along with disgust and a hell of a lot *I could have been spared the details and been a happier person for it.*

I gave him the phone back. "Dad, that's disgusting." I was sure my mother-to-be radiance died on the vine. "She seriously got around."

"While you were still in diapers."

I blanched. "She started *that* early in your marriage?"

"Fool on me, right?"

"Dad, no." I was infuriated. I got to my swollen feet and started to pace. "I knew she'd cheated because of your arguments, but from the beginning? And with how many men in total? No." I raised a hand. "Don't tell me. I don't want to know; you don't want to say it out loud. Damn, Dad. This is such crap." I shook my head. My fists balled at my sides. "I get that it's somehow cool these days for nannies and porn stars to Tweet and Facebook about their celebrity affairs, even if the celebrity is married. Somehow there's no backlash for them when they start shopping their tell-all books. So what does my mother have to lose?"

"I didn't come here to upset you, Ari. Sit down."

"No, Dad. I'm not upset—I'm livid. Because she came to me claiming that she'd write a book about her exploits and she demanded money to keep her quiet."

"Aria." He eyed me with that concerned-father look that made my heart hurt. "Do not tell me you gave her a penny. Not one red cent."

"Dad." I plopped back onto the sofa. "What else could I do? Let her launch her tales so that everyone on the planet found out she betrayed you? No way."

He suddenly sprang to his feet, anger rolling off him in waves. "I only came to give you a head's-up. This is not *yours* to deal with, Ari."

"Yes, it is, Dad. When she's trying to attack you and there's the tiniest bit of hope that I can thwart her, of course I'm going to do whatever I can. It's just never enough." I stood again, thoroughly irritated. How could I even be related to this woman? "Look, when she first knocked on my door, it was for five grand. I gave it to her."

"Sweets." His eyes squeezed shut briefly. "That is *not* your responsibility."

"You're my dad," I countered as fury and pain rose within me. Along with the shame that *my mother* should feel over her adulterous actions—but which she clearly considered juicy and scintillating instead. Not embarrassing or slutty, at all. Because of the famous names she could associate herself with; somehow they elevated her above scarlet-letter status?

I asked, "What was I going to do? Let her gut you all over again? No. I lived with your agony. For *years*. If there is anything I can do to keep her from tormenting you once more, I'll do it. In a heartbeat. But this is her third attempt, Dad—"

"*What?*" He stared at me, incredulous.

I forced myself to unclench my fists. No simple task.

"Number three, Dad. And we're going to have to figure out how to make it her final attempt. There has to be something we can do. Soon. Because if she ever finds out I'm married to Dane she'll never stop coming at us."

He lifted his hands in the air and said, "So maybe I just need to say it doesn't matter, Ari."

"What doesn't matter?"

"If she wants to tell the world what a whore she is, let her." I knew that one word hurt him greatly—because he'd been in love with my mother. Yet he accurately called the spade a spade.

"Dad, as much as I appreciate your desire to simplify this, that viewpoint isn't what's really at stake. No one's going to balk at how many professional athletes she slept with—the egg will be on your face, not hers. And I can't let that happen."

"Just because I was married to her at the time—"

"It's *all* about the fact that you were married to her at the time. Despite how solid *you* were in the relationship, she'll twist the cheating around to be a *woe is me* thing. *He left me lonely; what else was I to do?* or some such shit. You know her. That's her favorite device. She excels at evoking sympathy. In the long run, you'll be the heel and she'll reap all the reward."

It was all I could do not to erupt in a fit of rage, but my dad didn't need that at the moment. What he needed was the reassurance *I* could give him.

"I'll take care of it."

"Ari, this isn't your—"

"Dad, just let me do this. I have the money. I can give her more than her greedy little mind could possibly fathom and then—"

"You said you tried that before."

"It'll be different this time. I'll put Jackson on this. Trust me, when he's done with Mommie Dearest we won't hear from her ever again."

"Ari." He stared at me for endless seconds. As though trying to figure out who I was.

I flinched. Okay, I'd officially done it. Gone to my own dark and dangerous spectrum, the way Dane sometimes did. The way

I abhorred him doing if it meant he was about to cross a line he shouldn't.

There was so much of me that was like him. I understood his need to protect me because I felt that same pull. With him. Our child. Kyle. My dad. This whole new family unit of mine.

I would have taken a step back from all of this, except for two things. One, Dane and Kyle had both come to my aid when my mother had threatened my reputation as much as my father's. And two, I absolutely wouldn't have him wrecked again by her. Not *ever* again.

This time, I'd put a halt to her scheming in a way that would ensure she never came back to haunt us. In fact, I should have thought of it sooner. Yet when she'd first turned up I hadn't been deeply involved with Dane, nor had I fully grasped the concept of my own parent blackmailing me.

I got it now.

"Dad," I said, projecting a calmer visage and tone. "I know what she's after. Not just fifteen minutes of fame. She needs an ego boost because you ended up with a great post-pro career as GM of an exclusive, private club she'll *never* get into and I moved on from her. She can't afford country club memberships, and I'm sure that kills her. So she's put out this ridiculous cry for help. We'll give it to her."

"I don't want you handing over yours or Dane's money, Ari."

"Don't worry about it, Dad. I just need you to do me a huge favor. I can't access the Internet all that often—you know, with the whole making certain we're not hacked/compromised thing we've got going on in this house. So I'll need you to keep your ear to the ground and make sure she's not leaking teasers about a book or, God forbid, stalking Oprah to read her tell-all."

His head jerked back. "Oprah?"

"Yeah. Mother's a fan. Anyway, just eyes and ears open. I can't manage all of that."

"No problem. I'll Google Alert her."

I started. "You know how to do that?"

"I have favorite PGA contenders to keep up on and that's the best way when I'm on the course so often, rather than strapped to my desk."

"Right. Of course. My tech-savvy dad." Even I didn't know how to Google Alert. "Anyway, we can double-team her. She's not getting the best of either of us."

He still didn't look all that comfortable with my new, aggressive demeanor. But I'd been backed into the corner too many times to let it happen again.

Two days later, Kyle came into the office, wearing nothing but his white pants from karate class with Amano and a towel around his neck. His muscles seemed to be more sculpted with every day that passed. He plopped into a chair as I rushed about. Relatively speaking. I wasn't exactly zippy in my pregnant state.

After five or so minutes, he asked, "Do I even want to know this time?"

"Probably not."

"That's what scares me."

I glanced at him over my shoulder. "You need athletic outlets; I need mental ones."

"Yeah, but why do I get the feeling you're mock-auditioning for *Castle*?"

"Nothing like that. Not really."

Liar.

Turning back to the wall, where I had photos and yarn from Rosa's sewing basket strewn everywhere, I explained the method to my madness, partially coinciding with the Lux rebuild.

"So." I gestured to the top row of four pictures. "Dane, Ethan, Qadir, Nikolai. Good guys of the secret society." I indicated the level below them. "Hilliard, Avril, Castcrelli, Wellington. Bad guys." Then swept my arm to the right. "Bent and Vale. Dead guys."

Kyle leaned forward and rested his forearms on his thighs. "What's with the two crescent moons abutting each other with the circle in the middle?"

My sketch. "That's Wayne Horton. Asshole."

Kyle snorted. "Nice depiction."

"You think you're the only one who's creative in this house?"

"*You* realize Dane is going to have a conniption when he sees all the tiny nails you've hammered into his walls?"

With a coy smile, I said, "I'll just have to convince him to get over it, now won't I?"

Kyle grunted. "I don't even want to know about that."

"Okay, then." My attention shifted to the printouts. "So here's the Lux." Off to the left side of Wayne. I hooked a piece of yarn around the head of the nail and pulled it tightly to my sketch of the Asshole and looped it around that nail. Then I continued upward, to the right, where Vale's picture was, effectively connecting three dots. "We're pretty certain Vale and Wayne conspired to destroy 10,000 Lux, even if there's no actual evidence to back up that theory."

"Not a news flash," Kyle tried to delicately tell me.

"No, not a news flash. However, we're not entirely sure of everyone's motives and who's fully responsible for all the destruction."

"I believe that's what the trials are about."

"Maybe," I said. "Don't forget that we're dealing with an Illuminati faction with a powerful network built around it. Lots of pieces to the puzzle."

I gathered three more printouts. I posted my hand-drawn rendering of Tom Talbot with a rifle, his stick figure–illustrated wife and daughter tied up, and the snake-tat guy we'd encountered who'd provided the rattler for Vale when he'd set me up in the stairwell at the Lux.

"You have way too much time on your hands," Kyle drawled.

"Just hang in there a few minutes more."

For good measure, I scrawled out the shadow of a likeness of myself—with an enormous belly—and tacked it up. Then I twined yarn from here to there to there and stood back, eyeing the web I'd created.

"Tom, Candace, Ruby—all connected to Wayne, I'm positive of it. Who else would have planted the snakes on our patio and held Tom's wife and daughter hostage—just as he left the snake for me in the stairwell and helped Vale kidnap me? It sure as hell wasn't Vale, because it was finally confirmed with DNA samples that he was splattered on the front of that freight train in Flagstaff," I stressed. "Snake-tat guy provided all the reptiles to torment and endanger me. He worked with Wayne, according to Vale. Then there's me, directly related to Wayne, because I'm always his target."

I raised my hands in the air in a *voilà* way. Then I grabbed my red marker and drew a circle around Wayne's "cheeks."

"It all leads to him, not Vale. Not Bryn." I concluded. "Just as Dane had begun to suspect. This chameleon, wraith, satanic bastard is our nemesis. And until we rope him in, *anything* could happen." I swept a hand over my body. "Look at me. I'm six weeks away from giving birth. Do I want that psycho out there, lurking in dark shadows? Hell. No."

Kyle stood. "Ari, you're not suggesting—"

"Not *suggesting*. We've discussed this before. Now it's time to take action."

Perhaps it was the conversation I'd had with my dad and the fact that I'd reached that point of no return where I couldn't afford to let—*wouldn't* let—anyone threaten us again. *Any* of us.

Kyle shook his head. "No, Ari. No way. I'm not about to—"

"We both know that we need a confession from Wayne. Because he links right back to this." I tapped the Lux with my finger. "And while he's out there, I can't fully do anything with the hotel, for fear he's going to sabotage it again."

"So let the Lux go."

"No," I insisted. "Not an option. Besides, I have more."

He eyed me curiously. Slowly said, "I'm not sure I want to hear more."

"Get a grip." I rolled my eyes for effect. "You know that all Amano has to do is gaze at a person and he can pretty much read their every thought. He totally figured out what I was up to when he came in here again the other day. So he did some of his own research. Turns out, Wayne Horton used to work at a new multiplex casino in Las Vegas." I smiled triumphantly.

Kyle stared at me as though I'd just declared I was the one to invent Post-it Notes. And couldn't convince him it was true.

"Follow me here," I said. "One of the high-rise towers had some damaged or misplaced rebar or some such thing that substantially weakened the structure and, after paying six hundred million to have it built, the owners had to reinforce the tower with concrete pillars within the lobby area. Apparently, it turned out to be quite the eyesore, and wasn't a sufficient solution anyway. No one has ever been allowed to set foot inside, let alone occupy a room. They're now taking apart the tower piece by piece. All that money and effort gone to waste."

"And that has what to do with . . . *what*?"

"According to Amano's findings, Wayne was a construction lead on the project. He could have easily been in charge."

"Of a six-hundred-million-dollar catastrophe? Wayne Horton?"

Not to be deterred or undermined by his lack of confidence in my reasoning, I said, "Might I remind you that Asshole Horton hijacked the Lux Web site at the most crucial time, deactivated my access badge *at the most crucial time*, so I faced a diamondback with no escape, set fire to a media room I was trapped in, helped Vale kidnap me, destroyed the entire security system at the Lux—and, oh, let's not forget that he was the one to devise the whole *wouldn't it be fun if Ari was stung by scorpions?* campaign." I stared unwaveringly at my friend. "Trust me, not so fun."

Kyle clearly tried very hard to keep up with me but fell short. "We already know he's a problem."

"No, he is the root of all evil. And he's not on *anyone's* radar! That's how fucking brilliant he is at covering his tracks." Fear rippled down my spine, but I maintained my steady footing.

"So let's sic Amano on him—he'll find Horton," Kyle assured me. "That lowlife piece of shit keeps coming back here, after all."

"Since Vale's dead, likely the reason for Wayne's return would be because if he's spotted in Vegas the hotel owners might want to have a dangerous word or two with him. Or . . . maybe his work *here* isn't done."

Kyle's strong jaw set in a hard line. "That's not exactly a comforting thought."

"Tell me about it." I snatched a fat, black marker and wrote *Vegas* on the wall.

He grimaced. "You are so playing with fire here, messing up the King of Everything's walls."

"We can repaint. I need to see all of this, mull it over." I climbed onto the sofa and drew a curving arrow from Vegas to Wayne's piece of paper. "There's something about him being involved in that tower debacle that's eating at me. Like, the guy knows too much. Has too much power for someone who worked at the Lux as a valet, grounds crew, gofer type."

"Those roles did allow him to have access to all critical touch points at the resort." Kyle offered his hand to me and helped me off the sofa.

"Exactly." Returning the marker to the desk, I added, "Now, if only I could figure out who he really is and what he's really up to—because it seems like it's much more than just being Vale's henchman. In fact, like Dane, I'm starting to think that maybe it was the other way around and Vale was the minion to Wayne's master—" My mouth fell open as a slight tug occurred between my legs and then a splash hit the floor. And my shoes.

"Ari," Kyle complained. "That's gross."

I glared at him, a hint of panic besieging me. "It's not pee,

Kyle. I think—" I shook my head. "No. I *know* my water just broke."

"Your *what?*"

"Oh. Shit." The panic morphed into full-blown horror. "I'm not at full term yet!"

While Kyle's blue eyes turned as large as saucers, I felt a kick. Then another. Not contractions. I was certain I could discern the difference.

I wrapped my arms around my belly. "It's like he's on the move."

"Whoa, whoa, *whoa!*" Kyle started his own freak-out. "You're a month and half early, Ari."

"No kidding. Call Macy."

As he reached for the landline—designated for emergency purposes only—to phone his aunt, I shuffled to the doorway and yelled out for Rosa. She appeared almost instantly. "Water broke." I indicated my shoes.

A hint of concern flitted over her face. Then she said in a matter-of-fact voice, "You could have an infection. Or you could be going into labor."

A third swift kick had me saying in a strained tone, "Doesn't feel like labor. More like he's run out of room or something. Trying to stretch."

Amano joined us, just as Kyle did.

Rosa said, "Dr. Preston might be able to stall the birth. I'll pack your clothes." Rosa rushed down the hallway.

"I'll drive," Amano said as he reached for his cell.

I grabbed his arm. "Don't you dare call Dane!"

"Ari." Amano gave me his warning look, reminding me of whom his loyalty ultimately rested with—my husband. For once, I was one step ahead of him. Maybe two.

"You'll only worry Dane and make him completely crazed. Plus, this could be nothing. And, let's face it—" I hated to do this, but I couldn't have Dane tormented even more because he wasn't here during a potential baby crisis. "You owe me."

Amano glared at me, taken aback. I'd pushed the boundary with that one, but he clearly couldn't dispute my logic. He'd been the one to rescue Dane from the explosion at the Lux—and had not told me that Dane had survived. For good reason, but still. Amano had perpetuated the lie that Dane was dead in order for him to work undercover with the FBI. Amano had known it'd ruin me, but he'd also seen the prime opportunity for what it was.

"I'm sorry," I said. "I wouldn't ever play that card, except what's the point of telling him when he can do nothing about this, even if he were here? He can't stop this baby from coming early, if that's what's going to happen."

"He'd still want to be with you."

I shook my head. "We have come too far—he has sacrificed *too* much to be distracted by something that could be nothing."

Okay, I played another card I'd never intended. Amano had absolutely no experience with pregnant women or premature babies. If I stayed calm—*appeared* calm, at any rate—he wouldn't get mired in the full impact of what could actually be happening. I'd read enough books on childbirth to be deeply distressed, because if my baby was born at this point he could suffer severe health risks. I didn't share that knowledge with Amano.

"I just need to get to the retreat," I told my bodyguard. "I need Macy and Dr. Preston to check me out."

Did I sound normal or was my voice an octave too high? I spared a glance at Kyle, who seemed to grasp what I tried to achieve.

With a nod, he said to Amano, "You know Ari. It's not a typical day in our world unless there's some drama. Seriously." He tried to look nonchalant. Though I had no doubt he was as wigged as I was.

Rosa returned with a bag and a towel to clean me up. Then the men helped me into the SUV. Rosa sat with me in the back, since Amano refused to leave her alone at the house with no protection—not quite considering the safeguarding offered by our FBI property sitters reliable protection. He was just that way.

Rosa patted my hand and whispered, "Babies don't need the water so much at this point in the term and more will be produced, so it should be okay."

I didn't dare pose the *or . . . ?* question while Amano was in earshot. Tried not to dwell on that prospect myself.

When we arrived at the medical retreat, it was handy to have Kyle with us to alleviate problems with the massive security his aunt was required to maintain for her accreditations. Though the guards knew me anyway, since I'd stayed there during my first trimester and returned for my routine checkups and ultrasounds with Dr. Preston.

Macy ushered me into an exam room as I explained what had happened. She had me in stirrups with a blanket covering me in no time. The guys promptly disappeared, though I begged Rosa to stay with me. Not that I'd really had to—from her determined expression, she wasn't going anywhere.

"Dr. Preston is on her way," Macy informed me. "She'll be about an hour."

My OB-GYN was based out of Scottsdale, south of us. Since I didn't believe I was about to deliver *right this very second,* I didn't stress over the travel time. I was relieved she could break free for me.

Macy made me comfortable and talked me through a few possible scenarios. She assured me delivering today wouldn't be the end of the world, though it'd be necessary to closely monitor the baby if that occurred.

"From the size of that belly of yours," Macy said in a playful voice, "I don't think there'll be a problem with his weight."

"It's like he sprouted a few inches the past couple of weeks. Even my dad was shocked by how big I'd gotten, so quickly."

"That's not out of the norm. And sometimes babies stop growing when they've reached a certain point, which will contribute to a premature birth," Macy explained. "That situation is actually rare, but it does happen."

"Believe me, nothing about this child is going to be ordinary. You've met his father."

Both Macy and Rosa laughed. Easily, not strained or forced humor.

Okay, that was good.

Rubbing my belly, I said, "So maybe you can help me kill time by offering up some baby names."

We spent the hour running through an impressive list. I had a few *ah-ha* moments, but they passed in a flash. Brock stuck in my head, but I wanted to use Dane's father's name for a middle name, which was also Dane's middle name. So Brock Bradley Bax just felt like a mouthful. I didn't fully discount it, though.

Rosa offered Cort, which had potential as well. Cort Bradley Bax. It was strong, masculine. Too trendy?

We kept at it until Dr. Preston arrived and did her usual efficient assessment, with some head nodding, some shaking, then a final decisive, "Everything's going to be okay."

I let out a lengthy sigh of relief.

"Although," she added, "you are having this baby sooner rather than later."

I eyed her sternly.

She said, "Ari, you have cervical insufficiency. Usually that can be determined up front, if you've had miscarriages, a D and C, or are otherwise at risk. You had no risk factors. I even examined your cervix at the beginning of your pregnancy, and it doesn't fall into the short category. But there have certainly been some changes with your body that caused the incompetency in this late stage." With a steady gaze, she told me, "This child of yours is so ready to be born."

"Macy mentioned he might have stopped growing," I said, swallowing a lump of fear. "And seriously, I feel like he's all scrunched up and trying to stretch, find more room. Lots of activity in there the past week or so."

"What's of biggest concern," she said in an earnest tone, "is that all of his organs are developed, he doesn't have breathing problems, lung complications, and the like. I don't fear his weight from the looks of you, and preemies do very well when they're healthy. We'll just have to keep an eagle eye on him."

"So you don't think it's too soon to have him?"

"Naturally, I prefer to hold this off at least a few more weeks. That's not going to happen, though. Your cervix has weakened, softened. You're rapidly dilating because of the baby's weight on this vulnerable part of your body."

"But I'm not having contractions. Again, just the kicking." I grimaced as another thump backed up my statement.

She grinned. "Sometimes, when they're ready, they're ready." Then in a more serious tone, she said, "Unfortunately, once the water breaks there's a high risk of infection for you and the baby. We don't want that."

"Definitely not." She scared me even more, though I could see that wasn't her intention.

"I just want to reiterate that there could be some concerns to address after the delivery. Or things could go very well. You're healthy and there haven't been any complications beyond your morning sickness and dehydration, and you haven't suffered either of those in months, so I'm not overly worried." She gave me a confident look.

I took a few deep breaths, then asked, "So I'm having this kid now?"

"You're having this kid now."

chapter 8

Induced labor.

Yeah. Not what I'd expected.

I was dilated and Kid was ready to make his grand entrance into the world without any contractions, and I was good with that.

Induction shattered my bliss.

Meds were administered, sharp pains ensued, and I felt justified in screaming at the top of my lungs.

Dr. Preston and Macy demonstrated the utmost compassion. Rosa appeared mildly disappointed that my threshold for pain wasn't higher.

"Am I giving birth to a fucking elephant?" I demanded at one point.

Rosa went into a dissertation about her twelve-pound, twenty-inch son and I nearly passed out.

Twelve pounds?

"Ari, the baby's not *that* big," Dr. Preston said, and shot Rosa a look.

Another contraction hit; I screamed and then glared at Rosa. She shook her head.

Macy, assisting Dr. Preston, told me, "The plus side of a quicker labor is that you won't have forty-eight hours of intermittent pain. The downside is that you'll experience forty-eight minutes of *constant* pain."

And I did. So much so, it was a good thing Dane wasn't in the room with me—or even in the same state. I turned a bit irrational, cursing all men for having the ability to do this to unsuspecting women.

No, I hadn't been unsuspecting. But I had been on the pill. I'd just missed several doses during exhaustive Lux pre-launch planning. That was moot in my mind at the moment. At present, as far as I was concerned, I was more than entitled to blame everyone but me for the agony I was in.

Rosa held my hand—until I squeezed so tight that *she* cried out in pain. I almost said it served her right.

"Get Kyle," I insisted. Not that I wanted to subject him to this, but I needed to know I wasn't going to crush bones. Rosa was reluctant to leave but did as I asked.

Kyle popped his head around the door. "You don't really want me in here?"

"Yes. Quick." I reached for his hand and clutched it tight.

"Your breathing's good, Ari," Dr. Preston said. "We're about to start doing some heavy pushing."

"She's warning you, not me," I told Kyle.

"Like you're going to hurt me."

"You've been here two seconds. Just you wait."

Sure enough, when things really got going I caught him biting back a few winces and I might have pierced an eardrum or two.

I had no idea how long this went on, but after one particularly grueling "push"—really, that didn't even begin to describe the massive shove I gave—Dr. Preston let out a delighted sound and then suddenly I heard a wail to match mine and there he was.

Kid Bax.

"Holy shit." I stared at him, a bloody mess but mine nonetheless.

"I think I'm going to be sick."

I spared a glance at Kyle, who'd turned a bit green around the gills at the sight of the newborn.

"He actually *is* big," I said to Dr. Preston and Macy.

"With all ten fingers and toes intact," my OB-GYN announced. "Some hearty lungs from the sound of things. Steady breathing." She looked pleased and that relaxed me a bit. I still didn't let go of Kyle's hand, though.

He muttered, "Vise grip, Ari."

"Suck it up." I closed my eyes, in desperate need of some rest.

"I'm going to examine him," Dr. Preston said. "I'll bring him back in a little while."

I didn't like the idea of being separated from something I'd been so intimately attached to for seven and a half months, but I couldn't fight the overwhelming fatigue. And was out within minutes.

I woke sometime later to the gentle sweep of hair from my forehead and the light dabbing of a cool washcloth on my skin.

"That's nice," I murmured. I figured Macy was playing nursemaid. She was perfect at it—when she wasn't challenging me to take better care of myself. Likely the reason she was so successful with her rehab retreat. A soft touch mixed with some tough love went a long way.

"You are absolutely amazing."

Not Macy's voice.

My lids snapped open.

"Dane."

Tears flooded my eyes.

He gave me his sexy half-assed grin. The one that only lifted one corner of his tempting mouth. "You think I'd miss this?"

"Damn that Amano."

"I only wished I could have gotten here sooner."

"It doesn't matter. You came." As adamant as I'd been about him not being distracted, nothing compared to having him here.

I wanted him here. I needed him here.

I said, "You won't believe how beautiful our son is."

"Haven't seen him yet. Dr. Preston had tests to run and she's monitoring his temperature."

"She didn't say it was low, did she?"

"No," Dane assured me as his fingers threaded through my damp hair. "She said he's fine. In fact, Macy told me we didn't have anything to worry about. They're just taking precautions while you sleep."

"I want to see him. I want to hold him."

Dane whisked fat drops from my cheeks. "I'll let them know." He kissed me tenderly, then asked, "Did you get enough rest?"

"Yes. I think I've been out for a few hours. Feels like it, anyway."

"I'll be right back." He kissed me again, then gazed down at me for endless seconds, his emerald irises glowing. "I am so blown away by you. Nothing stops you; nothing holds you back. You are unbelievable, Ari Bax."

His eyes deepened in color and a light mist covered them. More tears flowed down my cheeks.

"All I did was have a baby," I said in my usual flippant tone, though it was tinged with emotion. "Tons of chicks do it all the time. In fact, I think I bored Rosa during labor."

He pressed his lips to my forehead, then whispered, "You're the most incredible person I know, and I love you desperately."

I twined my arms around his neck and held him tightly to me, soaking in his heat, his masculine scent, his strength. Everything about him teased my senses and wrapped me in bliss. He made me so happy. Our entire family made me deliriously happy.

"Bring me our son," I muttered against Dane's temple. "Let's get a good look at him together."

Dane left me and I shifted in the bed I wasn't even cognizant of having been moved to. I wore a nightgown Rosa must have packed. As I glanced around the room, I realized Macy had put me in the bedroom off the courtyard that I'd occupied for three months when I'd had so much trouble at the beginning of my pregnancy—and I'd believed Dane was dead.

I sighed. I'd have to make amends with Amano. I didn't like that I'd told him he owed me. Though he hadn't exactly played into that hand.

Or had he?

Who had called Dane? Amano or Kyle?

Hmm.

Would Kyle have done that again, just to make me feel better? Probably.

He was a bit too awesome for words, after all.

Dane came back to my room and took the chair next to the bed once more. "Macy's checking in with Dr. Preston."

Butterflies fluttered in my stomach. "Think he'll like us?"

Dane chuckled good-naturedly. "We'll see, right?"

I inhaled deeply. "Let's hope so."

A few minutes later, Macy came in with a thick bundle in her arms. My heart nearly burst from my chest. My toes curled.

"Oh, God," I breathed.

I was excited. Nervous.

So very excited. So very nervous.

It was like awaiting an interview for a dream job, filing a mortgage application, praying for approval from the private school you wanted your child to attend, and meeting the parents of your significant other all at once.

I felt ridiculously on display. Wanted a mirror to check my hair and face. Wished like hell I could brush my teeth and slap a coat of polish on the nails I'd gnawed to the nub while pushing and heaving and otherwise trying to give birth without freaking Kyle out too much.

I knew it was crazy—it wasn't as though our son had any clue who Dane and I were, let alone how disheveled I looked. Perhaps it was because Dane looked so sensational, as usual, that I feared I'd fail by comparison.

Macy leaned close and carefully placed the baby in my arms. She swept back the little beanie he wore and I gasped at the thicket of black hair on his tiny head.

"Holy cow," I gushed. "Look at that."

The strands were the same obsidian as his father's and just as soft. He even had Dane's dark complexion. The blue eyes were mine.

Dane said, "My mother was from Madrid. He has her coloring. But that hair. It's just like my dad's."

"He's so beautiful." I stared in awe. Nothing had prepared me for this moment. I hadn't really considered what it would be like to hold my son in my arms for the first time. This itty-bitty guy with his small balled fists and his perfect cupid mouth that sort of gaped like a fish out of water. He gurgled and gasped and I fell in love with every sound he made, as well as the sight of him.

"Too perfect, huh?" I asked Dane.

"Just perfect enough." His voice was filled with emotion. Pride. Joy. Love.

I glanced at him. He was mesmerized. I didn't blame him.

We both admired our little creation, who wiggled and squirmed, but in a way that made me think he was just looking for that cozy sweet spot in my arms.

When he found it, he settled in and let out a sigh. Or so I thought. Who knew? Could've been gas. It was cute either way.

"Amsel," Dane said in his low voice.

"Hmm?"

"It's German."

Like Dane's father.

"Means 'blackbird.'"

My gaze landed on the tuft of hair again. "Apropos."

"Yes."

"Amsel Bradley Bax," I quietly announced.

"He'll change this world."

My attention shifted to Dane. Had his father thought the same thing when he'd laid eyes on Dane for the first time? Had he innately known of Dane's potential for greatness?

I stared a while longer at my husband, a new puzzle piece forming in my mind.

Who was Dane's father? Rather, who had he been? And had he known his son would be someone so significant, influential, powerful?

Was this genetic?

The society popped into my head. Dane had been recruited outside of the circle, when the others had been inaugurated by virtue of heredity.

Except for Vale Hilliard. His father was part of the society, yet Vale wasn't. Were there others who hadn't made the grade? What happened when they fell short? Did they take up a role similar to Vale's? Serve as part of the network, on-hand to do whatever was demanded of them because they were the soldiers, not the leaders?

"Hey," Dane said as his lips grazed my temple. "What are you thinking?"

I didn't want to spoil the moment with the subject of the Illuminati, so I said, "Just that we've been given the most precious gift imaginable. Honestly, Dane, he's so fantastic." My head dipped and I brushed the tip of my nose against my son's. "Amsel," I whispered. He cooed.

Dane's fingertips brushed along the baby's plump cheek. "He's definitely something else. We're really lucky, Ari."

"Yes. We are."

He kissed me. Softly, sweetly, passionately. I could have just skated away with the soulful moment. But Amsel stirred and made a small distressed sound that I figured was related to the need for food.

Pulling away from Dane, I asked, "Would you mind getting Dr. Preston? I have a lot of questions about feeding and burping and changing Amsel. All that."

"Mind if I sit in on the lesson?"

"Of course not." A second later, my brow dipped. "But don't you have to get back to Quantico or wherever the FBI is hiding you?"

With another sexy kiss, he said, "It's not Quantico. And I can hang a while longer."

He left us briefly and I returned my attention to little Amsel Bradley Bax. My blackbird.

"So, Kid," I mused as he kept up the adorable gurgles. "What do you think of your family so far? Lots of people, all willing to do anything in their power to keep you safe. They're pretty fabulous. And wait until you meet your granddad. He's a golfer. Very laid-back dude. You'll learn a lot from him." I suddenly couldn't wait to introduce the two of them.

As I went all gooey over my dad and my son bonding, there was a small knock on my bedroom door. I barely heard it.

"Come in."

Lisa entered first—she was one of the specialists for the little autistic girl, Chelsea, whom Macy accommodated for inpatient care. "We're not interrupting, are we?"

"No. Great timing, actually."

Lisa moved farther into the room. Chelsea followed suit, though stuck to the fringes. She was a petite blonde with a frail frame and springy curls. A gifted child whose mother had done everything she could to raise Chelsea in a secure and nurturing environment but hadn't quite been equipped to deal with the complexities of autism.

The more I'd gotten to know Chelsea during my stay, the more I'd come to realize how fascinating she was—and how specific her needs were. I'd set up a foundation for autistic children as a result and one for single-income mothers, such as Chelsea's, in the small community of Sedona, where the cost of living could prove challenging.

Chelsea benefited greatly from Macy's retreat. Dane and I had paid for two years of her future care, which I now considered extending, seeing what good it did for Chelsea. When I'd first met her, she never would have made this bold of a move, coming to my room for an amiable visit. I prayed others reaped similar advantages from our efforts.

To the delicate little blonde, I asked, "Are you here to see my baby?"

She hung back, as was her nature. She didn't like anyone invading her space. I could relate. I'd never liked it, either. Hadn't been able to get over the affliction until I'd met Dane, actually.

"His name is Amsel," I offered in a soft voice. Like me, Chelsea was averse to loud noises. For entirely different reasons, of course. I'd heard enough slammed doors and shattered glass to last a lifetime.

I waited a few moments, not saying anything. Lisa remained silent as well. This was how Chelsea acclimated.

Mostly, she spent her time at a large table just inside the solarium that overlooked the gardens and courtyard. Chelsea had the phenomenal ability to replicate landmarks out of Erector Sets and Legos. If we could channel that talent into rebuilding the Lux, we'd really be in business.

Five or so minutes passed with no one rushing Chelsea or making a move. Amsel stopped fussing and slept in my arms. I was captivated by the sight of him, the feel of him, the smell of him. I resisted the urge to lift him to my nose and inhale deeply.

Finally, Chelsea inched forward. Slowly. She eyed Amsel from various angles. Subtly.

I watched, while trying to appear as if I weren't.

When she reached the bed, she tilted her head, checking out

the minuscule package. Then she climbed onto the mattress. That was a surprise, her being the spatially conscious type. I didn't say anything, didn't make as though this was a shock.

She crawled toward Amsel, sat on her knees, then very gently poked at my son. His leg. His arm. His shoulder. Not jarring him in the least, just sort of feeling him out.

I bit back a laugh. Lisa shot me a warning look—as though to remind me of how not to upset Chelsea with raucous sounds or sudden movements.

I whispered, "He's brand-new. Cute, huh?"

She studied him closely. Didn't say a word, not that I was surprised, because she rarely spoke to anyone other than her specialists. And Kyle.

"Smells nice, too. I'm keeping him."

She glanced up at me.

"I'll bring him to see you whenever you want. If you want."

Chelsea took a few moments to visually inspect Amsel a bit more. Then she nodded. She gave a couple more faint jabs and smiled.

"I promise he'll be awake next time."

Still, she didn't seem to mind. She climbed off the bed and wandered off.

Lisa said, "She definitely likes him."

"I think it'll be mutual."

chapter 9

We were all back at the creek house three days later. Dr. Preston didn't feel the need to keep Amsel under close observation at the retreat after that period but requested she be allowed to check in on him twice a week. I agreed wholeheartedly, and with Dane's approval Amano didn't have much choice but to acquiesce as well.

I felt a chill factor between my bodyguard and me that was distressing. I knew I'd pushed the limit when I'd wanted him to keep the premature birth from Dane, but I'd been thinking of Dane's safety—all of the coming and going made him a moving target and that worried me.

Dane stayed a couple nights more. The baby didn't seem to miss a beat when it came to eating, doing his little business, and sleeping. All the activity in the house garnered his attention, exhausting him. Everyone loved holding him. When they could pry him from my arms, that was.

I would sit and stare in wonderment at him for endless amounts of time, until someone came along and wanted to take over. Rosa mostly, but Amano was clearly hooked on our bundle of joy, too. Kyle was equally infatuated, which surprised me. I wouldn't have thought he'd be so keen on Dane's son. Typically, anything related to my husband made Kyle grumble. But Amsel was addictive, all cuddly and squeaky clean and only slightly fussy.

Of all the people fascinated with the baby, it was Dane who amazed me the most, as he cataloged every single detail when it came to our son. Dane watched me care for Amsel, but didn't shy away from feedings, changings, bathings. And he talked to Amsel about how incredible his life would be, how fortunate he was to have me as a mom, how much we all loved him.

Dane was smitten. Over the moon, smitten. He obsessed over me, certainly. But his admiration of Amsel was so incredibly endearing, my heart melted every time I happened upon father and son, sharing affectionate moments I knew would help to shape Amsel's life.

A tinge of envy also washed over me. My own dad had never failed to make me feel loved and wanted. Yet he'd never been particularly demonstrative, physically. My mother, of course, had exhibited zero warmth for either of us, so I'd grown up lacking those hugs and cheek kisses most kids found doting when they were young, annoying when they were teens, and reassuring when they were older.

Dane did not possess that reserved emotional sensor that kept him from expressing his feelings. It choked me up. I honestly couldn't have loved either one of them more than I did. And I literally just wanted to eat them both up. It was such a bizarre craving, this need to be with them, to watch them, to absorb them.

Dane tolerated my hovering. He didn't take offense, or fear it might be that I observed in order to make sure he didn't do anything wrong with the baby tasks. He seemed to like the tight family unit we'd become, even if it did include Kyle.

I had to admit that we all were a bit overprotective of the new household addition. Even as Amsel slept in his crib in our bedroom, Dane and I stood alongside the railing, unable to take our eyes from him.

Our son had been asleep a good half hour one evening when I finally admitted, "Okay, we are officially creepy."

Dane chuckled. "Not creepy. Mesmerized."

"And staking him out just to make sure nothing happens to him if we turn our backs for two seconds."

"He's just so—" Dane shook his head, appeared to search for the right word.

I offered, "Yummy?"

"Now you're creepy."

I playfully shoved at him. "You know what I mean," I whispered. "I want to hold him 24-7. Snuggle nonstop."

"I like hearing that. Except . . ." Dane wrapped his arms around me—having made a full recovery from the gunshot wound—and pulled me close to him. "I told you a long time ago that I wouldn't share you."

"You have no choice now."

"And I'm not complaining. At all. But I still get my time with you."

"Do you ever." I encircled his neck with my arms, pressed my body against his. "Take me to bed."

He kissed me. Deeply, passionately, possessively. Then he said, "To sleep. Because you're exhausted and need to rest. And I want to hold you while you do."

He didn't have to say the words *before I have to go.* They always lingered between us. Painfully. Tauntingly. Regretfully.

I swept my fingers through his lush hair. "You're Husband of the Century."

He snickered, though not in jest. "You know my stance on that. I wasn't even with you during the delivery."

I knew better than to mention that Kyle had been. That would only twist the knife. And I needed Dane to understand that all of his angst over not being with me, about us not having a normal relationship or marriage, was wasted energy. Because I loved him. No matter the circumstances.

Keeping the mood light, I told him, "Soon to be Father of the Century."

"Right."

Scooping me up in his strong arms, he carried me to the bed.

"And might I add, you already have Lover of the Century covered."

He placed me gently in the bed and I cuddled under the covers with his hot and hard body next to mine.

"I plan to take that concept to all-new levels," he told me. "When you're ready."

"I'll be taking you up on that pledge very, very soon."

After Dane left, I went back to my work in the office. He hadn't stepped into this room while visiting, so preoccupied had he been with me and the baby. A relief. I didn't have to explain my crazed methodologies to him or feel guilty about having taken over his space and ruining the walls with nails and permanent marker.

I really did feel bad about the latter, but I could fix it all up when the current FBI predicament was said and done.

When . . .

I followed news of the trials and generally tried to keep an even temperament, regardless of all the memories of the explosion they stirred up. Kyle was a little tenser than normal, and I wondered if that was for the same reason as my stress or if he was deliberating over what he'd do once the corrupt society members were behind bars and we were all free to go about our business. I didn't get the impression he'd figured out yet what to do with his future.

I struggled a little with that as well, if things didn't pan out with the Lux. By that, I meant if Dane decided he didn't want to keep the resort. I'd loved it from the time I'd first set foot on the grounds, and now that I was engaged in top-secret revival planning I felt even more a part of the exclusive hotel. Amsel's legacy.

Luckily, the two main contacts I worked with understood my need for secrecy, having partnered for numerous years with Dane on his various projects. They didn't mind that I changed e-mail addresses and phone numbers every week when I touched base with them. I'd gotten pretty good with the covert stuff and did everything I could not to take any chances with security or compromise my progress.

The late-summer monsoon season started and Amsel seemed to enjoy the sound of the heavy rains as we sat on the covered back patio most afternoons. We were admiring a vibrant rainbow over the tops of the trees when my dad made his first visit to see the baby.

"Look at that," Dad said in his casual tone. "You have a kid."

I laughed. "His name is Amsel. No nickname as of yet—other than Kid." To my son, I said, "And he's pretty much just going to be Gramps. Nothing fancy."

"Definitely nothing fancy," Dad agreed as he took my son in his arms. "Aren't you something else?"

I beamed. "Pretty awesome, huh?"

"He's incredible. Look at all that hair."

"I know. It's crazy. He already looks just like Dane. He's going to be a handsome devil, and all the girls will go nuts over him."

"That'll be fun for you," Dad deadpanned.

"Yes, well, they'll have to get past me if they want to date him." My dad laughed heartily. "I'm scared already."

"So am I."

He settled into a chair across from me. Oak Creek rushed along the smooth rocks just beyond the terrace, filling the silence. In addition to Amsel's normal cooing. He seemed to amuse himself wiggling gleefully and making silly little noises. I was dying to know what went on inside that tiny head of his. I was completely enthralled. And, knowing how brilliant Dane was, I wouldn't be surprised if our child was currently working out algorithms in his brain.

While my dad was held spellbound as well, I asked, "Any sign of Maleficent?"

He gave a half snort at my reference to my mother. "She has a literary agent."

"What?" My blood pressure likely just shot into the stratosphere. "You have got to be kidding!"

"She felt it was the courteous thing to let me know."

I fought a gape. "So she's serious about this book?"

Christ. I'd fallen down on the job with this one. I'd been so wrapped up in my web on the wall, nursery decorating, the Lux, and then having a baby that I hadn't reached out to Jackson to get him to divert my mother's bad intentions.

"Dad," I said, feeling like a huge heel. "I'm so sorry. This is all my fault. She literally slipped from my mind with everything else going on. I promised I'd take care of this, and I will."

"And I told you, this isn't your concern. It's mine."

"No. We can work this together."

With a grim expression on his ruggedly handsome face, he said, "Apparently, she has a ghostwriter. No deal has been made yet by her agent, but she's confident it's just a matter of time."

As much as my dad was mesmerized by his grandson, I could see he fumed over my mother's scheme to publicly air all their dirty laundry.

"She said something of the probable chances of it going to auction once they submit to publishing houses, and the seven-figure advance she's now hoping to get."

"She's such a pain in the ass. What did you say?"

"Nothing. I hung up on her."

"Dad!" I let out a small laugh because I could imagine her huffing about that when he'd so pointedly dismissed her. Still. "That's not going to solve the problem."

"Ari," he said, keeping his voice level so as not to disturb Amsel as he slowly drifted to sleep in the crook of my dad's arm. "What more am I going to do?"

"Sue her?"

He shook his head. "Whatever she has to say about me isn't going to be slanderous. I didn't win a Masters. No lie there. It's already public knowledge. If anything, she should be worried about the names she's including and how their wives—or ex-wives—are going to respond. Frankly, I'm shocked anyone would touch this project. Then again, maybe some of those big names she's slinging around are getting something out of it. More notoriety. A lot of these guys are retired—this could spark renewed interest in them, give them a fresh shot of adrenaline."

"Granted, it's not a new concept to spill bedroom secrets for cash. But, geez, she could really turn a lot of lives upside down." I frowned. "Ours included. The media would pick this up and start contacting you, Dad. Hounding you at the club. Following you around the course." I let out a sharp sigh. "What a fucking nightmare."

"Sweets," he lightly scolded, "don't swear in front of the baby."

I nodded. "Right. I'm going to have to curb the profanity. Wait'll I tell Kyle. He'll go through the roof without his own daily dose of colorful words from me."

"He's still here?"

"He and Amano are practically besties, and he's learning karate and all about guns and security systems and blah, blah, blah. He's totally into the ninja warrior thing. Unfortunately."

"This worries you?"

"I don't want him to get hurt. He's my closest friend, and he's done so much for all of us. He's such a great guy. I wish he had the chance to meet someone and—" My brow jerked up. "Whoa."

"What?"

I suddenly recalled a conversation with another friend of mine, the night Dane had flown us all to the Grand Canyon for a special dinner. Tamera Fenmore was a striking blonde who had the most elegant yet saucy British accent and was currently single since, according to her, "Mr. Right's GPS is skewed at present."

Her eyes had bulged at Kyle's solid build, all the muscles nowhere close to being concealed in the suit he'd worn that night. And before that at my and Dane's wedding.

Speaking of weddings, my high school pal Grace, who bartended at the resort where mine and Kyle's friends Meghan and Sean Aldridge had married—the exact place I'd met Dane for the first time—had taken a liking to Kyle as well.

"Maybe I should do a little matchmaking when we're all out of this mess."

My dad gave me a cautious look. "That can be dangerous."

"Danger seems to be my middle name—haven't you noticed?"

"Not exactly something I'm happy about."

"Well, it is what it is. For now. And you did have to go through two FBI agents and Amano to get to me today so it's not like I'm an open target." I sipped my tea and tried to appear nonchalant. I didn't want my father agonizing over me. He had enough on his plate, especially with this latest flare-up from my mother.

I wondered how best to handle that predicament. Dane had written her a check—so she'd gotten the initial hefty chunk of change she'd been looking for when she'd first come to me. He'd also strongly advised her to stay away from us. That warning had been heeded, until Dane had been presumed dead. Then she'd considered me weak enough to prey upon under the circumstances. She'd been correct with her assumption.

But my mother wasn't my only current dilemma. The distance

between me and Amano was palpable. It ate at me, because he'd felt horrific about keeping from me the fact that Dane was actually alive—and I'd used that guilt against him.

I wasn't proud of that. Or happy with the outcome. But approaching him with an apology wasn't as easy as one might think. He was a strong, resolute man who didn't like to show emotions or vulnerabilities. The fact that he was wracked with remorse over how deeply I'd been wounded because he hadn't shared with me that Dane had survived the Lux blast was his weakness. When I was pretty sure he felt he shouldn't have one.

There wasn't just a web growing on my office wall. One was woven throughout this entire house. And the strands continued to grow despairingly tenuous.

After my dad reluctantly relinquished his hold on Amsel, he left us to return to the golf club. I fed the baby and put him down for a nap. As I was heading toward the inner portion of the house where the office was, Amano approached from the opposite direction, his long stride purposeful.

"I have news," he said.

My stomach tightened at the way he glowered. His jaw was set and his eyes were dark and flat.

I followed him into the office and he turned up the sound on CNN.

Cameras were trained on the Vegas hotel being carefully dismantled until it was safe for an implosion.

"What's up?" I asked, shooting for amiable, not tense. I wasn't sure I succeeded.

"Bodies," he caustically replied.

I started. "Excuse me?"

"There are bodies in the concrete."

My clenched stomach now roiled. "Care to elaborate?"

"When it was determined the rebar was substandard or improperly placed or whatever the hell happened to make the structure unstable, concrete was used in the center to fortify the tower.

Which you already know. However, as they've taken apart the hotel, they've begun to closely inspect the crutch in place by chipping away at the concrete pillars. A body wrapped in plastic tumbled out. Followed by two more."

"Holy shit." I gasped. "That's scary as hell."

"It gets worse."

"How?" I demanded. "Because that's plain sick and wrong."

"The bodies are intact and identifiable. Names have been released. Jess Nichols. Mike Donaldson. Xander Horton."

"Horton?" I stared at him, deeply perplexed.

"Wayne's brother. He worked for me. He was the one who told Wayne about the openings at the Lux when we first started hiring."

Kyle had joined us, standing behind me initially, then moving around me to be included in our small conglomeration. He'd quickly caught up with the discussion, if the *oh, crap, here we go again* expression on his face was any indication.

Amano said, "There's another connection."

"Of course there is," I mumbled. Though I wasn't sure I wanted to hear it.

"Nichols and Donaldson were employed by the Lux, too. They were a couple of our original hires. Then they quit—out of the blue. And right around the time Wayne Horton came on-property."

A chill ran through me.

Kyle asked, "What'd they do at the Lux?"

"Nichols worked with the grounds crew. Donaldson was on the security team and Xander was the one to build the resort's Web site."

"All key positions for the mayhem Wayne created," I said. "And that explains how he ended up being the self-proclaimed jack-of-all-trades."

With a nod, Amano continued. "I suspect he disposed of the

three once he gleaned all of the information he needed from them to do his damage. Or they were on to him and he had to eliminate them."

"His own brother?" I knew I shouldn't be so shocked—not when it came to anything involving Wayne Horton. Still, the bile rose in my throat.

"The timing all fits, falls into place perfectly," Amano explained. "If he killed these three, right around the time they left for undisclosed reasons, it was also the same period when the concrete was being poured at the Vegas hotel. He had access to that property as well."

"Why the hell is that monster still on the streets?" I hissed out.

Kyle said, "He hasn't been on the FBI's radar—not at high alert, anyway. Like Strauss said. As far as they've been concerned, he's small potatoes, the marionette. They've been going after the puppet masters."

"He's not some dummy in a ventriloquist sideshow," I insisted. "He knows what he's doing. And I'm willing to bet he really is acting on his own more so than taking direction. Power trip to the extreme."

"He's still slipping through the cracks," Kyle said, "because nothing has firmly been connected to him."

"That ought to change after the FBI gets all the facts," Amano said. "Associating Horton with the Vegas hotel and his brother's death will help to break this piece of the syndicate wide open."

I shook my head. "He's a total weasel. The FBI needs *more* than a brotherly connection. They need a confession. Wayne has to admit to everything he's done since he started at 10,000 Lux. Because if you hired him, Amano, I'm sure he had impeccable credentials. And still does."

"Clean as a whistle."

"What if the Feds view him as above reproach, with the exception of his aliases? Can't really find anything significant—*significant enough*—to pin on him?" I asked. "Won't they just back-burner him as they've been doing?"

"This is serious stuff, Ari." Amano gave me a sharp look. "They're not going to discount all the intertwining variables." He tore his gaze from me and gestured toward my wall of webbing. "You pieced it all together, but only because you've had up-close and personal experience with Horton. You've been caught in his traps."

"Traps the Feds believe were set by Vale." This from Kyle. "So we're not really in danger in their minds when it comes to Horton—he's just a nuisance who may or may not have aided Vale."

"And since Vale's dead," I concluded, bringing it all back around to the inevitable, "Wayne's not of concern at the moment."

"Yeah, but what about his potential involvement with Tom Talbot?" Kyle countered.

I fumed. "We have to *prove* he's a key player in this game."

"He blew up the Lux," Kyle contended. "Come on. We're all sure of it. So it'd be a damn shame to let him get away with something evil of that magnitude."

Amano glared at us both. No doubt, the conversation he'd walked in on at the estate, when Kyle and I had first plotted to get a confession from Wayne, flashed in his mind.

"We could get him to admit that he's brilliant at setting people up," I said, a thought forming in my head. "That *he's* our Heisenberg—not Vale."

Amano scowled at the fact that I'd all but OD'd on *Breaking Bad*. "Perhaps a little less Netflix in the future," he muttered.

I grinned. That he was snarky with me was a good sign. "Sometimes we miss the tree for the forest, right? And let's face it, Wayne Horton is one squirrely bastard. He's operating in the shadows, with the exception of one weakness. We know some of the places he frequents."

I wagged my brows. Amano continued to scowl.

Kyle chimed in. "Bubble burster: Horton hasn't been at the casinos or in Sedona lately. He was in two poker tournaments in Reno that were moderately publicized. I caught the news on-line."

"That's perfect," I said, perking up. "Good job keeping tabs on him. With the bodies being discovered there, he's not going to stick around Nevada. He's too wily for that kind of exposure. And where does he always return?"

"Here," Kyle said.

"And where does he gamble when in town?" Excitement now swept through me, chasing away the chill.

"Cliff Castle," Kyle answered again.

I gazed up at Amano, giving him a hopeful expression. He stared me down.

But I wouldn't be deterred. Not even by his biting expression— the *oh, hell, no* stamped across his hard features.

"You're the one who tracked him down in the first place," I reminded Amano. "Really, it wouldn't be out of the ordinary or suspicious at all if I accidentally ran into him at the casino. He hasn't been seen or heard from since that day at the estate—that was nearly three months ago. Out of sight, out of mind is how we could play it. Plus, it would be easy for us to come off as not considering him a threat, since his *el jefe* is *el muerto*."

The dark eyes narrowed on me. "You are getting way too excited about this."

"Amano, Vale is dead! Wayne is in *our* crosshairs. Why wouldn't we take the shot?"

My bodyguard groaned. "You know what this is? Out of hand." He turned and stalked off.

I shifted my attention to Kyle. "It's not exactly crazy, admit it. We have two FBI agents outside. You don't think that if I pulled

them in here, showed them my wall and the Breaking News on
TV, they wouldn't back us up? Hell, they'd wire me in a heartbeat!"

"*You?*" he demanded. Roared, actually. Then very slowly and
succinctly said, "Abso-fucking-lutely not."

I'd heard a similar sentiment from him before. It didn't give
me pause.

"Kyle. We've had this discussion. You won't get squat out of
Wayne because you're too aggressive, too threatening. I, however,
can use the ploy of being taken aback to see him, intimidated,
slightly terrified. He'll buy that and won't think for a second that
I'm recording my conversation with him."

"Ari," Kyle said with exasperation in his tone. "There's a very
good chance he murdered those three guys—his brother, even!
You think he's going to let little ol' you trip him up?"

"Most everyone has underestimated him, but not me. And he
doesn't know we've actually figured him out. Though we really
ought to act fast, before he thinks we have a chance to put the
alive Horton and the dead Horton together."

Folding his arms over his massive chest, my friend demanded,
"And what about Bax Junior? You're going to willingly put yourself in jeopardy when you now have a son?"

"Kyle!" It was a bit of a low blow, but I reminded him, "We'll
have the FBI with us!"

"There is *no way* Amano is going to let you out of the house if
he believes you're up to something."

"He won't know. You take one of the FBI agents and stake out
the casino again, to see if Wayne has returned and what his pattern
is. Then we'll have Rosa schedule a grocery run at the same time
Wayne's at the casino. Amano always takes her, sometimes with
Amsel. We'll make sure of it on this particular trip."

"Ari. Goddamn it," Kyle said as our gazes locked.

"This is foolproof."

His intense look didn't waver. "I do not like how devious your mind has become."

"Why? Because it's a little too similar to *your* devious mind?"

He stormed out.

I took that as his acquiescence.

chapter 10

Our day of reckoning came all too quickly and my nerves were jangled. I figured that would work in my favor. As long as Wayne wasn't on to me—and my anxiety would definitely prove I wasn't in some cocky frame of mind over confronting him—I could likely get him talking. The FBI would get the information they needed. Justice might actually be served when it came to the Asshole.

The stakeout agents, Johnson and Price, hadn't been difficult to win over. Babysitting the creek house bored them to tears; I could see it in their eyes. Plus, they'd taken an interest in the Vegas developments. They wanted to nail Wayne just as much as the rest of us did.

So one dreary afternoon Kyle and I sat in an SUV atop a hill adjacent to Cliff Castle Casino, also perched on a hill in the Camp Verde area. While he popped Tater Tots, since we were parked at a drive-in space at Sonic, he surveyed the casino with binoculars.

Mid-day on Tuesdays seemed to be the prime time for Wayne

to hit the poker tables. The older folks who didn't plop down enough of their Social Security to waste time on were heading to their early-bird dinners, and the evening crowd of carefree revelers hadn't yet rolled in. The rounders were upping their own antes and getting rousing games going that would lure a few unsuspecting suckers to take advantage of.

All of this was relayed by Kyle, who'd spent some time at the tables himself. Apparently, he'd learned a thing or two in Monte Carlo that had funded half of his summer backpacking excursion through Europe and a first-class upgrade back to the States. I didn't ask who'd been the pretty girl to give him the pointers.

"So," he instructed, "you just stay outside the casino, right by the valet station, in broad daylight, where I—and everyone else—can see you. If Horton asks you to talk inside or in his car, just blow him off. Pretend you're rattled by the unexpected sight of him. Walk away."

"Got it." The FBI had grilled me incessantly already, with every *what if* scenario under the sun.

What will you do if . . . ?

What will you say if . . . ?

What happens if . . . ?

Granted, they had a lot on the line. The wrath of Amano and Dane included, if anything went wrong. Even if it didn't, everyone knew we'd be in hot water as soon as the stoic and stoicer found out about this latest field trip.

Dane and Amano might be impassive when it came to some of my more harebrained thoughts and ideas, but they both seethed beneath the surface at times. And if that simmering erupted—

Panic ran through my veins and I shuddered. Especially when I knew Dane's vulnerability over not being the hero husband (in his mind) that I believed him to be. That was definitely a sensitive subject that needed to be addressed after all was said and done with this Wayne Horton and secret-society bullshit.

"You're nervous," Kyle commented.

"Of course I'm nervous. Dane is going to be monumentally pissed off."

"Yeah, I'm sleeping with one eye open from here on out."

"I'll tell them it was all my doing. That you had to go along with it to keep me out of trouble."

"Right. They'll *so* believe that."

I wrung my hands in my lap. Kyle popped a few more Tots.

"How can you possibly eat at a time like this?" My stomach churned.

"Eating's never the problem. Taking a few intentional blows to the ribs in my next karate session with Amano will be the problem."

"Might want to lay low for a while. Till he cools down."

"You really think he has an off switch?"

"Doubtful."

Yes, Kyle and I were digging a very deep hole for ourselves. But I was convinced this was the most viable plan. No one else was going to corner Wayne and get him to admit to the tsunami-worthy waves of destruction he'd left in his wake. I wasn't a hundred percent certain I could do it, either. Not even 50 percent sure. But I optimistically clung to the 49, having no other strategy.

An FBI investigation could be drawn out for months. Wayne was too crafty and I had a feeling he'd covered his tracks well. Again, that was why the Feds weren't sniffing around him. They'd wanted Vale. Not Wayne.

But if I could give them Wayne—

"Hop to over there," Kyle suddenly said to me. The FBI was listening in, since I was already wired. "Horton just pulled under the porte cochere to valet park. He's wearing a red T-shirt, untucked. Denim jacket. Jeans and aviator glasses. Prick."

"He has every reason to be arrogant. So far, he's gotten away with murder and blowing up a luxury multi-billion-dollar hotel."

"Wouldn't be surprised if he's got offshore accounts galore."

"Doesn't he have to launder the money he's collected from Vale?"

"Beats the fuck out of me," Kyle said. "I don't get that part at all. Like, why couldn't Walt and Sky spend their drug money on *Breaking Bad,* but it worked out fine for her to hand over six hundred and some odd *thousand* dollars to the guy she'd had an affair with in order for him to pay the IRS? The IRS didn't wonder where the hell he came up with that kind of dough?"

"It's a TV show, you two," Price interjected.

I sighed. "Amano's right. We watch way too much Netflix."

Kyle lowered his binoculars and consulted the clock on the dash. "You have an hour and ten minutes until he comes out of the casino." That was precisely how long Wayne would sit at a table, win or lose. It was the only thing he did with any sort of predictability. "Sure you don't want a hamburger?"

"Why not?"

I nibbled while keeping my eye on the clock. As we inched toward showtime, I wrapped up the half-eaten burger and spruced up. Grabbed my *Poker for Dummies*–type CliffsNotes and willed my hands not to shake as I clutched it.

Kyle backed out of our space and headed down the hill, navigated the roundabout, and drove up the road to Cliff Castle. He parked in the east lot. One of our agents was in the west lot and the other had left his car under the valet ramada as he loitered by the entrance, sitting on a bench and reading the paper. Nothing out of the ordinary there. Plenty of people had stepped out for some fresh air and a break from pouring their money into the slots.

I'd be lying if I didn't find the intrigue a bit exhilarating. Maybe it was because I felt I had decent coverage with Kyle and the agents. Maybe it was because this was *my* revenge. If I could help to nail Wayne, I'd get a bit of vindication after all he'd done to us.

That did not quell my fear over how badly I could screw this up—or how furious Dane and Amano would be when they discovered what we'd done, or attempted to do.

But I simply couldn't step away from the flame. Dane had taught me to be tough, to stand my ground, to stay strong. Amano had as well. Kyle, too.

So I took a few calming breaths as I lingered around the corner of the building, waiting for Agent Price's cue from his bench. He'd alert me as to when to head to the entrance.

I waited impatiently. It seemed as though a few too many minutes ticked by.

"Kyle, what time is it?" I whispered into the mic implanted in my bra.

"Take it easy." I heard him through the tiny earpiece my long hair covered. Thankfully, it was a moderate day, temperature-wise. Gloomy, but not windy or rainy. No storm to create disruptive background noise or gusts to blow my hair back, away from my ear.

"Are you sure we didn't miss him coming out?" I wondered.

"Not a chance," Price said. "He must be winning."

I paced along the walkway. Amano had told us Wayne didn't break stride with his gambling routine. I would have guessed he'd slipped out the side entrance, but Kyle would have seen him, since that was the lot where he'd parked.

My exhilaration waned, to be replaced by apprehension. The more appropriate response, I knew. I shouldn't have been excited over this confrontation to begin with. Now I worried whether it would even happen.

I forced myself not to mangle the booklet in my hands. I smiled at passersby, practiced looking normal, not paranoid or guilty as sin because I was up to something.

Be cool, Ari. Breathe. Maybe Dane won't kill you. Amano will understand, right? It's all for the greater good, the—

"Game on," Price suddenly said.

I snapped to attention. Took one more deep breath.

Then I rounded the building and headed toward the entrance, my attention on the manual in my hands that I'd flipped open. I mumbled to myself about the difference between the river and the turn, and various betting techniques.

"Now," Price instructed.

I closed the booklet, tried to look completely overwhelmed from my crash course, and then allowed my gaze to fall on Wayne Horton.

I gasped and jumped back, my eyes widening as I did a double take for emphasis. I prayed I looked shocked—and petrified. The latter wasn't actually too far-fetched.

"Wayne Horton. What the hell are *you* doing here?" I demanded, letting my voice break.

"I could ask you the same question. Slumming, Ari?"

I ground my teeth. "Boredom without a job is more like it." I shook my head, as though annoyed with myself that I was actually starting a conversation with this man. I stepped around him and headed to the door but then pulled up short and whirled around. "You know, you've got some nerve staying in town."

He raised his hands casually in the air. "It's a free country."

"Asshole!" I blurted with sufficient angst. I closed the gap between us, moving in much closer than I'd been schooled.

"Ari, back up," came Price's warning.

I didn't heed it. Instead, I lowered my voice, though dropped my chin so I effectively spoke into the hidden mic, and said, "You should be long, long gone after all that you've done."

"I don't know what you're talking about. It was all Vale. Every little bit." Wayne gave me his criminal smile, the one he'd flashed while distracting me so that I'd climbed into the Venom F5 at the Lux, thinking it was Dane's car when in actuality it'd been Vale behind the wheel. "And what trouble has there been since he became a stain on the front of a train? None."

"Oh, let me refresh your memory," I argued. And took a stab in the dark: "Tom Talbot?"

With a shake of his head, he said, "I have no idea who or what you're talking about."

Okay, this was going to be more difficult than I'd guessed. In my mind, I'd convinced myself that Wayne would want to take credit for his ploys, gloat over how ingenious he'd been. The Heisenberg Effect, I'd contended when I'd explained to Dane that bad guys oftentimes fucked up because of their own ego, their own need for glory. I'd be dumping *Breaking Bad* from my queue the second I returned home.

If I returned home.

"So Tom didn't let you on to the estate grounds to plant two rattlers on my patio?" I demanded. I didn't broach the subject of the watchtower guard pointing a gun at me—and Dane—in the event Tom hadn't discussed with Wayne the way things had gone awry. I didn't know what the follow-up had been on their end, so I played dumb for the moment and tried to engage him with a less hostile topic.

He slid his glasses off and tucked an arm into the neck of his T-shirt. "Let's just say that your boyfriend's security isn't nearly as solid as he once believed." A glint of mischief in his beady brown eyes chilled me.

But I latched on to a golden nugget. He didn't know Dane and I were married?

Sure, we'd covered our tracks well. Apparently well enough that Wayne hadn't learned the truth.

I did some quick mental calculations and determined that unless he'd been watching me closely in very recent months he wouldn't have known I was pregnant, either. I hadn't started showing until later on, and no one else knew, not even Tom. At least, not until the kitchen/shooting incident.

Was it possible Tom hadn't told Wayne a single thing, assuming Wayne was the orchestrator of the latest events? Had Tom rallied to our cause in ultimate loyalty to Dane and Amano? And because Dane had gotten the FBI to find Tom's wife and daughter? Could I consider Tom an ally as I tried to shake down Wayne?

My head spun a little, but I held tight to the possibility that this could all work seriously well in my favor.

This notion gave me a shot of courage—and adrenaline. If Wayne didn't know about me and Dane marrying or that I'd had Amsel, then my son was safe. So I pushed the envelope.

"We discovered the chink in the security armor when you blew up the Lux," I said.

He made a menacing tsking noise. "Such a shame. All that money invested, and the hotel never even opened."

"Nor did the one in Vegas that you worked construction on, which is currently being dismantled."

"Just a hotel." He shrugged a shoulder.

"Sure. Like it was just a Web site you took offline, security wires you cut on Lux property, a bug you planted in my office, a rattler you put in the stairwell, scorpions you dropped from the terrace, onto me." I thought back to that night and rage built within me as it had when I'd revisited the harrowing episode with Kyle. "Have you ever been stung by a scorpion? Fucking hurts, like a Mack truck has just run over that particular body part."

"I'm not that careless." There was cunning in his eyes. Was he on to me?

"Why the attacks on me, specifically?" I demanded in a quiet voice. "Even the fire you set in the media room—I was the only one in there at the time."

"I heard the whole thing was caused by a leak."

"Someone created that leak in the pipes. Then punched a hole in the wall above live outlets when I was inside and the door was stuck shut."

"You really ought to pack up your toys and move along, Ari. You can't play with the big dogs. You've been a vulnerability all this time. A liability. A weakness for Dane."

I did another mental rewind. When had I last seen Wayne?

Did he even know Dane was alive, or was he speculating? Speaking in general terms to see what *he* could glean from *me*?

I tried to recall what Tom had said that morning in the estate kitchen, but the fact was, I'd been so scared, I really wasn't sure what specifics had been discussed, what pertinent information divulged.

So I took a wild guess, banking on Wayne not knowing Dane had survived the blast. "That's not really a problem now, is it?"

"Don't blame me that you ended up with nothing."

"You lousy son of a bitch. You can't really expect to just walk away from a reign of terror. You blew up a goddamn hotel. People died."

"Boo-fucking-hoo." He glared at me. "Do you really think I was going to be Vale's bitch after everything I learned at the Lux, after all the shit I pulled off that no one could pin on me? *Still* can't pin on me? I was able to bypass Vale after his massive fuckup. Go directly to his dad and tell him I'd finish the job. And I did. No more 10,000 Lux. No more Dane Bax. *Boom.*"

My jaw fell slack. The air rushed from my lungs. I couldn't breathe.

But then I realized my ace in the hole.

I glared at Wayne, hoping to evoke his anger—I had a feeling I'd need it to get to the heart of the matter. To make the exact words fall from his mouth that would secure this confession.

I said, "So Bryn Hilliard is pulling your strings. I thought you were smarter than that. Because now you're *his* bitch."

There it was.

Fury flashed across Wayne's face. "I am a *master* at what I do. And guess what? When those idiots who wanted back into the Lux—Bryn included—get their balls nailed to the wall because they were too stupid to cover their tracks and the FBI and IRS caught up to them, I'm going to take my millions and drift away. Disappear into thin air. *Poof!*"

He was beyond sinister and insidious. He was evil. Chillingly so.

But also delusional. That was *his* weakness. I wouldn't be dumping *Breaking Bad* so quickly.

"You're missing some marbles, Wayne, that's for sure. First, those 'idiots' will point fingers at the person who actually planted the bomb. They'll want to take you down with them. Second . . . have you watched the news lately?"

He eyed me suspiciously. "I don't have time for the bullshit on TV."

"That's too bad. Because that hotel you worked at in Las Vegas—overseeing some of the construction—was about to implode because it was so shoddily built. Except that suddenly it became a crime scene."

His jaw worked for a moment. I'd thrown him for a loop. He said, "I knew they were bringing down the hotel. What's the crime?"

"You really are a moron of epic proportions. A sneaky moron, but a moron nonetheless. While disassembling the tower that can no longer stand on its own and will topple over and kill thousands of tourists and wipe out some of the Strip workers discovered bodies in the concrete pillars. *Bodies.*" I gave him a knowing look. Time for *my* full-court press. "All three were ID'd. They used to work at the Lux, right at the time you signed on. One of them happens to be your brother, Xander. Or should I say, *used* to be your brother."

His head jerked back and he stumbled away from me, reeling. That was my brass ring!

I inched toward him. "Yeah, good in theory hiding the bodies in thirty stories of cement. Until those thirty stories have to come down."

"Shut up about my brother, Ari." His tone was ominous, foreboding. His jaw tightened. His shoulders bunched. His fists balled at his sides.

But I kept at him. "What happened, Wayne? Was Xander on to you at 10,000 Lux? Did he know how you were sabotaging the resort so it couldn't open? Did he know you were working for the investors who'd been cut because they were corrupt? They turned to Vale Hilliard to come up with a plan to cripple Dane—and Vale hired you to do that dirty work. Xander knew, didn't he? So did Jess Nichols and Mike Donaldson. How? Did they help you, or did they just catch you in the act? Are you really not as brilliant as you think?"

"You fucking cunt!" he erupted. Heads whipped in our direction. Price leapt to his feet but didn't move in.

I felt the clock ticking down. I was about to lose Wayne. He'd storm off. This was my one and only chance, so I went full throttle.

"You killed those three men—your brother included. Why? Because you didn't cover your tracks as well as you'd thought you had?" I demanded, plunging in the knife. "Then you helped Vale kidnap me and you blew up 10,000 Lux—for the money? Or to prove you were better than Vale Hilliard—a billionaire by heritage? While you're a nickel-and-dime loser."

"He was a waste of a goddamn trust fund!" Wayne bellowed.

Around the periphery, I saw men—general bystanders—starting to move in, cautiously, apparently ready to jump to my aid but not sure at what point to intervene. Probably wondering if Wayne and I were just having a lovers' quarrel over losing money at the casino. Wayne looked crazed. Likely what gave my would-be heroes pause.

And, clearly, Price was waiting to see how far this would go. What other information I could pry from Wayne. Not a comforting thought, though at the same time I wanted to see how far I could take this.

"Was it even Vale's idea to plant that bomb at the Lux?" I asked.

"Right. Like he'd think of that? He was a pussy," Wayne hissed. "Plain and simple."

"You could have killed about forty people that night."

"Do you think I care?"

"Of course not. You'd already murdered three. What's forty more?"

"Or forty-one?" he demanded cryptically, under his breath, as he glared at me.

I choked on fear.

"Hey, pal." One of the guys who'd just handed over his ticket for the valet to bring his car around finally decided enough was enough. "Why don't you back off?"

"Why don't you mind your own goddamn business?" Wayne shouted.

Then his hand shot out and he grabbed my upper arm, tight, jerking me to him.

My heart stammered.

"You are just too stupid for words," he told me in a low, menacing voice.

"Ari," I heard Kyle in my ear. "What the hell is happening?"

"Big, bad Wayne Horton thinks he's going to whisk me out of here and properly dispose of me," I taunted. Against my better judgment. Yet I had to tip Kyle off without giving away the fact that he was listening in.

Still, panic seized me. But I only had one chance to finish this.

"You actually killed your own brother." That seemed to be Wayne's most vulnerable spot, so I twisted that knife.

"Yes, you dumb bitch," he seethed in his quiet tone. "I killed my own fucking brother." He leaned in close. "You're next, pretty girl."

A part of me wondered if there was still a card left to play.

What could it be?

Barely breathing, I managed to say, "You think this will close the loop. Complete Vale's botched mission. Then you can vanish with whatever money you've collected, as you mentioned. But that's not going to happen. You won't get very far, what with all of these witnesses."

"I am *exceptional* at disappearing."

He had me on that one. But he didn't know about my insurance policy—Kyle and the FBI.

"I'll admit that you're a slippery little sucker. Yet you made a huge mistake losing your cool just now."

Agent Price brandished his weapon and was raising his arm to take aim at Wayne and likely demand he release me when Kyle suddenly rounded the corner of the building and said conspiratorially in my ear, "Go for the knee, Ari."

I was at the perfect angle, partially aligned alongside Wayne. Without a second thought I raised my foot and slammed it against the outside of my captor's leg. With all the rage he'd incited within me from day one.

"Fuck!" Wayne yelled in agony.

"Sucks to blow out a knee, doesn't it?" I ground out, recalling Kyle's stance on that particular injury.

Wayne called me all manner of colorful names—but also lost his grip on me. He staggered from the solid hit. Only momentarily, though, because Kyle launched himself at Wayne and tackled him. Kyle had Wayne on his stomach with his hands behind his back in no time flat. Quite impressive.

Agent Price now pointed his gun at Wayne's head, whose face was plastered to the sidewalk as he continued to wail over the damage I'd inflicted.

With sufficient angst—and a dose of his own warranted arrogance—Kyle said, "Meet our friends from the FBI, motherfucker. You're under arrest."

I continued to stare at Kyle, rooted where I was, my eyes popping, my heart thundering. Agent Johnson's SUV came barreling toward the porte cochere, horn blaring. He drove up onto the walkway, skidded to a halt, and jumped out. I remained paralyzed by the lightning-quick convergence. And the fear gripping me.

Kyle glanced my way. "This FBI shit is *insane*." His handsome face lit up.

"Oh, no," I said as I slowly shook my head, more fear clawing at me. I still couldn't pull in a decent breath. "Don't get any ideas."

"I kinda like it," Kyle told me with a grin, adrenaline practically glowing in his vibrant blue eyes.

"All right, honorary Agent Jenns," Price said dryly. "You can let us take over from here. Thanks for the backup."

I was finally released from my shocked state.

Backup? Ha!

Kyle had just kicked my ass.

chapter 11

Home life left much to be desired when you were in the dog-house.

Amano didn't speak to either of us. Kyle and I exchanged *oh, shit* looks, and I found myself pacing in the foyer, stealing glances at the front door, waiting for Dane to burst in. I kept Amsel close by. Mostly in my arms, even when he squirmed a little and wanted Rosa. Or his bassinet. Like he could sense my tension and understood I deserved to be in the hot seat. As I'd suspected all along, he was going to turn out to be one intuitive Bax.

I knew that, in addition to the risk I'd taken, Dane would be angry that Kyle had been the one to save me. Ironic, really, because not so long ago it had been Kyle who'd felt bested because Dane had always heroed up whenever it came to me being in tricky situations. Starting from that first night we'd met, when the snake-tat guy had grabbed me. Dane had swooped in without a moment's hesitation. He literally refused to let anyone hurt me.

Which made my little confession scenario with Wayne an even more challenging endeavor to justify.

Kyle went about his daily routine, monitoring the grounds physically and via the iPads. He chatted it up with Agent Price from time to time, which did not go over well with Amano. Or me. Something we silently had in common.

I worried the FBI was recruiting Kyle. I'd been concerned not too long ago that he might consider the Secret Service, given how into all of this intrigue and danger he'd become. I didn't like the idea of him being in the line of fire with either agency. But I had to admit, he demonstrated skill and steely resolve in a way I admired.

Still, I didn't want him continuing the dicey lifestyle we'd all fallen into. We'd had way too many close calls. Even our planned run-in with Wayne Horton had turned precarious.

If Dane found out—

Ugh. What was I talking about?

When Dane found out.

Rosa was under fire, too. She'd unwittedly played along when I'd stashed diapers and other baby paraphernalia. She'd told Amano they needed a grocery run. They'd taken Amsel with them. That was when Kyle and I had slipped out.

Now we all lived under the dark, ominous cloud.

Several days passed. While the rain pelted the windows and beat down on the roof, I settled Amsel in the crib I'd set up in my office, next to my desk. As my son amused himself—he currently found his bootie-covered feet fascinating—I did the only thing I could do. Continue my off-site supervision of the Lux lobby re-build. I had plenty of photos and updates to wade through. I also kept up with my secret-society puzzle.

I recalled Amano telling Kyle that he'd been shot in the shoulder at a social-economic summit in Mexico one year. The revolutionaries had been particularly riled and, unfortunately, armed. Dane's father had been at the conference, and Amano had been his bodyguard. He'd taken the bullet for the senior Bax.

I was curious about all of the socio-poli-econ affiliations of Dane's family. Even more obsessed over the lack of details on the Internet regarding Bax history. I already knew that Googling Dane and his dad would prove futile, so I tried a different tactic, because my curiosity about the family—and their extreme secrecy—never abated.

I researched international economic summits. Captured all the documentation and let the laser printer spit out page after page.

I had no idea what the purpose to that was. But then again, my entire life with Dane had been about finding the needle in the haystack. Like him at times, I never really knew what I searched for—it just always hit me when I found it.

So while one hand made funny little gestures at Amsel, distracting him from peeling off his booties, and he let out puffs of air and tiny squeals, I grabbed the sheets of paper, looked at the images, and then tossed them into the recycle bin.

A half hour passed. Kyle joined me.

"Shit, you're more bored than I am." He plunked down into a chair, wearing nothing but sweatpants.

"Just a friendly tip," I told him, "but you'd be better off showering and dressing—like in a parka and ski pants—in the event Dane shows up. He's going to be in a mood, and seeing you half-naked and hanging out with me and Kid . . ." I shook my head. "You think Amano worked you over?" My gaze landed on the bruises on Kyle's midriff. "That's nothing. And remember that Dane could have gone into professional boxing, he was that good."

"I gave Amano the shots he was due. I deserved it. He's pissed and I don't blame him. But he wasn't all I-could-kill-King-Kong-with-my-bare-hands like normal. He tried to get me to change up my thinking a little, like he's forcing me to learn counter-moves. It's kind of badass."

I glared at Kyle. "You're *enjoying* getting the crap kicked out of you?"

He chuckled. "It's called training."

"Well, you still need to be living in fear of Dane finding out about our excursion."

"You have a point there."

I discarded another stack of papers. What had I been thinking, printing out all of this? I didn't know what I searched for and was killing trees for no valid reason.

"He won't let this one slide," I stated the obvious. "Not even given the advantageous fact that I'm still breathing." I shook my head. "We're in deep, buddy. Like up to our chests in quicksand and sinking fast. All it'll take is one call from Amano to Dane and—" I lost my train of thought as I studied a photo with a stage setting, a podium, palm trees in the background . . . and a semifamiliar visage in the foreground.

"What's wrong?" Kyle asked.

I handed over the printout. "Doesn't that look a bit like Ethan? I mean, a million years ago, but still."

"Yeah. Sort of."

Recalling that Dane had once said Ethan was a renowned financial forecaster, I realized it wasn't out of the ordinary for him to be at one or more of these summits. So this wasn't exactly a clue for me to latch on to.

I set the page aside. Sifted through some more.

"Anyway," I continued, picking up my previous stream of consciousness. "Just because our adventure with Wayne Horton yielded excellent results—seriously, that asshole will be doing more time than Manson if all goes well—Dane will likely go postal on us himself."

"So this would be the time for you to use your feminine wiles, marital charms, whatever." Kyle smirked.

I balled a piece of paper and tossed it at him. "Smart-ass. It doesn't work that way."

Well, most of the time it did.

I considered the predicament. Then said, "You're right. I'll have to calm him down before he gets crazy. Especially when he sees you. He'll want to blame you for corrupting me."

"I rocked that last part of the confession scenario with Horton," Kyle reminded me. "Don't I get props for that?"

"From me? Certainly. From the FBI, sure. From Dane and Amano?" I gave Kyle a dubious look. "You can't tell me you aren't feeling the freeze-out from Amano when he's not punishing you under the guise of mentorship."

"Yeah." He scowled. "Not so cool. At the same time, why can't Dane be impressed? Glad that Amano taught me so well? Thrilled I was able to channel all of that tutelage into something worthwhile?"

"Because we went against his wishes. And because it could have been much more dangerous. Wayne could've pulled a gun on me."

"Not in front of all those people. And Price and Johnson were there, anyway." Kyle turned angsty. "Dane'll think I went off half-cocked after I swore I wouldn't, right?"

"We both took a chance," I said, commiserating with him. "Am I proud of us living a little too much in the red zone? No. I'm pretty rocked to the core about the whole thing. I have Dane and Amsel to think of. What am I doing playing Lara Croft when I have so much at stake? Then again." I shook my head and moved away. Amsel had zonked out and the room was quiet. I sank into my chair and said, "Don't I have the right to protect my family, too?"

"I'm not exactly in favor of you putting yourself in jeopardy," Kyle confessed. "But I understand the reasoning behind it. And something had to be done about Horton. Sooner rather than later."

"Deep down, I'm hoping Dane and Amano will realize how impossible it is to just 'sit tight.' To do whatever we're told when someone like Wayne Horton is out there wreaking lethal havoc."

I tapped my fingertips on my leather blotter. "I'm not cavalier about this. But since I started at the Lux I've been a target. At some juncture, you stop being the victim. You stop cowering in a corner or praying you'll never face a hissing rattlesnake or pissed-off scorpions. You accept that being terrorized just feels weak and wrong."

I stood and glanced down at Amsel, so sweet and peaceful. So beautiful. "Nothing can happen to my son," I told Kyle, "just because I was too frail or too scared to protect him. My husband has heavy weights on his shoulders—they're really not his to bear. But he takes on whatever he has to in the name of justice. And, yes, vengeance. I won't lie about that or dismiss it. Yet the bottom line is that when you're wrapped up in the stuff we are—even inadvertently—you have a choice. Hide under a rock and try to pray away the danger. Or take a stand."

"You're going all *Tombstone* on me now." He laughed softly. "I'm not saying that's a bad thing. I hear you, Ari. On the one hand, I want to give you a *hell, yeah!* shout-out. On the other hand, I want to cover your mouth and drag you off where no one can hear your rant. By *no one*, I mean Amano."

I nodded. "I know. And I'm sorry. You do so much to keep me safe. But just thinking of all that Wayne could have gotten away with makes my blood boil. Honestly, when I saw him at the casino, as much as I was scared, all I could think was that he had to pay. If I could help make that happen, it was worth any price."

Amsel sighed contentedly in his sleep. I groaned.

Kyle said, "Not *any* price, Ari. You have to stop thinking you have nothing to lose."

"You're right." I contemplated this further, then asked, "What about you? It's not like you're an orphan. Maverick. Lone dove. You have a lot at stake, too."

"Such as?" He pinned me with a blank stare.

"An entire future. You're twenty-three now." We'd recently celebrated his birthday—and my twenty-seventh. Unfortunately, without Dane, but that was the reality under which we lived. "You can't tell me you don't have thoughts of a family in your head—a pretty wife and gorgeous children? You sure as hell have the genes for them."

He waved me off with a hand.

"What?" I said. "You've already proven to be very good with babies."

"As long as I don't have to change them."

"There is that." Whenever Amsel pitched that sort of fit, Kyle promptly handed him back.

"Anyway," Kyle told me, "I'm thinking of investigating a field career with the FBI. Or the CIA."

My chest pulled tight. "Don't you think it's time for another desk job?"

"And let everything I've learned go to waste? Be serious, Ari. Agent Price has already given me the rundown on the process. It'll be a bitch to go through all the background checks, but—"

We both heard the front door slam shut. From this far back in the house.

"Oh, joy," I deadpanned, jolted. I promptly reached for the baby. Dane wouldn't yell—quite so loud—with Amsel in my arms.

Kyle jumped to his feet. "I'm out." He disappeared down the hallway. A wise decision, since he hadn't taken my advice and put more clothes on.

I stepped into the hallway, meeting Dane halfway. The expression on his chiseled-to-perfection face said it all. I really was in deep.

He stalked toward me, all dark and brooding. Sexy as hell in a black Armani suit and tie, but that was moot at the moment.

"Smart tactic, bringing my son to try to calm me down."

"He misses you."

"He'd be missing *you* if you'd gotten yourself killed."

"But I didn't." I spoke softly so as to not upset Amsel more since I'd just woke him—or set off Dane further.

"It was much too big a risk to take, Ari. And when I get my hands on Kyle—"

"It wasn't his idea, Dane. But we agreed we had to do something. When the bodies were found—"

"The FBI would have been on it."

"When it comes to the society and the network, he was at the bottom of their list, and you know it." Amsel wiggled in my arms and I handed him over. "Hold your son. You don't get to often enough."

"This'll only work for so long, Ari. He'll fall asleep, and then you and I are going to have a very lengthy conversation."

"I'll get a bottle." I walked off, a bit concerned about the tension radiating from Dane and the lecture coming my way. I knew he'd be furious that I'd put myself in danger. Yet, in the end, after we talked, I was fairly certain he'd understand why it had been so important to me.

I joined him in the great room and took Amsel from him briefly while he slipped off his jacket, loosened his tie, and rolled the sleeves of his dress shirt up his powerful forearms.

Then I gave him the baby again, and the bottle.

All of the tall glass doors were open and the rush of creek water wafted in, along with a cool breeze. The rain fell past the eaves, the fat drops splashing on the leaves that rustled gently. There was a hint of humidity in the air but nothing stifling, since the temperatures remained moderate.

Unfortunately, the flashes of lightning and the crackle of thunder seemed to punctuate Dane's broody mood. One more thing I found damn sexy about him. Mostly because his intensity was rooted in passion. And love. For me—and now for our son.

I kept quiet while Dane fed Amsel, and admired how striking they were together. Not just in that they resembled each other so much, but the contrast of the tiny baby cradled in such a strong, steady arm. Dane was a mountain of a man to begin with—holding Amsel made him appear even more mammoth. More formidable, because a protective vibe enveloped him.

What called to me was that he was riled over more than his wife being in jeopardy. I was the mother of this incredible little creature, and I knew Dane would tell me I had to stop thinking in terms of just me or just us as a couple. We were a family and I needed to focus on raising Amsel while Dane did what he had to do.

I bit back a sigh. I'd just recently learned this lesson, had been conflicted by it from the time Kyle and I had hatched our full-blown plan to trap Wayne.

Seeing Dane with Amsel, though, and thinking I could have painted myself out of this precious family scenario made it hit closer to home.

"I'm sorry," I said. "I know that doesn't exonerate me, but I couldn't let the opportunity slip, and I need you to understand that." I explained everything to him the way I had with Kyle in my office.

Dane nodded as I spoke, though the tension remained. He wouldn't be letting me off the hook anytime soon, that was for damn sure. But I had a niggling suspicion he comprehended my logic as I continued to unravel my feelings about staying put when there might be something I could do to help out.

Kyle steered clear of us. Eventually, Rosa took the baby to bathe him and then put him in one of his cribs. Dane paced in front of the fireplace.

Finally, he drew up short, raked a hand through his hair, and gave me a grave look. "You're a strong person, Ari. The things that happened to you at the Lux—because of Horton and Vale—weren't signs of weakness on your part. In fact, you handled it all very well. But this . . ."

"I know I took a big chance. But Dane. I had Kyle with me and two FBI agents."

"All of whom took too great a risk with your life. But that's a different issue entirely."

I sat rigidly on the sofa, anxiety tripping through me.

Dane said, "This relationship, this marriage . . ." He shook his head. "It's not right."

My heart nearly stopped. My stomach revolted, jarring me.

"Dane." I stared up at him, every inch of me about to come apart at the seams.

"I haven't been with you, the way I should be. Not since that night the Lux blew up. And all this time, you've been tucked away. At the retreat, the estate, here."

"Trust me, the accommodations have not been feeble or lacking any amenity." I tried to keep us on an even keel, because I didn't want this conversation to go in the direction in which I feared it was headed.

Dane said, "You're not living a normal life, Ari. Because of me."

"Whoa. Not this again." I jumped to my feet and crossed to where he stood. Splaying my palms over his heavily muscled midsection, I held his intense gaze as I told him, "First of all, you once told me life's too short to settle for normal."

He glared at me for the tactic I'd just employed.

With a small shrug, I said, "Well, it's true. That's exactly what you said. Second, you are a fantastic husband, provider, and father."

"When I'm here."

"Oh, hell, Dane." I let out a long breath. Tried to explain that I understood our predicament for what it was in a reasonable light. And I had a great example when it came to that sense of family abandonment he was feeling.

"Every Service member that's ever been deployed feels something similar, I'm sure. That they've left loved ones behind to fend for themselves," I said. "But these courageous people have a sense of duty to serve their country. They make the sacrifice to do whatever is necessary in order to get the job they're assigned done. I have immense respect for them. And for their families, who keep it all together, as best as they can, back home. You do what you have to do, no matter the situation, whether it's fighting terrorism or working with the FBI."

"It's not just that, Ari."

I was getting a little alarmed that he was forgoing all the terms of endearment he typically used, in lieu of sticking with my name. Even when he was deathly serious about something, he'd still call me baby or sweetheart.

Not so now.

"So what else is it?" I dared to ask. Somewhat reticent to do so. I wasn't quite sure how far the pendulum would swing with this sensitive, potentially detrimental, subject.

And that made it difficult to breathe.

He said, "We're not thinking of ourselves as parents with something to lose."

Kyle had pointed that out to me earlier; I'd already reprimanded myself for the slight. But I reminded Dane, "Amsel wasn't even a thought in our heads when all of this started."

"Well, he needs to be *the* thought in our heads now."

Dane backed away and stalked over to the wet bar to pour himself a glass of scotch. He turned back and handed over a crystal tumbler for me as well, with water in it, since I was breastfeeding.

Then he said, "When I was a child, I didn't fully grasp the concept of having a bodyguard. I knew Amano stuck close by. He was family, though, so it wasn't anything out of the ordinary. He offered a paternal presence—taught me how to ride a bike, throw a punch, all those things. When I was entering my teens, that's when I started to rebel a bit."

My brow crooked. "You?" He'd always been so stalwart and

grounded. I hadn't considered that his unique circumstances of being an orphaned billionaire at just one month old might have had more adverse effects on him than not ever knowing his parents. And the imminent threat of someone wanting to get their hands on his inheritance.

He said, "I wanted to be able to do things on my own, not constantly be shadowed. At that point, obviously, I understood why it was so important for Amano to keep an eye on me, but that didn't make it any easier to digest, when most of my friends had more freedom."

Dane's gaze locked with mine.

With a slow nod, I said, "You think I'm rebelling against all this protection?"

"I wouldn't be surprised and I sure as hell wouldn't blame you."

I sipped, then told him, "I'll admit it's been an adjustment."

"The thing is, Ari, I understand. Back then I got restless . . . and reckless." His emerald eyes clouded with guilt.

My head cocked to the side. "And someone got hurt?"

"Mikaela."

"Oh." I really didn't know what else to say. Wasn't so certain I wanted to hear the details. He gave them anyway.

"When I was fifteen, I wanted my driver's permit. Like every other fifteen-year-old in the country. But Amano and Aunt Lara were against it, insisting I already had a driver. Amano."

"I suppose you wanted a car of your own, too. Not the family limo."

"Yes. Had it all picked out, in fact. I could afford it, obviously, so there wasn't a reason in my mind why I couldn't get my license."

Now my gut twisted. He was delivering a very important message.

"So what happened?" I tentatively asked.

"Mikaela and I slipped out one night at her estate. Took her father's new Jag for a joyride. And I put it in a ditch."

"Wow." That must have wrecked more than the car. His trust with Amano. His pride. And . . . "What happened to Mikaela?"

"Broken nose from the passenger side air bag. There was blood everywhere."

"Freaked the hell out of her, didn't it?" The Heidi Klum look-alike was all about appearances.

"Yes. She was very upset."

I was sure that was putting it mildly.

"You were, too." An easy conclusion.

"It's not exactly the kind of lesson I'd hoped to learn."

I could grasp his frustration and his remorse. And heard precisely what he was saying to me. He knew how I felt. Because he knew me.

Still, I said, "I've always been able to come and go as I please, rarely ever telling anyone where I was off to or where I'd been when I returned. My dad was mostly on the course, and my mother was never interested in anything other than herself."

"You're extremely independent and resourceful. I admire those traits. I wouldn't want to stifle them. That's not what I'm getting at here. The fact is . . ." He paused to take a long drink. Perhaps to further contemplate his stance. Then he continued. "You and I are similar in a lot of ways. I wouldn't have been able to sit on my hands, either, if I thought there was something I could do to better a situation. You knew Horton's patterns and you knew the right buttons to push—and you had *every* right to go after him, given all that he's done to you. I'm not discounting any of that. I want the bastard to pay as much as you do. *More*, Ari," he said with conviction. "So much more."

My eyes watered. My throat tightened.

I tried to keep my composure, difficult though it was. I knew my husband was deeply wounded by every single attack on me. His pain and regret broke my heart.

Dane swallowed down another gulp of scotch, then told me,

"At the end of the day, however, we have a bigger picture than ourselves that we need to learn how to see more clearly."

Tears tumbled down my cheeks at that crucial reminder. "I get it," I said on a shaky breath. I heard him loud and clear. And felt the same way when it came to factoring in our son with all of this mayhem. Yet I recognized another critical variable. "There's also the matter of us."

"We're not your typical couple."

"Not by any stretch of the imagination."

He swept away fat drops on my skin with his thumb. "We're going to have to strike a balance. So you're not trying to prove your value and I'm not telling you what I do and don't want you to do. I love you. I want you to have everything you desire—whatever kind of life you want."

It was a lot to process. I'd actually seen the power struggle coming on. It was more than just about going after Wayne when Dane had told me not to. There was a lot to sift through when it came to all of this—us being separated so that I had to make decisions on my own, and Dane making his own decisions independently of me. The predicament we'd instantly been thrust into since getting together.

Everything between the two of us had happened so quickly. Meeting, falling in love, encountering danger at the Lux, getting married, losing each other, having a baby when we hadn't even fully discussed starting a family . . .

Now I was living in this beautiful house with my bodyguard, my best friend, our house manager, and a child. Occasionally my ghost of a husband.

Quite the whirlwind existence to experience over the course of just one year.

Swallowing down a bit more of my water, I tentatively suggested, "Maybe we ought to try a few sessions with Tamera. She's a couples counselor, in addition to being an officiant."

He nodded. I stared curiously at him, a little surprised he agreed. And so promptly.

"Seriously? You'd consider that?"

His thumb continued to stroke my cheek. "I'll do whatever I have to in order to make you happy. To keep you here with me."

"I'm not going anywhere," I vehemently insisted.

"I hope you'll always feel that way."

My heart wrenched that he'd ever doubt my conviction.

But then I recalled a time when I had left him.

So I tried to reassure him, simply saying, "Count on it."

We gazed at each other a few moments more. I knew this wasn't wholly resolved. There was more he needed to say.

I waited patiently.

Dane's hand fell away from my face. His jaw clenched briefly again.

"You need to make amends with Amano," he told me.

My heart constricted further. "I know. I went behind his back. He's furious, and I don't blame him."

"That's not all, Ari."

I easily conceded, "I put him in a difficult spot, asking him not to call you when we went to Macy's retreat, after my water broke. I didn't actually think I was about to have the baby, but it wasn't a fair situation for him. He'll do anything for me. He's already proven that. But he's loyal to you, first and foremost."

"No, that's not the point I'm making. He isn't loyal to me above you—or Amsel," Dane insisted. "He's committed to *all* of us. That's the way he is. He knows what's most important to me and that's what he protects. No matter what."

"So . . . ?" I raised a hand in surrender, this time not quite sure what he was getting at.

"Beyond turning the tables on him to try to get him to keep a secret from me, you snuck out with Kyle when Amano was with Rosa and Amsel. You have to understand how crazed that makes him—to discover you were out of his reach, out of his protection, without him even knowing about it. Ari, that's not the way the concept of a bodyguard works. And it's not how Amano operates."

"I was with Kyle and the FBI," I reminded Dane in my defense. "I didn't intentionally put myself in harm's way."

My hand dropped to my side. That was a lie, wasn't it?

Kyle and I had formulated our own strategy. We'd sent Amano off with Rosa and the baby so that he wouldn't stop us.

Therefore, our actions had been premeditated.

Damn. I had some owning up to do. This really had become a complicated family scenario.

"Look," I said. "I'll admit it wasn't the perfect solution. Kyle and I aren't as seasoned as the rest of you, and our plans aren't always the savviest. But I will find some way to make it up to Amano. I didn't mean to upset him."

"It's a failure on his part, Ari," Dane told me. "That's how he sees it. Even if you were with Kyle and the FBI. Amano should have been informed of *exactly* what you were up to and he should have been able to ensure your safety. Whether that meant keeping you here or going with you, he still needed and deserved to know your intentions so that he could do his job."

"I understand."

"Do you?" Dane challenged.

I nodded.

His cut-emerald irises softened. "Amano genuinely cares about you."

"I know that as well."

"Damn it," Dane continued. "As much as it perplexes me, Amano thinks of Kyle as part of this family, too. His new protégé. You know that grinds."

I fought the pull at one corner of my mouth. This was hardly the appropriate time to crack a smile. But I could tell Dane was trying to not be quite so stern, so harsh. Not that he'd let Kyle and me off scot-free. I knew Dane too well. Recognized that I'd better stay on my best behavior.

What I'd do about Amano I wasn't so certain. I hated that I'd compromised his own integrity in his eyes. That he felt he'd somehow failed Dane. All of us.

I'd suspected Amano was angry with me but hadn't considered that he'd also be irritated with himself for not keeping a closer eye on me and Kyle.

Amano shouldn't have to keep a closer eye on us.

We weren't exactly the reckless types. Just this once.

Well, and that other time with the switchbacks. Though that wasn't totally our fault. Another Wayne Horton fucked-to-high-hell escapade. But he was no longer a problem for any of us.

"It won't happen again," I swore to Dane. "And I'll speak with Amano."

"Remember all that's at stake, Ari."

"Yes, of course. I really am sorry. I didn't mean to make either of you worry—or piss you off. It just felt like too good a setup to let slip by. And it was."

Even he couldn't dispute that.

Yet he did remind me in a tense tone, "This family doesn't work without you."

I sucked in a breath. Here came the power struggle again. "It doesn't work without you, either."

We stared at each other for endless moments. Finally, Dane nodded.

"Okay, then," I added. Fury still oozed from him, but I surmised it had more to do with circumstance and that bigger picture he'd mentioned than what Kyle and I had done about Wayne Horton.

I set my glass on the mantel. Did the same with Dane's. Then stretched on tiptoe to kiss him. A cautious gesture, to further gauge his mood. Whether I might be able to sway him from his angst. When I pulled away, he smirked. The sexy, bad-boy one that made my insides sizzle.

"Really?" he challenged as he crooked a brow. "*Now* you play it safe?"

"Just testing the waters. You can be very intimidating when you want to be. Which is like all the time."

A heartbeat later he swept me into his arms and marched off to the bedroom.

Amsel wasn't in his bassinet, so I figured Rosa had him nestled somewhere close to where she worked. Her current vice was sewing clothes for the baby. Given her creativity and skill set, I was on the verge of offering to help her financially launch her own clothing line, if that was what she wanted. I didn't even bother shopping for Amsel, because he had several new outfits every week, thanks to Rosa.

Dane kicked the door shut behind us. He set me on my feet and then swiftly pinned me against the wall, his hard body pressed to mine. Gripping my wrists, he raised them above my head. His eyes blazed with heat, residual rage, and need. The heady combination made my blood sing, my body tremble.

"Understand that I can't live without you." His green irises were piercing, hypnotic.

"I can't live without *you.*"

"We can't take any more chances. If you're burning to help in some way, talk to me."

"The only thing I'm burning for right now is you."

His mouth crashed over mine, claiming me in a possessive kiss.

He held me captive with one large hand around my wrists while he palmed my breast, squeezed roughly, exciting me even more. Then he worked the buttons on my lightweight sweater and hastily brushed the material aside. His warm fingers blazed a trail down my stomach to the button fly of my Levi's. He ripped open the flap and shoved a hand inside my panties.

I was already ridiculously wet for him. From the moment he'd pinned me to the wall. *Oh, hell.* Long before that.

All of the passion and ire radiating from him was a huge turn-on.

Maybe I was too much of a ragged-edge girl after all. I couldn't seem to help it, and knowing how worked up Dane was only made me hotter for him.

His fingers glided over my dewy folds, stroking wickedly. His tongue twisted with mine in a searing kiss. With his brick wall of a chest against my breasts I was virtually immobile, and that heightened my arousal.

I was his. I belonged solely to him. He owned me. Every inch of me, inside and out, to the depths of my soul.

I spread my legs wider and he plunged two fingers into my pussy, the sizzling, erotic invasion ripping through me. I broke the kiss and gasped for air. He stroked faster, with skill and determination. The heel of his hand rubbed my swollen clit.

"Oh, fuck." It'd been so, so long since we'd been this caught up in each other, this intimate.

I knew I was going to come quickly. And I was going to come hard.

His mouth skimmed along my neck. He bit me, suckled the skin, swept his tongue over it.

My fingers curled into my palms, my nails digging as the urge to claw at him seized me. I was restless and squirming slightly against him, as much as I could. His erection pressed to my hip and it made me even wilder, knowing how hard he was for me.

His fingers pumped and I could have screamed from the ecstasy building fervently. But the sound lodged in my throat along with a lusty moan.

"I need to feel you, Ari," he said in a strained voice. "I need to feel you lose it for me."

"So close," I muttered harshly. "Dane, you're making me crazy."

He found that magical spot deep within me and massaged with just the right tempo, just the right pressure. Swiftly, heartily. Until an intense thrumming took hold of me, an incessant, demanding beat.

"Oh, God," I rasped. My body writhed, my pulse raged, my heart hammered. "Yes, oh, God, yes. Right there. Don't stop. Oh, fuck. *Right. There.* Dane!"

I erupted, every inch of me going up in flames, quaking from the powerful release.

"Damn it, Ari. Baby."

Ah. There was the coveted term of endearment. Dane had forgiven me for going against his wishes.

He continued caressing that perfect spot while I soared. He said, "I love it when you come undone for me."

"So fast," I semi-lamented. I didn't mind how rapidly he got me going. It was just a little embarrassing that I lost myself so easily.

"You're fantastic." His lips slid over mine. A whisper of a kiss. "And I'm just getting started."

Elation trilled down my spine.

My gaze narrowed on him. "You're not planning on making love to me, soft and sweet, are you?"

Mischief glimmered in his emerald eyes. "No."

I let out a delirious sigh as the tingles ran rampant. "Feel free to make me pay for disobeying you."

"Oh, I will." He released me but scooped me into his arms again. He strutted across the room and tossed me not so gently onto the bed.

Excitement shot through me.

I went up on my knees and reached for his tie, unraveling it. Then I freed the buttons on his shirt from their small holes and ran my fingers over his hot skin. His sculpted muscles flexed beneath my touch. Leaning forward, I kissed his chest, flicked my tongue over a small nipple. He let out a low, sexy sound.

His fingers tangled in my hair, loose about my shoulders and cascading down my back. My lips trailed over his pecs, then along the valley in between, to his cut abs. The beauty of him never ceased to astound me. To arouse me.

Dane's edgy perfection had drawn me in from the very beginning. Touching him and tasting him hitched my excitement. I inhaled his enticing, stimulating scent, so dark and virile.

As I made my way back up to his collarbone, his neck, his strong jaw, I asked, "How long do we have?"

"However long you want," he told me in his desire-roughened voice.

"That'd be forever."

"Then forever it is."

I stared quizzically at him.

He gave me a shadow of a grin, though it was mostly a scorching look. "I provided depositions. Juries are deliberating. The FBI wants me to stay under their surveillance, but there's no reason to remain in their safe houses when I can be here. We have state-of-the-art security, FBI agents along the perimeter. And with Vale dead and Horton soon to be on his way to prison, I don't see a problem with being here. I'd *rather* be here."

"I'd rather you be here, too." I kissed him, our lips slowly tangling. Then my tongue slipped inside to sweep over his. A groan escaped him.

I got a bit more aggressive, wrapping one arm around his waist, my palm flattening against the rippling muscles of his back. I raised my other hand and threaded my fingers through his hair.

He didn't let me keep the lead for long, of course. He toppled me until I was flat on the mattress, him partially on top of me. His tongue delved deep into my mouth and he turned our kiss into a smoldering, soul-stirring one. I simply gave myself over to it—to him.

When restlessness set in, I shoved his shirt over his broad shoulders and down his arms, tossing the material aside. He divested me of my sweater, reached around to unfasten my bra, then palmed my breast again, caressing firmly. My spine arched as I pressed against him, loving the feel of his skin, his hunky body.

His thumb whisked over my taut nipple, back and forth, tightening the small bud. His kiss went on and on, until I'd all but forgotten my own name, where I was, what our argument had been about earlier. I had a feeling I was in for angry sex, and that was perfectly fine by me.

Dane's head dipped to my breast and he curled his tongue around my nipple. Then the tip flitted against the pebbled peak, making the sensitive flesh tingle.

"Dane," I urged, "I need you inside me."

"Not yet. I have a little lesson to teach you."

A shiver of delight ran through me. He was good at his "lessons."

Still, I taunted him. "You haven't made love to me since Amsel was born. Don't you want me?"

He harrumphed. "That's not even worthy of a response."

"Don't make me beg."

"Oh, but I like it when you beg. And you will."

He scooted off the mattress and removed the rest of my clothes. I lay sprawled diagonally, the thick duvet beneath me.

Dane pulled the long silver satin sash from my robe, draped along the bench at the foot of the bed, and rounded the corner. The headboard was a low ledge with polished wood on top and the rest covered in tufted distressed brown leather that matched some of the oversized chairs scattered about and the sofa in front of the fireplace.

He crouched down and, I presumed, wrapped part of the sash around the leg of the bed frame to secure it. Then he eyed me seductively and said, "Arms above your head."

A tickle along my clit made me press my legs together. He'd tied me up before. On more than one steamy, erotically tormenting occasion. It was always a challenge to keep my cool when I desperately wanted to touch him. But what he did to me took a backseat to the desire to have my hands all over his body.

So I gave him what he wanted—knowing he'd give *me* exactly what I needed. All of him.

He bound my wrists as I wondered what creative tactic he had up his sleeve. Dane was capable of going to great lengths to pleasure me until I reached the breaking point. Was an expert at it, in fact.

I loved his bedroom antics and, given the tension still exuding from him, I had no delusions he intended to teach me a thing or two about defying him when it put me in the line of fire.

Sure enough, he snatched the silk tie I'd heaped on the floor with his shirt and then placed it over my eyes like a blindfold, securing the ends.

I bit back a grin of anticipation. Clamped my teeth down on my lower lip to keep from blurting out how insanely turned on I already was.

This was his game, and I let him play it.

Until I heard the ice cubes plopping into a glass.

"Hey," I protested. "You restrained me and then went for a cocktail?"

"It's well deserved," came his confident tone. "The punishment and the cocktail."

"The only point you're making is that you can resist me." I added a little pout, for good measure.

With a low, sexy chuckle, Dane said, "Trust me, baby. Resisting you is impossible. That doesn't mean, however, that I can't make you burn a bit brighter for me."

I heard him circle the bed, then felt the mattress dip at my hip. His heat enveloped me as he leaned in close and brushed his lips over mine, giving me a taste of glorious him and his expensive scotch.

"You are such a tease," I playfully complained.

"You can't imagine how damn gorgeous you look, naked and tied to my bed."

"I thought it was our bed."

"I'm being territorial at the moment."

"You're territorial *every* moment."

"Do you intend to make me drag out the suspense?"

I sighed. I desperately craved him, wanted him more than I wanted my next breath. "For God's sake, touch me."

He laughed softly again. The rich, sensual sound seeped through my veins, turning my blood molten.

"For the record," he told me, "it's difficult to just observe. Trust me when I say, you're pushing all of my buttons."

"Yet another reason for you to get on with this."

"Hmm. So eager. But I am enjoying the show. The way you're twisting and twining that luscious body of yours." His tone dropped a notch. "And those tempting breasts . . ."

I literally felt his heated gaze on me and the moisture pooled between my legs. "Dane, you're not playing fair." I couldn't see him, after all. Couldn't watch him watch me. Couldn't touch him. "You're making me crazy," I repeated.

"Then I'm better at teaching you a lesson than I thought."

"I get it. You went nuts over something happening to me. Now *I'm* going nuts over *nothing* happening to me!"

"Nothing?"

I could envision his quirked brow. With a moan, I said, "Okay, plenty of things are happening to me right now. Most notably, my insides are blazing and my pussy is throbbing with a very demanding need for you."

"Know that I want you just as much. In the meantime . . ." He seemed to settle more comfortably alongside me, without really touching me. Though I sensed his presence, smelled him. Wanted him more and more with every second that ticked by.

"Dane."

"Shh." His warm breath blew over my skin.

Every tantalizing moment that passed had me antsier, held me more spellbound. He was a master at making me forget everything else but him. I was fortunate in that I had a houseful of self-sufficient people who all vied for baby time. I didn't have to worry about Amsel, knowing he was in excellent hands. I could drown in the bliss Dane created in our private slice of heaven.

He said, "I've waited an extremely long time to just enjoy you again, without looking over my shoulder. Without worrying who was betraying me or how it might impact us."

"Agreed," I said, slightly breathless. "That would make me think you were more inclined to have your way with me."

"Oh, I intend to have my way with you," he assured me in a dark, rousing tone. I only wished I could see his eyes, because I loved the intensity that glowed in them.

While I wrested against restraints and the overwhelming need for him, I felt him shift once more. Heard him sip from his glass. The cubes jingled.

Then . . . nothing but silence.

I caught my lip again. Held on to my breath. Was bathed in suspense long enough that every fiber of my being cried out for him.

Finally—*finally*—Dane's mouth whisked over my temple. He whispered, "This is all that matters to me right now. You and me. The way we used to be before all the danger. The way we will be after the verdicts come in and we're all in the clear and I don't have to fear for your life, or our son's."

"Or yours," I added.

"Never worry about that, baby."

I didn't anymore. This was all different. He'd accomplished what he'd set out to do. Now all I wanted was for us both to reap the reward.

"So fuck me already," I insisted.

With another sexy laugh, he said, "I'm getting there."

A heartbeat later I felt the cold, wet edge of an ice cube whisk over my nipple.

"*Oh*," I said on a long sigh. "You're going to play dirty."

"It's an ice cube. I think that means I'm keeping it clean."

"You never keep it clean."

"You're right." He grazed the cube over my other nipple, drawing small circles around it, as the droplets spilled over the mound and warmed against my flushed skin. Then his lips and tongue soaked up the moisture. My insides rioted in that crazy-wicked way that made me hot and bothered . . . and so close to pleading with him.

But I held on to the desire welling within me.

The tip of the cube traced the undersides of my breasts, then lightly traveled the groove between my rib cage, down to my belly. My flesh quivered.

I gasped. "Dane."

"You like this."

"What's not to like? I'm on fire and liquefying ice."

He sucked up the pool in the indentation of my stomach. "Let's see what happens when I go lower." The melting cube skimmed my nearly bare mound, then skated over my slick folds.

Exhilaration rippled through me. "Oh, God."

Two of his fingers slipped inside me, along with the ice. The fiery sensation collided with the crisp one and I cried out.

My back arched and he caught my nipple in his mouth, sucking deep. A moan fell from my parted lips.

Dane murmured, "You're getting slippery. I could slide right in and—"

"Yes. God, yes. Please."

He groaned. "But not yet."

"Dane," I begged. So soon. I couldn't help it.

My hips rose to meet his strokes. Hot and cold proved to be a dynamic combination, and I felt the tension build as I sought more of what he offered. I thrashed about, loving the anticipation and need that mounted because I was restrained, loving that he kept pumping into me.

"You're pushing me right to the edge, baby," he said in his intimate tone.

"That can't be. Otherwise, you'd get rid of the rest of your clothes and be inside me when I come."

"You're that close?"

"Closer."

His fingers withdrew from me. I heard the rustling of pants and shoes. Then his arms hooked under my knees and he spread me wide. The anticipation I'd felt previously escalated to all-new heights as he held me open and I anxiously awaited the crown of his cock pressing into me, his thick shaft filling me.

"Dane," I nearly wailed. "Oh, God. Please! Now!"

He thrust deep with no warning and I cried out. Electric currents snapped and hissed in the most delicious, sexually charged way.

His hands clasped my waist and he lifted my hips, angling me so that he could drive deep, fast.

My fingers gripped the satin sash and I held on tight.

"Yes," I urged. "That's so perfect, Dane. Just like that." He pumped into me and nothing registered but the incredible sensations he evoked, the pinnacle he took me to.

"Christ, Ari." He bucked wildly, fucking me hard.

I clutched him firmly, deep inside. I needed him like never before. Couldn't get enough of him.

My heavy pants of air filled the quiet room, mingling with his. Echoing in time with each other.

He slid against my wet walls, gliding smoothly save for the prickle of friction created by his width in such a narrow space. It was an enticing sensation. One I reveled in, luxuriated in, as the intensity increased, the desire flamed, the pressure crested.

"I can't hold on," I told him, complaining and exhilarating at the same time. If I could only keep this sensation brimming, I'd be so thrilled. Yet it was too overwhelming to not give in to it. A twisted fate.

Dane said, "Squeeze me tight," at the exact moment I let go and called out his name.

My inner muscles contracted around him, pumping the same cadence.

He growled, his heat igniting an inferno so that I felt another orgasm piggyback the one I still savored.

I lost myself on one long, *"Ohhhh!"*

Dane thrust once more. Then his cock surged inside me as his body convulsed. "Yes, just like that," he ground out as his hot seed filled me, sending more wicked zings through my veins.

"Oh, God," I whimpered as every inch of me continued to blaze.

I'd been right all along. Angry sex rocked.

chapter 12

"Are you really home for good?" I asked Dane when the passion-induced haze in my brain subsided. At least partially.

"Yes," he said before kissing my forehead. "I can't stay away another day, Ari. Not another minute. And I don't need to."

We lay sprawled across the California king we shared while I still tried to grasp the fact that this was over. The threats against us, the witness protection he'd sort of succumbed to—though on his own terms—the trials, everything.

Really, the only thing I could fully latch on to was the fact that we could finally be a family. Not a typical one. I wasn't delusional or anything. Especially not after the *come to Jesus* meeting we'd had earlier in the great room. But we could finally live together under the same roof.

I could fall asleep in his arms every night. Wake in them every morning.

Emotion swept through me. It seemed as though I'd waited forever for this moment. Truly, my life had begun when I'd met this man. And despite the fact that I'd found more inner strength and certainly gained a greater worldview because of the danger we'd faced, it now hit me incredibly hard that being safe in his embrace, with our son, was all I wanted.

Not the bottom dropping out of my stomach and the heart palpitations Dane had given me when he'd started down the path of our relationship and marriage not being right.

I had to make it right.

We had to make it right.

The downside was that neither of us had ever been in love before, had ever done the romance thing, had never been seriously involved with anyone. Until that day our eyes had locked.

I wasn't one-hundred percent sure how to smooth the waters. But I began with the basics.

"I love you," I said as I snuggled close to him, my eyes misting.

"I love you, too." He held me tight. "I'm sorry about all of this, baby." Apparently, that conversation still festered in his mind, too.

"Dane, we've had plenty of perfect moments. We've just had to deal with a lot of other stuff along the way that isn't even your doing, but that of the society."

"I don't want to talk about the society," he said, his tone terse. "Honestly, Ari, if I never have to think again about all that went wrong—"

"Don't think about it, then." I shifted out of his arms and climbed on top of him, straddling his waist. "No more secret society, no more danger. Put it all out of your mind and make love to me again."

He did. Yet I could tell he stewed over all that had happened and remained just tense enough that I didn't let my guard down.

I wasn't a fan of having Amsel out of my sight for more than a short span of time when he was off with Rosa, but for the first few days Dane was home with us I didn't mind so much that she liked tending to Amsel and using him as a human mannequin for her latest creations. Kyle also apparently found it safer and wiser to whisk my son off when Dane and I wanted time together—that meant Kyle wasn't visible and Dane was too preoccupied to consider Kyle was the one looking after Amsel.

That didn't last long, though. After a few days of really hot sex—our own version of the honeymoon we'd never had—Dane was less inclined to let Kyle have his fair share of Amsel time. And clearly felt the need to stake his claim. Focus on familial obligations.

He came into our bedroom one morning and said, "We ought to consider a baptismal ceremony."

"Oh?" This took me by surprise. I'd been baptized but had no idea if Dane had. In fact, I didn't even know what religion he was. So I asked, "How'd Lara raise you?"

"Methodist."

I smiled. "Crazy. My dad did the same."

"Warrants a baptism."

With a nod, I said, "Sure. We can do it here. I wonder if Tamera can officiate that sort of thing." I didn't know enough about it to say for sure, but she'd been the one to marry us, so she was the best candidate. As for our guests, I asked, "The usual suspects?"

He chuckled, and it was music to my ears. Though he maintained that natural edginess to him, a few moments of levity here and there made me feel as if we were finally coming to terms with everything we'd been through and seeing at least a small light at the end of the tunnel.

Dane said, "Ethan, Jackson, Eleanor, Amano, your dad, Kyle, Tamera, Rosa. Yes. The usual suspects."

Amsel started to squirm, and Dane read the sign that he needed to be changed. As Dane fixed up the baby, I asked, "What about Mikaela?"

Dane finished and delivered Kid to me before he cleaned up in the bathroom. I remained deep in thought when he returned to the sitting area of our master suite and went into full-on pacing mode. I didn't interrupt. He had plenty to deliberate over.

Eventually, he came to an abrupt halt and admitted, "I feel like the biggest asshole on the planet for keeping her in the dark about what happened at the Lux—that I survived."

"Dane." I gave him an empathetic look. Much milder than what went on inside my body. My heart hurt for the pain he still endured over everything related to the society. "Please don't put this all on your shoulders."

"I've wanted to tell her, Ari. Of course, I wouldn't want someone upset over my presumed death. When I think of you believing I was dead—"

"Dane," I repeated, my chest constricting. I couldn't even bring myself to revisit that horrific time of our lives. "You never intentionally deceived anyone. You've had to keep so many secrets. To save us all. Nothing is your fault. Mikaela will understand that. All I'm saying is that if someone—like my dad—cared so deeply for me that my absence would cause them great pain and I could ease it a little by letting them know I was okay I'd want to take that step. I'm sure you want to do that as well. There are risks, yes. But at the end of the day—"

I gazed at Amsel, nestled in my arms, completely, contently zonked out. Trusting me to keep him safe.

Tears suddenly burned my eyes, the emotional impact of the past year intensifying now that Dane had returned to us. And the fact that we now had to confront how everything that had happened had changed our relationship.

I said, "You don't have to shout, 'I'm alive!' from the rooftops. The media will spill soon, anyway. Mikaela should know. She's been in your life since you were both children. This isn't something you should keep from her any longer. Or let her find out from someone else." I gave this further thought and added, "She doesn't even know we're married. I never told her. Nor does she know we have a child together."

"I'm not happy about all of the secrecy, but I'm still trying to play this hand to the best of our advantage. Mikaela is one more innocent bystander." He took a few additional seconds to consider the situation, then said, "All right. We'll include her. We'll just have to find some sensible way to break the news to her that I didn't incinerate with the lobby of the Lux."

Later, I caught up with Kyle in the kitchen, making dinner, while Dane and our son were busy working on a new dangling mobile. That entailed Dane crafting and Amsel cooing. I didn't bother explaining to my husband that the baby cooed over everything. Dane would figure it out on his own soon enough. And that would turn into an amusing tale I looked forward to hearing.

"What can I do to help?" I asked Kyle as he set out veggies.

"The salad should be mixed greens and romaine, asparagus tips, avocado, broccoli, cherub tomatoes, onion, and mushrooms. There's green goddess dressing already whipped up and in the fridge."

"I think I can handle this."

Meanwhile, he prepped a pork tenderloin that looked to die for before he'd even popped it into the oven. As it cooked, he sliced apples and baked them. The aroma in the kitchen had me salivating. Unfortunately, my good mood came to a grinding standstill when Dane appeared in the kitchen.

Not that he was gritchy. In fact, he looked taken aback—and I didn't get the sense it had anything to do with Kyle and me cooking together. Especially as Dane handed over the baby to Kyle, who sat at the island, sipping a beer as the food baked.

"Something wrong?" I asked. I read Dane that well, which became the source of my instant consternation.

Dane looked as though he couldn't quite compose himself. That was odd unto itself.

Had he reconsidered the baptism? Or letting Mikaela in on our secrets—*all* of them?

"Dane?"

"Let's take a walk, shall we?"

I exchanged a look with Kyle, cuddling the baby, as my nerves suddenly jumped. More Wayne drama? *What?*

I pulled in a long breath. On a slow exhale to prepare myself for *anything*, a deeply disturbing thought flitted through my mind.

Had Dane learned of my mother's latest extortion effort? The New York agent, the ghostwriter, the book?

Because Dane liked my dad so much, he would be as furious as I was that she'd go to this extreme.

Worse, Dane would wig because he'd done a damn good job of taking care of the problem initially. Until my mother thought he was dead—that was when she'd come back at Dad and me hard, because she didn't have Dane to worry about.

He was foreboding; Dad and I were not.

"Fuck," I mumbled under my breath. I shot a look toward Kyle and mouthed, *My mother.*

He went a little pale. Not at the thought that she was some monstrous creature to fear—though I was actually beginning to think that might be the case—but because he obviously had pieced together the fact that enough was enough as far as Dane was concerned. And this discussion wasn't going to be a pretty one.

I didn't disagree with that sentiment. But I wasn't quite sure what Dane's breaking point with my own parent might entail.

Even beyond that was the concern that *my* breaking point might be even more tenuous. He could at least tolerate her. Yes, I knew he'd love to bestow upon her that ultimate *if you ever make my wife cry again* . . . threat, but he curbed his aggression for my sake.

However, as it related to my feelings on the subject, after that visit from my dad—when he had yet again been put in that humiliating place where he had no idea who was going to find out how many men his wife had slept with while married to him and he was about to be thrust into the turmoil it had taken decades to escape—I wasn't sure I could approach this ongoing issue with a cool head.

A huge part of me wanted to tell Dane to deal with it in the most absolute terms.

Conversely, I didn't want to know what those terms might be.

Not that he'd physically harm my mother. That was a given. But he definitely had menacing down to a science, and it was possible she'd check into her own witness protection for fear of him.

Hmm. Unlike the first ominous thought that had jumped out at me, this facetious one held great appeal.

Which was why I loathed being in this position. I shouldn't have such thoughts when it came to my own mother.

"Are you coming with me or not?" Dane asked in a curious tone as I hedged while debating over this latest predicament.

"Sure." I glanced at Kyle. "Assuming you don't need me for dinner?"

He smirked.

"That's what I thought." I followed Dane through the oversized doorway.

We traveled down the hallway, took a few twists and turns, my stomach plummeting as we navigated the large house. I knew where we headed before we even entered the cavernous office.

Okay . . . not about my mother at all.

"So what happened here?" he asked. It was the first time he'd gotten a good look at the room since returning.

Trying to cover jangled nerves, I crossed my arms over my chest and said, "You did tell me to make myself at home when I first moved in."

He gave me a sardonic look. "Sure, that's absolutely what I want. But what's with all the holes in the walls?"

"Right. Those. Lots of holes." I spied the entire left side of the office that was dotted with pockmarks. Then my gaze landed on the huge sweeping words I'd scrawled in black marker to the far right. "I was doing some visualization that required a few pinups. Also, I'm not really crazy about this color on the walls. You wouldn't mind if I changed it?"

"You know I don't care about any of that," he said. "I was just wondering what happened." He still eyed the left side, not even addressing my collage/web to the right.

I stared at the blank space where I'd tacked all of the photos for the nursery and for the Lux. I'd taken both sets down. Since he didn't know anything about what I hoped to accomplish with the hotel, I didn't bother mentioning those depictions. I wanted to surprise him when the time was right.

Things were going smoothly on-site, and I was already at the stage of contacting key personnel previously employed at the Lux who could help me with the whole start-up process of hiring staff and getting word out about us taking memberships.

Since there was a database full of international VIPs who'd clamored to purchase the exclusive rights to stay and play at 10,000 Lux when Dane had initially constructed the resort, we had a lengthy list of former members we'd returned money to, who'd never gotten the chance to enjoy the property. We could reach out to them privately, and I suspected they would be even more zealous about signing up.

The drama surrounding the Lux was one of our hottest marketing angles. Above the exclusivity aspect that had originally drawn in celebrities, dignitaries, tycoons, and the like, people loved owning a piece of history and legend—especially Vegas-style legend.

I wouldn't be surprised if we sold out of memberships at a world-record rate. Despite the exorbitant cost to have the privilege to rent a suite or casita there. Host a wedding or special function. Be invited to attend an over-the-top Lux-sponsored event.

Really, I could hardly wait to jump back into the role of Event Director and bring the place to life with the absolute best of the best parties.

But that was still a ways off. I didn't want to get ahead of myself. So I focused on the topic at hand, saying, "I needed to get a good visual for Amsel's room before I ordered anything. I tore out pages from catalogs and magazines and pieced it all together."

Dane shrugged. "You and your collages."

"Yes! Exactly."

He didn't appear the least bit put out or act as though he were on to me when it came to revitalizing the Lux. Honestly, it shocked the hell out of me that Amano hadn't clued him in. I *knew* Amano knew. He was just that way. But perhaps he understood that I wanted to give the Lux back to my husband as a gift. So *mum* was currently the word.

Dane's attention finally shifted to my web. He'd already experienced everything that I'd puzzled together there, so it was really just a matter of taking it all down, tossing the printouts, and redecorating the office in a way that suited us both, since I intended to keep some of the space he'd graciously offered me.

"We should probably discuss color schemes," I contended. "I was thinking something just a little less severe than pewter and perhaps more cheerful."

He eyed me speculatively. "When did you become all about cheer?"

"I am a mom, now."

"And the nursery is certainly zip-a-dee-doo-dah-day," he said in a dry tone. "*Jungle Book* run amok?"

"It's an African safari theme. Those lions and tigers and bears are supercute."

"Despite being predators."

"There are giraffes and elephants, too," I pointed out. "Gazelles and monkeys. So all good there. I was just going with the—"

"Wait a minute." Dane's full scan of my wall documentary came to a screeching halt.

"What is it?" I asked, moving alongside him, scanning the layout. Nothing looked out of place. All the dots were sufficiently connected.

He stepped away from me to get a closer look at the puzzle. "Why do you have a picture of my father?"

"What?" I gazed at the wall, confused. "Where?"

"Here." He ripped a computer printout from a small nail and handed it over.

I said, "That's Ethan at an economics summit in the early eighties. If I recall the year correctly, it was 1983."

"No," he said, still staring at the sheet he held. "That's my dad."

I looked past the visage I'd constantly homed in on when working on my web and suddenly saw the second man in the photo. *Really* saw him. Dark hair, strong jawline, squared shoulders. I couldn't discern his eye color or get a full read on him, since I only saw his profile. But the more I stared, the more I saw the similarity to Dane.

My brows knitted. "That's odd, don't you think? Your dad and Ethan in a photo together?"

Dane examined the picture for endless moments. Then he shook his head. "That can't be Ethan."

"Dane, that man looks *exactly* like Ethan. Thirty years ago, but still. That's Ethan."

"Has Amano seen this?"

"He hasn't stopped by in a while. When he used to, he'd leave shaking his head, likely trying to erase from his mind whatever insanity he thought I was up to."

"This *is* insane."

I let out an exasperated sigh. "Why does everyone keep saying that?"

"Not your montage," Dane corrected. "It makes total sense. But how is my father in a photograph with Ethan?"

Okay, there was *that*.

I took it from him again and studied the piece of paper. "I was looking at social-political-economic summits around the world, with no real concrete reason or goal in mind. I was just thinking about the story Amano had shared with Kyle about him being a bodyguard for your dad and taking a bullet in the shoulder during one of those global econ conferences. Pretty ironic, in a not-so-nice way. You two have matching holes in your shoulders."

"A definite similarity I could do without."

"Agreed," I muttered. "Anyway, I didn't come across anything of value—that I could tell might be of value, that is. I kept this picture because I was surprised to see Ethan in it. And now that we're talking about this, don't you find it odd that Ethan probably knew your father? Did Ethan ever mention that to you?"

"No."

"Well, I'm sure there's a reasonable explanation for that. Perhaps he just never put two and two together."

"Perhaps."

I could tell Dane chewed on this new revelation as we left the office and joined everyone for dinner. I studied him closely while I poured the wine. I got the sense he didn't want there to be one more secret-society nuance to dissect, now that all was finally almost said and done. Evidently, he mulled it over, anyway.

"We're planning a baptism for Kid," I announced, in hopes some good news would break the tension created by Dane's internal ruminations, Amano's chill factor still directed at me and Kyle, and my feelings of walking a tightrope in my own home. Rosa and Amsel were the only ones currently oblivious to the strained atmosphere, but I surmised that was because it was feeding time and my son was deeply entranced by his bottle.

Kyle said, "I suppose you're going to ask me to wear a suit."

I smiled. Leave it to him to know exactly when to inject a dose of humor. "As a matter of fact, yes. It'll be a formal affair. Same group as the dinner we had at the Grand Canyon. Though with one addition."

This piqued both Kyle's and Amano's interest.

"Mikaela," I said. "Dane agreed she should hear from us that he's alive, before it's broadcast globally. Which really could happen at any time now."

I hadn't put much thought into how that would drastically change our lives—yet again. One more issue to confront. There would be massive media interest and that might also cast the spotlight on the Lux, prematurely revealing its resurrection.

Damn, I really needed to consult with Amano about all of this, but I wasn't exactly getting the warm and fuzzy vibes from him these days. Not that Amano ever exuded the warm fuzzies, but he definitely wasn't looking to chum it up with me of late.

Kyle asked, "Do you think Mikaela can keep all your secrets?"

A legitimate question—I'd mentally posed it myself.

"I trust her," Dane said. "It'll be a leak related to the trials that outs me. I need to be ready when that happens. Tying up loose ends ahead of time will be helpful."

"When's the party?" Rosa chimed in, already knowing we'd make an event out of the baptism. With her help.

I spared a glance toward Dane. "Saturday night?" Just a few days away, but between Rosa and me, we could nail down all the arrangements.

"If that's what you want," Dane said, his prominent features softening.

My stomach fluttered. "That's what I want."

He grinned.

The backs of my eyes prickled, but I blinked away actual tears. This whole new family scenario stirred a lot of emotions, but

I tried to remain collected. I'd had enough of the drama and the freak-outs.

"Seven o'clock," I told everyone. "We'll have a cocktail reception, then the ceremony, then dinner."

I could see Rosa begin to make checklists in her head, the way I did for every festivity. She'd demonstrated on numerous occasions her ability to match my event-planning style and we complemented each other nicely. I was thrilled to have something celebratory to work with her on.

No more gloom and doom.

It would be a fun evening. Lots of champagne. Lots of food. Lots of laughter.

Precisely what this house needed.

chapter 13

On Saturday morning, Amano and Kyle picked up the elaborate arrangements I'd ordered from the florist I'd frequently worked with on weddings. I placed them, along with dozens of candles, throughout the foyer and the great room. The floor-to-ceiling glass doors were opened to let in the fresh, rain-scented air. I added soft background music as Rosa stocked the wet bar and then nestled bottles of champagne in the strategically placed standing chillers throughout the large space.

We set up several hors d'oeuvres stations with fancy finger foods on silver platters and a seafood tower. The tasks occupied my mind and kept my anxiety at bay over seeing Mikaela. I'd called her to invite her to the reception, leaving the actual occasion vague. A get-together I thought she might be interested in attending was all I'd said. She'd been surprised when I'd given the creek house address and gate code, so I'd briefly mentioned Rosa's involvement and that seemed to appease Mikaela's curiosity.

I couldn't drop Amano's name, of course. He was supposed to be dead as well. This was all tricky and delicate—like every other part of my life with Dane. But he'd agreed that including Mikaela in the circle of trust was the right thing to do. If Kyle had been presumed dead I'd want to know if he was really alive.

While Rosa went to work on dinner, I ducked into the enormous dressing room Dane and I shared. He was stepping out of the shower and I admired the view. He caught me gawking in the reflection of the mirror of the double vanity and gave me a cocky grin.

"Nice to see I still enthrall you."

"I'm sorry," I said. "Was there drool pooling in the corner of my mouth?"

"Funny." He wrapped a thick towel low around the hips and tucked in the end.

"Must you cover up?"

"Yes, I must. You keep eyeing me as though I'm the Last Supper and we'll never be ready in time."

Yes, I feasted upon him with my gaze locked on his mouth-watering body. Fat drops rolled along the side of his neck, a few collecting in the indentation between his clavicle, others trickling down his expansive chest. One coated his small, pebbled nipple, and I couldn't help stepping toward him and flicking my tongue over his hot skin, licking up the moisture.

He let out a sexy sound.

I gloated inwardly. Maybe I shouldn't worry so much about Mikaela's model perfection and worldly sophistication.

My fingertips skated over his abs, a whisper of a touch, but his muscles tensed.

"You know that will get you into trouble."

"This is exactly the kind of trouble I like getting into," I countered. I licked another drop from the rivulet along the valley of his hard pectoral ledge.

He fisted strands of my hair and gently tugged my head back as his mouth crashed over mine. Our lips parted on the same breath, our tongues tangling. My heart slammed against my ribs, my pulse ignited.

He backed me up against the wall and shoved my yoga pants and thong down my hips and thighs. I toed off my sneakers and wiggled out of the clothes with a little dance, kicking the garments away. Then I yanked at the end of his towel, unraveling it. He was already hard for me.

His hands shifted to my ass and he cupped the cheeks as he lifted me. I wrapped my legs around his waist, and a heartbeat later he plunged inside me. I tore my mouth from his and cried out from the heat that rushed through my veins.

"That's what I want to hear," he murmured against my neck. "You crazed for me." He nipped at the skin. "And don't worry about digging your nails in."

I gripped one of his bulging biceps. My other hand combed through his damp hair. "I've long since given up that concern. Seems to turn you on."

"Because it tells me how turned on you are."

"So very," I muttered.

He kissed me deeply as he thrust forcefully, quickly. I clung to him, my thighs clenching to hold me in place, my pussy clutching him as he slid along my slick walls, my fingers coiling around as much of his arm as I could manage, the tips pressing in.

His darkly passionate kiss and aggressive strokes stirred my soul, singed me to the core.

I broke the kiss again and said on a sharp breath, "I'm going to come."

The erotic sensations swelled and surged. A powerful release raged through me and I called out his name as I lost myself in those all-consuming moments when ecstasy overruled everything and the fiery bliss devoured me.

"That's it, baby," he murmured in a strained voice. "Just like that."

I had no control over the way my inner muscles milked his thick shaft as he expanded within me. I felt the throbbing sensation of his cock mix with the incessant beat of my orgasm and then he said my name on a lusty sigh and filled me with his essence.

I continued to hold him firmly, nowhere near ready to let my climax languish or give up my claim on Dane.

"Ari," he said against my lips. "You have no idea what you do to me."

"I think I do." I grinned.

Our breaths were labored, our chests rising and falling together as my breasts pressed below his pecs. I wore a tank top but could feel his heat. I reveled in the absolute masculinity of him.

He was a strong, commanding presence and yet I could turn him inside out with a look, a touch, an explosive go-round when we really should be getting ready for a baptism.

I kissed him, then said, "I like this new arrangement."

"I had better find something to occupy my time or you'll be my 24-7 hobby."

"I would *never* complain about being your hobby." I kissed the corner of his tempting mouth, then his jaw. I flicked his earlobe with my tongue, suckled on it. "Or your obsession," I whispered.

He groaned, low and deep. "You're about to get me going again."

"We don't have time for that." I tenderly bit his neck. "It's just that you're so delicious, I can't resist."

"I'll be cutting this party short tonight."

With a soft laugh, I said, "No, you won't. I want everyone to enjoy themselves. These are our closest friends, Dane. We don't get to spend enough time with them as a group. I want that to change." I gave him a pleading look. "We're extremely fortunate to have people in our lives who understand how critical your work has been, how imperative it is to keep your secrets. They've supported us the entire time. They stand by us. We're very, very lucky. And I want them to know we feel that way."

He pressed a kiss to my forehead. "You are the best thing that ever happened to me, Aria Lynne Bax. I am not only forever indebted to you for all that you do, but I am eternally, hopelessly devoted to you."

"I'm the one who struck gold." I kissed him again, then added, "And I'm the one who needs lots of mirror time."

"You're perfect," he contended, love shining in his gorgeous green eyes. "Every second of every day."

"I want *us* to be perfect," I told him. "I'll do whatever it takes."

Our gazes remained locked for endless moments. As usual, it was easy to forget the outside world existed when we were together. Save for one thing.

"We have a son to baptize," I reminded Dane.

"And he'll be sleeping with Rosa tonight, because I'm going to do some very wicked things to his mother when we're alone again."

I could hardly wait.

While anticipation flowed through every inch of me at the promise Dane had made, I managed to focus on getting ready before our guests arrived.

Tamera was the first to step through our doors, looking lovely as always in an ice-blue strapless minidress that did everything to make even *my* eyes pop.

"Geez," I said as I took her coat. "If I weren't thoroughly addicted to my husband, I might consider switching teams."

She laughed in her throaty, sensual way. "Darling, you never fail to make my day. And you're one to talk." Her cultured

British accent gently punctuated her words. "Where *do* you shop, Ari?"

"Since the first time Dane invited me to dinner, my hot spot has been a boutique in Tlaquepaque that collects one-offs, so I never feel as though I'm shopping off-rack." In fact, I wore the emerald mini I'd selected for that dinner a little over a year ago. I'd chosen it because the color almost matched Dane's eyes. He'd been mesmerized that evening, and I tended to pull it out on special occasions in hopes of keeping him captivated.

"I know precisely the boutique," Tamera said. "By René, which is a fabulous restaurant. Let's have lunch there soon."

"And then we'll shop."

"I'm not sure I can afford your taste," she said with a wry smile. "I'm just an ordained officiant and counselor. I haven't married a billionaire."

"Clearly, you don't need to in order to look like you did. Seriously, astounding." And I couldn't wait to take her into the great room where Kyle was sipping scotch with Dane and Amano.

I gently clasped her hand and led her that way. I already knew Tamera found Kyle attractive. Perhaps that was why she'd dolled up for a baptism?

We entered the room and I very happily announced, "Look who stopped by to show off her fabulous legs?"

"Ari!" She swatted at me, her tawny eyes widening. "Are you out of your mind?"

Dane laughed. "Come have some champagne, Tamera."

My friend glared at me before crossing the room to join the men. Amano was already pouring her bubbly. Kyle eyed her over the rim of his glass. He played it cool, but I caught the flicker of interest in his sky-blue irises. And bit back a smile.

He'll get over me.

I'd do everything in my power to make sure of it. He deserved to be as deliriously happy as I was—and Tamera was too fantastic for him to pass up. I didn't mind trying to convince him of this, though Tamera in her tight, short skirt and with her mile-long legs might do the trick all on her own.

The bell chimed again, and I excused myself to answer the door, since Rosa was busy in the kitchen. She had the baby in there as well, likely giving Amsel his first cooking lesson.

My dad arrived, looking dapper in a navy-colored suit. While Kyle and Dane filled theirs out in a way that suggested a tailor had to work some serious magic around the rock-hard biceps and powerful thighs, my dad was lean muscled and clothes hung naturally on him. He handed over a bottle of fancy sparkling water I favored and kissed me on the cheek.

"You look beautiful," he told me.

"Thank you. I was just thinking how well you wear a suit. Kind of funny, since you live in polo shirts and Dockers."

"One of the perks of running a golf club."

"True." I'd pretty much grown up in golf skirts and shirts. Sometimes in high school I'd reach for the spikes instead of tennis shoes before heading off to class and would catch myself as I walked out the door and change. Came with the territory of basically being raised on the links.

And since I missed them with the recent sequestering, I said, "We need to get out on the course soon. My swing has probably gone to pot since I've been tucked away here."

"How's Wednesday afternoon? The rain's supposed to let up."

"Perfect. Dane will get a kick out of being on his own with Amsel. Though Rosa will likely only be a soft shout-out away. She's not big on letting the baby out of her sight for long. Same with Kyle and Amano. It's really very endearing."

"In a few more years, we can start him on the putting green and driving range."

"He ought to be a natural, what with the golfing genes I might have passed on and the fact that his father is so dexterous. If Amsel takes to this sport, he might actually give you a run for your money."

I winked. My dad laughed heartily.

"I wouldn't mind," he said. "Your son can school me on the course—just not your husband."

With a smile, I told him, "Dane knows that. If you were anyone else, he would have dedicated sufficient time to improving his already great game, given his competitive nature. But beating his father-in-law . . . No, not a smart move."

We headed toward the great room, but I sent my dad ahead of me when the chimes went off again. He knew his way around the house, so I left him in order to greet our next guests. Jackson and his very lovely wife, Eleanor, joined the festivities. Then Ethan appeared, bearing gifts.

"Holy cow," I said as I eyed the enormous basket he carted in both hands. I had him set it on a foyer table with the other presents. "This is so gracious—but so not necessary."

"I'm the godfather," Ethan declared, his now-empty arms spread wide, in magnanimous fashion. "You think I'm not going to spoil this child?"

I laughed. "The very reason we chose you."

"Smart alec."

Dane had phoned him after our decision had been made to go through with the baptism. Ethan was a natural selection for godfather, a total no-brainer. Easier to peg than how we'd let Mikaela in on the mystery of our family.

Ethan kissed me on both cheeks, then handed over a sealed envelope.

I gave him a piercing look. "Let's not get carried away."

"My dear Mrs. Bax," he said, knowing how much I loved hearing that moniker—and how infrequently it was ever used, given our circumstances. "I only have one godchild. Don't ruin my fun. This is mad money for when he wants to buy a Harley before he's old enough to access his trust fund and you say no."

I playfully squeezed Ethan's arm. "You're so bad."

Of course, I considered the "joyride" story Dane had told me.

But I honestly didn't feel our son would have any reason to feel rebellious at that same age; he wouldn't have anything to rebel against. We weren't in danger, and our little blackbird wasn't an orphaned billionaire. There wouldn't be any wolves to keep at bay while Dane and Amano were around.

Ethan's tone turned serious as he said, "Amsel is going to be an amazing kid, Ari, and I'm both honored and humbled to be such an important part of his life."

"We're the ones who are honored, Ethan." Myriad feelings overcame me. I supposed I'd have to get used to this aspect of my life that I hadn't experienced growing up—or within my first year of marriage. More and more people around me who cared for me, whom I cared for in return.

What I focused on was how incredible it felt to have all this warmth filling the hallways of our home.

This wasn't like my dad and me being on our own after the divorce, when he'd struggled to pay the bills because his PGA career was over and he hadn't quite had the wherewithal at the time to admit it, especially with my mother taking him to the cleaners, both financially and emotionally.

This was friendship—family—rooted deep.

And I loved it.

With a smile, I told Ethan, "Everyone's in the great room. Dane will pour you fifty-year-old scotch or eighteen-hundred-dollar champagne. Take your pick." I winked.

"Always the overachiever," Ethan quipped of my husband.

"And never one to do anything half-assed."

"Agreed. I've never heard of a baptism over cocktails."

I laughed. "Wait until you see what Rosa and Kyle have whipped up for dinner."

Ethan went in the direction of the reception. I lingered in the foyer, awaiting our final guest. I should have had my own glass of eighteen-hundred-dollar champagne in-hand, because I was suddenly wracked with nervous anxiety.

How, exactly, did one break the kind of news I had to break to Mikaela Madsen?

Visions of her slapping me Joan Collins/*Dynasty*–style flashed in my mind. I could almost hear Mikaela saying—out of heart-wrenching agony because she couldn't accept the reality of my words—*How could you be so cruel, Ari? How could you blatantly lie to me about something that has tormented me for so long?*

My throat tightened. She'd be right in the accusation, even though it'd never been my intention to keep this from her—it'd been a necessity. Imperative. Out of my hands.

Would she understand that?

I wrung my hands now as I paced the wide hallway, my tall black heels clicking on the heated stone floor. The elegant chandeliers lining the long corridor and vast entryway were on a low setting. The cut-crystal-and-glass adornments caught the light and cast glittery rays over the silvery-blue hue filling the house. There was a large fireplace in the foyer, with roaring flames to take the edge off the autumn chill. The crackle lent a soothing quality.

Dane preferred gas fireplaces in every other room, but at the point of entry this wood-burning one created a very homey, inviting ambience to the otherwise expansive house. I wanted Mikaela to feel welcomed. I wanted her to understand that she hadn't been excluded from our clandestine efforts because she was any less important than the others in our circle. Circumstance alone had dictated who learned of Dane's existence. And when.

As I rationalized this in my mind, the vibrato chimes echoed in the hallway. I jumped, since I'd been deep in thought and the sound caught me off-guard. It wasn't a normal occurrence for people to come knocking on our door. We were set way back in the woods, along the creek, extremely difficult to find.

But everyone currently in the house had our gate code because they had reason to come and go from our inner sanctum. Mikaela would have that right now as well. Dane trusted her and so, too, did I.

I pulled open the door and was instantly enveloped in a rich aroma that nearly hypnotized me, except that Mikaela was so stunning, the sight of her overpowered the scent of her.

"Wow," I said. "You take cocktail reception attire to all-new levels."

"Ah, Ari." She affectionately gave air-kisses to both cheeks. "Ciao, *bella*. Emerald is your color!"

"I'm pretty fond of it." I ushered her in and carefully slipped the full-length fur coat from her shoulders. "That dress is sensational." In fact, it looked straight out of *Dynasty*. That didn't bode well for me, did it? I'd streamed a few seasons, and the diamonds dripping from Mikaela backed up my assessment. Her gown was liquid gold, clingy with strategic cutouts. Heidi Klum herself couldn't have worn it better.

"Rosa always did like formal gatherings," Mikaela mused in her Italian accent. I had yet to discern how she'd so quickly acquired it, since she'd been born and raised in Philadelphia, "next door" to Dane. According to my husband, that meant miles away, given the size of their respective estates.

"More like cocktail formal, but whatever. You're gorgeous."

"So are you." Her gaze slid over me. "You've lost weight."

The last time she'd seen me, I'd been pregnant. Not noticeably pregnant, but definitely plump. I thought of how Dane had admired the curves and knew he preferred them to the stick figure I'd been when I'd thought he was dead and I couldn't keep anything down.

Thinking of that time made my brain churn with harrowing Lux thoughts and brought the anxiety back full force when it came to squaring up with Mikaela.

I asked, "Would you mind joining me in the study for a drink?"

"Of course not." She beamed. But as we walked toward the center of the house, her vibrancy dimmed. "You know, I haven't been in Dane's home in years. Not since he broke ground on the Lux. He, Ethan, Qadir, and Nik celebrated. I happened to be in town and got to hear all of Dane's grandiose plans for the resort. See the schematics."

A flicker of pain over her delicate features made my insides roil.

"I was so proud of him," she continued, "for building his dream. And so happy that he never let anything hold him back. I'd always respected that about him."

She dabbed at the corner of her eye with a French-manicured fingertip and that nearly made me burst into tears.

Oh, God. How was I going to handle the big reveal in the most humane way, without her thinking I was some sort of monster for keeping Dane's existence from her?

I'd insisted I be the one to tell her. To share the news gently with her. If Dane just strutted into the room, all perfectly intact and hotter than ever, she'd likely hit the floor like a ton of bricks. I know I would have done the same the first time I saw him after the explosion, had I not figured out on my own that he was alive.

We couldn't just spring this on Mikaela. I had to ease her into the reality of the situation. Especially since she knew nothing of the Illuminati and Dane's role in the secret poli-econ society.

This would blow her mind, I knew.

So I headed straight for the wet bar and poured her a snifter of brandy. I handed over the Baccarat glass, steeling my nerves as she sipped.

It took me a few minutes to collect myself, but I finally said, "I'm so glad you came. But I guess you're wondering why *I'm* here. Why Rosa is hosting a reception at Dane's house."

"I assume he left it to her. She's been quite dedicated to him and this place always seemed to suit her. I honestly can't imagine this house without Rosa in it."

"Yes. That's true."

We exchanged a look. One that suggested we were on the same page. Which made my gut clench. Because we really weren't.

I said, "Rosa has definitely been a significant person in his life. Dane didn't trust many others and—"

"Ari." Mikaela's expression turned perplexed yet solemn. "Are you trying to soften me up for some reason?"

"I—um—*huh*." Did she know what I was up to? Had she figured it all out?

I shook my head. Anyone could speculate that Dane was alive, wish it was so, feel a glimmer of hope. I'd done that myself. But until I'd seen him in reality, my wishful thinking had been simply that.

"Ari," she said again. "I understand you worked for Dane and that you were close to him because of that association. We're nearing the anniversary of the devastation of the Lux and his death and, well, I think you and Rosa memorializing the effort he put into the launch of the resort is extremely thoughtful."

I stared at her, taken aback. That was what she thought tonight was about?

Granted, she had no other ideas to go on. But we were still a couple months away from the observation of that horrific time of our lives. Not something I wanted to think about, though I had to admit that recognizing the tragedy would have been on my mind had Dane not survived—making Mikaela extremely astute in this situation.

I sucked down my small glass of water and set the tumbler on the massive table in the middle of the room. Then I snatched the receiver on the landline and hit a button for an internal number. Rosa picked up and I quietly asked her to bring Amsel to the study.

I turned back to a confused Mikaela.

"Truly, I do want to thank you for coming," I said. "I'm sure it's not easy for you to be here, what with the memories and all that. Dane's entire presence permeates this house."

"Yes, it does."

"Beyond all the pleasantries," I told her, "I'd like to share something with you. I couldn't do it over the phone."

She finished her cocktail and returned both glasses to the wet bar. Then she told me, "Ari, I think I know what this is about."

My brow rose. "You do?"

A soft laugh escaped her glossy lips. "Certainly. I saw how Dane looked at you when I came across both of you at El Rincon in Tlaquepaque. And then at the reception Anthony Delfino hosted for his daughter and her husband in Scottsdale. *That* time, Dane looked territorial. Like you were his. You have to know that's why I wanted to get better acquainted with you."

I hadn't considered that, given the way she'd treated me initially. I'd operated on the assumption she was following the adage of keeping her friends close and her enemies closer. But I had to concede that I'd misjudged her from the get-go. Because I truly had been envious of her association with Dane. Especially the fact that she'd known him most of his life and likely was privy to secrets I previously wasn't.

The tables had turned significantly. Now I was the one holding all the cards. It wasn't a comfortable or even powerful position to be in when I felt the turmoil rage low in my belly.

Rosa came into the study with an animated Amsel in her arms. His little fists moved about as though he was rocking out to his own tune. He gurgled and gave a few half snorts. I seriously wished I could crawl inside his brain and figure out what amused him so. Perhaps he'd bypass his father's Harvard footsteps and go into stand-up comedy.

I took the baby from Rosa. She gave Mikaela a hug and they each said it was good to see the other. Then Rosa stepped out of the room to give us privacy. I pulled in a long breath to steel myself before I peeled away the blanket and the beanie from Amsel's head to show him off.

To show off the resemblance to Dane.

"Oh!" Mikaela actually jumped back a few inches, teetering slightly on her six-inch stilettos. "He's fantastic, Ari! And he looks just like—*oh!*" Her hand pressed to her chest, over her heart. Then she lifted it to her mouth as astonishment flitted in her eyes. Finally, her palm flattened over her left breast again. "I suspected there'd been something between you and Dane but I had no idea—"

"I know. We didn't really tell anyone. And when I discovered I was pregnant . . . I kept that an even bigger secret." I hadn't told Ethan, Qadir, Nikolai, or Jackson in the beginning. My dad and Kyle had known because they'd been with me at the hospital following the explosion, when tests had revealed the unexpected condition.

"He's Dane's son," Mikaela said in bewilderment. "I can't believe it. Except that he looks exactly like Dane when he was a baby. I've seen pictures. At the mansion in Philadelphia."

"Would you like to hold him?" I offered.

She looked momentarily taken aback. I suspected it wasn't a normal occurrence for anyone to ask if she wanted a kid in her arms. I'd been the same way, until recently.

Recovering somewhat from her shock, she accepted Amsel and inspected him closely. Not poking at the baby in the way Chelsea had done at the retreat, but definitely curious about him, fascinated by him.

"His name is Amsel," I said. "Apparently, it means 'blackbird' in German."

"Dane's father was German."

"Yes. He's very proud of his heritage."

Her gaze snapped from my child to me. Panic flashed through me. I'd just referred to Dane in present tense.

"Um, so, maybe I should take the baby," I carefully insisted as I reached for Amsel. "Because I have more to tell you. In fact, you might want to sit down."

Her gaze never left my face as she eased into a plush chair.

I pulled in a deep breath. Let it out slowly. Then plunged forward.

"Dane and I married last fall. The day after Thanksgiving, to be exact. Ethan, Amano, and Jackson were all present as witnesses. Guests. Whatever. We kept it covert because of the problems happening at the Lux and some complications with the original investors. Dane wanted to protect me. This was before I was pregnant and before the blast at the resort."

Mikaela's sculpted brows furrowed. "I can't believe he didn't tell me. He didn't keep things from me as a rule. We were very close."

"I understand. It was just a really tense time, a volatile time. It wasn't a trust issue, Mikaela. It was survival tactics. Nothing personal."

"Sure. Right." Though she didn't look convinced. And the hurt feelings were not only etched across her stunning features, they also laced her tone. I felt wretched.

"The thing is," I forced myself to continue. "Life following the explosion has been insanely precarious. *Dangerous*, mostly."

"I don't understand. Why? The Lux was destroyed. Dane was killed. What more could possibly have happened?"

"A lot." I didn't have the heart to outline all of the insidiousness. As it was, I could see she struggled to make sense of what I shared with her. "Suffice it to say that Kyle—whom I'm sure you remember meeting when we visited your market in Old Town—

has taken it upon himself to protect me and Amsel. As Amano did for Dane after Dane's parents died."

"*Dio mio.* That's a horrible history to have repeated."

"Yes. Except . . ." My stomach knotted. Here came the really tricky part of this tell-all. I squared my shoulders, looked her in the eye, and said, "There's a bit of a difference in the scenarios. A twist, if you will. A fortunate one, even."

From her mystified expression, I could tell she had absolutely no idea what I was getting at, even with my earlier slip when referring to Dane.

I licked my gloss-covered lips out of nervous habit. She wouldn't strike me while holding a baby, I was sure of it. Yet I had no doubt she'd have an explosive reaction to my news. I wouldn't blame her.

"You see," I began. "There was a lot of debris and confusion and chaos that night the lobby of the Lux went up in flames. Thankfully, I was the only employee hospitalized. Others were injured, but not as badly as me. Or Dane and Amano. Dane especially." My eyes squeezed shut as I tried to block out the sight of him with angry, fresh scars and a severe limp. Even the gunshot wound of late flashed in my mind, the sight of all that blood making me instantly queasy.

"Ari, darling. You don't have to torture yourself by explaining the details. I know how devastating—"

"There's more," I interjected, my lids flying open. "And really, I'm not going to draw this out and torment you. I'm just going to rip the Band-Aid off. Quickly. Anything I can do to spare you more agony."

"Please, whatever it is, I'm dying to hear. Without you suffering any more than you currently are."

We were both suffering. I saw it clearly, painfully.

Our gazes locked and all I could think was that if I were in her shoes I wouldn't want a lie to keep me from a relieving truth. A life-altering truth.

I took a deep breath.

"Ari," she implored.

This was no easy revelation. But what choice did I have?

I gave her an unyielding look and blurted, "Dane's alive!"

chapter 14

I gasped.

Oh, crap.

This required such delicacy and I'd just opened my mouth and spewed!

Mikaela's smoky-accented eyes widened. Her jaw slacked. Then promptly shut. "Ari."

"I know. I'm so sorry. I could have said that much more eloquently. Eased you into it. I panicked." I stared helplessly at her. "It's just that . . . we invited you here tonight so that you'd hear it from us, not on some ten o'clock newscast when the rest of the world finds out Dane actually survived the explosion."

"Survived the explosion." She said this slowly, tentatively, speculatively. As though I might be crazy and she suddenly feared for her life. "Ari, is there anything else you'd like to tell me?"

"As in, am I on medication? A nut job?"

"That's not at all what I said."

"Yet that's exactly what you're thinking. I'd feel the same if I were currently in your shoes."

"Ari."

"I know. It seems impossible. Implausible. Lunacy, even. I experienced the same shock at first, when I discovered the truth. But then again, this is Dane we're talking about. And Amano. He's alive, too. Amano saved Dane. He was really, really messed up and in a coma for a long time and I didn't know they'd both escaped; no one knew either one of them had survived and that played out well for Dane so that he could—oh, Christ. Just . . . Let me show you."

I took a step toward her. She shrank back in her seat.

"I promise I would never, *never* lie about this to you or anyone else," I insisted. "It's not something I've made up, Mikaela. And Dane can better explain it all. Just, please. Come with me into the great room. Let me show you," I repeated.

She'd gone a bit pale. I saw a tremor run through her and her eyes glistened with the threat of tears.

It tore me apart. I knew her pain. I knew exactly how she felt.

Mikaela wanted to believe me. But it was so far beyond comprehension that it bordered on cruelty that I'd say something like this. Give her misguided hope or make light of a traumatic situation.

I understood completely. And that pained me even more.

"Mikaela. You of all people know that Dane's life has always been extraordinary and that with him you have to expect the unexpected. In this case, the unexpected has turned out to be cause for celebration. Don't you want to take a leap of faith and see him?"

"I—" Her mouth gaped the way Amsel's sometimes did, gulping in air or otherwise floundering, because no words verbalized.

"Please," I said, balancing the baby in one arm and reaching the other toward her. "Believe me, you're going to be pleasantly surprised." I offered a smile through my own tension, the tears that flooded my eyes. "It's another ball of wax when you actually see him in person."

Several suspended seconds passed. She worked down a hard swallow. A few drops trickled over her high cheekbones. I wasn't even sure she noticed. Her gaze locked on me, and she apparently tried to discern how detrimental to her it might be if she accepted my reality—and it turned out to hold no validity.

Again, I could relate. I'd once been there myself.

"Mikaela."

Finally, she placed a slender hand in mine. Got to her feet.

Still eyeing me with trepidation, she said, "Amsel is a gorgeous child."

"With a gorgeous father. He was worse for the wear at first, but you know Dane. In what world would he ever be defeated?" Kyle and I had previously declared this, which had made it a bit easier to accept the fact that everything I'd believed to be true about Dane's death was actually false.

We left the study, Mikaela walking briskly beside me, though I could sense her reservation, her inner turmoil. This wouldn't be easy for her to reconcile, but once she saw Dane she could begin to fully process it all.

The hallway seemed longer than ever before, like it just might take forever to reach the great room and Dane. A heavy weight settled in my chest and my stomach continued to roil. As we finally approached the front of the house, I feared Mikaela might bolt.

I wouldn't blame her, since she probably still worried about my mental state. Perhaps wondered how dangerous me being off my rocker might be to her own life.

But her pace didn't speed up; rather, it slowed. She hung back a bit as we neared one of the oversized entryways into the great room.

Laughter wafted into the wide corridor, mingling with the music I'd turned on earlier. Mikaela spared a glance toward me. I smiled and nodded encouragingly.

She seemed to swallow down another lump of emotion. Then preceded me into the room.

I heard another gasp from her—this time a sharp, shocked one—as Dane stepped away from his conversation with Amano and Ethan to greet her.

A litany of what I presumed were Italian swearwords flew from her mouth and she swayed a little, so that I gripped her arm to steady her. Rosa rushed over to take the baby, saving me from a juggling act. Particularly helpful in the event Mikaela fainted. I didn't know if she was the sort, but there was just enough drama surrounding us that I wanted to be prepared for anything.

"This really can't be happening," she said on a harsh whisper. "*How* could this happen?"

"I'll explain everything," Dane assured her. "Just believe us that it was necessary to keep this all a—"

"Oh, my God! Dane!" The Italian accent vanished and Mikaela all but launched herself into his arms.

Thankfully, he had lightning-quick reflexes. He caught her soundly and held her while she burst into a crying jag I felt was wholly justified. So much so, it got me going a bit. Ethan handed over a handkerchief for me to blot my eyes. Even Rosa looked moved. That was saying something.

Eleanor came to my side and gave me a gentle squeeze about the shoulders. "I'm sure that wasn't an easy conversation to have."

"I'm actually glad he doesn't have sisters," I said in a raspy voice. "I'd never make it through."

She laughed softly, soothingly. "Mikaela's a close second, so I'd say you did a fantastic job."

Tamera joined us. "Really, Ari. You constantly amaze me with all this resiliency. You used to be the solver of wedding crises, and now look at you. Taking on all of these family obligations and strengthening the entire foundation you and Dane started building last fall. I'm so proud of you—and so in awe."

As I gazed at her, I saw the emotion in her eyes. The admiration. Along with a hint of something elusive, forlorn. I knew Tamera didn't have relatives in the States, nor did she date often, given the limited availability of young, single men in our community. I almost felt her lonesomeness, and it shredded me as much as Mikaela's pain did.

I'd been right all along about not coming out of this insanity unscathed. We were all caught up in something too fragile and heinous to carefully extract ourselves from, but I had to find those silver linings Dane always credited me for latching on to.

And, in all honesty, I wasn't above admitting the vulnerabilities growing within me over how to strengthen my marriage and my bond with Dane.

I said to my friend, "I'd like to have a lengthy conversation with you in a few days. Once I've composed myself following all of this."

Tamera eyed me curiously, then slowly nodded. "Of course, darling. This hasn't been an easy ride for you. Whatever I can do to help."

I gave her a faint smile. "I could use a little perspective."

Eleanor gave me another squeeze. "I'm happy to lend an ear as well."

"I just might take you up on that." I could use marital expertise in addition to moral support.

Mikaela collected herself and I moved to her side. Placed an arm around her narrow waist. "I really am sorry we had to keep this from you. Dane had important work to do that necessitated the lie, once he pulled through from the surgeries and coma."

"Ari," she said as she patted dry her cheeks with a tissue my husband supplied. "I would never doubt yours or Dane's intentions. In fact, I suppose I helped to perpetuate the lie by orchestrating his memorial service. So, in a roundabout way, I was involved to a small degree."

That was a little more along the lines of what I expected from her. "Thanks for finding an upside."

She gave me a quick hug, then said, "I'm happy for you. For both of you. That's all that really matters."

"Well, there is one other thing," I said.

"Oh, naturally," she quipped, though her tone was a bit strained. "This is Dane's World we're all living in."

"Indeed," I concurred. "So he and I have discussed this, and I know we're springing a lot on you all at once, but it would be such an honor for us if you would consider being Amsel's god-mother. I realize this is the first time you've met him and the circumstances are certainly unorthodox, but you've known Dane your whole life and so I thought—"

"Ari." She beamed through her residual tears. "I'd love to be Amsel's godmother."

"Really?" I gripped her hand. Perhaps a bit too tightly, though she didn't let on.

"Of course." She smiled.

"Phew." I sighed as the tension eased. "Thank you. We're so grateful."

"No. Really, this is an honor for *me*."

I was finally able to breathe normally. "We're so happy."

Amano served cocktails to help break the ice, and a more re-laxed atmosphere ensued, with the exception of Mikaela con-stantly shooting glances Dane's way, as though fearing she'd bought into a ghost story and he was no more than a figment of everyone's imagination. Hers included.

A half hour later, Tamera proceeded with the baptismal cere-mony. Then Rosa served a stellar sit-down dinner on the patio. It was a beautiful evening. Nothing hindered the stars from twin-kling like diamonds against the night sky. The heaters kept the autumn chill at bay. Dom flowed, the conversation was light and lively, and I was thrilled that we'd all come together again. That Mikaela was a new addition to our circle.

I knew the time we all spent together wouldn't be limited to rare occasions but would become more frequent.

I gazed at Dane, sitting to my right at the head of the table. He leaned over and kissed my cheek, then murmured, "I've told you before. You're everything."

His intense, appreciative gaze chased away all of the consternation I'd been feeling. This evening had shaped up perfectly. We'd achieved everything we wanted and now were able to benefit from Dane's hard work—having our friends rally around us for a special cause.

Although Amsel had long since crashed out, this was a night I'd be sure to tell him about again and again. So that he'd know he was a part of something special, something significant.

I had no misconceptions that, in the back of Dane's mind, he wanted our son to be as powerful as him, to possibly be a member of an Illuminati faction that didn't go awry. I'd prefer that didn't happen, but if greatness was in Amsel's future who was I to squelch it? My job was to make sure he understood that whatever direction he took, it was a positive one that served a higher purpose than himself. Like his father's endless plights.

Dinner segued into decadent desserts and espresso, then more mingling. At one point, I went to check on Amsel, though Rosa had been keeping a close eye on him. As I left his nursery, I caught sight of Mikaela and Ethan in a secluded nook. They appeared engaged in a heated discussion, with her hands flapping agitatedly and him scowling.

Since I was ensconced in shadows, I knew they couldn't see me. I watched a few moments more, as whatever argument they were embroiled in seemed to escalate. Then, unexpectedly, Mikaela raised an arm and slapped Ethan quite soundly. The Joan Collins slap I'd anticipated as I'd awaited her arrival earlier in the evening.

I held my gasp in check, not wanting to draw attention to my presence.

Ethan's jaw clenched as he glared at her.

Mikaela slapped him again.

All I could think was that she must be pissed that Ethan had known Dane was alive—and hadn't told her. That might warrant the same reaction from me, given the circumstances.

I'd held Amano accountable to a degree, after all, when he'd kept the secret and I'd suffered for it.

I discreetly left the area and returned to the patio. The festivities wound down until it was just Kyle, Amano, Rosa, Dane, and myself loitering about.

Rosa excused herself to finish cleaning the kitchen. Then Amano and Kyle went about their surveillance work. Dane took my hand and guided me toward our bedroom. On our way, we stopped into the office to dim the lights and the fireplace.

As my gaze swept over the web still hanging on the wall, my consternation returned.

I told him about the Mikaela/Ethan encounter in the hallway.

He stuffed his hands in the pockets of his pants. He'd already discarded his jacket and tie. Had rolled up the sleeves of his dress shirt. He'd also undone a few buttons at his neck, giving me that tantalizing view of the pulse point at the base of his throat that always enticed me.

Finding him too tempting by far, I closed the gap between us and splayed my hands over his abdomen. "If I recall correctly, you planned to do wicked things to me this evening."

His head dipped and his mouth sealed with mine. I twined my arms around his neck and pressed my body to his, loving the strength, the heat that surrounded me. My fingers curled in his lush locks. An inferno instantly ignited within me.

Dane palmed my ass and held me to him, his thigh wedged between my parted legs, hitching my skirt and rubbing insistently, making me burn brighter. When we came up for air, I shifted my hands and slipped the rest of the buttons on his shirt through their small holes. My lips skimmed along his throat, down to his chest.

I tongued his nipple and muttered our new favorite words. "Let's take this into the bedroom."

"Definitely."

He turned back to the lamp on my desk to switch it off but paused. His gaze swept over the web once more. Mine followed.

He stared at the photo of his father and Ethan that I'd retacked to the wall.

"What's bothering you?" I asked.

Shaking his head, he said, "Nothing." He turned off the light and reached for me.

I sidestepped him and flipped the switch back on. "Something."

Dane's devilishly handsome face darkened. "Now's not really the time—"

"Now is always the time," I insisted. "So nothing festers." I gave him a hard look, despite the desire coursing through me. The urge to say to hell with it all and let him take me to bed. I knew better. I couldn't get past ominous thoughts when they lingered between us. Not anymore. That was our new reality. "Spill."

His mouth quirked up on one side. "So demanding."

"Yes." I didn't back down.

"Fine." He didn't appear pleased that I'd diverted our intimate rendezvous, but clearly something weighed on his mind. He crossed to the webbing and pointed at the photo we'd both eyed days before. The one of Ethan and his father. "This isn't right."

"You don't know that."

"True." He blew out a long breath. "But you can feel it, too. Even if just subconsciously. Otherwise, you wouldn't have added this printout to the puzzle."

With a shrug, I told him, "I've considered various angles. You and I both know there's a reasonable explanation."

Dane turned away. Started to pace. Never a good sign.

I wasn't exactly in the frame of mind to dig deeper, was drained emotionally from the ordeal with Mikaela. Yet when Dane and I encountered something to piece together, neither of us could let it drop without investigating all possibilities.

So I said, "If Ethan and your father were at a summit together and were standing next to each other on a stage, you know they would have been introduced to each other. They'd shake hands, exchange a few pleasantries, that sort of thing."

"That'd be my guess."

"For that matter," I continued, my mind starting to whirl. "They were probably at cocktail receptions or dinners together during that conference. They'd likely swap business cards, right? And what about the fact that your dad was wealthy and influential? A billionaire? No one can overlook all of that. Ethan would certainly remember him."

Dane folded his arms across his massive chest.

I continued, the momentum building. "People don't just 'forget' meeting someone of that financial stature. And what about your family name? It's not like Bax would slip one's mind. I mean—"

"Ari, stop." He was already way ahead of me. I saw it in his eyes.

But I gave him one more thought to ponder. "Where was Amano? Did he work for your father at that point?"

"In 1983?" Dane thought about it. Nodded. "He was in the family employ, but that was the year he spent in Minsk because both his mother and father had come down with pneumonia and neither was expected to survive. Nor did they."

"Minsk?" I resisted the urge to say, *It figures.* Our exotic ninja was from Russia? I didn't think Amano was a Russian name. Had never actually looked up the origin. Which made me suddenly burn with curiosity to do so. Especially since I'd always considered there was a hint of Japanese in the man. Perhaps that was just because of his impressive karate skills?

Mr. Miyagi had nothing on Amano.

Though I couldn't fathom him having too strong of an Asian background, mostly due to his intimidating size.

I continued to stare at the wall, wondering why this web only got stickier. How was I supposed to deconstruct the intricacies when the threads grew of their own accord, mysteriously weaving together to hint at more untold stories and intriguing, sometimes suspicious, connections?

With a shake of my head because I wasn't able to answer my own question, I said, "You think Amano *didn't* know Ethan back in the day?"

"It would have come up long before now."

"True." I gnawed my bottom lip a moment, then added, "Maybe." I carefully ventured, "You didn't know Ethan had met your father before now. How is that possible? Why wouldn't he have mentioned it when you started at Harvard? You had him freshman year, right? I can't understand why he didn't take one look at the student roster and say, 'Hey, a familiar name.'"

Dane held up a finger to stall me. He poured a scotch for himself. Offered me a bottle of FIJI that I bypassed. I'd nearly drowned myself with sparkling water all night long.

"Guess I'm not the only one who finds this completely mind-boggling," I mused.

"It makes no sense," he agreed. Then he gave me a contemplative look. "You're absolutely right. How could there not have been a click in Ethan's mind when he heard my surname?"

"It is kind of unique." Like the man himself.

He said, "There'd never been even the tiniest flicker of recognition in his eyes. Not a hint. And he'd spent that first year and a half courting me the way professors do with favored students." He drained his tumbler and splashed in more scotch.

"I wouldn't really know. I'm not a financial whiz or a rocket scientist."

He grinned. "You're plenty smart. And resourceful."

"I do like complicated puzzles. Now, you were saying about Ethan . . . ?"

"Right. So he spent the first few semesters dazzling me with his own economics knowledge. We attended faculty-student networking functions, lectures, global presentations. He seemed to have no idea who I was, and that *did* make sense, because I'd wiped the slate clean on the Internet, as far as my family was concerned."

"Which is a mind trip unto itself."

"With Amano's help and contributions to the right organizations I made sure I wasn't the least bit relevant on the Web, aside from a few approved articles from the *Wall Street Journal*. I'd covered my tracks. By the time I'd arrived at Harvard, I was just a smart, rich kid who'd broken the code to get in when he had no family connections and no real history to draw upon."

"Your father didn't go to Harvard?"

"No, he was a Yale man."

I did a little pacing of my own. "That alone would keep the Board from letting you in, I'd think."

He chuckled. "It doesn't exactly work that way. Anyway, since my parents died when I was just a month old, there wasn't any family obligation, connection, funding, whatever. Amano and Aunt Lara were cognizant of how to ensure I got into the right schools, but they were more practical about it than political."

"Meaning they didn't suck up?"

"Exactly. GPA, student body standing, extracurricular activities, volunteering—those were crucial and I focused on them. Naturally, I had the money to buy my way in, but then again, so do a lot of kids."

"What made you stand out?" I had to ask.

"From my understanding, it was the volunteering and charitable donations. I was able to devote free hours not related to school activities to community service. Ivy League universities want well-rounded, socially conscientious students. The difficulty in that affects students who can't keep up their GPA, activities, and fund-raising efforts for tuition all at the same time. I'm not a fan of the system, but it's a respected institution regardless."

"And you did what was required of you. That's admirable, Dane."

He seemed to grind over this. "If Amsel wants Harvard, I don't know how I feel about that."

I stared at him, incredulous. "You want our kid to go to one of the best universities, right? And wouldn't you advocate from the get-go that he follow your educational path? Continue your Harvard legacy?"

"What if Stanford offers him a football scholarship or Duke wants him on their basketball team? Am I going to say, 'No, you have to go to Harvard because that's where I went'?"

"Point taken." And I acknowledged it as a selfless one on Dane's part. "But let's put that aside for the moment. It'll be at least sixteen or seventeen years before he goes to college, if he's on the Dane Bax schedule. Though chances are, we'll end up with a genius who pushes a decision at twelve." I had no doubt our son would be absurdly ambitious. Though I added, "That's currently neither here nor there."

Not that a hint of panic didn't creep in on me. I'd married a brilliant man, after all, whose father had also been brilliant. Sort of went without saying that our son would follow in those significant footsteps.

But I digressed.

"Okay, so you got into Harvard. You kicked ass. Ethan took notice. But again—how did he miss the connection between you and your dad?"

Dane set aside his glass. "I don't know, truthfully."

"What about the hard drive Ethan brought back from Switzerland? Anything of value on it?"

Dane's entire demeanor went rigid. A chill ran through me. "Dane?"

"This has been bothering me all night."

He shoved a hand through his hair, further mussing the strategically tousled locks. Momentarily distracting me. He was breathtaking at any given second of the day, but when fury tore through him his strong features darkened and raw intensity exuded from him.

"Tell me what you're thinking," I said.

"When did he deliver the laptop?"

"While we were at the retreat, after I had the baby. Ethan brought the hard drive here, to Amano, who locked it in your safe. Guess he didn't mention it?"

"Amano? No. He wouldn't at the time, when I was wrapped up in the fact that you'd just given birth."

"Yeah, he was a bit worried—like how could a Bax be born prematurely?" I pulled in a sharp breath, pain lancing through me. Something could have gone horrifically wrong with my delivery. Our child could have died. That did not sit well in my heart or my gut.

"Ari. Baby." Dane gave me a long look, then asked, "Is that what's going on between the two of you?"

"The two of who?"

"You and Amano."

"I don't follow."

"Did you freak out that you might be going into labor six weeks early and that's why you told Amano not to call me?"

"I—" Had nothing to say to that.

"Ari." He carefully gripped my shoulders. "Did you really put all that pressure on yourself? Thinking if something were to go wrong that it'd be *your* fault?"

Tears prickled the backs of my eyes.

"Answer me," he gently insisted.

"I don't know," I said honestly. "I just . . . I . . ." My eyes closed for a moment. Then snapped open, a bit misty. "Maybe. Yes."

"Baby." He pulled me to him and held on tight.

I fought back tears. I wasn't prepared for this. It wasn't something I'd put substantial thought into. My water had broken, I'd been rushed to the retreat, and Amsel had been born.

Sure, I'd been stressed out over having him early. But Dr. Preston had been more than forthcoming about all the risks, hazards, what have you, and I'd not felt as though I were floundering in the dark, uncertain of my son's health.

But Dane did have a point. I had put a lot of pressure on myself. That was moot at the moment, though, no matter how it percolated in Dane's head. His thoughts were likely centered on his not having been there to help or offer support. A massive conflict to overcome on his end. One I fully understood yet had no idea how to broach.

So I let it go for the time being.

"Back to the hard drive," I said as I pulled away and swiped tears from my cheeks. "Ethan returned it, but Amano didn't mention that to you."

"Chances are he assumed I'd already had discussions with Ethan."

"But you obviously didn't."

"Not until this evening," Dane confirmed. "He mentioned it repeatedly. In fact, he seemed eager to know if I'd found anything noteworthy in my files."

"But you haven't even looked at them."

"It wasn't necessary during the trials. Plenty came out in the courtrooms, even prior to my testimonies. I can't imagine anything on the hard drive could compare. Really, I wasn't certain of what I'd downloaded or documented, which was why I wasn't in a huge rush to get my hands on the laptop. It was, literally, just for backup purposes—in the event there might be something worthwhile stored on it."

I sank into my chair and tapped the end of a pen on the leather blotter. A nervous habit.

Dane asked, "What are *you* thinking?"

"Nothing really. This'll all be over when the verdicts come back, so what else is there to deliberate over?"

He shrugged, not the least bit nonchalantly. "Other than the fact that Ethan might have known my father thirty years ago and it somehow slipped his mind?"

"That's been eating at you all this time, hasn't it?"

"Yes." He reached for his cell.

"Wait." I jumped to my feet. "Just wait."

"Ari, I need to speak with him."

"I agree. But let's make sure we have all the facts first."

I didn't blame him for being disturbed by the turn of events, this unexpected twist of fate. But this wasn't just anyone we were talking about—it was Ethan. Dane's best friend. His mentor. His business associate.

The godfather of his son.

I knew Dane was one to confront adversity head-on, not beat around the bush. But I was nervous about this new anomaly.

Ethan being that anomaly.

"Can we maybe just take a peek at what's been hiding in Switzerland?" I asked. "You know, get a little ahead of the curve, if possible?"

Dane clearly didn't see a problem with that. He crossed to the wall by the fireplace and removed an original van Gogh. He worked the combination to the safe I had no idea was concealed behind the painting, pulled open the door, and handed over the laptop.

"You want *me* to check it?"

"An objective third party."

Intrigue trilled down my spine.

No, I shouldn't still get a kick out of the Lara Croft stuff. But I did.

I sat at my desk and he gave me the password, *bagan*. Standard fare for him. It was German for "to fight." Also the origin of his last name, Bax.

Not having any idea what we really trolled for, I asked, "Did you take note of how many files you had before locking this thing up?"

"Six hundred and seventy-two."

"Wow. Way to pin it down. Okay." I accessed the Documents folder and scanned it, then checked the number of files saved. I frowned. "Sure it wasn't more like five hundred and twelve?"

"No," he said in his confident tone.

I glanced at him. "You don't have to be right on the money, Dane, but we should be in the same ballpark."

With a shake of his head, he repeated, "Six hundred and seventy-two."

My stomach churned. "Hmm."

"What?"

"There's only five hundred and twelve now."

"*What?*" He strode toward me and leaned over my shoulder. "No, Ari. Check again. I made sure I knew how many files I'd downloaded before I put it in the safe-deposit box, not long after Vale had kidnapped you."

"Dane, one hundred and sixty files are missing."

I shoved back my chair. He stealthily moved out of the way.

"Take a look for yourself," I said as I gestured toward the computer. Then I circled the desk. "What might have been on there that has now disappeared?"

"I'm not sure. I told you, I arbitrarily collected information that just seemed reasonable to privately document. But it was bits and pieces here and there. Nothing I'd ever pulled together for a big picture."

"And nearly two hundred files were deleted after the indictments and Bent's suicide? Before the trials even began?"

"That's impossible," he said. "Locked up in Switzerland, remember?"

"Right." I frowned.

"Except . . ." Dane pushed back my chair and vacated it, then said, "Take a seat."

I didn't question him, just did as he asked. "What now?"

"I didn't need all this information for the trials. The evidence I'd gathered and handed over to the FBI, beyond e-mails, was sufficient to show what was happening with Hilliard, Avril, Casterelli, and Wellington. Even the admiral."

"So why send Ethan for this?"

"Just in case."

"Well, *just in case* isn't necessary, so we're kind of chasing our tails, right? It doesn't really matter what's on this hard drive—or not."

He nodded. Paced. Nodded again. Then stopped in front of my desk and flattened his palms against the polished wood. He gave me a steady look as he said, "Check for deleted files."

I opened the recycle bin. "Empty."

"How else, on a PC, would we know when someone last accessed this hard drive?"

"I'm not sure there's any bearing whether PC or Mac based, but . . ." I investigated the restoration date, were we to reset to the last period the hard drive had been backed up.

I stared at the date and my frown deepened.

"Ari? What is it?"

"It's—I don't know. Weird." I shook my head. "Two days after Amsel was born."

Dane's brow dipped.

I said, "You stayed at the retreat with me. Kyle was there, too. Amano and Rosa came back here. That's when Ethan dropped off the hard drive."

Something foreboding flashed in Dane's eyes and, before he even asked me to see if I could discern who'd last accessed the database my fingers were already skating across the keyboard and alternately clicking the mouse.

But there was nothing to share with him. No evidence Ethan had even logged on.

And for that matter . . .

"Dane. Ethan is your closest friend. Your mentor. Not a suspect."

"No." He shoved away from the desk. "Not a suspect. What

the hell is wrong with me?" he mumbled, and walked the office in frustration.

I kept up my search for good measure, though we both knew Ethan was not a rabbit to chase. Someone else was. We just didn't know who.

As I scanned the hard drive and then pulled up the Computer function, I fought for a viable option to offer Dane. The best I could say was, "This is a dead stick. There's absolutely nothing here. No leads, no nothing. I can't even—" I stalled out mid-sentence.

"What, Ari?" Dane demanded. "What is it?"

"I don't know," I repeated. "Hold on a sec." I stared at the screen as he came around to stand behind me, peering over my shoulder again.

"Something caught your attention."

"Yes. This." I pointed at the icon on the screen. "Devices with removable storage." I clicked on the official-looking shield with initials in the center of it and a new page came up with *Encryption Launcher* stamped across the top.

Dane asked, "What are we looking at?"

"It's a program that launches an encrypted, password-protected thumb drive."

"I don't have one of those."

"We should definitely get you one, then. For all this top-secret stuff you collect."

"I'm officially out of the spy business, remember?"

"Maybe, maybe not. Because I'm willing to bet that Ethan has an encrypted thumb drive and used it with your computer."

"Ari." There was a hint of warning in his tone.

I knew I was about to cross a line. Again, this was Ethan we were talking about. Dane trusted him above all else—with the exception of Amano.

Still, I flashed Dane a look that I hoped conveyed *my* confidence in what I was doing.

I explained, "What happens when you use one of these stor-age devices is that you plug it into the USB port and the program automatically downloads so that you can put in a password and move files onto the external drive—without them ever hitting your recycle bin, so you don't really know what's been copied over. Or removed."

"Fuck," he mumbled.

Continuing, I told him, "When you're done, you eject the device. Now, if you do it correctly, shutting down the thumb drive through the icon option, I think the program goes away. If you just pull the device out of the USB port, the program remains installed."

"As it currently is." He straightened.

"Yes."

I felt the rage instantly radiate from him but still jumped in my seat as he bellowed, "Son of a bitch!"

chapter 15

"This can't be right, Dane."

He prowled the office once more. I didn't disturb the flight path, letting him mentally dissect this new twist for a few minutes.

When the suspense became too much to take, I asked, "What purpose would Ethan have for moving files from the hard drive to another external source?"

"Must've been something on the laptop that he didn't want me to see."

"Are you suggesting he spent the entire trip back from Switzerland going through all that documentation you'd collected and somehow felt threatened by some of the information?"

"I can't think of a better explanation." He gazed unwaveringly at me. "Can you?"

My spirit sank. What could Ethan possibly be doing behind Dane's back?

"Obviously," Dane said, "Ethan is keeping things from me. Like knowing my father."

"That is odd, I'll admit. Questionable. Once again, what purpose would he have for not mentioning it when you first arrived at Harvard?"

"I can't think of a single reason. So my father was a Yale man. That wouldn't have any bearing on why he wouldn't tell me they'd met seventeen or so years prior to me showing up on the Harvard campus."

"No, it wouldn't. At least, not in my mind."

Our eyes remained locked. I could practically see his brain churning. Likely, he thought back to the time he'd met Ethan, his years at Harvard with him, the business investments they'd shared, the secret society they'd served.

My brow furrowed.

"What?" Dane asked.

My lips pressed together as I contemplated that last little item—the secret society. I said, "The Illuminati faction he recruited you into was supposed to be a generational thing. No outsiders. And considering Bryn Hilliard is pushing eighty and his son, Vale, was never inducted in to take his place—"

"Because he proved to be a colossal idiot."

"Right. Anyway, if there's no Hilliard to step in, Bryn remains a member. Unless Vale were to have a son who had some sense in his head. Then he could succeed Bryn. Is that all correct?"

Hypothetically, of course, since Vale was no longer alive to proffer an heir.

Dane said, "Yes."

"So the rules of the society are finite? The exception being you?"

"The exception being me."

"Hmm." I mulled this over a bit further, then suggested, "Or not?"

His gaze narrowed. "You're not saying . . . ?"

With a small shrug, I offered, "Is it possible that your dad was part of the society thirty years ago—and any of the members who knew kept it quiet and those who came into the society later, such as Qadir and Nikolai, never even met him? Never knew anything about him? Because, let's face it, the secrecy pretty much remained intact until I came along last year."

"That's one hell of a conspiracy theory."

I nodded. "Question is, why go to all of the trouble to hide your father's involvement? Why would Ethan and the others *not* want you to know your dad was one of them?"

"Ari, this is impossible. I trust Ethan. I've always trusted him."

Unfortunately, I detected the broken conviction in Dane's voice.

"This is risky territory for us both, Dane. I understand that. But is it really so impossible to believe that he might know more than he's ever shared with you?" I challenged. " 'Cause, honestly, a secret society is a pretty crazy notion unto itself. One that's turned corrupt—and that corruption is rooted deep . . . Well. I'd say there are no inconceivable theories."

"I'm having trouble denying it myself." The angst flashing in his eyes backed up his statement.

I opted to tread lightly with a tentative tone as I suggested, "Who's to say your father didn't know these guys were doing wrong and tried to stop them? Instead, they cut him out, as you did to them later on with 10,000 Lux? Vicious cycle to the extreme, sure. But nothing is impossible with these people. We've learned that the hard way." I gave him a firm look. One that screamed, *They conspired to blow up a megaresort!*

Dane whirled on his heels and stalked toward the fireplace, taking up his pacing with his hands on his waist. Tension and frustration permeated the room. My heart ached for him.

This was a monumental betrayal we might have happened upon. Not just another deception from the society members, but from Ethan Evans. Of all people.

And for that matter . . . "What if Qadir and Nikolai aren't on the up-and-up, either?"

He spun back around to face me. "Ari, Ethan is *not* a criminal."

I didn't shrink away from his silent fury, understanding it wasn't directed at me. "You don't really know that for sure. Do you?"

His jaw clenched. I remembered the first time I'd met him I'd found that small gesture intriguing, desperately wanting to know the source of all his dismay. I was now wholly aware of that internal strife—and it deeply pained me.

Dane was a strategic sort, calculating when it came to risks and whom he could trust. There were very, very few people he'd let into his life. Very few he'd relied on or considered solid. He'd been a part of Ethan, Qadir, and Nikolai's pack since he was nineteen years old, when he'd been recruited. To learn twelve years later that those friendships and that tight camaraderie could be false, an intentional setup—that had to rip the rug from underneath him.

Once again.

So of course he'd be reticent to believe the worse.

Yet Dane was neither naive nor easily snowed. Therefore, I knew he'd evaluate every nuance and work it from every angle in his mind.

I felt compelled to help out. "Let's say, for argument's sake, that your father really was with the society three decades ago. How could we prove it?"

"Not via the Internet, that's for damn sure."

I hadn't even been able to discern when Dane's parents had passed, let alone from what cause. I'd finally asked, when Dane and I had gotten a bit closer. A plane crash on their way back to Philly from a night at the Met in New York.

Contemplating this, I asked, "Your parents were the only ones on that plane, right?"

He eyed me curiously. "Yes. It was my father's Learjet."

"Weather or mechanical problems?"

"Ari." His emerald irises deepened in color. "You're going to your own dark place now."

"And you're not already there? As usual?"

He pinched the bridge of his nose. I'd hit the nail on the head.

"You said yourself that the crash that night, their deaths, was ironic," I noted, "since they'd gone to see *Todd Sweeney*."

"*Sweeney Todd*," he corrected.

"Anyway, he murdered people. And when you told me that, there was something in your voice. Remember, I even asked if you thought there'd been foul play?"

"Actually, you didn't ask. You hinted." The man had a mind like a steel trap. "And I told you absolutely not."

"But were you just saying that to appease me? Do you really believe it?"

A bit irritably, he conceded, "Yes, it was mechanical failure that brought the plane down. Yes, there were some questionable engine parts that were investigated. In the end, they were deemed faulty, but not tampered with."

"*Faulty* doesn't guarantee they weren't tampered with."

"No, it does not."

We stared once more, as though gazing deep enough into each other's eyes might somehow solve this mystery. As if we searched hard enough into the other's soul we'd suddenly have all the answers.

That was never going to happen, of course, because neither of us knew any sort of truths when it came to the society—or the deaths of Dane's parents.

Finally, he asked, "Is there any way to tell what files were moved onto the thumb drive, since the program is still installed?"

I shook my head but went back to the computer nonetheless. I double-clicked on the shield and it launched, triggering the need for a password.

That prompted me to ask, "Would Ethan even know your initial password—the one to get into the laptop?"

"It's always been *bagan*."

"The same as the Wi-Fi in the house, which he knows."

Yet when it came to Ethan's password for the thumb drive I couldn't even begin to guess as to what it might be. I hit the hint button.

NOS popped up.

I asked Dane what it meant.

He came around to stand behind me once more and gazed at the screen.

"Damn it," he growled.

"What? You know what the password might be for the thumb drive?"

"*Novus ordo seclorum.* It's Latin for 'new order of the ages'— what the society members dubbed themselves."

I crooked a brow. "Seriously?"

"Yes."

"Wow, pretty heady stuff." Literally.

He explained, "The term comes from the fourth Eclogue of Virgil:

" '*Now comes the final era of the Sibyl's song;*
The great order of the ages is born afresh.
And now justice returns, honored rules return;
Now a new lineage is sent down from high heaven.'"

He reached around me and grabbed a gold coin from the velvet-lined tray that was also home to his more expensive fountain pens. He slapped the coin down on the desk, and there was an engraved pyramid, with *Annuit Coeptis* stamped above and *Novus Ordo Seclorum* below.

I frowned. "I don't get it. '. . . Justice returns, honored rules return . . . ?' These guys are corrupt. There's no justice or honor there."

"Remember, the society wasn't always bad. They had noble, legit goals from the beginning. They came together to effect positive change, not promote their own agendas for personal gain. That came later. Around my time."

"Unbeknownst to you at first. But did Ethan know?" My brain shifted into high gear. "How long had he been with the society before you came along?"

"A little over thirty years," he reluctantly admitted.

"Back when he knew your father." I stated our *new* obvious. I firmly believed there was a tie there that needed to be explored.

"Christ." Dane pulled his phone from his pants pocket and hit a speed dial number. Then he tersely said, "Get the plane ready. I'm going to Philadelphia."

I leapt up. "*We're* going to Philadelphia."

"You're staying put," he told me. "You'll remain here with Amano and Kyle. The baby."

"Amano and Kyle can protect the baby perfectly well. I'm going with you."

His gaze turned steely. I knew better than to push when that look entered his eyes, but this was much too important to pass up. First, I'd never been to his family estate in Philadelphia. In fact, I was curious to learn why he'd chosen to keep the mansion after his aunt passed away four years ago. Especially since he'd never once mentioned that we'd visit or live there.

Second, this was all too painful for Dane to suffer through alone. I wanted to be with him no matter what he discovered. If we were way off-base or dead on the mark, I didn't want him having to reconcile it all by himself when I could be there with him.

"Ari," he said. "We've had a conversation about seeing beyond the two of us, sweetheart. We have—"

"Amsel to consider. I know."

Leaving him wasn't a comfortable or easy decision, but our son had three other devoted people to pick up the slack for a day or two. I had no qualms about his safety—that was the least of my worries.

Dane, however, was at the top of my list when it came to the final piece of this puzzle.

"Listen," I said as I wrapped my arms around his waist and stared up at him. "I have heard every word you've said about us and the need to factor in our baby. Every. Single. Word. But we agreed to be in this marriage for better or for worse. We agreed to deal with this entire nightmare together. You can't suddenly shut me out. I'm perfectly aware that there's shady stuff going on and I am all too familiar with how dangerous this is. But we made a pact when we exchanged vows. Whatever happens is between the two of us—it involves us *both*."

He swept a plump curl from my temple, his long fingers tangling in my hair. "Baby, this isn't something I want you even more embroiled in."

"Too late," I said. "I'm packing a bag and I'm going with you."

His jaw worked rigorously. I didn't back down. I *wouldn't* back down.

Our standoff dragged on for several minutes. Finally, I untangled myself from him and said, "I'll get ready. You tell Amano."

I skirted Dane and rushed off, being quick with my packing because I didn't want Dane to slip away without me. For my own good, he'd later contend. But I'd had enough of the separation. I wanted to be with him from here on out. Particularly during an emotional time such as this.

After I explained the situation to Rosa, I stalked down the hallway. My cell rang. It was Mikaela.

"Hey," I abruptly said.

"Hi, Ari. I just wanted to thank you so much for inviting me this evening. For letting me know about Dane."

I cringed. Christ, once again, she didn't know the half of it. "I'm so glad you're now aware he's alive."

"Can we get together tomorrow for lunch? I owe you."

"You don't owe me. Really. And the truth is, I'll be out of town.

We're flying to Philly for an impromptu trip. But I'll call you when we're back."

"Sure. Of course. Let me know what works best for you."

"I'll be in touch."

I disconnected the call and tucked the cell in my bag.

I was actually kind of surprised when I found Dane in the foyer, waiting for me. I preceded him out the front door, wondering briefly if he had a plan to ditch me before we even left the property. But he opened the door to the Mercedes McLaren he'd had restored following the harrowing day Kyle and I had needed to dump it in the forest when Wayne Horton had chased us up the hairpin switchbacks of Oak Creek Canyon, toward Flagstaff.

I buckled up and Dane climbed in next to me.

"Are you okay?" I asked.

"I'm ready to bash in some heads."

"That's not exactly out of the ordinary for you," I commented, hoping to lighten the mood.

He shot me a look. I smiled.

I couldn't bait him, though. He remained grim. "This could get really ugly, Ari." He started the sports car and backed out of the garage. "I'm not happy that you're with me."

"I'm done *not* being with you," I countered. "I'm sick of us being torn apart at every corner because of this damn society. I want it all to end, Dane."

"I understand that, baby. But just because we nailed the others doesn't mean this new scenario is any less dangerous. I don't know what Ethan is up to. I don't know if Qadir and Nik are involved. I can't believe it, but then again, if Ethan did remove files from my computer, if there's something he's trying to hide—"

Dane's hands gripped the steering wheel a bit too tightly. I feared he might rip it from the dash.

"Maybe we're wrong about this whole thing," I offered. "It is possible."

With a sharp shake of his head, he said, "*NOS* as the password for an encrypted thumb drive inserted into my laptop? When I specifically told Ethan I wouldn't even send the FBI for it because I didn't want the information compromised?"

"And he so quickly jumped on retrieving it for you," I recalled with a sinking feeling in the pit of my stomach. "Clearly, he wanted to know what secrets you kept."

"Clearly, he wanted to know if they involved *him*," Dane expounded. "Or if I'd inadvertently gathered information against the society that he didn't want leaked—again because it would tie back to him."

"So what, specifically, are we searching for in Philly?" I asked as the trees whizzed by at a rapid rate. The sky remained sparkly and unhindered by clouds. A break in the moody monsoon weather was a small blessing, since we'd be flying this evening. Unfortunately, that little tidbit did nothing to calm my frazzled nerves.

Dane said, "All of my father's files are in a vault in the mansion. I'm the only one who can get in."

"Have you ever looked at his files?"

"Never had a need. My father was a political strategist. A global consultant. While I was interested in his work, it wasn't fully geared toward economics, which was always my focus. He gauged caucus climates and influenced politicians. My forte is financial forecasting."

He delved deeper into the trending and bending of socio-poli-econ environments, most of it going over my head. But it seemed to keep him on a more even keel to talk, so I posed a question here and there to give him something to concentrate on, other than the dismal prospect of Ethan's potential betrayal. Or an even sharper knife in the back if Dane's own father truly had been a society member—and had turned to the dark side, along with Ethan and the others.

Or, conversely, had Ethan stayed the legit course but known Bradley Bax had not?

Could that have anything to do with Ethan covertly removing electronic files? Keeping the truth of the senior Bax's involvement with the NOS from Dane? Was Ethan trying to protect him from a reality that would devastate Dane?

I reeled over this new possibility. And its ominous, detrimental implications.

I prayed I actually wasn't the least bit good at conspiracy theories. I hadn't come up with anything I wanted Dane to endure in reality.

We reached the airport and boarded the Learjet he owned—*we* owned. Still a surreal concept. I sat next to him on the sofa and he continued discussing all the beneficial things the society had once achieved and what their purpose was supposed to have further evolved into, with the changing times.

I heard the hope in his voice—that perhaps the wayward society could be redeemed, somehow. There'd have to be a whole new faction adopted, obviously. But it was apparent Dane had found value in the Illuminati bloc once upon a time. When they'd all been on the straight and narrow.

As the jet gained altitude, he draped an arm around my shoulders and pulled me toward him, so I leaned against his chest. He kissed the top of my head and said, "I'm so sorry we're caught up in all of this. Again. I swear, if I'd have known a year ago how badly things would get twisted around I—"

"Don't say you never would have gotten involved with me," I urged. "That you wouldn't have pursued me—or married me."

"You'd be much better off without me."

"How do you figure?" I quietly demanded. "I have everything I could possibly want. You. Amsel. A gorgeous house I love. Our own little family with Amano, Rosa, and Kyle—stop scowling—and oh, yeah. I have you." I smiled, despite my own tension. "I *definitely* would not be better off without you, Dane. You've changed my life and—"

"Put you in jeopardy."

"If you haven't noticed, I'm pretty good at achieving that all on my own."

"Still," he said with unmistakable torment. "Kyle would be a much safer alternative."

I gaped. It took a few seconds for me to recover. "Did I just hear you right? *Now* you think I should have hooked up with him, when you employed great effort into scaring the shit out of him every time he got close to me?"

"It was sort of fun."

I laughed softly. "Yes, I noted how much fun you were having with all that grimacing going on and all those menacing looks you sent his way."

"I don't like how he hovers, always waiting for a chance to be alone with you."

Then I would certainly never mention the fact that Kyle had told me he loved me before we'd returned to the creek house. It was something he and I would eventually have to address, deal with. I felt bad that he still harbored feelings. Feelings that had always been and always would be unrequited.

That was a complicated mess I'd have to sort out once Dane and I ascertained what the hell was going on with Ethan and the others. What might or might not have been when it came to Dane's father.

I'd also have to devote some time to my own family drama. Try to help my father and keep his reputation intact by extracting Mommie Dearest from our lives. Perhaps when she discovered Dane had survived the Lux blast she'd run for the hills again. One could only hope. Though I couldn't count on it and my fear was that, any day now, she'd land a book deal and then all hell would break loose.

Too, I wondered incessantly what she'd done or was doing with the money Dane had given her to stay away from me. Had she blown through it already? In a year?

Honestly, I had no clue as to how my mother's mind worked,

what her ultimate goals were, and why she simply wouldn't just exist the way she used to without me in her life.

The remainder of the flight was just as unsettling as the beginning of our day had been. I tried to keep out of Dane's head, for the most part. And he urged me to sleep, since we'd be landing around seven in the morning, East Coast time.

But I was too keyed up to get my mind to shut down. How had everything gotten so fucked up this past year? Dane's dream of 10,000 Lux had been shattered. Our life together had been shattered. Now his trust had been shattered.

That had to rub him raw.

I was certain his mental state wasn't the best, and that hurt me all the more. I didn't know exactly how to comfort him. I couldn't assure him everything would be okay. I'd learned that from the onset, from the first time I'd met him.

The bottom line now was that I hated the constant torment. Even as he tried to hide it from me. I could fully comprehend the demons taunting him and that broke my heart. Made me even more apprehensive when we made our descent into Philadelphia.

What would we find here?

chapter 16

The Bax estate was comprised of a Colonial-style mansion sitting majestically on thirty acres of manicured grounds with three pools and several fountains, gardens, and courtyards. Tennis courts, a solarium, a greenhouse, the list went on and on. All of it was surrounded by shiny black wrought-iron fencing that was shrouded by tall, lush foliage.

The house itself was more like a hotel. Or the Louvre. The marbled corridors were wide and stretched endlessly in various directions, depending on to which wing you were headed. I needed a compass to navigate it all, though I'd still get lost.

I didn't exactly grasp the need for three formal dining rooms and four casual ones. Thirteen bedrooms and nineteen bathrooms. More living rooms, studies, and sitting areas than I could process as we passed them. A ballroom. A conservatory with a grand piano and various other instruments. That wasn't the only grand piano. I counted six others as we made our way to one of the back staircases that curved both upward and downward from the main floor.

As we went downstairs, I asked Dane, "You seriously grew up here?"

"You get used to it after a while."

"I can't see how. I'd have to leave bread crumbs to find my way to the bathroom. God forbid I should attempt to find one of the kitchens. You'd have to send a search and rescue team for me."

He chuckled, though it was a bit strained. The dark thoughts lingered—or likely intensified when it came to what we might discover in his father's vault.

I followed along as Dane headed into a mammoth library with floor-to-ceiling shelves, similar to what we had in our great room in Oak Creek Canyon, but this room was nearly the size of our entire home and the shelves spanned about twenty feet in height.

There were numerous metal railings with ladders attached for retrieving books. I figured there had to be a computer system that kept track of all the titles and their locations—or one just randomly climbed a ladder and scanned the novels until they found something of interest.

The room was also filled with sofas and chairs, end and coffee tables, lamps of varying sizes and heights, interesting artifacts and knickknacks. A bookworm could move in and never be heard from again.

And not mind the solitude.

Dane crossed to the far wall and selected a novel that he pulled out of its slot. Then he hooked his fingers in the side of the unit and gave a swift yank so that a narrow portion of the shelves opened like a door.

"Oh, no way." I scurried across the hardwood floor, instantly intrigued. "A secret passage?"

"The vault."

I joined him and stared at the massive metal door with a keypad along the side. Dane plugged in a series of numbers, got a green light and a beep, then repeated the process. The lock sprang free and he slid the metal pocket door to the side. We entered the vault, which probably could have doubled as a panic room or a fallout shelter. It was bigger than my first apartment. And obviously fully secure.

As I took in all the drawers and titanium-looking containers, Dane sought out a series of cabinets and entered another code. Then he started sifting through drawers.

Exhilaration pumped through me. "Can I help? I'm really good at discovering stuff I didn't even know I was looking for."

"Yes, you are." He opened another cabinet and said, "We're searching for anything related to the NOS, Ethan and the others, or even the summits my father might have attended."

"What about anything on Yale, in the event Ethan made visits there—or, for all we know, taught or even guest-lectured there?"

"Sure."

We dug in. Thankfully, we'd eaten on the plane with fresh catering or I'd get a little worried about the afternoon ahead of us. As it was, four or five hours slipped by with us finding absolutely nothing of value related to our quest.

There were some pretty interesting theories and documentaries Dane's father had drafted, and he kept just about everything related to primaries and elections on-hand—for decades. Not just locally and nationally, but worldwide. He had correspondence from some of the most famous leaders of the twentieth century and even had a healthy stack of information on Nixon and the Watergate scandal, which I would have devoured if Dane and I weren't on a more specific, imperative mission.

A TV or movie producer would have a field day in this room, with infinite possibilities screaming at them.

Unfortunately, *we* didn't find much benefit to our trip.

And I was starving.

"Can we take a break?" I asked.

He left his chair at one of the small tables and joined me on the other side of the vault. He kissed me, then said, "Of course. Let's eat."

While we had lunch on one of the many patios I did a little Web research, even though I knew that was likely pointless. But there had to be something we were missing—there had to be a clue somewhere that would give us a direction in which to go.

I considered some of Dane's investments—the ones that actually were linked to a few *Wall Street Journal* and the like articles he hadn't felt inclined to remove. That made me say, "Your father didn't necessarily have to be connected to Ethan via the society, though that would make sense, since Ethan later recruited you. But very simply, they could have been involved in joint ventures together. Business opportunities. No secret-society ties necessary."

"Most of his holdings are under his corporation, not joint ventures." Dane gave this more thought as I went back to surfing.

Neither of us came up with anything more significant to ponder. We spent a few more hours in the vault, with no substantial results.

After dinner, Dane showed me to his bedroom. He employed full house staff who maintained the mansion and grounds and kept clean linens on the beds and in the bathrooms. There were plenty of spirits and wines stocked throughout and food in the freezers and pantries, all in the event Dane dropped in unexpectedly, as he said he was prone to do from time to time. Whenever he traveled abroad, he flew out of Philadelphia so he could spend the night at the mansion.

I got the feeling he missed it. Mostly, he probably missed his aunt Lara. But since he'd grown up here, I could see how the memories would anchor him to the estate.

We showered, then got ready for bed.

As we settled under the covers, I asked, "Did your parents have this house built?"

"No, it's a family estate. My great-great-grandfather bought the land and constructed the main portion of the mansion. My great-grandfather added the west wing. My grandfather added the east wing. My father built the solarium and greenhouse."

"Hmm."

"What?"

"So much family history," I mused. "Generations intricately connected. Seriously, Dane, it would only make sense for your father—and maybe his father and so on—to be involved with the society."

"Too bad there's no one I can covertly ask. My ancestors are dead and I don't trust anyone in the network at this point. We're pretty much on our own, baby."

My fingertips glided over his temple and chiseled cheekbone. "You're not used to this. You're more accustomed to knowing exactly who to call in any given situation."

"It was a lot different having a network at my disposal. Especially one I helped to build."

"Is there any chance network members would come after us at this point?"

He was quiet a few moments. His silence did not bode well for my nerves.

"Dane," I eventually prompted, unable to handle the suspense a second longer.

"There's always a chance of something like that. Even Tom turned on me, when his back was to the wall. Others could feel threatened by what I might have offered to the FBI, the IRS, and international agencies."

As much as I'd convinced myself that Dane returning home meant the end of the danger, I should have known it wouldn't be that easy. That cut-and-dried.

With all the sinister machinations to brood over, I decided now was as good a time as any to give Dane some potentially happier news. Maybe something to take his mind off the chaos for at least a few minutes.

So I told him, "All those holes on your office wall weren't just for my web or the nursery decorations. I had another project I started while you were away. I removed all the evidence before you returned."

One dark brow lifted. "I'm not going to like this, am I?"

"Hear me out first. Then decide." I remained cuddled alongside him, my head on his chest, my fingers gliding lightly over his warm skin and hard muscles.

"I'm listening," he said. "Though you know how much you're distracting me, right?"

"I can't resist touching you."

"I'm not complaining. But you'd better tell me what's on your mind, because mine's wandering in a totally different direction."

The sensual tinge to his voice almost made me forget what I had to say. Almost.

I bucked up. Dove right in. "You know that when we all thought you were dead everything you owned became mine. All that money, all those investments."

"You started another foundation," he guessed. "Ari, that's not a problem. I told you, my money is your money, whether I'm alive or not. If you found another cause you want to support, I'm fully behind you. In fact, I'm impressed with your philanthropic nature."

"I am extremely grateful I was able to set up the autism and low-income, single-mom foundations to help others, Dane. I have you to thank for that, because, at the end of the day, it's your cash flow supporting both."

"No, Ari." His arm about my shoulders held me tighter. "Baby, I told you. It's yours. Ours. And you dedicating funds to something meaningful and worthwhile is never, ever going to be an issue with me. You don't have to ask. You don't have to worry about getting my approval. I trust you. Implicitly."

Emotion welled within me. As of now, I was just about the only one he trusted, aside from Amano and Jackson. So I knew what a monumental statement that was for Dane to make.

"You really deserve some sort of reward for all that you've done," I told him. "For all that you've sacrificed. That's why I wanted to do something for you, Dane. I wanted to give you something. But what do you give the amazing man who has everything?"

"Are you pregnant again?"

The spark of hope in his eyes lit my insides. And my heart skipped a few beats.

"Would you mind?"

"Are you kidding? I was thinking another two or three or four would be just fine."

My eyes bulged. *"Four* more?" I wasn't sure how I felt about that many kids. Luckily, I didn't have to dissect that conundrum at the moment. But I did say, "I would love to have a daughter. Have a real relationship with her, you know? Not the atrocious one I have with my own mother."

"Oh, God." He grunted. "Not her again."

"Yeah, my thoughts exactly. Believe me, she's the last person I want to discuss right now. And for the record, no, I'm not pregnant. That would be like one of the quickest conceptions in the history of the world."

"I've always been an overachiever," he said with a cocky grin.

"I'm well aware of that—and the fact that your arrogance knows no bounds. But currently, stud, you haven't knocked me up a second time."

"Hmm. I'll have to work on that then."

He made a move to roll over and position himself between my legs, but I pressed a hand to his chest.

"Just wait. I'm not done."

His lips brushed mine and he murmured, "Can you make it quick? I have a lot of lost bedroom time to make up for."

My stomach fluttered. "Glad to see that's a top priority for you."

"Never doubt it."

He kissed me. Seductively. Enticingly. Igniting a slow burn that spread outward from my core, making my inner thighs quiver and my pussy thrum. Need and excitement rippled through me as his tongue slid over mine, curling and teasing.

My hand shifted from his pecs and threaded through his hair. I pressed my body to his, wishing I'd bypassed the satin nightgown so I could feel his skin against mine.

Dane's thoughts apparently mirrored mine, because he fisted the material close to my knee and gathered the long, full skirt on one side and pushed it up to my waist. His fingers skimmed over the front of my lacy thong and my hips jerked in silent demand for him.

His mouth left mine and skated along my neck, down to the tops of my breasts, where he left feathery kisses that teased me further.

"I love how you taste," he whispered. "Not just here."

He moved lower. His fingers twined in the thin strands of my panties and he gave a yank, so that I raised my butt.

"These are nice, but they have to go." He dragged the lace down my legs and tossed the lingerie aside. Then his lips swept over my flesh, up the inside of one thigh, and to my sex.

His warm breath blew across my dewy folds, making me squirm. I spread my legs wider for him. He wedged his large frame in the vee I created and his head dipped, his mouth grazing my cleft.

"Dane," I muttered as I clasped his shoulder. "Make me come."

His tongue flitted over my clit, lightning quick. A moan fell from my lips as a searing sensation blazed through me. He tugged on my sensitive flesh with his mouth.

"Oh, God." My eyelids grew heavy. All previous thoughts fled my mind. "That's so good."

He used the pads of his thumbs to massage my folds, then the tip of his tongue flickered against that knot of nerves once more. I writhed beneath him as exhilaration raced through me.

I held him close with my hand still on his shoulder and the fingers of my other hand buried in his thick hair. My hips lifted and I pressed myself to his mouth as he skillfully licked and then deeply suckled.

"Dane. Christ. I love this. You are so damn talented."

He rimmed my opening with his tongue; then it pressed inside me. I gasped. My body jerked.

"Oh, yes. God, yes, Dane."

He went back to the wicked flicking of the tip of his tongue against my clit. He eased a finger into my pussy and pumped steadily, making me whimper, making my pulse soar.

I quaked under his expert touch, my lids drifting closed. My chest heaved and my breasts felt tender, heavy. My puckered nipples tingled and ached for his attention, but I was held enrapt by the way he diligently licked my pussy. He worked in a second finger and stroked forcefully, pushing me right to the edge.

I let out a throaty moan as the pressure built within me. Dane picked up the pace and suckled my clit again as his fingers drove deep.

"That's perfect," I rasped. "So fantastic. God . . . Oh, God! I'm going to come." The erotic sensations swelled, then burst wide open, burning through me. "Dane!"

I came on a fevered rush that stole my breath and sent tremors tearing through my body. Little white orbs flashed behind my closed lids.

"Holy cow," I whispered. "Unbelievable."

I opened my eyes and found him watching me, a hint of satisfaction in his smoldering eyes, but mostly I saw the need to be inside me.

I relinquished my grip on his shoulder and crooked a finger at him. "Come here. Let me show you how much I appreciate the effort you put into getting me off."

He slipped from the bed and divested himself of his briefs. I crawled toward the edge of the mattress and eyed his thick, erect shaft. I licked my lips, finding him tempting, tantalizing.

My fingers encircled the base of his cock. I ran my tongue along one side of him, up to the tip. Then swirled around the crown, causing him to pull in a harsh breath. I closed my mouth over him and took him deep, sucking hard.

"Oh, yeah," he said in a gruff voice. "Just like that."

His fingers tangled in my hair. He rocked slightly, pumping into my mouth.

"Baby. Goddamn, you get me going."

I cupped his balls and gently rolled as I continued sucking him.

After a few more seconds he pulled away. "I want to come inside you." His tone was dark and sexy. My pussy ached for him.

I stared up at him and fluttered my lashes. "You can have me however you want me."

It was the next morning, after Dane had made love to me again, and I lay on top of him, boneless and euphoric, when I said, "I didn't get around to telling you my news."

His fingertips stroked my spine. I was propped up by my forearms on his chest as I gazed at him.

He said, "I figured you'd get to it after two or three orgasms."

"Try four."

"Not even a personal best." He made a soft tsking sound. "I'm slacking off."

With a smile, I assured him, "Each one was more spectacular than the last. I'm quite pleased."

He chuckled. "Okay, then. Give me your news."

I took a few deep breaths, letting them out slowly. "I told you I wanted to give you something, Dane. That something is 10,000 Lux."

He stared at me, the wheels in his mind clearly spinning, though he didn't appear to latch on to a sane explanation for what I'd just sprung on him.

I said, "I have documentation that shows the land and the hotel were willed to me when you 'died,' and I gave that documentation to the original engineer and architectural teams and told them I wanted to rebuild the lobby, offices, and suites that were destroyed. I want to open the Lux, Dane. For you."

He continued to stare, completely at a loss for words.

I gave him a few moments to let my news sink in.

A few more to process.

Several more to form a coherent thought that I hoped wouldn't include *you fucking did what?*

"Dane?" I tentatively asked when it seemed a couple of minutes had ticked by.

He opened his mouth to speak. No words came out.

I repositioned myself, sitting up and straddling his midsection. "Say something," I urged.

I'd never stumped him, rendered him speechless. Not even when he'd found out I was having his baby. Dane Bax was not a man you caught off-guard or left stupefied. That was his job, actually. Particularly when it came to me.

"Dane?" I waved a hand in front of his face. "You okay? Honey?"

He suddenly came around. His hands clasped my waist and he moved me slightly so that he could sit up, with me still in his lap. "You only call me honey when you think you've done something I won't like."

"Have I?"

"I don't know."

My stomach took a dive south. *Shit.* Maybe I should have asked his permission first. Warned him well in advance of my intentions.

What had I been thinking?

He moved me again and climbed out of bed. Did his token pacing while I watched. And resisted the desire to gnaw on my lip or my nails. My stomach stayed hunkered down around my knees, all twisted up.

When I couldn't take the silence any longer, I said, "Look, Amano told me you'd probably mow the whole thing down since the lobby had been destroyed, and maybe that's because it'll never be the same. I mean, even with the same team and the same plans, it's not going to be exactly the same. I had to order specially crafted fixtures, but they're very similar, Dane, and so very, very stunning. I swear. I wouldn't put a trash receptacle on that property if it wasn't the most artistically designed container imaginable. You know I'd never—"

"Ari." He held up his hand, effectively cutting me off. His tone had done that just as well. "You're rebuilding the Lux?"

"Yes."

"My hotel?"

"Yes."

"You?"

"Well." I let out a nervous laugh. "Not me personally, obviously. But I am overseeing the whole thing remotely. After all, it was constructed once. It's not as though the people I rehired haven't already connected Part A to Part B and so on. Even better, it was determined that the main building is structurally sound. I have certification for it. We're currently rebuilding the center section. No small undertaking, but at least we don't have to—"

"Ari." Again with the hand. "You're rebuilding my hotel?"

"Am I not speaking English?" I inquired, a bit perplexed.

"Our hotel," he mused. "You're rebuilding *our* hotel."

"You did make me sign papers at our wedding that gave me half of the Lux," I reminded him. "All of it, in the event anything happened to you. And for a while, I did think something had happened to you, so—"

"You are unbelievable."

I gazed at him, not at all sure what went through his mind. My apprehension mounted. "Is that *unbelievable* in the good sense . . . or the bad sense?"

"Baby." He grinned, yet his eyes burned with a different emotion. Not just delight, but . . . awe. "You never cease to amaze me."

He joined me in bed again and cupped the side of my face with his hand. I'd seen a myriad of feelings cross his devilishly handsome features over the past year. The expression I thought was reserved strictly for the birth of his child apparently applied to the Lux as well, because Dane was as equally fascinated, grateful, and filled with wonderment now as he had been when he'd laid eyes on our son for the first time.

"You know how much 10,000 Lux means to me," Dane said as he stared deep into my eyes. "It was my dream—my only dream. Until I met you. What happened to the resort . . . It devastated me, Ari. Not as much as losing you would devastate me, but I couldn't bear to think about it, envision it in my mind, consider what the hell I'd do about it, without wanting to kill Horton and Vale."

I sucked in a breath. "You know how I feel about that, Dane."

"I didn't do it, did I?" he said. "But I wanted to. I've spent endless nights lying in bed plotting my revenge. The one thing I didn't strategize was how to revive 10,000 Lux. I really couldn't bring myself to consider it."

"You don't have to," I assured him. "I'm not saying I totally know what I'm doing, but again, I'm working with the people who *do* know what to do. And once it's structurally complete, Amano can help with all the functions that will bring the hotel back on-line. Dane, we can still have our grand opening. You can still have your dream hotel."

He fell silent again. My tension didn't ease.

"Are you happy about this?" I finally asked.

"Hell, yes, I'm happy," he said emphatically. "I'm just . . . blown away. My God, is there anything you won't take on?"

"I think we already know the answer to that."

"Rattlesnakes and scorpions," we said at the same time.

He shook his head. "Jesus, Ari. I'm just floored. I can't even fathom how you've managed to do this."

"It's only a start, Dane. Don't get too excited."

"Doesn't matter," he told me. "The fact that it means enough to you to do this—"

"It *does* mean a lot to me, Dane. Because it means a lot to you. And because I love the Lux, too. I couldn't stand the idea of it abandoned and left sitting to rot. Or being completely demolished. That broke my heart. I had to do *something*."

He kissed me fiercely. I was breathless when he pulled away and he said, "I honestly didn't know how I would face the Lux when the thought of what happened makes me so irrational and—"

"Not homicidal." I pressed my finger to his lips. "I'm not saying you don't have the right, but you know how that disturbs me. Greatly."

Pushing my hand away, he said, "I know. Doesn't mean I'm not going to feel it, though."

"Vale is dead, anyway. And Wayne Horton will get what's coming to him. The society members you cut from the Lux have no vested interest and are going to prison as well. The only thing you have to figure out is what to do about Ethan, Qadir, and Nikolai. Jackson doled out the equal amounts of insurance money, based on their percentage of investment. I don't know how it works going forward, since you all were committed together at varying degrees, but now—"

"Shit, Ari." He scooted away and stood again.

"Yeah, I get it. They might still hold an interest in the hotel, but Jackson will—"

"No, wait." Dane dragged a hand down his face. "You just hit on the one thing we didn't look for yesterday."

I eyed him curiously. "Sorry. Not following you."

"My father's investments."

"We did talk about that. He had strictly corporate holdings under his own umbrella."

"Sure, for his major businesses. But maybe there actually were joint investments I never knew about."

I caught on quick. "Like investments he might have held with other society members? Or . . . Ethan?"

"I know Ethan's conglomerate names and investment groups. Where's your iPad?"

I slipped from the bed and rushed to the sofa in the corner where I'd left my tote bag. I pulled out the tablet and handed it over. Dane settled in next to me again and started surfing. I kept quiet, not interrupting or sidetracking him, because he looked like a man on a mission.

I watched him plug in names on various state incorporation sites. Owners' names popped up, but nothing connected to his father. Dane continued for an hour or so, clearly racking his brain for all the possibilities he could recall. Then, suddenly, his fingers stopped tapping. His entire body stilled.

I'd just emerged from the shower. "Dane?" I asked. "What?"

"I found it," he said. "The investment group they all belonged to—all of them, the entire society. Formed in 1978."

"Ethan knew your father that far back? And never said anything?" I could strangle the man myself. "Asshole."

"I think it's worse than that."

I stared quizzically at him. "Why?"

"This is about more than just an investment group."

"Sure, the secret society—"

"And the fact that no one has mentioned to me, in twelve years of being with the society, that my father was previously a part of the faction. That he was a member as well. I *am* a generational member."

Yes, that was bad.

Mysterious and . . . devious?

"There's a hell of a lot more going on than them wanting a piece of 10,000 Lux. And I'll figure it out if it's the last thing I do."

The breath rushed from my lungs.

I *so* did not like his words.

chapter 17

Dane left me to go run several miles on the treadmill and then beat the shit out of his punching bag. I considered tagging along, because I didn't want to be away from him, especially when he was so volatile. But I needed food—and he would, too, when he was done expending some of his aggression.

So I made my way to one of the kitchens, with some guidance from a housekeeper or two. The staff from last night offered to cook breakfast and I decided that was a good idea, since my mind was much too hyperactive at the moment. I would have burned anything I'd tried to prepare as I mentally waded through everything that had happened in the last twenty-four hours. Like Dane, I was a bit mind blown myself. For a number of reasons.

I ate without him and then headed back down to the vault. I'd search one piece of paper at a time until I found what we needed.

Dane joined me sometime later, after he'd showered. He started on the opposite side of the vault and we worked our way around the room, not even close to meeting in the middle when

Dane jerked an entire file folder from the drawer. A thick one. Three more followed.

"Whatcha got there?" I asked.

Dane sat across me from where I sifted through my own files.

"EBHACVHBWM Holdings. The most god-awful corporation name to register, but all the right initials. Evans, Bax, Hilliard, Avril, Casterelli, Vasil, Hakim, Bent, Wellington."

"That is monstrous."

"Doesn't really matter. I highly doubt it was ever put on a business card or commercial real estate sign. Though they apparently had numerous investments."

"What about the M at the end? You didn't have a name associated with it."

He glanced back at the documents. "Right."

"What state was the company incorporated in?"

Digging around some more, he eventually said, "A Delaware closed corporation."

I Googled the Delaware trademarks site, pulled up the exact link I needed, and had Dane rattle off the litany of initials once more. I entered the registry. Nothing came up. But there was a section for dead registrations, so I copied and pasted the name into that form.

Bingo!

I scrolled down to the principals listed as investors. Found all of the members Dane had pinpointed. The last name, however, made my stomach plummet and my heart twist.

"Shit," I mumbled.

Dane took the iPad from me and scanned the page onscreen. His entire disposition hardened as he stared at a very incriminating piece of evidence we'd never pondered. Would never conceive of pondering.

"William Madsen," he said through clenched teeth.

My mind worked a little too quickly on this one. Mostly

because I was getting used to the threads of betrayal, even if every strand shocked me to the core of my being.

"Brought into the investments by your father?" I queried. "Or planted in your lives by Ethan?"

Dane's head snapped up. We stared at each other.

I let the idea sink in.

Then I asked, "Exactly how well does Mikaela know Ethan Evans?"

Tension visibly gripped Dane. So much for working out his aggression.

He said, "I introduced them when I started work on the Lux."

"Are you sure that's the first time they met?"

"I can't really be sure about anything, now can I, Ari?"

I winced. "No. But it seems they'd have to have a significant connection for her to smack him twice at the baptism—and not have him react."

Dane's expression turned grave.

I added, "I saw them, in a nook, remember? Intense conversation, smack. More intense conversation, another smack. The TV drama-type slap, like one woman finds out her best friend is sleeping with her husband and he's decided to leave her for the friend—and the pre-nup sucks."

"Jesus Christ."

"Sorry. Just giving you the severity level."

"No, it's not you." He shook his head. "I'm just trying to figure out how this could all be."

"When did the Madsens buy the estate down the road?"

"They moved in when I was five or six. Amano drove Mikaela and me to and from school for Mrs. Madsen. That's how we became such close friends."

"Close enough that she would know all about your comings and goings, your plans for the future, how well you did in school, what your special talents might be, like financial forecasting?"

"Ari—"

"Just hear me out," I rushed on. "She could have easily been a spy for the society without even knowing it. All she had to do was answer casual, unassuming queries from her father, all posed under the guise of taking interest in her day. Since you two were friends, it wouldn't have been out of the ordinary for her to tell him everything she knew about you."

He pressed a finger and thumb to his brows, as though fighting off a migraine. I felt wretched for him.

"That still doesn't make a direct connection with Ethan," Dane said. "Madsen wouldn't exactly have had him over for Sunday dinner—not if they were both society members; the ties are meant to be secretive. And besides, Madsen was rarely ever home, because he's been a U.S. ambassador since I've known him. He's always been overseas."

Thinking back to the baptism, I said, "I can understand Mikaela being upset that Ethan knew you were alive and didn't tell her. But enough to hit him? If anything, I thought that rage would be directed toward me. It wasn't. In fact, she was shocked, but not volatile in any way. So why erupt with Ethan?"

"I have no idea. But you can be damn sure I'm going to find out."

I set aside the iPad. Dane went back to plowing through the files, his frown deepening until it turned into more of a menacing glare. A lot of head shaking ensued.

A good hour or so passed and I said, "Dane, you can't leave me in suspense here."

"Sorry." He groaned his disgruntlement. "So, they all went in together on several joint ventures from '78 to '83. But there are all of these receipts"—he held one up for me to see—"that show reimbursement to Bradley Bax for his percentage of the initial investments. One per venture."

"So he was involved initially, then they cashed him out?"

"Because he backed out?" Dane wondered.

"Possibly. If he started to suspect something fishy."

Dane got to his feet and prowled the vault. "I was born in 1983. My parents died in 1983."

"And the last reimbursement came in 1983. Just two weeks before you were born." I waved the slip from the very back of the last folder in the air.

"Six weeks before they died."

We stared at each other. Sure, my conspiracy theorist mind went in all different directions, but inevitably it landed on one particular thought. "Is it conceivable that your father realized things weren't going the way they were supposed to with the society, he pulled out, and they let him, for appearance's sake? Even went so far as to give him the money due. And then six weeks later . . . ?"

"They killed him. And my mother was a casualty of war?"

"Victim of circumstance. There's no justifying it. But let's extrapolate."

He gave me a teasing look, despite the gravity of the situation. "Do you have any idea how sexy it is to hear you use the term *extrapolate*?"

I laughed. "Only a brainiac such as yourself would find that sexy."

"Okay, maybe it's just you in general."

"Stay focused."

"Right."

"So you said that Ethan had wooed you from the beginning, when you arrived at Harvard. Is it really too far-fetched to assume that he and the other members of the society kept tabs on you from birth? Using Mikaela as a source of information."

He considered this.

I continued. "Were there indications that you'd end up at Harvard instead of Yale or Princeton or wherever? Did Ethan follow your progress and align himself accordingly, so that the two of you were 'destined' to meet? And then he recruited you without ever having to mention that you technically *did* fall within the generational rule of the Illuminati?"

"At this point, nothing is too far-fetched. And all of it is fucking bullshit." Angst rolled off him in waves as we got closer and closer to an absolute revelation he might have to accept. The emotion was mixed with something even stronger—a rage I suspected was related directly to the implication that his parents might have died by society hands.

That would be more excruciating for him to face than Ethan's betrayal.

I kept sifting through the files Dane had extracted from drawers.

"Unfortunately"—I loathed admitting the reality of the situation—"the plot thickens."

"Ari!" he ground out, tormented.

"Dane." I'd located the last needle in the haystack. Extracting the gold coin from an accordion sealed folder, I flattened it on my thumb and then flicked my thumb with my index finger, sending the coin Dane's way.

He caught it with one hand. Kept his gaze on me as he opened his fist.

"Final proof," I simply said.

He tore his emerald eyes from mine and stared at the NOS insignia in his hand.

"Fuck!"

I nodded. I could see how this gutted him, and that pained me, too. But there was no way to hide from this, no way to shove the files and the evidence into the drawers, seal the vault shut, and pretend we never pieced together an insidious puzzle that went well beyond my web on our office wall.

We'd just thrown onto the table the very real possibility that Dane's entire life, his entire existence, was based on a lie.

Worse . . .

It'd been orchestrated from birth until this very second.

I drifted in and out of sleep while Dane scoured more paperwork, agonized, analyzed, internalized. I couldn't even begin to fathom what churned through his system at this point, while he spent hours grinding over every little tidbit unearthed.

I had known from the age of five what my mother was all about and what my home life would be, how the interactions would play out, and what to expect. As hostile as the environment had been because of her, at least it was predictable.

Even as shitty as my childhood had been when all of my father's money had gone to Maleficent and he hadn't been able to continue to compete professionally because of his shoulder injuries and everything in our life had turned dark and dismal, there had been a huge amount of certainty.

That certainty had all been centered around the fact that my mother was a selfish, money-hungry bitch. There'd not once been any proof otherwise, and she hadn't put any effort into correcting the image or our opinion of her over the years, the decades. If anything, she'd found creative ways to exemplify and perpetuate the role she apparently loved playing.

Unfortunately for Dane, he'd never had a demon staring him so squarely in the face—that demon being the society he'd believed in. Vale Hilliard and Wayne Horton had come damn close to tearing him apart with their Machiavellian plots against me and the Lux, but this was Dane's parents we were talking about.

Chances were very good his father hadn't crossed to the dark side along with Ethan or anyone else. For the most part, all evidence pointed to Bradley doing exactly as Dane had done when he'd discovered things had gone horrifically wrong—finding a way out.

Yet Dane had no one to confront, no one to question. If there'd been a generation of Bax men who'd occupied a seat at the table, they were long since dead and buried. Dane couldn't consult them. And it wasn't as though he could ring up Ethan and ask *him*, right?

Not blatantly at any rate. Not without repercussions we were not at all prepared to deal with at the moment, as we acclimated to this new scenario. This new peril.

To that point, I grew infinitely agitated as we showered and got around the next morning, after packing up all of the documentation Dane had collected and we put the vault back together.

I didn't like being away from Amsel for so long. It made me even more nervous since Dane and I had encountered additional sinister doings. Dane spoke with Amano and assured me all was well back home, but I'd never fully accept that until we were in Sedona and my son was in my arms. So, with no other reason to hang around Philly, we flew home.

Dane was abnormally quiet. Not that he talked much on a regular basis. He was a brooder by nature. I could easily amend that and consider him a ruminator by nature, because he was deep in thought, as usual. I didn't interrupt. I couldn't offer anything to tip the scales for him, so I flipped absently through magazines while he mentally debated everything we'd discovered, his jaw and his fists clenching from time to time.

Dismay set up permanent residency low in my belly, keeping me unsettled.

The matter of what had really gone on between 1978 and 1983, what the Bax family's involvement was with the society, and what had truly happened to his parents were confounding enough. But one other issue reared its ugly head in my mind.

If Ethan discovered we'd pieced the puzzle together, what then?

If he was in cahoots with the corrupt members who'd conspired to destroy the Lux, who'd executed attacks on me, who'd do anything to get what they wanted or thought they deserved or were owed, then all of this *wasn't* over. We'd just added another layer to the danger that darkened our doorstep.

"Don't look so worried," Dane finally whispered as he leaned toward me and kissed my cheek.

"I can't help it. There are roots buried deep that neither of us ever considered, because you trusted Ethan and didn't know your father's connection with him or the society."

"I'll figure this out. We'll deal with it."

"Dane." I shook my head, let out a long breath. "If Ethan's been the puppet master all this time, for over three decades . . . What's going to stop him now?"

"Not what. *Who*." He gave a solemn look. "Me."

My eyes closed briefly. "I just got you back. You did everything asked of you, everything you could do in order to bring down the society. And still it's not enough."

I felt the tears build, but I pushed them back. I was angry, hurt, scared. And so very, very tired. I just wanted everything to be normal. Everything *should* be normal. Dane had gone through hell to make sure justice was served. Yet he still wasn't free of the corruption. If anything, he was trapped further. Like there was no escape for him. For us.

"This is crap!" I blurted.

"Yes. But I've got some ideas."

"Do I even want to hear them? Why can't you just be done with this?"

"Because *it's* not done, Ari. Understand, I can't just let this drift."

I shook my head.

He pulled me to him, tucking me against his rigid body. "Just sleep, baby. You need to sleep."

I did, but as soon as we landed I was at it again with the questions. Dane didn't have anything new to say, not that I expected him to. I was just too agitated to let it all slip.

When we reached home, I couldn't get Amsel in my arms fast

enough. Dane was practically breathing down my neck, but it took a bit longer than I'd imagined to relinquish my hold on our son.

I gave him over and said to Kyle, "More trouble headed our way."

"Ari." Dane glared.

The ominous news seemed to perk Kyle up. Not a good thing. He needed to get over this adrenaline rush he was riding.

"What's going on?" he enthusiastically asked.

"It'd probably be a good time for you to make a decision on the FBI or CIA," I told him. "Start your training. Leave all of this behind. Because it's burned deep—into a lot of lives."

"Whatever it is, bring it on," he said, his chest puffing out. He looked all studly and determined and it made me admire his courage as much as I loathed him not getting a break from the danger any more than the rest of us. Worse, he seemed to crave it these days, thrive on it.

I left Dane, Amano, and Amsel and dragged Kyle into the kitchen. "I need ice cream," I told him. "Drowning in chocolate. Stat."

"Easy enough." He whipped up sundaes while I explained the current predicament.

"Whoa," he said when I was done. "Did *not* see that one coming."

"I know, right? Ethan playing double agent? And since 1978?"

"That sucks for Dane."

The bit of empathy stunned me, coming from Kyle. But I appreciated the sentiment.

He continued. "To not really have a clear family history and then to have something this severe heaped onto you? Very uncool."

His compassion touched me. "It's all a pretty big blow to him, yes. I can't quite figure out what he's feeling, though. He has his moments of angst, but then he tries to conceal it all and pretend it's just a math equation to work out."

"Some equation. His best friend and mentor fucked him royally."

"Probably did the same to Dane's father, too. And I strongly suspect Qadir and Nikolai have no idea they've been played by Ethan as well. They weren't part of the society at that time. Their fathers were, though. And included in the investment group."

"So now the secret society implodes. Good riddance to a faction that should have stayed the course and didn't. Dane testifies against Ethan with the evidence he has on the hard drive and that asshole goes down, too."

I swirled some hot fudge around the tip of my spoon and asked, "Got any caramel or butterscotch? I need it."

"The double whammy?" His gaze narrowed on me. "What gives?"

I sighed, not the least bit thrilled to drop the bomb. "There is no evidence. Whatever might have served Dane well in this scenario is missing from the laptop Ethan retrieved from Switzerland. He removed a hundred and sixty files before he handed it over to Amano."

Kyle stared at me as though I'd just grown a third eye.

"Kyle?"

"Oh, no way."

"Way."

He whirled around and went for the butterscotch, which he warmed up and then added to my sundae.

"Come on, Ari," he said. "Your dude and I do not gel, but now I'm feeling the sucker punches myself. Ethan, of all people, betrayed Dane—*all* of us?"

"I know. It's pretty painful."

"And deadly."

"There is that." I dug in, not sure what else to say.

Kyle seemed to absorb my revelations, at a loss as well. Finally, he said, "You know I'm not just walking away. You've still got a red dot on your forehead."

My head jerked up.

"Figuratively speaking," he was quick to say, bringing my pulse down a notch. "Because Ethan knows you're Dane's weakness."

I dropped my spoon in the empty dish. "Ethan knows about Amsel. Don't forget that."

"His own godson? He'd target his own *godson*?"

My heart thundered. "You know the kind of people we're dealing with here."

"But Amsel?" Kyle gripped the side of the counter, dropped his head, and shook it.

"Deception cuts deep, doesn't it?" I was feeling it to the core of my being. Kyle was just as tangled in the barbed wire as the rest of us.

"It's downright vicious," he said.

"Yes."

"So what's your husband going to do about it?"

"I don't know," I admitted.

"And that scares you?"

"Of course."

Kyle backed away from the counter and paced. "You realize Ethan is a worse threat than Vale or Horton? He has more money, more power, more connections, more motivation—and a hell of a lot less of a soul if he can pull this sort of shit."

"I've reached that conclusion, too."

"And Qadir and Nikolai?"

"There's absolutely nothing that suggests they're involved," I said. "And they joined the society right before Dane. Like within months. It seems as though they have no idea Dane's father was once a member. The code is absolute secrecy—even amongst family. Dane broke that code for me, because I insisted I needed to know."

"Maybe you ought to rethink your boundaries on what you find acceptable, Ari."

I let him get in the digs he felt he deserved. Then I said, "I have two favors to ask you." I shoved aside my bowl. "I want you to carefully consider them both and then do the absolute right thing. What's best for *you*. Not me. Not my family. Not even my son. Just you."

"Ari." He halted and stared deep into my eyes. "Don't give me ultimatums."

My stomach coiled. "I don't have a choice, Kyle. You and me . . . we're a lot alike. We do what our heart tells us to do. We follow our gut reactions. Sometimes we're right. Sometimes we're wrong. But we always have good intentions."

He groaned. "Already, I'm not liking this."

"Kyle," I began, dread and tension gripping me. "There's a difference between honor and stupidity. Sadly, neither of us knows that difference."

His jaw clenched.

I continued. "Dane doesn't do anything without thinking it through from start to finish. And he's wicked-fast about it. When it comes to the two of us . . . We know when something needs to be done, but we don't always think the solution through to its natural conclusion."

"Get to the point, Ari," he said in an agitated tone. "What are the two favors?"

I stood and planted my hands on the counter. "I want you to leave. Now."

"Not going to happen," he said without missing a beat. "Next?"

I closed my eyes again, shook my head. "I asked you to give careful consideration to—"

"Next?" he softly demanded.

My lids fluttered open. We gazed at each other across the kitchen island. He was my best friend and I trusted him with my life. I trusted him with my son's life. That meant my second favor would not be a small one. "Stay and protect Amsel. Not me, not Dane. Not even Rosa. I'm sending her away. Just Amsel."

"Ari—"

"Just my son, Kyle," I insisted. "He is your only concern, your only focus. No matter what. I can have five red dots on my forehead. Your only thought is protecting my son. And keeping yourself alive."

He gave me a strange look. Then asked, "You're really hoping I'll just walk away?"

"For your own safety, yes."

"But what would be the point?"

"You'd still be alive next week."

His shoulders bunched. His jaw tightened again. "And you might be dead. Your son might be dead. In what world could I possibly live with that?"

"Kyle—"

"No," he said, cutting me off. "Maybe you and I will never be." He threw his arms up in exasperation. "Okay, yeah. You and I will never be," he huffed while tears stung the backs of my eyes over this very touchy conversation. "But that doesn't mean I could just leave. Whatever danger you're in, whatever danger your son is in—that's *my* danger, too, Ari."

His conviction was punctuated by his hostile and adamant tone. Kyle clearly had no intention of backing down.

He told me, "We've been in this together from the beginning and we'll continue to be in it together. Until this is done, Ari. That's *our* for better or for worse."

He stormed past me, out of the kitchen.

I stared after him, trying to catch my breath.

chapter 18

Later in the evening, I met up with Kyle once more. This time on the terrace.

He sipped Dane's good brandy while staring out across the creek, into the dense forest. Silver streaks from the moonlight filtered through the trees and cast glittery sprays over the rapids.

"You know I wasn't telling you that I want you to leave, right?" I asked as I joined him at the wrought-iron railing. "Not in the *it's time to move on* sense. It's just that you've made it this far without fully taking a bullet for anyone. I'd like to keep it that way."

"I know what you want," he said, still gazing out into the heavily wooded area beyond the steady stream of water. "It's what I want, too. For us to somehow be friends, despite it all."

"I've always loved Dane." I couldn't allow Kyle to have any delusions about that. "I always will."

"I know."

"I love you, too, Kyle. Just not in the same way. Never in the same way. From the first time I saw Dane, something happened to me. Something changed inside and it can't be changed back. It won't be changed back, ever. I wouldn't want it to."

"You could end up dead, Ari."

"I realize that." In a gentle tone, I said, "But I still choose him."

Kyle's gaze finally slid my way. "I get it. I don't agree with it, and personally, I think you're making a huge mistake by passing up my witty repartee and smooth moves, but . . . I do get it. The heart wants what the heart wants, right?"

"You'll do much better than me," I promised. "Someone with slightly less drama would be nice, huh?"

He chuckled, though it was a bit strained. "Slightly less."

"Just a tiny bit."

"Otherwise, I'd be bored?"

"You do seem to handle insanity without being too traumatized by it."

"That's what the brandy is for. And when it happens to be your husband's favorite, extremely expensive label I'm about to polish off, that makes it even better."

"You do love the ragged edge, don't you?"

"Beats a desk job any day."

I was afraid he'd feel that way. "So I guess you won't be rejoining the Marketing department when we open the Lux."

"You told Dane about your grand plan?"

"Yes."

"And?"

"He was happy. Really happy. And so am I." One thing I could breathe a sigh of relief about. Too bad it was the *only* thing.

Kyle let out a notably irrate sound, then said, "Except for that minor, pesky detail of Ethan Evans wanting to kill you."

"There is that."

We were both quiet a few moments; lost in ominous thoughts. Eventually, Kyle murmured, "I'm not the only one who likes the ragged edge."

I couldn't argue the point—had already considered it myself

some time ago. But told him, "The difference is, I will be thrilled to go back to my event planning."

"Of course. Because bridezillas are even scarier than secret-society members who bomb hotels. You really should seek help."

"Pot. Kettle. Black." I crooked a brow at him.

He gave me his megawatt smile. "I keep telling you that we're meant for each other."

I narrowed my eyes.

Kyle grinned. "As friends."

"Friends." I gave him a long hug, feeling torn between my relief that we still had him on our side and fear of anything happening to him.

When he pulled away, he said, "There are two fingers of brandy left, and they have my name on them."

"Enjoy." I left him on the terrace and went in search of Rosa.

I wasn't sure what direction to give her for her own safety, so I'd leave that up to Dane and Amano. I just wanted her to know how much I appreciated everything she'd done for us and that I couldn't have her in danger. We'd send her away with enough money for her to sail off on the cruise of a lifetime, for the rest of her life, if she so chose. And if she wanted a bodyguard, we'd provide for that, too.

Not that I anticipated her having any trouble. She'd never been a target and wouldn't be of interest to anyone once she left this house and was no longer anywhere near me or Amsel. Still, she meant too much to all of us to not ensure she was protected and taken care of.

After I explained everything to her, she said, "I don't have to leave."

"Rosa, it's too dangerous for you to stay. Maybe once this is all over and done with—if it all works out the way it's supposed to and we're safe again—then, naturally, we'd want you back. That's if you're not too enamored with the margaritas, sunshine, and gorgeous tanned men on the beach."

Not buying into my levity, she stood and paced her bed-room. "I don't scare so easily, *chica*," she told me in her thick accent.

"We've already discovered that. And, believe me, we all ad-mire how devoted and coolheaded you are. But this is so much more than anyone should have to endure."

"So Kyle is leaving, too?"

"No. Kyle is staying."

"Then I stay." She crossed her arms over her chest. Pinned me with a look. Really dug in her heels.

"Rosa."

"I grew up in Juárez, Mexico. Drug wars, shoot-outs, border attacks. I've seen it all. I can handle this."

"You shouldn't *have* to handle this, Rosa," I insisted. "It's not normal. It's not right. And if anything were to happen to you, we—"

"Ari," she said, finality in her tone. "I stay."

The backs of my eyes burned once again. How could Dane and I be so unfortunate when it came to external forces threaten-ing our lives and yet so damn blessed by the circle we'd built around us?

Still, as much as Rosa's determination and commitment to our family touched me, it worried me incessantly. The fewer heads on the chopping block, the better. But at the moment, I didn't have the heart or the wherewithal to argue with her.

So I said, "I appreciate your honor." I hugged her. "But Dane will want to speak with you as well."

"My decision will still be the same," she said with her steely resolve.

I swiped at a wayward tear. "You could give my mother a few lessons in loyalty. But I wouldn't subject you to her any more than I want you subjected to the rest of this."

"I agree that it's not right that this isn't finally over," she con-curred. "Eventually, though, it will be. Dane will see to it."

I was grateful for her faith in my husband. "Just stick close to Kyle, okay? He's on baby detail."

"We'll be fine," she assured me.

I left her room, somewhat tormented. As I chewed on our latest precarious situation, I came across Amano in the great room. He had two iPads and his phone spread out on the table of the Parisian bistro set Dane had picked up at auction in Paris. Apparently, Marie Antoinette had sipped tea at that table.

I would have laughed at Dane's eccentricity, but I didn't have it in me. I had one more tense conversation to have. I didn't look forward to it.

Joining Amano, I asked, "Mind if I take a seat?"

He made a vague gesture toward the chair opposite him.

"Monitoring the property?"

"That and downloading the programs for each of the GoPros Kyle mounted in all of the vehicles."

"What are GoPros?"

"Video cameras. We can live-stream them on our wireless devices and the TV. There's audio, too."

"Clever."

"Just keep in mind that sneaking off is no longer plausible, since I control the on/off switches. You and Kyle can't take your joyrides without me knowing about them."

Our gazes locked across the table. I didn't have to ask him to elaborate. He'd be alerted the second Kyle and I took off if we did anything crazy again, as we'd done when going after a confession from Wayne Horton. Or taking Dane's Mercedes McLaren up the treacherous switchbacks in hopes of evading Wayne when he'd baited and trapped us.

Swallowing my pride, I said, "Point taken."

"Are you sure?"

I accepted Amano's anger over what he obviously considered our carelessness. I knew he was furious because we'd gone behind his back too many times and opened ourselves up to even more danger, well out of his reach.

Not to mention, the fact that he'd used the term *joyride* told me he was additionally upset with our actions because Dane had once done the same. To Mikaela's detriment.

With a nod, I told my bodyguard, "I assure you, we won't be out of your sight without you knowing about it."

"I've seen that you take precautions, and I'm not saying you haven't done a good job. But my responsibility is to protect you. I can't do that when you run off with Kyle."

"I understand," I said, contrite. "And I'm sorry. I know we worried you—pissed you off—when we went after Wayne's confession. That was never our intention. Never my intention. I was feeling hopeless, Amano. Worthless, even. Like all of this stuff was happening around us and I couldn't do a damn thing about it. Then this opportunity presented itself, and I needed to step up. Can you at least accept that?"

"The way this arrangement works," he said in a stern tone, "is you stay put and I keep you safe."

I shoved back my chair and stood. "Maybe I'm not the stay-put type. Maybe it'd be okay if I were a bit more proactive than reactive."

He set aside his iPad. "What do you want?"

That was a bit too point-blank. I didn't have an answer. Except to say, "You didn't tell Dane about my plans for the Lux."

Amano simply stared at me.

"Come on, I know you know what I've been up to. You keep giving me phones."

"I'm glad you want to rebuild the hotel. I knew Dane would be happy about it, too. You're managing it remotely, not putting yourself in any danger. I don't have any problems with the way you've handled the project. So I didn't feel the need to tell him."

"And you wanted him to be surprised, didn't you?"

"He deserves some good news."

"Yes, he does."

I sank back onto the cushioned seat. "I'm sorry I caused you trouble and worry. It won't happen again. And I apologize for asking you to not call Dane when I was about to have the baby. I didn't want him freaking out because I was delivering early. Nor did I want him to know—" I shook my head. This confession was even harder to make. "I was concerned about having Amsel prematurely. It scared me. For all the obvious reasons—his health and well-being. But also because I considered it a shortcoming that I couldn't carry Dane's baby all the way to term."

"Ari." Amano gave me a firm look. "That is *not* a shortcoming."

Tears stung my eyes. I was having quite the emotional night. "Are *you* married to an overachiever?"

He actually cracked a smile. "Thankfully, no."

My tension didn't abate. "Does make for difficult times on occasion."

He regarded me a few moments, then said, "Maybe you shouldn't put so much pressure on yourself."

"And if someone were to say that to you?"

With a smirk, he said, "I'd ignore them."

"Hmph."

Perhaps that was one of the reasons we got along so well. We shared the same fabric.

We sat in silence a little while longer. Eventually, he asked, "Do you want to learn how to stream the GoPros?"

"Oh, hell, yes."

"Where have you been?" Dane asked when I finally retired to our bedroom.

"Making the rounds," I said as I changed into my nightgown. "We have quite the loyal crew. I couldn't scare them off."

"That's funny. I couldn't *pay* them off."

"Neither Kyle nor Rosa?"

"I tried. Lots of zeroes on the checks I wrote."

I settled under the covers with him and said, "It's just money I guess is the way they think of it. Not a family. Not a purpose."

"We'll see how they feel in the morning. Give them both some time to sleep on it."

"That's exactly what I said."

We exchanged a look.

Dane told me, "They won't change their minds."

I was grateful for the strong ties. But also wary of anything happening to the people I cared so much about.

Dane said, "Rosa was more than happy to move in when Amano and I approached her with the full-time gig when we all came back to this house. It was for her protection as well, but what it all boiled down to was that she used to go home to an empty house at the end of the day—now she's got a family, with us. Nonstop activity."

"And danger," I reminded him.

"We'll deal with that. Ethan won't win."

I cuddled against Dane's side and rested my palm on his cut abs. "What about Qadir and Nikolai?"

"When I finally share all of this with them, I think they're going to be as shocked as I am."

"As equally betrayed?"

"Not as equally." Ethan had been Dane's mentor and best friend since he was nineteen, after all. "But it'll be a cold, hard slap in the face, nonetheless."

I gave this some thought, then offered, "So it'd be okay to keep the two of them on as investors in 10,000 Lux? They really took a personal interest when it was being sabotaged. It was more than just the money, right? It was because they supported your vision, your project."

He didn't speak for some time. I didn't press.

For a little while, anyway.

After a couple of minutes of silence, I took a guess at what he might be stewing over. "You want to keep them onboard because of your relationships with them, and because it makes good business sense."

"Naturally."

"But you can't afford another stab in the back." I wasn't talking monetarily.

He reached for the bedside lamp and switched it off. The moonlight filtered between thick branches on the trees and streamed through the unadorned floor-to-ceiling windows. That, along with Amsel's night-light, provided enough illumination that I could see the hard set of Dane's jaw.

I said, "I understand how you feel. For something like this to come out of the blue with no warning. From such an unexpected source."

"Kind of like what your mother did to you?"

"And what she's doing to my dad."

Dane's arm tightened around my shoulders. "So that problem hasn't gone away."

"It's the least of our worries."

"Not if it affects your father. I know that'll eat at you. I'll speak with Jackson. We'll resolve this once and for all. Safely, I promise."

"My dad doesn't deserve this attack." I kissed Dane's cheek. "Any more than you deserve everything that's happened to you."

Dane pulled me closer to him. My lips glided along his jaw, then brushed over his mouth.

He swept hair from my face as he engaged me in slow, sexy, tongueless kisses that made me burn for him.

His hand moved downward and he gathered the nightgown on one side, while his other arm kept me anchored to him as I eased on top of him. I felt his erection between my legs and I guided him inside me.

"You always feel so good," I whispered against his lips.

"Mm. This is my favorite spot."

I smiled. "Mine, too."

We moved together, languidly, in no particular hurry. He palmed an ass cheek and pressed me firmly against him as my hips rolled leisurely and he thrust deeper into me.

He kissed my chin, then his warm lips skimmed along my neck. His breath teased my skin as he murmured, "I love you so much."

Then he sat up and I felt him even thicker, fuller, deeper within me.

"Dane." My head fell back on my shoulders as he lightly nipped at my throat, working his way down to my collarbone and across the tops of my breasts. His head dipped farther and his mouth closed over my hard nipple, suckling through the satin covering me.

My fingers threaded through his lush hair. My eyelids fluttered closed. Erotic sensations blossomed in my core, ignited my nerve endings.

I rocked against him, feeling him swell in my pussy. We found an exciting yet sensuous rhythm that had us both breathing heavy and gripping each other tightly as the electricity arced between us and the sensations intensified.

His lips blazed a trail back up to my neck and he suckled the erogenous zone below my ear.

"I'm going to come," I whispered.

"Yes."

His arm around my waist kept our bodies pressed together as I rocked faster and the tension mounted.

"Dane," I repeated.

"Now."

"*Yes*." Everything inside me pulled tight, then exploded in a heated wave that rushed through my veins.

"Ah, Ari," he said on a low growl. "Just like that."

I milked his cock as my climax radiated, bright and beautiful. Then I felt him convulse and erupt as he came hard and fast, still holding me tight.

Dane's heat and muscles surrounded me as he embraced me, his chest to my back, our bodies melded together. I lingered in a blissful state, all warm and cozy in our intimate cocoon.

It hadn't taken more than a few minutes after Dane had made love to me and I'd fallen into a peaceful slumber, thankfully devoid of menacing thoughts and haunting images.

Around 3:00 a.m., I wasn't quite as deep in sleep and heard Amsel stir. I listened carefully, but seconds later he went back to making his cute little cooing sounds as he drifted off again.

Still wanting Dane, I was tempted to wake him.

I didn't have to.

Kyle did it for me.

"Dane! Ari!"

I heard Kyle's booming voice down the hallway. The sharp edge to it wasn't necessary. He'd only once come this far back in the house, to our master suite—when he and my dad had brought me home from the hospital, following the Lux explosion and the news Dane and Amano hadn't made it out. Kyle had needed to collect my necessities, because I hadn't been able to bring myself to enter this room at that time.

So now I was instantly alarmed.

"Breach!" was all Kyle had to shout out and my blood turned to ice.

A heartbeat later the moonlight was shrouded and shadows covered the wall we faced. Everything happened at once. I heard the ominous sound of helicopter blades and then the *pop, pop, pop* of automatic weapons and the shattering of glass as the doors and windows comprising the far wall exploded.

Dane shoved me out of bed and I hit the area rug covering the stone floor, his body shielding mine.

"Amsel!" I cried out in terror.

Kyle dove through the opened doorway and crawled over to the bassinet to collect my now-screaming child.

Dane yanked open the nightstand and grabbed his gun.

"You okay?" he asked me, his voice tight.

"Yes. Keep our baby safe."

On his belly, Dane maneuvered to the end of the bed and partially rounded the corner to take aim. He quickly emptied the magazine, and the gunfire from the other side ceased.

Kyle handed the baby to me and pulled his own gun from the waist of his jeans, at the small of his back.

Dane stood in a fluid move and shoved his feet into his shoes. He'd put on a pair of black drawstring pants before we'd curled in bed. I still wore my nightgown. He took me by the arm and helped me up before we rushed from the room. We heard Amano toward the front of the house, yelling for Rosa.

Then another round blew out all the glass in the great room, from the sound of it.

Kyle said, "They're all over the damn place. Like fucking cockroaches." He flashed his iPad mini, with various surveillance camera angles on-screen at once.

"Not for long," Dane said. He stormed into the great room, Amano at his side.

"Dane!" Fear seized me.

A steady barrage followed. Amsel wailed in distress. Rosa came running into the hallway in her bathrobe and slippers, swearing up a blue streak in Spanish.

Seconds later a chilling silence filled the house. Though my heart hammered in my ears and my breath lodged in my throat.

Dane and Amano stalked back into the corridor.

"Goddamn it!" Dane roared.

Kyle flicked his thumb over the screen of the mini, checking more camera angles. Then ground out, "Fuck!" All eyes landed on him. "They're inside."

I gaped. Held Amsel even tighter.

"How many and where?" Dane demanded.

"Three through the kitchen. Two through the laundry room." On opposite ends of the house.

Kyle added, "One at the front door."

Panic sliced through me. "They're surrounding us."

"No," Kyle said. "The one barreling through the front door right now is Agent Price."

I would have breathed a sigh of relief he was still alive . . . if I could actually breathe.

Amano gestured for Price to follow him into the kitchen. Dane marched toward the laundry room.

Kyle stayed with Rosa, Amsel, and me in the center of the house.

"Where do you think the helicopters went?" I asked, finding the silence bone-chillingly eerie. I tried hard not to squeeze Amsel so firmly to my chest.

"Your guess is as good as mine. I haven't gotten around to satellite monitoring of our airspace."

"Jesus Christ." Even his sarcasm couldn't lessen the terror gripping me. I handed the baby to Rosa before I suffocated him, and then searched one of the hallway tables for a suitable weapon, settling on a silver letter opener with a sharp tip.

More gunshots made me jump.

Kyle said, "Laundry room is secure." He kept scrolling. "I don't see anyone else invading us. Just—oh, shit!"

More of the sharp, ear-piercing popping and then Kyle erupted again with the profanity. Dane crept back into the hallway, checking rooms as he made his way toward us.

Kyle called out, "Price and Amano are down. There are four—*four!*—in the kitchen, moving . . . Goddamn it!"

His head whipped around. Our gazes followed. Ethan and three others rounded the corner from the kitchen, guns drawn.

Dane raised his arm, taking aim at Ethan.

"Dane, no!" I screamed.

Ethan carried one of those rifles with the scopes on top I'd hoped to never see again in my lifetime. And the infrared dot settled on the baby's forehead.

My heart launched into my throat.

"Not Amsel," I said to Ethan as hot tears rolled down my cheeks. "*Not* our son."

chapter 19

"Don't *even* fucking think about pulling that trigger, Ethan." Dane's tone was deathly serious.

"What choice do I have?" Ethan demanded. "You couldn't leave well enough alone, Dane. I had everything under control once I got my hands on that hard drive. I destroyed all the evidence against me. I was in the clear. But you had to go to Philadelphia, didn't you?"

Shock reverberated through me. How the hell did he know? We'd just gotten back!

With a challenging look, Dane asked, "You know what I found there?"

"You never had a need to delve into your father's records or files. If you just would have left it be, if you just would have let it all lie—"

"How the fuck was I supposed to do that?" Dane bellowed. "I saw the photo of you with my father. Of course I was going to start piecing this all together."

"That's always been your problem," Ethan said irritably. "You can't overlook anything. You can't just turn a blind eye."

"To everything the society did to ruin lives while making a profit? I was supposed to *pretend* that wasn't happening?"

"You're just like your father."

My eyes squeezed shut. So we'd been right all along. Bradley had taken the same stance with the society as Dane had, only thirty years before him.

When I opened my eyes, Dane still had his gun trained on Ethan. The red dot still flashed against Amsel's forehead. My insides were still a mangled mess.

Amano and Agent Price had been shot and were either dead or bleeding to death in our kitchen. And we were all at an impasse.

"What good will any of this do?" I somehow managed to ask Ethan.

"Well, Mrs. Bax, I could have easily brought down your private jet on your return flight from Pennsylvania. Leaving your son to suffer the same fate as Dane did right around the same age. I could have let history repeat itself."

I felt an insidious ripple along my spine.

Ethan continued. "That, however, would mean I'd have to start from scratch, since your husband felt compelled to do everything in his power to ensure my colleagues were incarcerated."

"You were working with them," I hissed out. "*All* of them?"

"Not Qadir and Nik," he said. "I recognized from the beginning they'd be impossible to sway, like Dane. But that was okay. I didn't need them. I had the other five—it's a majority rules society, so I never even had to cast a swing vote, never had to risk the smallest hint of where my allegiance lies."

"You just reaped all the benefit," Dane said in disgust.

"I understand you're upset," Ethan told him. "I wasn't exactly thrilled to have to go behind your back, Dane, but once you got your feet under you at Harvard I could see I wasn't going to win you over to my plight any more than I did your father."

"So you killed my parents."

"Yes."

"And you think you're going to kill my son?"

"That depends on you and your wife."

I swallowed down a lump of emotion—and horror.

I knew how all of this had started.

I knew how it would end.

"You want 10,000 Lux," I said.

"Sign it over and your son lives. So do the two of you."

My blood turned to ice. "And Kyle and Rosa?" I didn't even want to think of Amano at the moment. For all I knew, he was lying lifeless on my kitchen floor, and that possibility nearly crippled me.

"No." Ethan gave a slight shake of his head in answer to my question. "Witnesses. You know I can't leave loose ends like that."

"You son of a bitch," Kyle spat.

"Sorry, kid. I like you and all—you've demonstrated a lot of potential. Unfortunately, you aligned yourself with the wrong side of the faction."

"There's no way I'll let you get away with this," Dane said.

"There's no way you're going to beat me this time, Dane. It's all very simple. Don't complicate it. You, your pretty wife, and your baby live. I get the Lux. It's really that easy."

"You're forgetting one thing," Kyle said.

Ethan gave him a sinister smile. "What's that?"

"It's not so much what, but . . . who."

Ethan's brow dipped.

Kyle grinned. "Amano."

My gaze flashed toward the direction of the kitchen. Amano was in the corridor, bleeding from the shoulder and leg. My stomach wrenched.

His first shot was to the head of the soldier at Ethan's side while Kyle simultaneously tackled Rosa—with the baby in her arms—as Ethan took his own shot at them.

I cried out.

Kyle's quick reaction saved all three of them, though Amsel wailed in distress.

Ethan jerked out of the way as Dane took aim, and Ethan caught the bullet in his arm. Blood splattered everywhere and continued to as one of Ethan's other guys shot at Amano, who dove behind a massive credenza. Kyle shot the other soldier flanking Ethan. Dane took out the final one.

But Ethan was a step ahead of them.

He pointed his gun at me.

And pulled the trigger.

A searing pain like nothing I'd ever known tore through me. A dozen scorpion stings all at once couldn't compare to the fire that lanced my leg. I screamed again and crumpled to the floor.

"Ari!" Dane was instantly at my side, dropping to his knees.

I watched, petrified and in sheer agony, as Ethan leapt forward, ripped the baby from Rosa's arms, and bolted for the door.

"Kyle!" I yelled.

A second later he was on his feet and racing after Ethan.

My attention snapped to Dane. "Go!"

"Ari—"

"Go!"

He tried to press his cell into my palm, but I couldn't grip it. He leapt up and chased after the others.

Rosa joined me, whipped off the robe she'd tied over her nightgown, and pressed the material to my leg. I was suddenly woozy but said, "Take care of Amano. I'll be fine."

She left me and I kept the pressure of the thick terry cloth against my wound. As best as I could, at any rate, because my body trembled violenty.

"Ari."

My unsteady gaze flitted down the hallway, in the direction of Rosa's voice. She shook her head slowly.

My breath caught. "No," I whispered. "Amano." Everything inside me seized up. Tears threatened my eyes. I closed them tightly, but the drops leaked from the corners.

Amano was . . . ?

No, no.

No!

"Fuck!" I yelled at the top of my lungs.

Then tried to focus, to think clearly.

What would Dane do?

My lids flew open. I reached for the phone, my shaky fingers dropping it twice before I was able to hold it steady enough to hit the speed dial number for Dr. Forrester. I relayed, as best as I could, as quickly as I could, what had happened. He promised he was on his way.

I fought body-racking sobs, choking them back. They weren't even related to my leg. The grief was purely about Amano and the fact that Ethan had my son.

Mustering all of my strength, since I had determined the day I'd confronted Wayne Horton that there was no way I'd cower in a corner, I partially crawled, partially dragged, myself toward the credenza.

Rosa's head popped up from the end of the enormous piece of furniture.

"*Chica*," she barked. "Stay."

"I'm not a dog, Rosa."

"You're going to make it worse."

"It can't get much worse than this!"

"He's breathing," she said.

"Oh, God!" I burst into tears. "Oh, *thank God!*"

"Barely."

"Urg!" I could kill Ethan myself. I was certain of it.

"This is bad," Rosa said. Her hands were covered with Amano's blood. "He's got lots of holes in him."

"Jesus. Amano, just hang in there. Dr. Forrester is on his way."

"Ari," Rosa said. "You don't look so good, either. You are much too pale."

I was afraid I might pass out. Or throw up. And the burning sensation didn't abate.

Amano mumbled something. I stared at Rosa.

"What did he say?"

"I don't know." She shook her head. "'Go . . .' something."

"'Go . . .'?" I waded through the haze in my mind. "Go where? What the hell?" I cried with sufficient anguish. Then suddenly I said, "GoPro!"

"What?" She had no clue what I meant.

"Kyle's mini—can you grab it, please?"

It was on the floor where he'd tackled Rosa and Amsel. She wiped her crimson-colored hands on her white nightgown, then rushed over, snatched the device, and gave it to me.

I employed last night's lesson from Amano and was immediately streaming the video and audio feed from Dane's McLaren. "Kyle, can you hear me?"

"Yeah!"

"What's happening?" I couldn't remain focused on the video with Kyle weaving in and out of traffic. It made me dizzy and nauseous.

"Ethan is several cars ahead of me."

"Where's Dane?"

"On his motorcycle behind me. Are you okay?"

"Been better."

"What about Amano?"

"Swell," came the bodyguard's response.

"Don't let him fool you," I said. "He's in bad shape. Dr. Forrester is on his way. Is there a GoPro on the bike?"

"No, the helmet."

I pulled up that video. "Dane!"

"What the fuck?" he roared.

"It's me! I'm in your head—your helmet," I corrected. "GoPro. Amano and Kyle installed it."

"Christ, Ari," came his tormented voice, loud and clear. "Are you all right?"

"Amano's worse off. Forrester is on his way. Damn, Dane, I can't watch you traversing all this traffic."

I set aside the mini and heaved onto the stone floor.

"*Chica!*" Rosa scolded.

I screamed again.

"All right," she grumbled. "If you must. I have to clean up all this blood, anyway."

She was a strange bird, but I loved her.

"Ari?" Dane demanded, since I hadn't turned off the speaker or switched to Kyle's system or whatever the hell I was supposed to do so that Dane didn't have to hear me wail.

"I'm still alive." Just drowning in pain and misery.

Luckily, Forrester and his staff came through the door minutes later. Apparently, he had the gate code. As had Ethan.

Damn it!

"Ari," Dr. Forrester said as he crossed to where I was propped up against the credenza.

I pointed to the other end of it. "Amano needs you."

Dr. Forrester saw to him, with one of the assistants, while the other tended to me.

"Don't you get tired of this?" I asked him, remembering him from the estate, after Tom Talbot had shot Dane and Kyle.

The assistant asked, "Don't you?"

"You have no idea," I said on a wisp of air. My breathing had turned shallow.

"I'm Stan, by the way. And this is going to hurt. Sorry."

My eyes squeezed shut for a moment. "More than it already does?"

"Yeah. For a little while."

He started in on me, I cried out again, and then . . .

Nothing.

I woke with a start. And another bloodcurdling scream.

"I gave you something for the pain," Stan instantly said. "You shouldn't be in so much of it now."

That wasn't the problem. "I blacked out."

"It's been like twenty, thirty minutes. The bullet wasn't difficult to get to. You're stitched up."

He'd also settled me on the sofa in the great room.

"Where's Amano?" I demanded.

"His room. He needs a bit more work."

"Will he be okay?"

"Are you kidding? Do you think Dane would accept anything less than a full recovery from either of you?"

I wanted to laugh, because I knew Stan was trying to lighten the mood. But I didn't have it in me.

"There's an iPad mini in the hallway, where I was sitting. Can you bring it to me?"

"Sure." He was gone for only a few seconds and handed it over.

As I hastily pulled up the video from Dane's helmet and streamed it on the flat screen over the fireplace, I could see they were still in hot pursuit of Ethan. Where the hell was he taking Amsel?

"Dane?"

"Jesus," he said. "You had me terrified, baby."

"Sorry. Blacked out. I'm better now."

"And Amano?"

I shot a glance at Stan, who said, "He's not going to bounce back quite so quick, but I'm sure he'll be fine."

Dane swore under his breath.

"It'll take more than a few bullets to stop him," I added, hoping to relieve some of the tension. "Where are you?"

"Heading toward the Lux." A second later he said, "Scratch that. Headed toward the estate."

"That asshole!" I ground out. I swore that place was cursed since the day Vale had kidnapped me and taken me there.

From the camera mounted on the front of the helmet I could see Kyle ahead of the motorcycle. The McLaren bounced along the red-dirt road, the headlights dipping and rising, dipping and rising, so that I thought I'd puke again. Then the high beams went dark and the car jerked to a stop in front of the massive gates, which were wide open.

"Ari," Dane said. "What do you see?"

"Straight shot through the front windows to the living room. Ethan and Amsel."

My breath stuck in my throat again.

"Perfect." There was a rustling noise and jostling of the camera and then it sat on the hood of the car, giving me the same view as before.

Kyle rounded the front of the car and handed over his phone and wireless earpiece. Dane immediately called his phone, which rang in the hall. Stan retrieved it.

"Dane?" I asked, putting him on speaker.

"Yeah." I watched him, on-screen, stuff the phone into his pocket, with me still on the line. "Tell me if anyone comes into the courtyard, gets near the front door, or comes into the living room. Can you see that much?"

"Yes. But if Ethan moves farther back into the house, I might lose him."

"Noted."

Dane and Kyle drew their guns and crept into the courtyard.

Thank God we had the cells, because they were too far out of the GoPros' audio reach.

I had no idea if Ethan knew they'd kept up with him or even followed him. Nor did I know if he had other soldiers at his disposal. I maintained a vigilant watch on the house, as did Stan.

"Kyle has the GoPro in the car angled to capture the entrance into the estate. Can you pull that up as well? Alert us if any vehicles join us?" Dane asked.

I did as Amano had shown me last night, using a split screen to get dual access. "Got it."

"Let me know if a convoy converges."

"Please don't even joke about that," I said.

"No joke, baby."

I'd suspected as much. "Be careful, Dane."

"Don't worry about me. You take care of yourself."

"I'm worried about all of us. And you need to give Kyle huge props for rigging up the GoPros."

"I'll be sure to pat him on the back," he said dryly. They reached the patio. "We're going in."

I sent up a silent prayer they'd be coming out—with Amsel.

Rosa joined us in the great room. I was moderately surprised she didn't have a bowl of popcorn in her hands as she settled in. Though from the worry lines etched on her face I was on to her. For all her bravado, she appeared as terrified as I was.

"How's Amano doing?" I asked her.

"Medically induced coma." She looked a bit pale herself. "He has a lot of healing ahead of him."

"Shit."

"He's tough as nails," Stan said in a reassuring tone. "He'll pull through."

I tried to buy into that theory. But my insides were all twisted and I was a bit loopy from whatever Stan had given me. It was difficult to concentrate on the TV, yet I did my best.

Kyle and Dane split up, each taking a different entryway into the living room.

Rosa said, "If he harms one hair on that baby's head, so help me—" She went off on another tangent in Spanish.

I was right there with her, even if I had trouble comprehending half of what she said. Her angst resonated deep within me.

Returning my attention to the screen, I told Dane, "It's still all good. I don't see any moving shadows."

A quick in and out would be a blessing. No more bloodshed.

Kyle moved in first. From where Dane crouched to the left I couldn't hear anything but muffled voices coming from the living room. I could only guess what Kyle had to say to Ethan. Something along the lines of, *You can hand over the baby peacefully, or I can kick the shit out of you.*

My tension ratcheted. I stared at the scene unfolding in front of me and was utterly hopeless to do anything about it—except watch their backs. That wasn't enough, of course. It was likely a good thing I was drugged, or I probably would have jumped in the SUV and sped over to the estate right behind Kyle and Dane. Not that I would have been able to since I'd been shot in the leg, but still.

I couldn't hear a damn thing and that made me crazy.

"Dane."

"Shh."

I wanted to scream again. But a movement in the bottom right corner of the screen diverted my attention.

"I think there's someone outside," I said. "By the fountain."

Deeper in the house, Kyle had his gun pointed at Ethan, but no progress was being made to get Amsel back. Ethan had to be waiting for his backup before he made his own move.

My stomach roiled. Chances were very good Kyle just might shoot him. Even though Ethan held the baby close to him.

"This is too much." I groaned. I wanted to pace but couldn't. I wanted to do something—*anything*. But couldn't.

I'd never had anxiety crawl through me like a million tiny spiders unless my mother was in the same room with me.

Though this was way worse.

My gaze remained locked on the TV. I was riveted, yet every fiber of my being burned for me to jump to my feet and somehow be involved. I wanted to swoop in and snatch Amsel from Ethan's arms. But I couldn't save my own son.

I had to just *watch*.

Whatever happened . . . I would see it all.

My heart pounded in my chest. My pulse echoed in my ears. It was a wonder I didn't black out again. Or go into cardiac arrest.

As the standoff between Ethan and Kyle ensued, tears streamed down my cheeks. Fury tore through me. How could this even be happening?

"Two o'clock," Stan suddenly instructed Dane. "Coming right at you."

I caught the shadow of a figure as Dane hunkered in the hedges.

I watched with bated breath as Dane took the fountain guy by surprise. I heard the gunshot and the guy hit the ground. It drew the attention of the other shadow, and he shot at Dane. I gasped. The bullet missed him.

Two shots later and the second gunman sprawled on the patio.

Dane didn't waste time waiting for anyone else to move in on him. He stormed the living room, gun pointed at Ethan's head. I frantically worked the controls to zoom in.

Rosa leapt to her feet and started to pace and swear some more, her arms flapping wildly.

I couldn't figure out what the plan was and suddenly yelled in frustration, "The baby!"

"Keep up your watch," Stan told me. "Amsel will be fine."

Stan said it to help me calm down, but of course it didn't work. Suspense clawed at me. My heart didn't feel right. It beat too fast. Was pulled too tight.

Unexpectedly, Kyle lowered his gun and took a step back.

"What?" I demanded. "*No!*"

But then Ethan stood and handed Amsel over to him.

Dane put away his gun.

"You just silently agreed to give up the Lux," I said. "Oh, my God." My head spun. Yes, our child meant more than a hotel. But . . . "How can you trust Ethan to stick to the deal? How can you trust him to not come after us again?"

He didn't answer me. I suspected he didn't want to blow our own surprise element—that I watched the estate.

But then the true source of the surrender came into sight.

Mikaela.

"Oh, God, no," I said on a harsh breath. "He's kidnapped her, too."

Ethan held his hands in the air, unthreatening, and crossed to the desk in the corner. Mikaela joined him.

"What the hell?" I muttered.

She stood by Ethan's side behind the desk. This perplexed me. Ethan retrieved a folder and held out a pen to Dane.

My heart broke all over again for him.

He'd lost 10,000 Lux once. I'd given it back to him just recently. Now it slipped through his fingers for good.

But Kyle had Amsel, and really, that was all that mattered. Somehow Dane would get Mikaela out of the sticky situation as well. He'd save them all.

Relief didn't edge in on me, though. I watched with rising fury as Dane signed the papers. Kyle backed out of the room and my attention shifted to him, my focus on the baby, though I slid a glance Dane's way when he straightened and tossed the pen onto the desk.

"Stay the fuck away from my family," he said. "And Kyle and Rosa."

"Fine," Ethan said. "It's over. I got what I wanted all along. You all leave Sedona, stay far away from 10,000 Lux, and this will just be a bad memory. No more."

Dane backed up as well. Kyle had almost made it to the front door. Ethan collected the paperwork and opened the drawer again.

The baby must have screamed, though we couldn't hear anything from that far off. It nabbed Dane's attention, though.

A split second later, Ethan pulled a gun from the drawer.

"Dane!" I cried into the phone.

Everything inside me seized up.

This was it.

Game over.

chapter 20

I stared at the flat screen above the fireplace, rocked to the core of my being. Horrified.

Dane must have caught the reflection of Ethan in one of the front room windows, because he whirled around while whipping out his own weapon.

My hands spasmed and I dropped the mini. It hit the floor and the TV went blank as though we'd lost the feed.

Except I heard the gunshots, and each one made me jump. Four times.

Rosa shrieked.

"Dane!" I called out again.

Who had just shot *who*?

Stan lunged for the mini and pressed buttons until the camera function worked again. Suddenly our big screen was filled with blood splattered everywhere, all over the walls behind the desk where Ethan had stood and covering the papers Dane had just signed. Dripping ominously.

My stomach lurched.

Then I saw Dane. He had his gun pointed at Mikaela, the nozzle pressed to her forehead. Her back was against the wall. She didn't move an inch.

"Dane? What the hell?" I demanded. Monumentally relieved he was alive but confused by this new course of action.

"Holy shit," Stan said, sounding traumatized. "What the fuck is going on here?"

Dane reached in his pocket and turned on the speaker function of Kyle's phone. Then he asked Mikaela, "How long have you been in on this?"

"Dane!" I froze, my eyes bulging. He couldn't possibly think she was directly involved with—

"I didn't have a choice," Mikaela said. No false Italian accent. Her eyes were also wide—with terror. Brimming with tears. Her voice cracked as she told Dane, "I was in too deep to walk away at the time I found out you were alive."

"What did you do?" he demanded, his tone sharp, filled with rage. "Why did you turn against me?"

"I didn't, Dane! I swear!" She choked on her words. "It all just happened—I couldn't stop it." She'd gone as pale as the light-pink sweater she wore with white leather pants, which had Ethan's blood splashed across them. "I had no choice. You have to believe me!" Tears streamed down her ghostly cheeks.

"*Tell* me."

She visibly quaked. "I needed his help. I was out of money. Flat broke before I even opened the market. Brizio's brother double-crossed us. We paid for imported goods and invested in his shipping business, but he never delivered. Never even started the business. We had to find another source and that cost us everything I had. I couldn't go to my father for the money. He'd never lend it to me, since I'd depleted my trust fund."

"Why Ethan?"

She swallowed hard. "I—I don't know. It just happened," she

reiterated, fear tingeing her voice. "That night of the Delfino party in Scottsdale. After you and Ethan talked to him about the problems I was having setting up shop in Old Town. You and Ari left afterward. I had a few drinks with Ethan. I explained the situation with Brizio's brother, and that we were having a cash flow problem. He offered me the money, Dane."

I could see my husband's shoulders bunch. This was about to get even uglier. If that were possible. He'd shot Ethan. Dead was my guess, since Dane didn't seem concerned that Ethan might rise up, gun in hand.

My insides churned over the reality of the situation and the trauma it would cause Dane when the adrenaline stopped pumping and it fully hit him that he'd killed his best friend and mentor.

Mikaela said, "He wanted a few favors in return."

"So you slept with him."

"Yes. But that wasn't all. Dane, he wanted my electronic badge for the Lux. I didn't understand why, but he knew I had one with no restrictions. There were only a few you'd issued that granted all access to every inch of the resort. Ethan's badge was only good for getting him to the top floor of the executive wing—your office suite, because that was all he'd ever needed. Yet I consulted with Chef D'Angelo and the managers of the various restaurants, so I had to be able to get to them for meetings."

"Oh, God," I breathed. I was about to heave again. "She was the one who let Wayne Horton into all those restricted areas after Amano fired him. She was the one who provided him access so he could plant the snake and the scorpions . . . the bomb."

I was certain I'd gone as ghostly as Mikaela.

"I didn't know what he was up to," she insisted. "I swear it, Dane. I didn't ask; he didn't tell."

"And that exonerates you?" Dane hissed between clenched teeth.

"Dane, please understand, I—"

"Ari was attacked. *Repeatedly.* On-site and off. Because of the access you gave to Horton. Ethan shot her, Mikaela. My wife! He kidnapped my child." His tone was low, lethal. His finger twitched against the trigger of his GLOCK.

"Dane," I said in warning. I could sense the dark place he'd gone to in his mind, knew what he saw before him was not his childhood friend but a traitor. Someone who'd destroyed everything he'd built, someone who'd threatened his family, someone who'd deceived him. "Put the gun down, Dane. Call the FBI. Daugherty will take over from here. I have all of this recorded. Just walk away. Bring our son home."

Fat drops rolled down my cheeks. I needed this to all be over. It was too much. Too painful, too harrowing, too impossible, to continue watching, experiencing. It needed to be done.

"If you kill her," I told him, my throat and heart constricting, "you'll regret it. You know you will. Maybe it'd be justified and you'd feel satisfaction right this very second, but when the reality hits you, Dane, you'll hate yourself for pulling the trigger. She doesn't deserve to die."

Ethan's death I had no qualms over. But this was different. Mikaela had gotten caught up in something much bigger than herself, something she likely couldn't wrap her mind around even if she tried, even if she had all the facts. I still struggled with it myself, and I'd been immersed in this life, this evil, for more than a year.

"Dane," I urged.

It took several more suspended seconds for him to respond. He didn't lower his weapon, though. In a menacing voice that left no question of what he'd do to her if they ever crossed paths again, he said, "I will make you pay for this. I will make sure that you live a very miserable life in prison. You will never get help from me again. I will nail your father for his involvement, for whatever conspiracy he partook of that killed my parents, for whatever the fuck I can do to make sure his life is over, too. You will both rot in hell. Do. You. Hear. Me?"

I gaped. Mikaela shed more tears. Her bottom lip quivered and her breath came in heavy pulls. Clearly, she couldn't speak. Only slowly nodded her head.

"You are dead to me," Dane said. "Whatever happens to you from this moment on will never, *ever* be of concern to me."

He took a few steps back. Didn't disengage the weapon but didn't keep it pressed to her forehead, either.

To me, he said, "I'm disconnecting the call. Kyle's bringing the baby home. I'm contacting Daugherty."

There was such a distant, detached note to Dane's voice that it sent a chill down my spine. Panic shot through my veins. "Dane?"

"I love you, Ari." He hung up.

I stared at the screen, my mind reeling, my insides shattering.

"Dane," I whispered as my own tears streamed. "Come home to me."

He didn't.

Kyle arrived a half hour later and promptly placed a distressed Amsel in my shaking arms. He actually had to help me hold the baby.

I was in a lot of pain, but it seemed to radiate more in my chest, deep in my core, than in my leg, which was sufficiently patched and propped up while I lay on the sofa. Stan stuck close to me as Dr. Forrester did whatever needed to be done to Amano. His assistant came into the great room frequently to give an update, since I was desperate to know how it was all going.

Rosa tried to occupy herself in the kitchen, but couldn't stay away for long, constantly checking in. I didn't bust her for showing her soft side, for letting me slide on the pain-threshold level I lacked. She was also visibly upset over Amano's condition, and in the back of my head I wondered if she'd grown fond of our fear-less bodyguard. Wondered if the feeling was mutual, since Amano never seemed to mind sticking close to her when the heat was on.

Kyle said, "I know Kid has no idea what just happened, but the noise and bad vibes have him really worked up."

I stared down at the gaping, squirming bundle in my arms. His little fists were in full swing, as were his tiny feet. He looked a bit flushed and that worried me.

"Can you get me a bottle?" I asked Kyle. "And then you need a hot shower and a hell of a lot of brandy. Dane's best label is in the wine cellar off the study."

"I don't think I should leave you."

"Stan will help me."

"Ari." Our eyes locked.

I could see how deeply disturbed Kyle was by everything that had happened this evening. Maybe everything that had hap-pened since we'd first met—it'd likely all caught up to him, hit him hard tonight. The way I suspected it had Dane.

My insides twisted at the thought of him. I desperately needed him to come walking through the front door, but there was a part of me that feared he would not. He was devastated by the entire fucked-up scenario from start to finish. Worse was that he'd killed Ethan. And that Mikaela had contributed to the entire explosive situation—even the destruction of the Lux.

It had to be tearing Dane apart, destroying him.

I told Kyle, "This isn't the way your life should be, Kyle. This is so bad and wrong. You should be out dating, meeting Meg and Sean for drinks, having fun."

"Yeah, that's totally me," Kyle deadpanned. "Living it up, hav-ing the time of my life, all fun and games."

"Kyle." I let out a long breath. "That should *totally* be you."

I stared several more seconds, my gaze unwavering. Then I asked, "Have you visited Amano in his medically induced coma? Do you really think I could handle it if that were you someday? I was devastated when I thought he was dead. And the feeling hasn't changed even knowing he's still alive."

"He did what he was hired to do, Ari. He went after the bad guys."

"And that's how you feel about Price? It's that cut-and-dried for you? Because he's dead, Kyle."

He grimaced.

"No. I didn't think so," I said. "You care about Amano and I know it has to crush you, too, to see him like this. And Agent Price—the two of you had become friends. So don't play tough with me."

"Okay, yeah, I'm hating this whole part!" He erupted. "But it was a damn good thing I was here. Even you have to admit that."

A few tears crested the rims of my eyes.

He raked a hand through his hair in agitation. Then he leaned toward me and brushed the fat drops from my cheeks.

"You're already a hero," I told him. "Many times over. That's not enough?"

"Come on, Ari. I never signed up for the carefree existence, remember? I had to deal with a major injury in order to keep playing ball, in order to keep my scholarship and get a college degree. I had to kick a very serious prescription-drug addiction. Goddamn it, Ari," he ground out. His eyes blazed with emotion and intensity. "I did a lot of shit just to get through life. And what kind of life was it, anyway? My dad was hardly ever around. My mother had a newborn to focus on from the time I was nine. I raised myself. I didn't have a family unit."

"I understand that, but—"

"I do now," he insisted with conviction. "I've been involved in something dangerous, yes. But also extraordinary. There's a whole universe I never would have been exposed to if I hadn't met you and Dane. Amano. And tonight, when that red dot was on Amsel's forehead . . . ?" He shook his head. The emotion deepened. "That was when I knew that what I've been doing has meaning, purpose. And that I am a part of a family. One I *choose* to be a part of. I belong here, protecting Amsel. You *know* it."

My heart swelled. I nodded, because I couldn't speak.

Kyle added, "Don't send me away. Amano is going to need some serious healing time. And damn it, he deserves a break. He's no spring chicken, you know? He's been doing this shit for three decades."

Another nod, because I simply couldn't get a word around the lump in my throat.

"So let me do what I'm getting good at," he pleaded. "I'll get even better. And all those dangers Dane had to face because he was born a billionaire that your son now faces because he's an heir to a huge empire—let me be the one to help protect him from it all."

I would have hugged him if my arms weren't full. I was pretty sure my eyes said it all, though. Told of my eternal gratitude and best-friend love and devotion.

He gently whisked away more wetness on my cheek and said, "Just nod again if it's okay that I stay."

I did. Emphatically.

With Kyle keeping his allegiance to me and Amsel despite the hell he'd been through, I was able to let him and Rosa look after my son while I drifted in and out and tried to heal.

Morning came and went, and though I knew Dane had a long haul ahead of him with the FBI to dissect, piece together, and tidy up all facets of the secret society run amok—and Mikaela's involvement—I stressed over him not calling. Not stopping by.

He'd trusted Kyle to return Amsel. But was Dane capable of coming home knowing I'd witnessed him killing someone? Knowing I'd watched him hold a gun to Mikaela's head and that he'd been seriously close to pulling the trigger—again—in his rage?

It was all justified, but still . . . He'd likely be freaked out that I'd had to see him go all dark and dangerous one last time.

I fretted over every minute that ticked by. Kyle appeared equally on-edge. As though he also wondered if Dane had slipped into some sort of rawer, darker place in his mind that precluded him from setting foot in his own house—from facing all of us.

It created a very tense environment. And incited a lot of anticipation.

All I wanted was for Dane to walk through the door. To be with me.

What had happened to us was something I could eventually put behind me. I could survive it, just as the rest of us would survive. And knowing Kyle planned to keep Amsel safe from any future threat settled me all the more.

With Amano in stable condition, all that hung in the balance now was Dane's absence.

I continued to doze intermittently. It was probably a good thing I was laid up or I'd be pacing the house incessantly, wearing a hole in the stone flooring Rosa had diligently cleaned of blood and glass. Stan and another of Forrester's assistants boarded the broken windows for us.

Unfortunately, there was no outlet for my anxiety as the activity ensued and I . . . waited.

I needed Dane. And every second without him burned my heart. Tormented me.

I battled a serious bout of apprehension and panic that pushed me almost to the point of hyperventilation. Stan wanted to give me more pills. I stuck with the bare minimum. I wanted to retain coherency and I still had Amsel to take care of and worry about. He seemed to pick up on my disconcertment every time he was in my arms and was fussier than ever. As though he knew a huge presence was missing from this house, knew it disturbed me greatly.

Another day passed and my spirits sank lower. Kyle found ways to amuse Amsel in his bassinet, distracting him from my suffering while I remained sprawled on the sofa in the great room. Kyle occasionally flashed me concerned looks.

Eventually, he said, "It's not like you to brood. You're the silver linings type, remember?"

"I'm entitled."

"Sure. But you're still not the type."

"These are extenuating circumstances. I'm due some melancholy."

"That's not melancholy. That's despair. Big difference."

"Should I break out in song and dance?"

"You have a broken leg," he pointed out.

"And a broken heart. So there."

"He'll be back."

"When? And what makes you so sure? Even you know that Dane's got to be mired in a dismal abyss neither one of us can fully comprehend."

"Hey, I've been pretty messed up over you and Amano."

"But you weren't the one to shoot us," I reminded him. "There's *your* big difference. And we survived. Even bigger difference."

"He'll pull it together, Ari."

"I don't know." My eyes squeezed shut to keep the waterworks at bay. "This doesn't feel right, Kyle."

"Keep the faith. That's what you're best at."

He took Amsel to the kitchen to feed him. I agonized a bit more, until I fell under the spell of pain meds and, yes, despair.

The next time I woke, it was to the sound of Amsel gurgling and making other silly noises. He'd clearly gotten over his unsettled state and was now oblivious to my anguish. My eyelids drifted open and I stared up at the ceiling.

I thought back to that horrific time in my life when Vale had kidnapped me and Dane had nearly killed him for it. I'd considered that a breaking point. I'd walked away.

What had I learned from that experience?

That I couldn't exist without Dane.

His presumed death had been even more detrimental to me. But I'd had a baby inside me to focus on. Now Amsel was in need of my rising above my own pain to tend to him.

So I *had* to exist without Dane.

Somehow.

I asked Kyle, "Who changed Kid, you or Rosa?"

"I did."

Not Kyle's voice.

My heart leapt into my throat. My head rolled on the pillow and I stared at Dane.

In an instant, the most important defining moment of my life returned to me. Kyle and Sean had been bantering over me in the bar of a Sedona resort, minutes before Sean and Meg's wedding ceremony had begun.

I glanced over my shoulder. And lost my breath.

The argument faded into oblivion as my pulse echoed throughout me, drowning out all other sounds, thoughts, everything.

In the corner up front sat two men, paperwork sprawled across their table. One salt-and-pepper-haired, distinguished looking, older. The other dark-haired and dressed all in black—jeans, boots, and a button-down shirt with sleeves rolled up to reveal impressive forearms. Late twenties, maybe thirty. He had a very mysterious air about him, and he was staring at me.

Right at me.

His onyx hair was sexily tousled as though he'd just rolled out of bed with a woman who'd enjoyed mussing the thick, silky-looking strands. His piercing green eyes held a hint of intrigue and a hell of a lot of don't mess with me. *Contradictory signals that sparked my interest.*

His face was a chiseled masterpiece. He had strong features with a stone-set jaw, balanced brows, not too thick, not too thin, and a nose that might have been punched a time or two, given the slight bump close to the eyes, but which still managed to look specially crafted to keep harmony with all the sculpted angles. A mouth that easily drew my attention, my gaze lingering on it until I caught myself.

All in all, he was devilishly handsome. Darkly beautiful.

It struck me that I would never consider a man beautiful, thinking it would undermine his masculinity. Not so with this one. He was beautiful and virile. Downright heart-stopping.

I felt a peculiar stirring deep within me. An innate reaction to his edgy perfection.

It seemed as though the blood moved a bit slower through my veins. Thicker, warmer. Molten.

My gaze lifted, our eyes locked, and I was riveted. I still couldn't breathe.

Something flickered in those hypnotic emerald pools of his. Something curious, like a warning to be heeded. Not menacing, but . . . definitely intimidating.

My breath was slow now, suddenly labored. I stared at Dane, seeing all the strength, power, determination that I'd noted in those first few seconds of meeting him.

Only this time, there was a warm aura surrounding him as he held our son in his arms and gazed lovingly at me.

"I—" My brain stalled out as myriad feelings rushed through me. Making the backs of my eyes prickle.

"Shh," he said to me. "Let me say something."

"I don't need words," I told him as I stared at him settled in a chair pulled close to where I lay on the sofa, Amsel cradled close

to his chest. "You're here. You have our son. There's nothing more
I need."

"But there's something you deserve," he insisted. His emerald
eyes glowed with affection and pain. An agonizing combination.
"I'm sorry I didn't come home right away. I needed some time. I
needed you to take some time to really think about what you saw
the other night. I shot Ethan."

"I actually didn't see it," I said through my tears. "I dropped
the mini and it cut the stream temporarily. I heard the gunshots
and I had no idea who'd fired. There were a few petrifying seconds when I didn't know what had happened. If you were dead
or alive."

"Jesus. I'm so sorry."

"Stan fixed the feed. I saw that you were alive." I pulled in a
shaky breath. "Dane. I lost you once when I walked away. I lost
you again when I thought you'd died in the Lux explosion. I
lost you just the other night. I can't—"

"You won't—"

"Ever lose you again."

"You *won't*."

"How can you guarantee that?" I asked as I choked on a sob.

Dane looked thoroughly devastated by my torment.

But he kept an even tone. "The FBI has everything, sweetheart. Everything I know, everything they need. I spent the past
twenty-four hours with Nik and Qadir. The society is done, dissolved, no more. The Lux is mine and yours—no other investors.
We'll open in the spring. Amsel will have a legacy. Our other
children will have a legacy. It's done, Ari. The bad shit . . . It's *all*
over."

"You promise?" I quietly demanded as tears tumbled down
my cheeks.

"Swear to God. And *this* is a promise that will not be broken.
Ever." He leaned toward me and kissed my forehead. "We won,
baby."

I stared at him for endless moments—minutes?—through watery eyes. I felt a shift inside me; embraced it wholly.

"We did it," I finally said with great relief.

And smiled at my husband and our son.

epilogue

KYLE & ARI

six months later . . .

kyle

I officially hated weddings.

The one I'd been best man at nearly two years ago was where I'd first met Ari. I'd seen her a few times at the bride-to-be's house. Later Ari had been all business at the rehearsal dinner. And then she'd hunted down the groomsmen at the bar just before the ceremony was about to start at a resort here in Sedona.

She'd blown in with a stiff breeze. It'd been impossible not to notice her, all flushed skin, bright blue eyes, and sculpted legs.

I wasn't the only one whose attention she'd grabbed. Dane had also been there that night. So had Vale Hilliard. And some asshole with a diamondback tattoo, who'd later helped Vale and Wayne Horton to terrorize her on-site at 10,000 Lux.

Fifteen minutes in that bar had set a series of dangerous games into play. Regardless, I hadn't been able to convince Ari that Dane was the wrong man for her.

The next wedding I'd attended was hers. A small affair in their creekside backyard. Six guests total, plus Rosa. I'd thought that was pretty pathetic. Ari was a wedding planner, after all.

My third wedding in less than two years—*really, guys don't dig this shit*—was about the most absurd event imaginable.

The aisle had to be a mile long and was flanked by huge arrangements of red roses and deep-green leaves and white fluff. Lots of fluff. Candles galore. Like set the whole damn courtyard on fire, galore. Decorative lanterns hung from iron stakes of various heights along the perimeter, the gardens, the fountains. Clear twinkle lights had been wrapped around all of the tree trunks. There was fruity music that I supposed women found romantic. They all seemed to gush over the decorations and flowers and, yes, the harpist and pianist.

My gaze swept over the small conglomerations as they crossed to the event lawn and selected seats. Some attractive blondes. Several pretty brunettes. A couple of fiery redheads.

Yeah, it was time I dated again. I definitely had to get over Ari.

After all, this was her wedding.

Again.

"Time for the best man to perform his duties."

I turned to find Tamera Fenmore, a leggy blonde with a sassy British accent, heading my way with a pearl-white smile on her face. She had big, tawny eyes and high, defined cheekbones. I'd put her in the knockout category and ask her to have dinner with me if I had half a brain.

"What do you say?" she asked as she straightened my tie.

Not the standard bow tie, but some fancy silk thing she made sure was tucked neatly into my vest. It was a formal black-and-white wedding. I felt as though I should be on a movie set with

Pierce Brosnan. But Ari was finally getting the wedding of her dreams, so I couldn't complain. Too much.

"I think I can handle the redo," I said of the nuptials. "If it makes Ari happy."

"She's deliriously happy. Perhaps the tiniest bit tipsy, but what the hell. She's earned the right."

I couldn't deny that.

"So," Tamera continued, "Grace will be at the altar, too, just like at last night's rehearsal."

Definitely a pretty brunette. She'd also been at the bar that fateful night I'd met Ari. Grace had been the one serving the tequila shots, as a matter of fact.

"You don't have to arrange Ari's monstrously long train or hold her bouquet. Grace will handle all that. But you do have to wipe the scowl from your face and pretend you're not annoyed she's getting married. Really, Kyle. She's already married, so . . ."

"I know, I know." I cleared my throat, squared my shoulders, bucked up.

"Ah." Tamera beamed. "Much better. You know, you're really quite handsome when you're not skulking about."

"I don't skulk."

"Oh, really?" She shot me a challenging look.

I laughed. "Fine. Whatever. Can we just, you know, get this over with?"

"No rush. This is Ari's big day. Guests are still filing in. The event staff members are having conniptions about, oh, everything, because they want absolute perfection. Dane's sipping scotch with his people. Ari's father is freaking out over being on such massive public display. All in all, I think we're doing just lovely."

"Maybe I ought to say a few words to the two-time bride-to-be."

"That would be sensational. Let me take you to her."

There were two tents erected for the bridal party—one for the men, one for the women.

I stepped behind the magic curtain and found Ari admiring, in the full-length, three-way mirror, the back of the wedding gown she wore. The design was intricate pearl and crystal lacing across her bare back. The whole thing was way over-the-top, but I supposed that was part and parcel when you were marrying—*were married to*—a billionaire.

"Hey," she said with a bright smile as she caught a glimpse of me in the reflection.

"Hey."

Tamera left us alone. I had no idea where Grace was.

"So," I said, "I hear you've hit the sauce already."

"Just a little champagne." It had turned her cheeks rosy.

"You look fantastic."

"So do you."

I shrugged. "I suppose."

She laughed sweetly. "Seriously gorgeous."

I had to skip over that. Time to stop reading too much—stuff that wasn't actually there—into everything she said. "I didn't realize you knew so many people. Six hundred guests. Seriously?"

"This is the short list. We didn't want to get too crazy."

"Right."

She laughed again. "A lot of them are Dane's associates, friends, acquaintances. People from the Lux. You know how it goes." Her smile faded and her expression turned contemplative. "If you've noticed, Mommie Dearest isn't crashing."

I eyed her curiously. "How'd you manage that? I think there was a wedding announcement in the *New York Times*."

"There was."

I shook my head. "I guess *normal* has officially slipped from your vocabulary."

"Well . . . consider who my husband is."

I couldn't come up with a rebuttal. So I said, "Tell me how you're keeping out the wicked Maleficent."

"Ingenious of me, really. And Jackson. He managed to get the agent to dump her by threatening lawsuits. Then I jumped in. She's not a fan of babies, so I decided to introduce her to mine."

"Oh, Christ. This ought to be good."

"During a fashion show at the Royal Palms Resort and Spa," Ari began, "where she was all dolled up with her socialite BFFs. I swept in with a VIP ticket Dane secured for me. Not only was poor little Amsel 'ripe,' as you would put it, but his diaper leaked."

She crinkled her nose. I resisted the urge to, just thinking of how this had likely played out.

Ari gave me a coy smile. "Leaked all over Mother's ecru-colored Prada dress to be exact."

"Gross!"

"I swear, it was practically on-cue! I knew he was a little gassy before we arrived. Was sort of banking on it, to be honest, since he'd just had a bottle."

"Remind me not to piss you off. Like, ever."

"Precisely."

"What was the reaction?"

"Picture, if you will, the ladies who lunch all prim and proper, sipping their Cristal and planning their summer wardrobe during the fashion show. The smell wafting their way was disturbing enough. But Mother . . . Wow. She pitched a temper tantrum the likes of which I have never seen—right there in front of Gucci, Dolce and Gabbana, Chanel, and everyone."

"Did you take the GoPro with you?" I had to ask.

"Damn, didn't think of it. Wouldn't that have been something? I could have uploaded the video to YouTube."

Okay, so she had the same warped mind as I did. Maybe that was why we were such great friends.

Ari continued. "I very sweetly let her know there'd be more to come if she didn't leave us all the fuck alone. I could see my tone scared her, but clearly the threat of baby poop or vomit—and the damage to her reputation when she threw her snit fits—trumps it all."

"You're kind of . . . disgusting, Ari. Anyone ever mention that?"

"I just homed in on *her* weakness."

"Okay, maybe ingenious." I gave this some thought and added, "You get props."

She searched around the immediate area, as though looking for something soft to throw at me.

"Come on," I said. "I'm in Armani. You don't want to ruin the tux."

"Consider yourself off the hook for the moment. But I'd sleep with one eye open, if I were you."

"I always do. I live under your husband's roof, after all."

"And he's a little less menacing these days, right?"

"Yeah. Right," I deadpanned.

"Anyway, what do you think of the decorations?"

"Um . . . plentiful?" I ventured.

"Kyle!"

"They're great, Ari," I assured her with a nod. "Really great."

"Phew."

I crossed to where she stood and pulled a small box out of the inside pocket of my tux. Handing it over, I said, "My wedding gift."

"Kyle, you didn't have to do that."

"I didn't get you one last time. And since I now hold a percentage of the Lux, I can definitely afford it." An arrangement Dane had made for me, Rosa, and Amano. Quite generous of Dane, even I had to admit.

Ari took the box from me. "This is nice of you."

"Don't get too excited. I'm not good at selecting gifts."

"My dad said the same thing. He gave me these earrings." She showed off the sparkly, dangly things that actually looked perfect with her gown.

"Not too bad," I said with a head bob.

She opened my gift and gasped. Likely just for dramatic effect.

"Kyle, this is awesome!" She lifted the delicate chain from the velvet folds and held up the platinum and diamond–encrusted locket.

"Open it," I quietly urged.

She did and another gasp filled the tent. A photo of Amsel was on one side, with his date of birth on the other. Not that she'd forget it or anything. I just didn't know what else to include.

"It's perfect," she said with tears in her eyes.

"Well, it's not the Hope Diamond or anything, so don't get all weepy on me."

"It's better than the Hope Diamond, you ass."

I gave a half snort. "Nice to see your sense of sarcasm is still intact."

"Always. Help me put it on." She swept a hand under the thick mass of curls that cascaded between her shoulder blades, and I latched the necklace. She admired it in the mirror and said, "A ring from Dane instead of a bracelet this time, earrings from my dad, a family heirloom from Amano—blue, no less—and a necklace from you that has a photo of Amsel. That covers the bases of all my favorite men."

I lightly kissed her cheek. "Happy second-wedding day."

She laughed. "A mulligan."

"I did call it a redo."

"So better luck to us all this time around."

"I think we're in for a pleasant surprise. No more bad guys."

"No more bad guys."

Tamera came back to fetch me, so I said to Ari, "Don't trip in those skyscraping shoes on your way down the aisle."

"I think I can handle it. Outpatient rehab for my leg at your aunt's retreat has done wonders." She reached for my hand and gave it a squeeze. "And you are the best friend, *ever*."

"Go get married." I rolled my eyes. "Again."

ari

I thought it'd be different this time around.

As though having all these people here to watch Dane and me joined in holy matrimony would make it more significant. As if all the decorations and the incredibly gorgeous courtyard of 10,000 Lux would *really* solidify our marriage.

I remembered when Dane had proposed the first time and had then told me it'd have to be a small, private affair no one outside our circle could know about. I'd been upset because, yes, as a bridal consultant, I wanted to plan my own picture-perfect wedding.

More than that, though, I'd wanted the entire world to know I was marrying the most devilishly handsome, amazingly tempting man on the planet.

But as my father had walked me down the creekside aisle that magical night, I hadn't even noticed the decorations or the guests. I was grateful for it all, of course. Yet the only thing I saw was what awaited me at the end of that aisle.

The only person I saw was Dane.

So breathtaking.

And all mine.

This time around was really no different, as my father escorted me toward the altar on the spectacular grounds of the recently launched 10,000 Lux.

"Breathe, sweets," he whispered beside me.

"Dane's just so perfect."

"And you're already married to him, so . . . ?"

"Dad," I said on a rush of air, my heart fluttering at the sight of what I walked toward. A future that finally shone bright.

"Fine." My father guided me to that coveted spot in front of my dear friend Tamera and then kissed me on the cheek.

Rosa sat on the end of the first row of chairs, with Amsel in her arms. I flashed my son a smile and gave him a little wave. In return, I believe he gave me his first fist pump.

Go, team Bax!

Then I faced Dane. My dad placed my hand in my husband's.

Amano, not quite fully healed, though no one would ever guess it by the way he carried himself, stood beside Dane. As did Jackson Conaway, once more.

Tamera started the ceremony and, as was the case last time, I barely heard a word. My entire focus, my full attention, was on Dane. And vice versa.

We exchanged vows and he slipped the mammoth skating rink he'd picked out for me onto my finger. Because now we weren't worried about who knew we were married. There were no more threats. Not to the Lux and not to us.

I admired the huge diamond, as did Tamera—with a gaping mouth.

"That is ginormous," she whispered.

"Ari deserves something spectacular," Dane whispered back.

I shook my head and said, "That adjective does not do this ring justice."

"Enjoy it." He smirked.

"If you say so." I beamed up at him and added, "By the way, I'd like to convert one of the extra bedrooms into another nursery."

His jaw fell slack. But he quickly recovered. "You're not—"

"Not yet. But I'd like to be."

Dane grinned.

Then Tamera said to him, "You may now kiss your soon-to-be pregnant bride."

I was pretty sure my dad squirmed uncomfortably as the scorching kiss went on and on. I didn't care.

When Dane and I finally came up for air, Tamera made her grand announcement.

"Ladies and gentlemen, I present to you Mr. and Mrs. Dane Bax."

And with that, the whole world knew we belonged to each other.

For the rest of our lives.

"There's HOT.
And then there's
CALISTA FOX."

—Erin Quinn,
New York Times Bestselling Author

READ THE ENTIRE
BURNED DEEP TRILOGY

AVAILABLE WHERE BOOKS ARE SOLD

St. Martin's Griffin

Don't Miss the

DIRTY
WICKED
BILLIONAIRE

e-book bundle!

Featuring short stories by
Opal Carew, Sheryl Nantus,
Calista Fox, and Christina Saunders.

AVAILABLE WHERE BOOKS ARE SOLD DECEMBER 2016.

31192021099534